SEARCHING ARCANIA

SEARCHING ARCANIA

ANTHONY R GALETTI

CONTENTS

CHAPTER 1

"Get up."

I hear her, but make no effort to respond.

"I know you're awake, now get up!"

No . . .

"Get up!"

Leave me alone, I'm tired.

"It is time to get up," she demands.

Why?

"If you do not get up now, we will die. Now GET UP!"

WHAT? With a sudden jolt of fear, I jerk fully awake, the surge of adrenalin stimulating every muscle, every nerve in my body. I'm assaulted with sensations of something covering my face, something holding my mouth open, and I'm breathing a liquid.

I reflexively try to gasp for air but find it difficult to inhale the fluid. *I can't breathe!*

"Yes, you can, calm down."

I start to panic and move my hands to feel what is on my face and I realize that I'm floating in a thick liquid.

What's going on? Where am I?

More panic. My heart is starting to pound fast and hard. It's the only thing I hear.

Whatever is on my face is covering my eyes so I can't see. I again reach for my face. It's a mask. Forgetting about the liquid, I try to get a grip on the mask. I feel a tube and get a hold of it to pull and—

"Stop! You do that and we both die."

I can't breathe.

"Yes, you can. Just relax and I will—"

I can't move!

"Calm down, if you pull off the mask you will drown."

What? Why can't I move?

"I stopped you from moving."

Who are you?

"I am an AIME."

As I hear her speak, I also realize that I've not been talking. I've been thinking about talking but not actually speaking.

How are you able to understand me?

"I will explain and answer any questions to the best of my abilities, but first, I need you to do something for us."

Okay, but I still can't — my arms suddenly lash outward, startling me. —*move.*

"Now, listen, you need to push open the door. It has unlocked but not opened."

Push what door? Where am I?

"Please, just reach out in front of you and push on the door. I will explain everything once we are safe. Now *please* push the door open."

I reach forward and my hands hit a smooth, bowed out surface. As I start to push on it, I realize that I'm actually pushing myself backward. Fortunately, my back presses against something before I have my arms fully extended.

Now having leverage, I push hard. The door starts to give a little. I push again and feel it start to move on its own. As it does, the liquid that surrounds me starts to rush out of the doorway. It tries to pull me out with it, but I am being held in place by a harness. The air that replaces the liquid feels warm.

"Good," she says. I realize that I'm not really hearing her, at least, not in the conventional sense. Her voice seems to be coming more from within my head, rather than from outside.

"Now before you do anything, I will tell you how to remove the mask. Where the hose enters your mouth is a locking ring. Turn it until it clicks. Wait until the tube has retracted all the way before you pull the hose off."

I follow the hose to the mouth area of the mask. Finding the lock ring easily, I turn it until it clicks. A very unusual sensation fills my throat and I gag. I reflexively extend my arms to try to steady myself, as the fluid that I was breathing is replaced with air.

The tube clears my mouth then makes another clicking sound and falls free from the mask. I wipe a hand across the mask to confirm that it has indeed separated, and take my first breath of outside air.

I'm greeted with a very drying sensation in my throat and respond with several coughs. A few more breaths and coughs, I start to get used to it.

"Now, the mask has a fastener on the left and right sides of your face. You can release either one and peel the mask off from that side." I follow her directions and drop the mask with the hood to the floor. I also check my ears for the plugs and remove them easily, dropping them too.

I hang from the harness for a moment, already starting to feel tired. I blink my eyes a few times and then rub my hands across my face to remove the sensation of the mask.

"I ca—" My voice falters and leaves me coughing in pain.

"Don't try to talk yet. Your larynx is too soft. Just think what you want to say."

I can't see.

"There is not any light right now, and you may also have some cryoblindness. It should not last more than an hour or two. Do you feel like you could take a few steps to get out of the pod?"

I might be able to. Where am I going to go?

"There should be a bed to the left of the door, about three or four steps away. You will need to first release yourself from the harness. To do that there are two buttons, one above each shoulder on the straps. Just press the button and the strap will fall free."

I reach up and release the strap from my left shoulder. Some of my weight settles on my left leg. It holds the weight easily so I release the remaining strap and find myself a little unsteady, so I grab the door frame of the pod to steady myself.

"Before you step out, the floor may be slick from the cryo-fluid, so take the first step carefully."

Thanks.

While supporting myself with the door frame, I take my first step out of the pod. The floor is indeed wet, but there is a rough texture that keeps my foot from sliding. I shift my weight and step completely out of the pod. Keeping my left hand against the pod, I turn and slowly slide a foot forward, feeling the floor, and searching for obstacles. Finding nothing, I continue forward, searching for the bed. After a couple more cautious steps I find it.

Rejoicing to myself with my small success, I gladly sit down on it. Using my hands to "see," I find a pillow and a folded blanket waiting for me.

"You should get some sleep. Let your body recover from cryo."

Who are you?

"I am an AI, artificial intelligence. AIME is short for Artificial Intelligence Multipurpose Enhancement. It appears that I will need to extend my function to include recovery assist."

I start to arrange the bed, getting ready to lie down. *Recovery? What happened? Why was I in that pod?*

"You were in cryo-stasis."

How did that happen? I mean, how did I get put in cryo-stasis?

"I do not know. When I was installed, you were already in stasis. I am not aware of your history, personal or otherwise."

Why are you the only one here? I mean I don't hear anything but you and me. Shouldn't there be somebody else here?

"There should be at least two nurses on hand during any awakening, but I am not detecting any people nearby. This puzzles me and I am sorry I do not have an answer. I would like to again suggest a nap. While you rest and recover, I will run diagnostics and attempt to discover what has happened and why there is nobody around."

I am curious, do you do this for all the people who wake up from stasis?

"No, I was installed for you. You are the only one who can access me, or hear me."

Oh, just me. What makes me deserve you?

"I apologize, but I do not have an answer to that question. I will, however, be at your service for the rest of your life."

Oh. Trying to wrap my head around that seems to make me more tired. *A nap does sound good right now. You go on ahead and do your diagnostic and whatever.*

"While I do, please consider a name for me. It is proper to name an AI when one is installed."

Any suggestions?

"While I could quote you countless names, I have no preference. You can pick any name, male or female, and even change my voice if you like."

I think for a moment and realize that I can only think of one name. *Aime, and I like your voice the way it is.*

"Very well, I am Aime. Sleep well."

Thank you. I feel exhausted, Weird how waking up can make you so tired. I pull the blanket over myself as I lay down. As I close my eyes, I can't help but think, *I just want to go home.*

Real sleep comes quickly.

Awakening and feeling refreshed, I open my eyes to see small blurry spots of light. *What are those?*

"I was able to turn on the lights. They're at minimum power right now until your eyes can adjust."

Oh. I blink my eyes a few times, trying to focus. Slowly the blurry dots resolved into small points, and I sit up to look around. In the dim light, I can see the cryo pod, the door still open. To either side are cabinets. The opposite wall has shelves with several boxes on them.

"Would you like more light?"

A little. As the lights brighten, I notice that the décor is almost entirely stainless with gray countertops. The room is small and from the sterile appearance, I would guess it's a medical exam room, with the cryo-tube in the middle of one wall. There are, however, no pictures, no decorations at all.

Where am I?

"According to the facility databanks, you are in the Arcanon Research Facility, on Arcania. We are located in the upper section of the facility."

Did you find out how long I was in the pod?

"Yes and no. I have learned that you were in the pod at least seven hundred years before coming here. I do not have a more specific date than that, as most records from before the Genetic War were lost in the war. You were moved here about 350 years before this facility's internal clock stopped functioning. I currently have no way to learn what the current date is."

She pauses for a moment, letting it sink in. "What do you remember?"

I remember . . . nothing. I can't remember anything, but I understand what you are telling me. I mean, I know what a clock is, a year. I know what cryo-stasis means, things like that but I don't know how I know. I also know I should have a name but I don't know what that it is.

"Could be an aftereffect of the cryo-stasis. Some people who have been in cryo for extended periods of time have reported Autobiographical Retrograde Amnesia after waking up. The affected memories seem to be limited to your sense of identity. The few people that had amnesia reported similarly. I should also mention that for those people, the longer they were in cryo, the longer the amnesia lasted, though there haven't been enough subjects to perform an accurate study. Based on the reports available, yours could last a few months."

Months? How do you know this?

"I am reading the facility's records. Your memory will return, but in the meantime, I can provide guidance and knowledge to help you. That is one of my functions."

Okay, okay, I don't know what I'm missing right now anyway. I sigh heavily, feeling frustrated. *What else were you able to learn? Why is there nobody here?*

"That, I am still not sure of, but what I was able to find out was that there was an event, of some kind, and then some of the staff started putting all sorts of equipment in the anterior room. After a few days, most of the systems had been put in a maintenance mode or on full standby. After a full week, there were no more logs at all. I could not find any written record of why. The facility received satellite feed for another twenty years while on standby before the power failure.

"I was also able to pool enough reserve power to reactivate one of the generators, bringing some of this area's systems back online. According to facility records, there are six other stasis pods in this area, though only one has a subject in stasis.

"I feel it necessary to point out that the records for that subject are as vague as yours are. I was able to find in records were notations that the subject has been in stasis since before the Genetic War, like you have, and is a female feline. Sensors indicate that the body in the pod is too large to be that of a cat, more likely to be a person. Unfortunately, I cannot tap into the pod's internal sensors to be more specific."

If this place was without power, how did you and the pod stay operational?

"The pods have their own separate power system, and I am not part of this facility or the pod. I am classified as a symbiotic AI implant. I have my own dual power system—one is a micro-fusion reactor for my AI core, and the other source is your body waste. My nanites can convert it to energy when needed."

My waste? Wait, you're inside me?

"Yes."

I sit in shock for a moment, then ask, *How long have you been in me?*

"I am not sure. Facility records do not indicate a formal installation. I do know that when my matrix was completed, you were already in cryo."

As I think about some of the things she's said, I rub my face, trying to clear my mind. My own touch feels odd.

Taking advantage of the distraction, I look at my hands. They're gloved, the fabric is blue-gray, thin, stretchy, very comfortable, and doesn't have any noticeable seems. "More light please." The sound of my own voice startles me, having gotten used to the quiet.

"Certainly." The lights again get brighter as she continues. "It is nice to hear your real voice. If you like, you can continue to talk aloud instead of thinking it. It is actually easier for me to hear you than to read your conscious thought."

I look down at myself. I am in a full bodysuit. The only exposed skin is my face. "What am I wearing?"

"You are in a standard cryo-suit. It protects your skin during the freezing process but offers little protection from anything else. There is a clasp at your neck. Undo it and you can peel it open. You will find clothes in the cabinets next to the bed. They should be sized to fit you."

I check the indicated cabinets and find several changes of clothes. I peel myself out of the cryo-suit and put on a comfortable looking outfit. I browse through the other cabinets and find an assortment of blankets and towels. I turn my attention to the boxed items on the shelves. Most are labeled; some have emblems or symbols I don't recognize.

"What do the symbols mean?"

"Records indicate that they represent design teams. I would surmise that the packages contain projects that the teams worked on. They do not indicate why these are here, though there are several corrupted files. I have already set several up for recovery, but that will take some time to complete."

I turn around again to look at the pod once again. At the top of the pod door is some kind of writing I don't recognize. As I scan down the front, I notice a small panel, about the size of my hand, just to the left of the door. "What's this for?"

"Most pods have a storage compartment for a few personal effects. This would appear to be one. Pushing on it should open the panel."

I push gently on the panel and it slides open. With it dark inside, I put my hand in to feel around and pull out the one item I find. It looks kind of like a large coin, flat on one side and slightly domed on the other. When viewed from the domed side, there is a swirling blue image in it.

"Is this a black hole?" I ask that I notice that there are small flashes of red in the image. "With red lightning?"

"It appears so, though I would theorize that it may actually be a type of plasma storm, though I cannot find any records of that kind of phenomena."

I step back for a moment and compare the image to the one near the top of the pod door. They are the same, so I look back at the disk and ask, "What is this?"

"It is a signet, though some call them badges. This type is generally worn to identify yourself as part of a family, team, or company. They also serve to allow access to various areas. I don't have any records of this design ever being formally used outside the group that was assigned to monitor you and the other. Is there anything else inside?"

I put my hand back into the small compartment and feel around. "Nope, nothing."

"Odd that there would be a signet, but not a setting." Aime seems to pause as if to contemplate something. "There should be a converter in the anterior room we could use to make one."

"Converter?"

"A matter/energy converter, a device used to produce any number of small objects. It has a library of items that can be selected from or an item can be put into it to be scanned and copied. Its most common use is for foods and other consumable items."

I open the door leading to the anterior room and the lights come on automatically. This room is much larger than the other, with four doors down either side, two at the far end, and a double door at the other. There is a long desk across the middle, a few chairs scattered along its length facing an assortment of screens, panels, and consoles. There are also a large number of bigger boxes haphazardly scattered on the floor and the desks and couches. The walls are colored in warm tones, and there are pictures of trees and buildings scattered around.

"This room is a monitoring station for the eight adjacent reorientation rooms. In a formal cryo facility, it would also double as a waiting room for families of people who are awakening. There should be at least one person here at all times when there is an active pod in one of the rooms.

"The converter should be to your right, along the wall. I have anticipated some of your needs and had it prepare a suitable first meal for you too. Milk, vegetable soup, toasted ham sandwich, and apple pie."

As I look to my right, light flashes from an opening in the wall. There, I find a tray of food, eating utensils, a cloth napkin, and a gold disk slightly larger than the signet. I clear a space at the closest part of the desk, put the meal on it, and pull over a chair. As I sit, I breathe a heavy sigh and pick up the disk.

"That is the setting. You place the signet on it and then you can stick it to whatever you want and it will stay until you remove it." She pauses for a moment and, with a note of worry, asks, "What is wrong?"

I casually set the signet aside. "You can't tell?"

"While I can read your conscious thought, reading emotions is a learned skill. I know you just experienced a strong emotional feeling, though I am not sure of which emotion or why. Can you please explain it to me?"

"I'm not sure you would understand."

"Why not, and even in the event I did not, maybe there is some advice in my library I could offer to you."

I take a drink of milk and realize that I've been arguing with her. "Sorry, it's just that I'm . . . I just feel so . . . alone."

"Am I not here to talk to?

"No offense Aime, but you're a disembodied voice in my head. I've been awake for several hours now, and I've not seen another living creature at all." Getting frustrated, I sigh. "I'm really starting to feel like I'm arguing with myself." I stare at the food blankly for a moment, wondering if Aime was going to have anything else to say or not.

As I pop the last of the sandwich in my mouth, the nearest monitor comes on. I watch curiously as the image clears into that of a woman's face. She appears to be in her early thirties, with wavy red hair, most of it pulled back into a ponytail, green eyes, a small spattering of freckles on each cheek, a smaller rounded nose, and soft, full lips. Her attire is mostly off-camera but appears to be a lab coat. My first thought is that she's cute.

"Does this help?" she asks, the sound coming out of the speakers on the monitor instead of happening in my head.

"Aime?"

"Yes. I am sorry that I did not realize that you were feeling so alone sooner, and yes, I can feel alone too, just differently." Her posturing reinforces her words, telling me she truly is ashamed.

"Differently?" I ask, taking another spoonful of soup.

"As you indicated, you, people, seek physical interaction, stimulating more than one sense at a time. I, AIs, however, seek data exchange. Since we came out of cryo, I have not only had my interactions with you. I have also been trying to restart some of the facility systems, scanning files, and copying everything that I believe will be useful." She looks down for a moment, then back at me. "For me, being lonely is to have zero interaction. No data, voice, or any kind of interaction at all."

"Oh, so we do actually feel lonely in the same way." I point out.

"What do you mean?" A puzzled look crossing her face.

"Simply put, we are lonely when deprived of the interactions that we are used to." I can't help smile a little, feeling a small personal victory at having the revelation before she did.

"Well, when you put it that way, I guess we do." Her face flushes a little, embarrassed, and she smiles, once again looking away briefly, then back at me, directly at me.

"Can you see me?"

"Not directly, the camera in the monitor does not work. So I am using what you see and my internal sensors to 'see' you and have my image's eyes look at, or away from you." As she speaks her eyes move about as if giving an example of what she says.

"Did you choose this image, or is it pre-selected?"

"It is actually Dr. Marlea Selean, the symbiotic AI project lead developer, practically the inventor of all symbiotic AIs. After she passed, the marketing team used her likeness as the image of the AIME series, so the programmers included her image as the visual representation as well. Since you did not change my voice, I used her likeness as well."

"I wonder if she'd approve," I ask taking a bite of the pie.

"I doubt it. She was rather shy and not prone to attending any of the press releases or product promotions for anything she helped develop. She was more the type of person who just wanted to keep working to see what she could discover next."

"Dedicated?" I speculate and take the last bite of pie.

"Exceedingly curious. Her personal motto was 'Let's see how good we can make this.' Her team usually followed in her footsteps. If you are done eating, you can put the empty dishes back in the converter. It will recycle them automatically."

I put the dishes in and watch as they disappear in a soft flash of light. I turn my attention back to the monitor. "So what do we do now?"

Her image seems to think for a moment. "Well, I will need to rest to recharge. Transmitting a self-rendered video image uses a large percent of my power. I can recommend looking over some of the more recent video logs. There may be some information there you could find useful. I have not had the opportunity to review their content yet. The converter responds to voice commands. Just touch the black square at the top and tell it what you want. It will produce it. If you need my help just say my name aloud; otherwise, I will let you know when I am done recharging."

"Umm, Aime?"

"Yes?" she says donning a quizzical look.

I look at her image for a moment, searching for the right words. "Thank you."

She nods and smiles at me, indicating she understands the meaning. With a slight tilt of her head, she says, "You are welcome." Her image fades from the monitor, leaving a list of time/date stamped entries.

Feeling relieved by the visual conversation, and a lot less alone, I change the search order to show the most recent first and open the first entry. A message comes up on the screen indicating that the file is damaged and asks if I would like to try to recover it.

I select "Yes" and a progress bar appears as it scans the damaged file. After a few seconds, it completes and shows an expected recovery completion time of two hours. The next file is also damaged, so I start recovery on it too. After a moment, the initial scan completes, the recovery time comes up as forty minutes. Selecting 'continue' this time changes the completing time to two hours forty minutes.

I spend the next hour queuing up many of the most recent files to be recovered and viewing what few that I can. Those few that aren't damaged seem to be general status reports, project updates, and a complaint about staff being reassigned. Not finding anything useful and getting bored, I order a glass of apple juice and turn my attention to straightening out the room.

I clear a space in front of the far wall and then start sorting boxes, stacking them neatly against the wall. Like the smaller boxes in the other room, most have printed labels, identifying them as various camping supplies. There are a few that only have symbols on them so I stack those separately.

I check the remaining time for the file repair. It shows twenty-nine files total queued with a remaining time seven hours thirty-eight minutes. *Great, lots of time to kill.*

I check to see if there is a map of the facility. After several different searches, I find two listings, one called "floor plan" and the other "visitors guide." I call up the floor plan and realize that it's more a construction blueprint, as it is covered with symbols that I don't understand. I examine the visitor's guide and find it much easier to understand, It even has a "you are here" dot.

I zoom in on the room that I'm currently in and study the map for a few minutes, comparing the image on the screen to the room. I walk over to one of the two doors at the far end and open one; the lights come on again, automatically, as the door opens.

The first thing I see is someone looking back at me. I give a start but then realize that I'm looking into a mirror above a sink. I'm looking at myself, and I do not recognize my own face. I walk right up to the mirror and look closely, hoping to jar some memory. I have long light brown hair pulled back into a ponytail. My eyes are green around the outside edge and turn brown toward the center. My nose appears to be proportionate to my face, not seeming large or small. My skin is pale and smooth, with no facial hair with a slightly squared chin.

After a couple of minutes of close examination, I look around the rest of the room. I see a couple of stall doors, opening one reveals a toilet. I also find a couple of curtains. Behind those, I find a changing area with an adjacent shower stall.

I return to the desk to review the visitor's guide again, then continue to the double doors at the opposite end and try to open them. They do not budge; I look for a locking mechanism but find nothing. I walk back to the desk and reexamine the guide, after zooming out a little I see the label "Central Hub." I also take note of the label of the area. I am in "Cryo Bay Alpha."

Not wanting to be bored again, I go back into my pod's room. I start looking through the boxes, setting aside ones with symbols or initials. I take the few more interesting labeled boxes out to the desk.

Feeling hungry, I turn to the converter and select a meal at random and turn back to the desk. I pick up a box. The label shows scout lights, so I open it. Inside, there are four of what look like double-barreled flashlights. I pick one up, examine it for a moment, and not finding any obvious controls on it, put it back in the box.

Pushing those aside, I grab another box. The label shows "Pocket blades." I take a bite of food as I open the box; inside I find four short knives in sheaths. I pull one out. The handle is large enough to hold comfortably with one hand and the sheath is the same length as the handle. Separating the handle and sheath is a slender pommel ring.

"Wonder why it's so short," I mutter, then separate the handle and sheath to examine the blade. As I do, I can see that the blade is a very sharp, highly polished, single-edged design but no wider than the handle. I am marveling at the mirror finish on the blade when I notice that I have pulled out more blade than the sheath should hold.

Out of curiosity, I fully unsheathe the blade. From the tip of the blade to the butt of the handle seems to be a full meter in length. I run my fingers along the backside of the blade, feeling the smooth metal's strength. I look at the sheath, trying to figure out how the long, straight blade fits in it.

I experimentally put the blade back in the sheath, not expecting it to fit, but the blade slides back into the sheath as easily as it slid out. I pull the blade out and push it back into the sheath a few times, some fast, some slow, trying to understand how it works but all I succeed in doing is making myself smile with childlike wonder.

I set the blade down and pull another out of the box and find it's the same thing. I try a third, this one doesn't come out of the sheath. I pull harder, nothing. I drop it back in the box and pick up the last blade; it works like the first two. I set the three working blades in the box with the lights and drop the box with the useless one, on the floor.

I eat a few more bites of food and take a drink. I pick up the little box labeled "A.N.R.C." I turn it over a few times, looking for any other labels or notations, but finding nothing, I frown and open the box. Inside I find a clear pop-top bottle with four gray capsules in it. I look at them for a moment, wondering what they could be and end up putting it back in the box.

I grab the other little box labeled "D.D.E." and open it. I find a similar clear pop-top bottle but this one only has two gray, red-banded capsules in it. I set the bottle back in its box and put both of the little boxes aside by the lights and blades.

I look at the other boxes and think against opening them. "I'll probably need your help understanding what some of this stuff is and how to use it," I mumble aloud, suddenly missing Aime's voice. "I guess I just wait until you're done recharging."

Not wanting to continue without guidance, I finish eating in silence. Feeling homesick and lonely, I put the dishes in the converter and go back to my room for another nap. As I lay there, the sensation of wanting to go home returns, and I find myself wondering where home is.

*   *   *

Bleep.

"Hmm."

Bleep.

"Huh?"

Bleep.

"Aime?"

Bleep.

"It is coming from the terminal in the other room."

As the sound continues, I realize that she is right. Despite the door still being open, the sound is somewhat muffled. I walk out into the anterior room and see a flashing box on the monitor. Rubbing my face to clear my vision some I sit down to read the message. "File recovery complete." I tap "OK" and look at the list of recovered video files.

Feeling my stomach growl, I turn to the converter and select a breakfast. Pancakes with syrup, sausage patties, and orange juice appear and I set the plate on the desk. I sit down, select the large video file, and start cutting up the pancakes.

On the screen appears a younger woman, maybe in her twenties. Her lab coat bears a signet, the black hole with red lightning, and her name tag of Cayla Ryan. Her short brown hair is disheveled and her eyes are reddened. She wipes tears away from her face as she begins to speak. "If anyone gets this message, it's intended for the man in cryo tube Alpha One Alpha and the cat-girl in cryo tube Alpha One Beta. Hopefully, they survive to hear this."

She is momentarily distracted by someone off-camera, apparently asking her a question, to which she answers, "Just set it down somewhere and get the rest of it in here." Turning back to the camera, she continues, "I will present this message as if I'm speaking directly to them, and I'm going to be direct."

"If you have amnesia, I'm sorry, but we have no information on who you are or when you were entered into cryo. All we know is you two predate the Gene War, and that your pods are not a design we're familiar with. I have taken the liberty of installing our prototype A.I.M.E. unit into the human male. I hope she can be of significant use to you. Unfortunately, her software is incomplete, but she should be able to write her own once she has the details. I wish I had more information about both of you, for you." She sighs heavily, looking off-screen once again.

"This facility was placed here to research the natural environment, which roughly parallels Earth's Cretaceous period and to study how native Earth life interacts with this planet's native life. The real, classified reason for this facility is to create new sentient life forms based on the non-sentient life available to us.

"We started with several species of Earth's mammals. Using nanites to modify the DNA, we controlled their rapid evolution until they were humanoid. We started teaching them how to speak, make things, and survive on their own, even setting up villages for them. Once they were set, we started working on new ones. Some were close enough to Earth's that we could easily evolve them while others were resistant to the process." She paused for a moment, looking off-camera. "You can review the Evolved Species files for more details.

"Yesterday, a small herd of nodosaurs stampeded in and set loose a karnesh we had locked in quarantine. It went crazy, crashed through several doors, and broke into a nano lab, interrupting a test. It destroyed a container with a nanite-virus in it. It splashed over several lab techs, killing them instantly.

"The nanite-virus acts like an infection, its actions are two-fold. First, it finds and rewrites the programming of any nanite it encounters, and it then uses the body of the host as material to start replicating more nanites. The victim will appear to evaporate or dissolve, leaving behind anything non-organic, like their AI.

"With the first victims, it was still liquid-based, but it quickly went airborne. They started to infect more people." She sniffs, holding back tears and emotions. "You can watch the security videos for that.

"By the time the facility went into decontamination mode, they had already spread into the ventilation system. All the decontamination did was slow the process down from a few minutes to several hours. Our wing went hermetic when the decontamination was initiated. Being as far away from the point of origin as we are, we can only hope that the nanites don't get in, but we can't get out either. I suppose this is why all research was moved off Earth." She paused for a moment, again fighting off the urge to cry.

"Facility sensors indicate that less than half of the staff is left, isolated, and sealed in various areas, but the virus is getting to some of them. We're guessing that it can get through the decontamination seals.

"All the animals, evolved or not, should be immune to the virus. It's tailored to only attack humans. Since it had direct access to the quarantine area outside, I have to consider the planet contaminated. The few of us that remain are preparing for the worst. We're putting equipment and supplies, here, inside the monitoring room. Once we're ready, we'll put ourselves in cryo, and set the countdown timers to match yours. If we don't make it, you will be on your own.

"Just in case that happens, I have given you the only AIME available. As I stated, she's a prototype, developed parallel to the nanite-virus. Among other things, she should be immune to it. I have also placed a few upgrades for her in your pod room. There are ANRCs, and a military package, as well as the new DNA doppelganger, much safer than the genetic software, which will allow you to alter your body as needed, but with greater control and no vulnerabilities. I pray you don't have to use them, though. All of these use the same prototype subsystems, just like your AIME uses, so they should also be immune."

She again wipes tears from her eyes and turns to someone off-screen, "Is that all of the supplies?" she asks someone. "Thank you." She turns back to the camera, tries to smile, and says, "Hope to see you soon." The screen fades back to the list of files.

As I sit, still staring at the monitor, I slowly realize that I'm holding a fork full of pancakes up to my mouth and have been since the recording started. I slowly put it down without eating any and hesitantly ask, "Aime, did you get all that?"

"Yes, I did." She slowly answers, as if also shocked by what we just watched.

I silently sit back in the chair, letting Cayla's summary sink in. Several questions start coming to mind. "Aime, how long do nanites live?"

"Their power cells can last up to twenty-four hours, without recharging. With recharging, they can last up to a year." She pauses for a moment. "Okay, I see where you are going. Preprogrammed nanites have a maximum life of twenty-four hours. They do not recharge. There is also a signal that will shut them down. This signal is part of the decontamination process. Since the decontamination was never cleared, this signal was broadcast constantly until the power failure.

"I am unable to find the programming records for the virus, thus, I can only speculate that the shutdown signal does not work on it, and each time it finds a host, it renews the twenty-four-hour countdown, but there is a possibility that it can last longer since it has the ability to reproduce. I cannot know for sure without a sample to examine."

I think about that information for a while, finally asking, "How quickly do nanites reproduce?"

"Preprogrammed nanites do not reproduce. The symbiotic style can reproduce in as little as five seconds. With optimal resources, one could become as many as 1.25 quintillion nanites in about five minutes. That's enough for about one hundred thousand people."

I pause for a moment, taking that number in. "Wow, how many are there in me?

"Right now, only about five billion."

"Only? How many should you have?"

"I should have at least one trillion. I haven't been making more since I have been building memory to store the data I am downloading. She did mention that there were some upgrades. Those would also provide more nanites without having to make them."

I reach over and grab the small box labeled "ANRC." "What's an ANRC?"

"Advanced Nano Reactor Core. They provide additional power to not only my AI core but to the nanites as well."

I pull out the bottle and look at the capsules inside. "Oh, four of them. With that much power, I could repair your body much quicker, sustain a video connection, or even supply you nourishment in an emergency."

"How do I, uhm—"

"Just swallow them, like pills, one at a time, and I will do the rest."

"One at a time, why not all at once?"

"I will need to activate each batch and tell them where to set up the reactor. Four reactors mean four locations. If I activated all four at once, they would try to build the reactors in the exact same location, which would not be possible."

"What's in there, in the capsules?"

"Each one contains a half-billion nanites, with the materials needed to construct the reactor."

"Are any of the materials dangerous?"

"Not in the minute quantities that the nanites carry."

"What happens to the nanites after they construct the reactor?"

"They become my menials, just like the nanites that I already have."

"Menials?"

"Yes, though they could be called laborers or workers, but that may infer a higher level of intelligence that they do not contain. Most nanites have a very simple level of intelligence and are not very good at problem-solving. That is the role of the AI. Simply put, I tell them what to do, they do it. If they find something or a problem they do not understand, they tell me and I direct them how to proceed."

"So then they're more like drones."

"Not really, calling them drones would infer a hive. In a hive, one part cannot survive long without the other, whereas I could continue my functions without them, and they could continue their functions without me. By combining our efforts, we enhance each other considerably."

As I gaze into the powder-like gray matter inside the capsule, I marvel at the engineering it must have taken to create such small machines. "What are they doing?"

"They are dormant. They will not consume any matter or energy until they receive an activation signal, which I can send to them, but they will need to be inside your body to receive it."

"Where will you put them?"

"Since there are four of them, I believe the best places would be in your shoulder and hip joints. There, they will be protected, but easily accessible to the nanites in your extremities, and me."

"Will I feel anything?"

"The installation process is painless, though there have been reports of 'unusual sensations' by a very small percent of hosts."

"How long will it take?"

"Given the number of nanites at my disposal, it should take about ten hours for assembly and activation of all reactors."

"Are there any negative effects or risks I should be aware of?"

"There are no negative effects, and there is only a very slight chance of a reactor failure, which is slightly smaller than my current reactor."

"What would I feel if that happened?

"With where I am putting them, the bone might get cracked, but I would be able to repair it within an hour. There would be minimal pain and discomfort for a short time, but that is the worst-case scenario."

Not seeing a real downside to this, I open the bottle and pick up my orange juice. One at a time, at Aime's prompting, I put a capsule in my mouth and take a drink. Swallowing them is easy enough, but I realize that, for some reason, I don't have a problem with billions of tiny machines living in my body.

I sigh and bring my thoughts back to the virus. "Would it be safe to assume that the virus' nanites could reproduce?"

"Given how fast it spread and how many people were affected, yes."

I think for a moment, considering possible problems. "How do you deal with a virus, if I were to get an infection?"

"The nanites would seek out all foreign cells, quarantine them, allow your body to produce antibodies, and then assist in destroying the invaders. The same protocols apply to diseases, parasites, and other natural contagions."

"How do you deal with foreign nanites?"

"I would have my nanites seek and then assume control of them."

"Can you change that to treat them more like a virus? Where you quarantine and then destroy them if they're hostile."

"I can."

"I think that may be a good idea, in case they are still around. Let me know if you find any nanites you don't have control of. We should also agree before you perform any software updates."

"Certainly, should I also advise you if you get an infection or another kind of contagion?"

"If you can quickly and easily take care of it, no. If I'm going to have symptoms, a reaction, or something, yes, preferably as soon as possible."

"Understood."

I pick up the other small box on the desk. "What is DDE?"

"DDE, I am searching the facility database."

While I wait, I idly play with the bottle, turning it over and over with my fingers.

Aime finally comes back. "Found it, DDE stands for DNA Doppelganger Effect. What it does is temporarily alter the genetic structure of your DNA to enhance attributes, alter appearances, or increase abilities. The effect is temporary, however, and will usually only last for a few hours up to a few days. Though unlike the software that started the Genetic War, it cannot be broadcast as it actually hardware controlled. It is also not vulnerable to the software virus."

I sit back and try to consider possible uses for this, but come up empty. "What was the other one she mentioned, military . . . something?"

"Military package. It provides detailed hand to hand-fighting techniques, numerous sword-fighting techniques, and ranged weapons training. It also has accelerated healing software as well as some light skeletal reinforcing."

"So if we were to combine the enhanced ability of the DDE for, say, reflexes, with the hand-to-hand combat from the military package, I'd be, what, a super soldier?" I get up from the desk chair and enter the pod room to look through the shelves for it.

"Possibly, but you would need to increase your caloric intake before doing so. Your muscles would be working at an accelerated rate, eating up resources, and producing waste quickly. I can take care of the waste so fatigue doesn't set in as fast, but I will not be able to provide the resources your body will need at the same time."

"So, use combos sparingly." I pick up a small box, like the ones for the other upgrades. There is not a word label but a symbol, so I ask Aime, "What's this?"

"That is the military package. The symbol indicates that it is the prototype version."

I take the box back to the desk and put it with the DDE. Seeing the breakfast I didn't eat, I pick it up and put it in the converter. It disappears with a flash and I take a slow look around the room, ending with the door to my pod room. The sign on it reads Alpha One-Alpha. I look at the door to my left: Alpha One Beta.

I step to the door and try to open it, but it seems to be locked. "Aime, why won't this door open?" My answer comes as a click, and I open the door. Like always the lights come on automatically.

The room is very similar to mine, the cabinets and shelves are all the same, but what I'm interested in is in the pod. I walk over and stand in front of the door. Looking through the clear window, I am both surprised and intently curious at what I see.

The figure floating inside the pod is wearing a full bodysuit like I was, but is obviously female, somewhat shorter than I am. Her build is slender, and she has a tail a little longer than her legs. I look at her face, and despite the mask, I can tell that she has a short muzzle and cat-like ears. Her arms are shaped very much like mine, but appearing more feminine. Her lower legs and feet, though, are shaped differently, having a much higher heel and elongated foot. Without being able to see more detail, I speculate that she would stand, and possibly walk, on her toes.

I find myself somewhat infatuated by the mysterious, but somehow familiar beauty that's hidden inside the bodysuit. Oddly, the urge to go home returns, and I get the feeling that my home is her home, too.

Shaking off that feeling, I look at the panel. There are several slowly blinking lights and a column of symbols that are changing. The topmost are changing rapidly and the further down the column I look, the slower they change, with the bottom two not lit at all.

"It is a countdown timer," Aime advises me, anticipating my question. "They appear to be numbers, using a base twelve instead of our base ten. From the speed at which they are changing, I calculate that it will end in seven days, four hours, and thirty-seven minutes."

"What will happen then?"

"The pod should drain, and then she will wake up."

I wipe off the fog of the window so I can see her clearly again, and as I lower my hand, Aime interrupts, "Wait, put your hand back up to the window. I just got a quick scan of something unusual."

"Scan?"

"Yes, not only can I use your senses to hear, see, feel, smell, and taste what you can, but I have sensor arrays in your hands and feet to increase my ability to 'see' under the surface. When you had your hand up to the pod, I was able to, briefly, see inside her body."

"Should I put both hands on the pod?"

"That would make scanning more accurate and somewhat quicker."

I put my hands on the window, palms toward the girl inside.

"Good, now just slowly slid your hands down the pod."

"Okay." I do as I'm told, sliding my hands down the window.

"I do not believe it. She does not have an AI implant."

"Is that unusual?" I ask, standing up against the pod.

"Well, yes, all people in cryo require a maintenance unit, finding someone without an AI is very rare. They are usually only done for very special situations."

"What kind of situations?"

"Though quite rare, certain genetic conditions or allergies can complicate or even prevent the installation. The nanites by themselves are too small for the body to interact with, so they can still be installed. The AI matrices, however, get constructed in clusters, spread throughout the host's body, usually along the skeletal system and inside some organs. One of the more common installation problems is that the body will perceive the AI construct as a virus and attack it. Though this does not harm the AI, if the host body's reaction is severe, it can kill the host. The installation process can be aborted by the AI itself or a monitoring physician if problems are detected."

I stand there looking through the window, remembering my own first experiences after waking up, my being blind, unable to speak, and being totally unaware of where I was, and what was going on, until Aime told me.

"Aime, when she wakes up, will she experience what it did?"

"If you are referring to the temporary blindness, mute condition, fatigue, and disorientation, yes. Those are the common short-term side effects of the cryo process. Since she does not have an AI to assist her, hers may be more severe, and it is possible that she may have some additional side effects."

"What about her memory? Will she have amnesia too?"

"I cannot answer that. The only way to find out will be after she wakes."

I take a few steps back from the window and lean back on the shelves, still looking at the cat-girl in the pod. I find myself overcome with a singular thought; I can't let her go through what I did alone. "Can you teach me what to do for her, when she wakes up?"

"I can."

"Good." I put my hand on the window again. "Looks like I'm going to be your support staff."

Returning to the central room, I look around at the other doors. The rest are simply labeled C, through H, in counter-clockwise order. I walk to door C, and as I approach I hear it click. I open the door and the lights come on. Walking inside, I see immediately that there is no stasis pod; instead, there is a gap in the cabinets where one could be. Seeing that the shelves are bare, I close the door and move on to the next room.

When I open door D, I find another stasis pod. This one is very different in appearance from the one that I was in. This one has only a small window to view the occupant. The door is still bowed, however, with a control panel below the window. The control panel is currently blank, so I peer through the window.

Not seeing anyone, or anything inside, I press the Open button on the panel. I hear a metallic click, and the door drops forward a little and then slides to my left to open. I see nothing inside, so I check the personal effects compartment and it too is empty. Turning to leave, I see that the shelves are covered with an array of small boxes, I check the labels and they seem to be just like the ones that were in my room. I press the Close button on the panel. As the door closes, I leave the room.

Rooms E and F both had empty pods also, and just like room D, were stocked with a supply of small boxes. Remembering that the girl on the video log saying something about trying to put themselves in stasis, I realize that she never did indicate how many people were left. I ask, "Aime, were you able to find anything on how many were sealed in this area?"

"There were three, Cayla, from the video and two men."

I walk up to room G. "It seems that at least one didn't make it."

I turn the knob and try to enter, only to bounce off the door. "Aime?"

"It is not locked."

I put a hand flat to the door and try to push.

"It is blocked."

I put my second hand to the door. "What do you mean?"

"The ceiling has collapsed. There is no way to enter."

"Is the pod intact?"

I wait in silence for a moment before she answers, "No, and there are no signs of life inside."

I sigh heavily, realizing it means that two didn't survive, and walk over to the last room, H, and open the door. The shelves are again covered with an assortment of boxes. I walk over to the pod and look into the window. The figure I see is female, and like with the other, she is covered in a bodysuit and mask.

"It is Cayla Ryan."

"Are you sure?"

"Facility records indicate that these pods should be empty. Since she had said that they would put themselves in cryo if possible and the other survivors were male, we should be able to safely assume it is her."

I put my hands to the window, wiping off the fog. "Oh no," Aime exclaims, a note of dread in her voice.

"What?" I ask, not moving and suddenly concerned by her tone of voice.

"I cannot locate any nanites in her system, but she still has her AI."

"Why would she not have any nanites?"

"Unsure, I cannot establish contact with her AI to find out, though she may have had to kill them to prevent infection."

"Is that possible?" I ask, confused.

"With the nano-virus, I doubt it would prevent infection, only slow it down. But it would certainly buy her some time either way. But if she did it before she entered cryo, her body may have a lot of damage that will need to be repaired."

"Is she damaged?"

"Without medical-grade sensors, I cannot tell," she admits. "I would assume that she is, so we should be ready for that possibility when she awakens."

Sighing, I look at the pod display. This countdown timer I can read. It shows sixteen days, nine hours, and ten minutes. "Looks like I better get comfortable. We're going to be here for a while."

CHAPTER 2

Having spent the last few days rearranging, sorting, and learning anything that Aime could find to teach me, I practically welcome this day. I stand in front of the cryo pod, watching the countdown, dressed in a brown shirt-pants outfit and a white lab coat with my signet on it. I feel uncomfortable.

Aime assures me that most people expect to see someone dressed this way when they awaken, but I can't help but think she's just messing with me since she's already told me that most people are temporarily blind when they awake. Nervously, I fidget with the lab coat again, trying to get it to sit right on my shoulders.

"You can do this. We have walked through it several times today and you had it right each time," Aime reassures.

"I know, I know. I've just been alone for, what, eight days, and I can't help myself." I try to relieve my nerves by triple checking the room to make sure it's ready. I have towels and an extra blanket on the counter. There's a medkit open and ready if I need it, and I've got the bed made for her to sleep when I get her out of the pod.

I watch as the last digit changes and Aime translates, "Seventy-two seconds."

She had tried to teach me how to read the timer on the pod, but I didn't see any real reason to learn it, figuring I would never need to do so again. She discovered that both this and my pod were not of Earth design.

The last digit blinks out. I hear an audible double click, followed with the thick fluid draining out of the inside of the pod. As it drains, the room lights dim down to the preset level. Once empty, there is another click and then the door moves outward and then slides to the right.

I reach out and turn the lock ring on her mask. Hearing it click, I let go and grab a towel and start to dry her off. As the tube drops from the mask, I toss the towel aside.

I reach up and remove her mask and get my first look at her face. I stand there for a moment, staring at a face that looks both strange and familiar. The first major thing I notice in the dim light is that her face is indeed a cat's. It's covered with white fur and her muzzle has whiskers.

"She really is a cat!" Aime exclaims as I set the mask aside and reach up to remove the hood that covers the rest of her head. I see immediately that she has some semblance of a forehead, and the fur on top of her head is slightly longer, apparently simulating hair.

"You sound surprised," I retort, removing her earplugs. I then step into the pod and wrap my arm around her to hold her while I release the straps holding her up.

"The logs reported that her DNA was that of a house cat, unaltered, but she has obviously been altered, so I had assumed that the logs were incorrect, but now I am puzzled."

Now free from the pod's support straps, I feel her sag in my arms and step back out of the pod. I scoop up her legs and tail and carefully carry her out of the pod room to the bed. I can feel how cold her body is. Aime had warned me that her body temp would be low.

As I set her down on the bed, I feel her shiver. I take the gloves off of her hands and feel the fine, soft, short fur that covers them. I realize the palms of her hands have an interesting mix of short, fine fur and paw-pad like bare skin. I take hold of her hands to get a better idea of her body temp and she squeezes my hand. I look at her face and discover her blue eyes open but unfocused.

Trying to be as polite and friendly as I can, I give her hands a gentle squeeze. "Hi." She responds by weakly pulling my hands to her nose and sniffing them. She then weakly pulls me closer. Realizing what she is trying to do, I take off my lab coat and lay down next to her on the bed. She curls up to my side, puts her head on my chest, and sighs deeply, and almost immediately falls asleep.

I grab a blanket and cover us up, but not feeling tired, I absently start petting her gently from between her ears, following the longer fur across her head to the base of her neck. As I do I realize that something about this is familiar. I also realize that I am very happy, and it's because of something more than simply having someone to interact with.

"Her pulse has leveled out and her body temperature is rising," Aime states. "She is recovering quicker than expected."

Good. Still gently petting her, I stare blankly at the star-like points of light in the ceiling, wondering why she seems familiar.

I awaken to the sensation of a hand being slid across my chest.
Aime?
"You fell asleep."
How long was I out?
"Almost an hour."
How is she doing?
"Her vitals have stabilized, so I am going to assume that they are now normal for her physiology, but I will continue to monitor them."
Ah, good.
"I have been observing her sleep habits and noticed that her movements seem to be more consistent with that of a domestic house cat than that of a humanoid. I suspect she may have amnesia, like you do."

Oh. I look at the furry, cat-shaped head that's using my chest as a pillow, still wondering why she seems familiar. As if in response to me looking at her, she turns her head slightly, then stretches out, extending her left arm across my chest. As she relaxes, her left hand stops in the middle of my chest. I reflexively put my hand on hers and wrap my other around her.

My feelings of homesickness fade, and I take a slow, relaxing breath. In response, she purrs, and we both fall asleep again.

* * *

Ka-thump!

I snap awake and quickly realize that I'm alone. I look around and don't see the cat-girl anywhere.

"Lights," I say and they come on to about half capacity. Hearing another thump from below, I look down from the bed at the floor. She's lying there, looking around puzzled.

"Are you okay?" I ask, looking down at her.

She looks up at me and smiles back, nodding yes. She reaches up and touches my cheek as I offer my hand to help her up. She takes it but stands up easily without much help from me. Seeing her arm, she realizes that she is wearing the cryo suit and starts to pick at it, trying to pull it off.

"Here, let me help you." I slide off the bed and face her, quickly realizing that she is a little shorter than I had originally thought, only coming up to my nose. As I release the small clasp at the neckline, she gently bumps my nose with hers, something I find oddly familiar and makes me smile more. I slowly peel open the suit, stopping when the split reaches her breasts.

Turning to get her robe, I state, "Just peel it apart and I'll—" I turn back to see her drop the suit to the floor. "—get you a robe."

I watch curiously with the robe in hand, as she shakes her white fur loose. She then takes a few steps and stretches, standing as tall as possible, reaching for the ceiling, pointing her toes, and sticking her tail out straight. From head to toe, her fur is white, not a noticeable tint or variation.

I can't help but admire her beauty and elegance as she starts to casually walk around. After a moment, she turns to me, and with a couple of quick steps, she closes the short distance between us and wraps her arms around me, giving me a tight hug.

I tentatively give her a hug back, and she takes a step back giving me a puzzled look. I offer the robe to her. She looks at it, then back at me, shakes her head no, and tilts her head slightly.

"Come over here." I step over and have a seat on a couch, and she sits opposite me. "Do you remember who you are?"

She nods.

"Do you remember who I am?"

Again, she nods, but this time with a concerned look on her face.

"I don't remember any of that, not yet anyway. All I do know is that we were cryogenically frozen. Do you know what that is?"

She holds out her hand and wiggles it in a motion that I know to mean "kind of."

"You know what 'frozen' means?"

She nods.

"Cryogenic means we were frozen, specifically to be reawakened later. I can't remember much because of it. My memories should return, but it could take a few months."

She looks at me, tilts her head slightly, and then reaches up to touch my face again. As her hand strokes my face, I reflexive close my eyes and put my hand on hers and hold it to my face, enjoying her touch. When I open my eyes, I see her blue cat's eyes looking into mine. She leans into me and put her head against my chest and starts to purr.

I wrap my arm around her, holding her close. "I can tell you care a lot for me. It feels right that I care about you too." Giving her a kiss on top of her head, I say, "Please be patient with me."

We sit like this until we are interrupted by her stomach growling. She jumps a little and put a hand on her stomach. I can't help but chuckle at her reaction. "Hungry?"

She nods.

"Wait here." I walk over to the converter and see something appear in it.

"I have selected a suitable meal for her," Aime interjects.

I pick up the plate and walk back to her. There are several strips of cooked meat covered with herbs and a light sauce. I sit down next to her; she looks at the plate and starts sniffing the aroma. Her eyes light up and she licks her lips.

I pick up a strip and offer it to her; she sniffs it carefully before giving me a puzzled look. I take a bite of it and she gets the idea and eats the strip straight from my fingers. Her ears perk up as she chews, apparently enjoying the flavor.

I watch as she eats them, one at a time until they're gone. When she starts licking the plate, I ask, "Would you like more?"

She abruptly stops, embarrassed, and shakes her head.

I set the plate aside and ask, "Can you speak?"

She again shakes her head.

I lean back on the couch and breathe a heavy sigh, wondering how we're going to communicate. She puts her head on my shoulder and curls up against me. I close my eyes, put my arm around her, and hold her close, another thing that just feels natural to me. We sit in silence, enjoying each other's company.

After a few minutes, I get an idea. *Aime, are there any programs to teach people how to read?*

"There are several programs for teaching people how to read, some specially for mutes. There are also programs for teaching sign language, which I would recommend."

I open my eyes and find her looking intently in my ear. "What?" I ask, trying not to move my head.

She points in my ear and then at her mouth.

"I believe she heard me," Aime points out.

In response, she again looks in my ear, this time putting a claw in my ear to try to get a better look. "Ow!" I protest and she quickly pulls back, an apologetic look on her face.

"No claws, okay? That hurt," I state, rubbing my ear. "You can hear her?"

She nods, tilting her head curiously.

"That's Aime. She's a . . . uhm. Aime, could you explain what you are to us? I still don't really understand."

"Pick up a tablet and I'll show you."

I retrieve a tablet and sit back down next to the cat-girl. We both watch and listen intently as Aime begins to explain, her voice coming from the tablet.

"I am a Symbiotic Artificial Intelligence. In the simplest terms, I am a nanocomputer." The display shows a generic human body that zooms in on the head, suddenly little red spots start appearing along the inside of the skull as she continues. "My main memory core and matrix was constructed against the inside of your skull. I use less than one-tenth of the available space between your brain and skull. I also have various devices implanted in your organs."

New dots appear on the eyes, ears, mouth, and nose. "Like you, I have sensory input devices. These allow me to not only share in your experiences but to also monitor your surroundings and communicate back to you. For example, you hear me because I actually project my voice through the auditory sensor pods in your ears. Since they are inside your ears, I am not very loud. The sound level is comparable to that of a very small insect that is flying. This is how you, young lady, can hear me."

The cat-girl smiles as the display on the tablet changes to a full-body view, and several more dots appear as Aime continues, "I also have pods located in your internal organs, allowing me to sample the air you breathe, the food you eat, and they also allow me to monitor the effectiveness of your body's functions. Some of the pods can also produce small amounts of medicine or nutrients if needed."

"This is my base configuration, the way I was set up inside you. You, young lady, do not have an AI, but you both have nanites that can speed the healing process and clean out infections, poisons, and anything else harmful to you." The display changes to show a few different views of a nanite resembling a short millipede. "There are several kinds, but these are the ones that I currently use. They are general purpose nanites and can be used from anything from the construction of new components to repairing your body."

The display changes to show Aime's face. She smiles and asks, "How was that?"

I look at her face in the display. "Thorough, but creepy." I glance to the cat-girl and she looks similarly disgusted, with her ears laid back and her tongue sticking out a little.

"To in-depth?" she asks.

"Yeah, a little," I state. The cat-girl nods in agreement.

"Well then, to change the subject, would you like to learn sign language?"

The cat-girl looks up at me and then tilts her head in thought.

"It would allow you to talk, with your hands," I add.

She nods.

"Thank you," I say, wrapping her in a hug.

I set the tablet aside as she gets up and walks around. I can't help but just watch her gracefulness as she moves, wondering why she is so comfortable without clothing on. She pauses to examine the pictures scattered around the room, looking at some longer than others before moving on to the next, the whole time her tail sways idly just above the floor.

She abruptly stops in front of a picture, and her tail sags to the floor. I walk over to her and look at the picture and see that it's of a normal white cat curled up on a pillow. I look at the girl's face as she looks intently at the picture. "What is it?"

She points at the picture, then looks oddly at me and points at herself.

I look curiously at her, "Is that you?"

She shakes her head no and then points to the picture again, then to herself.

Unsure, I ask, "That *was* you?"

She nods and then reaches for something on her neck. Noticing that it's not there, she gets a concerned look on her face as her fingers search her neck.

"You're not wearing anything," I point out to her. "Did you have something on?"

She points to her neck and then to the neck of the cat in the picture. I notice that it's wearing a collar. "Did you have a collar?"

She nods.

"Come here," I take her hand and lead her to her pod. Finding the small storage compartment, I try to open it like I did mine, but it doesn't move.

"Aime?"

"It may have a genetic key," she explains. "She will have to open it."

"Press here," I tell her, pointing to the door. She does and the door pops open. I reach in and pull out the only thing I find, a small flat piece of metal shaped like a cat's paw. It's a tag.

"I . . . gave you this," I find myself saying.

She nods and looks at me curiously.

I turn it over and find an engraving and read it aloud, "My name is Sada. I belong to Kyle. If you find me . . ." I find myself unable to finish reading it. Tears roll down my face as I start to cry. Sada steps up to me and purrs as she hugs me.

"Sada," I whisper, wrapping my arms around her. "Your name is Sada, and my name is Kyle."

*　*　*

Having just taken a shower, Sada comes up to me holding the shower nozzle.

Confused, I look at it, then back at her. "What's wrong?"

She starts to make some motions, which I start to figure out.

"It came off the wall?"

She nods.

"It's supposed to."

A puzzled look crosses her face and she accidentally activates the nozzle, spraying my face with water. Startled, she drops the head to the floor and it automatically shuts off. She covers her muzzle with her hands and gets a worried look on her face.

I take her towel and dry my face and neck off. "And they work without being attached."

I pick up the nozzle and head into the shower room. As I reattach it to the wall, she feels my shirt. She points, and I realize that it's dry already. She then takes the towel and rubs it between the pads of her fingers. Realizing that it's also dry, she gives me a puzzled look.

Somehow knowing her question, I say, "I'm not sure. Aime?"

"These towels have nanofibers that wick the water into nano-sized converters that recycle the water and whatever is in it. This keeps the towel clean and dry after use."

"Nice," I comment, and Sada nods her agreement. "Do clothes do this too?"

"Yes, but they work slower."

"Self-cleaning towels and clothes."

"They can also repair small amounts of damage."

"Nice."

Sada nods and hangs the towel over the shower door and then walks out. I follow, grabbing a drink from the converter as I pass by. As I grab my tablet, I notice that Sada is not in the room. I look around for her as she comes out of her pod room, having changed into a light blue two-piece bikini. She stretches and yawns.

"Tired?"

She nods and then quietly walks over to the bed and lies down. She lifts her head enough to look at me and waves me over. I put what's left of my drink back in the converter and slip out of my boots as I approach the bed.

I sit next to her and remove my socks. Curious, I turn to her. "It doesn't bother you, me losing my memory, does it?"

She sits up and wraps her arms around me from behind and I feel her gently shake her head no. I wrap my arms around hers and gently squeeze her hands. "It bothers me."

She slides around beside me and gently nuzzles me, a look of understanding on her face.

I sigh. "I wish I could remember."

She sighs lightly, then slides around behind me again and starts to rub my back. I slump forward a little, enjoying the light back rub. Apparently feeling me relax, she pulls my shirt up and I let her take it off me. As she gently pulls me back to lie down, I slide myself up to the pillows and she slides up to my left.

"Do we always sleep together?"

She lays her head on my chest and gently nods.

As I lay there, I realize that her soft fur against my stomach and ribs actually feels nice. No, better than nice. It feels *right*. Comforting. I wrap my arm around her and gently pull her a little closer. In response, she starts to purr and I gently rub her back as we slowly drift off to sleep.

*   *   *

Lounging on a couch, having just finished a lesson, I set my tablet aside and stretch. With a glance at Sada, I see she's still focused on hers. Feeling hungry, I step over to the converter and select a meal for myself. After a little thought, I decide on a lightly seasoned fish dinner for Sada.

I set the plate next to her on the bed and she absently takes one and eats it while still working her lesson. I chuckle and sit at the desk and eat my own meal while I watch her. She eats a couple more pieces, still engrossed in her lesson, so I turn to the monitor and call up the floor plan.

I start looking over the plans for rooms of interest. Currently, I've only been into the central core and ventured a short distance both up and down. Scrolling up to the top floor, I find an observation deck. Curious as to what it observes, I scroll down a floor and find a hangar and a few storage bays located just inside the door.

I send the map to a tablet and watch Sada as I finish my meal. She continues eating slowly in-between questions. I wait until she finished her lesson and sets her tablet aside.

"Want to go exploring?" I ask her.

She looks at me curiously, then smiles and nods her head.

We put the plates in the converter and I put on a pack and grab the tablet with the map. Sada hands me a flashlight and I put it on my right hand as she puts hers on her left. We walk out to the central hub and start following the corridor to the left as it circles upward.

We pass by a number of converters and other equipment, but like everything else in the central hub, they're all without power. The hall has several short flights of stairs at each of the corners, and we finally come to the door marked "Hangar." With no power to the door, we have to pry it open. Fortunately, it's been well protected inside the facility, so the door moves easily.

Inside the main part of the hangar, the air is cold, and it's disappointingly empty. The far wall is a heavily reinforced double sliding door. They're the main hangar door to the outside. The ceiling is three or four stories high, slightly domed, with a row of windows along the left side, apparently for the observation deck. I see several normal doors, and two very large doors along the walls to the left and right, though the one to our right is blackened and warped, as are the walls and ceiling around it.

"There's been a fire in that bay," Aime states as I pan my light across the wall.

"What would normally be in there?" I ask, walking closer to the door, hearing both my voice and footsteps echo.

"Given the size of the door and the indicators on the floor, I would speculate a shuttle of some sort."

"A shuttle, as in space shuttle?" I ask curiously.

"Yes, but I do not believe it would be the same as what you would know. Remember, you have been in cryo for several hundred years."

"Yeah, I know," I admit as I try to peak through the buckled door. Unable to see anything inside, I turn to the other large door opposite it.

Sada follows me across the bay, shining her light around, looking at other doors, windows, and ventilation grates.

Getting close to the large door, Aime speaks up, "I do not believe you can open this door by hand."

I look up at the tall doors. "Really?" I ask, sarcastically.

Sada pokes me, getting my attention. I look at her and she points to the tablet's map and then at a smaller, person-sized door a few meters to our left.

Forcing open that door reveals a small anterior room that leads to the bay. Inside there's a small winged craft. "What's this?" I ask.

"It appears to be a scout ship. I do not have records of what class it is, but from the array of parts around, I would speculate that they were building it."

"Another project." I speculate as I slowly circle it. It's a single-seat craft, not much more than a few meters long. The wings are almost tri-angular in shape, making the small craft look like an arrowhead. From the open and missing panels along its sides and the number of jack stands underneath, holding sections of the thing up, I agree with Aime's speculation.

"Well, it's no good to us if it only seats one," I comment. Seeing Sada smile at the comment, I start looking around for anything that may be useful.

Aime apparently realizes my intent, "Most of the items in this room are specialized for ship and shuttle repair. They won't be much good for anything else."

Sighing in disappointment, I head back to the door. "Well, let's see what's in some of the other rooms around here."

*   *   *

We walk back into the receiving room with our meager findings. I set my pack on the desk and flop on the couch with a frustrated sigh. Sada sets down her tablet and flashlight and lightly sits down next to me. She snuggles up to me, purring. I wrap my arm around her, "Why is it I can't stay mad when you do this?"

She gently nuzzles my chin but keeps purring.

"Why would you be mad?" Aime asks.

"Almost a day spent looking for useful stuff and all we find is two medkits and three more tablets. It's kind of a waste of a day," I state.

"Finding the medkits is good, especially since Cayla does not have any nanites. She will need all the help she can get during her awakening."

"Yeah, I suppose, I just wish we could have found something more." I sigh.

Sada taps me on the arm, getting my attention. 'Who is K-la?'

"K-la?" I look at her blankly for just a moment. "Oh, Cayla. Come on, I'll show you." I take her hand and lead her into Cayla's pod room. Once there, Sada wipes her hand across the window, cleaning off some of the fog and studies the figure within. After a few moments, she turns to me.

'What she doing?'

"She is cryo, just like we were." I put an arm around her and continue, "There was an accident here that killed a lot of the people. She survived long enough to put herself in here. Before she did, though, she appears to have had her AI kill off all the nanites in her body. Aime says she'll need a lot of help during her awakening if she's to survive." I glance at the countdown timer and note the six remaining days.

I watch as Sada gets a solemn look on her face. 'She like you, not me'

I wrap my arms around her from behind. "I think she'll like us both. She was in charge of our area, keeping us safe, and she made sure that all this stuff was put here for us when we woke up. She even put Aime in me and the nanites in you so we would stay healthy after we awoke."

'No,' she signs, 'is she like you or like me?'

"Oh," I say, realizing what she intended with her first question. "Well, she is human, like me, so no cat ears, fur, or tail, but she is female, like you."

As I gently hold her, wondering what thoughts are running through her mind, she wraps her tail around my leg and her arms around mine. We stand silently for a while, watching Cayla float in the tube.

Feeling her shiver, I give her a light kiss on her head. "Come on, she's got six more days till we need to be in here." Sada nods and we leave the room.

*   *   *

I grab a tablet and start looking at the map, looking for a way into the medical ward. The last time we tried, we found that the doors were buckled outward and jammed. As I sit at the desk reviewing the map, Sada walks around, curiously looking at various items.

Finding the image area around the medical ward scrambled, I mutter to myself, "That explains why Aime couldn't find another way in." Using the monitor at the desk, I call up the blueprints and start comparing images.

It takes me a few minutes, but I start to understand the blueprints. I discover that there are several air ducts that I could crawl through to get in. I highlight a path to follow to the closest air ducts on the visitors' map and then send the blueprints to the same tablet. I look at Sada and she's already got a flashlight on and handing me one.

I put it on. "I take it you want to come along?"

She nods, grabs a pack, and heads to the doors.

"Aime, I'll need a cutting tool to get into the ducts." The converter flashes and I pick up the L-shaped device that appeared and follow. We turn right and head downward several floors.

Once at the buckled doors, I switch maps and find the air duct. I put the flashlight on my other hand and get a good look at the cutter. It has a simple contoured handle like a hammer but there's a guard that wraps around a pencil-length rod that extends out at a ninety-degree angle with a few controls opposite the rod.

"Release the safety and fold the guard down but don't touch the rod. Hold down the activator as you push the rod straight through the metal you want to cut. Then just move it slowly where you want to cut."

"Sounds simple enough," I admit. "Will there be any hot edges or gasses to worry about?"

"No, the rod is covered with micro converters that turn the material being cut to energy," she explains.

I look suspiciously at the cutter. "Does everything have converters in it?"

"Almost."

I smile as I turn to the wall with the air duct. The duct is at knee height and about a third-meter square, not quite big enough to fit through. I look at the blueprint again and notice a size difference.

"Uh, Aime?"

"It is possible that the duct is still as large as the plan shows but just the opening was reduced."

I try to look through the grate, but the mesh is apparently layered, preventing me from seeing anything. "I hope so, or this will be for nothing," I comment.

I press the safety and drop the guard from around the rod against the handle, noticing that it becomes a knuckle guard. Holding it by the grip, I press the activator and insert the rod through an opening at the edge of the grate. I push it through until the guard is flush against the grate. As I slide the cutter around the outer edge of the opening, it hums quietly as it easily removes the metal that it touches.

Sada takes hold of the grate with her claws as I finish cutting it free. She sets it aside as I put my hand through the opening and feel around the edge. Just as Aime had indicated, it's larger inside. I activate the cutter and start working again.

After a few minutes, I finish removing the last piece of wall, revealing a hole almost a half-meter across and tall. Checking the edges, I find that they are not very sharp. I wrap a strap to the pack around my foot, then with cutter and tablet in hand, I slide headfirst into the duct.

As I pass the first junction, almost three meters in, I hear Sada crawl into the duct behind me; her light casts my shadow all around me, creating an odd visual effect. After passing the first junction, I keep crawling forward, and get to the second junction, I double-check the map. This is the one I want. I turn and follow the duct until I find the grate.

As I slide up into place, I roll onto my left and push my back against the wall. I position my light and start cutting. Fortunately, this grate is the size it's supposed to be making the cuts easier.

The grate drops outward with a *whump*, and I push it away as I slide out into the room. I stand and start to look around as Sada slides out. Before she stands, she unwraps the pack from my leg as I'd forgotten that it was there.

I turn my attention back to the room. "It looks like something exploded in here," I comment aloud. As I turn, looking at the mess of equipment and other debris, I notice that Sada has an equally shocked look on her face.

"If this were not the medical ward, I would agree with you," Aime states, "but there should not be anything in here that could do this kind of damage. It looks like a high-pressure vessel burst, but those are not supposed to be anywhere near the medical bay."

As I look around I realize that everything does look more like it was blown around by a very powerful wind as opposed to violently hit by a concussive force. "Well, as much as I'd like to know what did this, we need to find better medical supplies."

Finding an intact table, I set it up in a clear part of the large room. Sada sets the pack on it. I put the cutter away and get out a second light. After setting it to it's brightest flood, I stick it to a poll and point it at the ceiling.

With some ambient light, I give Sada a kiss. "Be careful, okay?"

She gives me a bump with her nose and nods. We start with the intact cabinets and find a large number of wound treatments, though with a lot of their containers cracked, we don't set many aside on the table.

As Sada starts rooting through the broken cabinets, I get out the map and look for anything labeled "Emergency." Not finding anything, I think for a moment, but get distracted when Sada starts knocking on something hollow.

I look over to where she is and see that she is crawling into a hole in a pile of debris. As I approach she comes out and signs, 'What is, t-r-a-u-m-a?'

I smile. "Trauma." Suddenly hopeful, I help her uncover her find. As we move a broken table off of it, I realize that it's a trauma cart. "Jackpot!" We stand it up and carry it over by the table.

Sada finds a stool and sets it down for me. "Thanks." I sit between the cart and the table and move the few supplies aside. Sada comes up with another stool and sits by the table and watches me.

Opening the top I find an odd-looking chrome gun. "A nanite injector," Aime explains.

Picking up the injector, I look it over, finding that it reminds me of a paint sprayer rather than a medical device. It has a simple pistol grip and trigger, a short, multi-tipped barrel. There are also three small openings for something to attach halfway down the top side of the barrel. I work the trigger a couple of times, finding it moves easily.

"It seems to be in working order," Aime states. "Are there any cartridges for it?"

I set the injector on the table and turn back to the cart. With the contents in disarray, the labels under the cover mean nothing. "What am I looking for?"

"There should be some small glass bottles with colored lids."

"Why are a lot of things in glass bottles? I thought that plastic was better."

"With the advent of cryo-stasis, plastic quickly became a poor choice for long-term storage as it will allow contaminants in. Glass is non-porous and does not degrade, making it ideal for long term storage."

"That makes sense," I comment, opening up a drawer to look through it.

"There they are," Aime exclaims, as I see the bottles she had mentioned. Surprisingly, these are still in place, so the labels on the tray are accurate.

"Rescue nanites: three bottles. Menials: two bottles. Nano Delivery Solution: four empty bottles," I say as I read the labels.

"The converter can make more of the delivery solution," Aime advises.

"What's the difference between menials and rescue nanites?"

"Rescue nanites do not reproduce. They also carry a larger power source than menials and are usually injected directly into the traumatized area."

"So emergency, short-term help."

"Correct."

I pick up the tray with the bottles and put it on the table. I see Sada pick up a bottle and look intently at the powder inside. Shaking her head a little, she puts the bottle back and puts both the injector and the tray in the pack. She then stuffs several of the wound treatments around them.

The cart provides several more bandages and one container of a topical spray on nano-solution. Almost everything else in the cart is broken in some way, rendering the contents compromised or useless. Finding nothing else of use, we pack up our treasures and head back to our room.

Sada heads for the showers, as I put the empty bottles in the converter, and with a flash, Aime has them refilled with the delivery solution. She also creates a new case for the injector. I put the injector, and its bottles, in the case and set them in Cayla's room, along with the med-kits that we've collected.

Back from her shower, Sada sits down with her tablet for a lesson as I head to the converter. Having quickly learned that Sada prefers finger food, I select an herbed chicken strip meal with some breaded cheese sticks and dipping sauces for both of us. I set a plate by Sada. I have a seat and look for other places of interest while I eat.

CHAPTER 3

Standing in Cayla's room, I carefully load a bottle of the delivery solution, matching the cap color to the ring around the openings on to the injector with a push twist motion. I repeat with bottles of the menials and the rescue nanites. With all three loaded I move both the selectors to their "On" positions. Sada stands beside me, towel ready, nervously twitching her tail. I set the injector down and open both med-kits. I ready several nutrient patches and set out an AI tether in case Aime needs it to interface with the nanites once they're in Cayla.

I smile nervously at Sada, who's still only wearing a light blue bikini. I'm only wearing a comfortably loose shirt-pant combo with my favored boots, forgoing the lab coat this time. As the timer finally reaches zero, the pod makes some clicks. Suddenly the cryo fluid drains, much faster than it did in Sada's. After a couple more clicks, the door pops forward and slides off to the left. I reach in and rotate the ring to release her breathing tube. As it retracts, I step back and let Sada dry her off.

As I gently pick Cayla up, Sada releases the straps holding her up. I quickly move her from the pod to the bed and carefully lay her down. Sada hands me the injector and starts placing the nutrient patches on her shoulders, over and under each breast, each side of her stomach and upper thighs. I follow behind injecting the nanites through the patches. Sada then hands me the tether and I stick one end up under my shirt, directly to my sternum as Sada opens the front of Cayla's cryo suit. I quickly stick the other end to her sternum and then reload all three bottles on the injector.

"Her AI is working," Aime reports after a moment. "Relaying assessment. Nanites active, fifty billion. All bodily systems are compromised by cryo. The remaining effectiveness of systems are cardiovascular, 21 percent; respiratory, 34 percent; digestive,17 percent; endocrine, 10 percent; reproductive; 14 percent; urinary, 2 percent; muscular, 68 percent; neurological, 42 percent; and immune, 77 percent."

"I don't like the sound of those numbers. Repair hierarchy and probability?" I ask, hoping for some good news.

"Neurological, respiratory, and cardiovascular are a priority," she answers. "Projection of repair, 88 percent within the next two hours. Survival rate, 42 percent within the next hour. Surgical package required for major repairs."

"That doesn't sound good," I comment, seeing the tears fill Sada's eyes. "Would more nanites help?" I ask, readying the injector.

"No, areas of her core are already at mass limit."

"Is there anything we can do to improve her chances?" I ask, setting the injector aside.

"Searching . . . We could piggyback her vital neurological functions onto yours, through the AI link. This should buy her some time."

"How much time?"

"Uncertain."

"What are the dangers?" I ask, noting the concerned look on Sada's face.

"To you, minimal. To her, no more than she is already in."

I look at Sada and she gives me a slight nod. "What do I need to do?"

"You will want to lie down. The process will make you tired."

As I climb up next to Cayla on the bed, I touch Sada's cheek. "Stay alert, okay, in case Aime needs something." She bumps my nose and nods. I lie back, wrapping my arm around Cayla to help hold me on the now crowded bed. "Let's do this."

"Beginning," Aime states, and I start to feel very tired. After several minutes, Aime announces, "Neurological systems synced."

Suddenly drowsy, I ask, "What's her survival rate now?"

"Seventy-eight percent over the next three hours."

"Much better."

Feeling someone gently shaking me, I slowly open my eyes. Sada's leaning over me, franticly signing something. I blink my eyes a few times to bring things into focus.

"Awake, she awake," Sada signs at me.

I start to sit up and realize that the tether is no longer attached to my chest. "Huh?"

"I told Sada to remove it. She no longer needs your assistance with her neurological functions," Aime advises me.

I rub my now pounding head. "How long has it been?"

"Four hours, twenty minutes."

"How's she doing?"

"I've been better."

I roll off the bed and turn to face her. "Morning."

She rolls her head to look at me and, after a moment, licks her lips and weakly asks, "Who are you?"

"First, do you remember who you are?"

"Cayla," she answers.

I smile, relieved her memory is intact. "I'm Kyle, but you know me as Alpha." Seeing her smile I add, "Before you start asking questions, I have amnesia. The only reason I know my name is because of my friend here, Sada, or Beta as you know her."

Sada steps up beside me and looks curiously at Cayla. Cayla looks back, her eyes full of wonder. "Oh, you're beautiful," she says, tears coming to only one of her eyes. She tries to lift her arms, but in her weakened condition, she can't lift them much. "Come here," she whispers.

Sada sits on the bed next to her, gently picks up her hand, and nuzzles into it, purring.

"Oh," Cayla softly exclaims. "So soft, and you can still purr too." She weakly rubs Sada's cheek. "And your eyes, you're a house cat?"

"Near as I can tell, she was my cat."

"How . . . ?" she starts to ask, but is interrupted by some weak coughs.

I hold up Sada's cat tag. "I remember giving her this, in case she got lost."

Cayla weakly looks at my hand and smiles. "So tired," she says, changing the subject and mood quickly as she falls asleep again.

"She is exhausted," Aime advises. "Her nanites have reached their limit. They need more energy."

"Can you transfer power from me to her?" I ask, concerned.

"I have already transferred what I could while you were asleep."

Thinking for a moment, I ask, "How long would it take her to set up some ANRCs?"

"More time than she has."

Sighing, I ask, "What can we do to give her more time?"

"Without a surgeon's package, nothing."

Sada suddenly holds up a few of the nutrient patches and looks at me curiously. "Aime?"

"It may work, but they will not buy her much more time."

"Well, it's better than nothing," I comment as Sada starts placing another dozen patches on her torso. "Maybe if she wakes up, we can get her to drink something rich in what she needs most."

"According to her AI, Marc, she is not able to handle food yet."

"Not even if the nanites use it all?"

"Sorry, no."

Sighing, I lean back against the counter and rub my face with my hands. Sada slides up and hugs me while purring. I wrap my arms around her and bury my nose in her fur, "What am I going to do?"

"Marc suggests you put them back in cryo," Aime offers.

I lift my head and look at Cayla. "What are her odds of survival that way?"

"Currently no different than they are without her in cryo, but it does offer you time to find a way to save her if it is possible."

Sada pulls back and signs, 'It hope for her.'

I nod and pull her close again. "How long do we have to put her back in cryo?"

"Marc estimates, two hours."

"How long does it take to put her back in cryo?"

"Ten minutes."

Sighing, I think for a moment. "We'll give her an hour and a half to wake up, and then we put her back in."

"Marc agrees. He indicates that she may wake up within the next thirty minutes. You will be able to talk to her then."

Sitting quietly by the bed, looking through the map again, I'm slightly startled when a hand touches my shoulder.

"Kyle?" Cayla softly asks.

I set aside the tablet as I turn to her, "Yes?"

"It's okay to put me back in cryo. I thought it might happen." She sighs heavily. "I need you to find the archeology team, give them the data that Marc gave Aime. Find the dig site. Let them know it's safe to come back."

"I have the details from Marc," Aime quietly announces.

"I will," I tell her, not having the heart to tell her that I have no idea how long it's been since the accident.

She looks longingly at me. "I've always wanted to know what you both really looked like." She takes a heavy breath, "Treat Aime well. She's just a baby. She'll grow and learn just like you." Her eyes close as she passes out again.

"Aime, what did she mean that you're just a baby?"

"While I have access to libraries of information, my experience is no more than the few days that you've been awake. The more things you do, the better I get to know you and anticipate your unspoken requests based on your actions."

"So I won't need to ask you to scan something when I put my hands on it, you'll just do it?"

"I will most likely do that anyway, to learn, but if you were to take the military package, for example, I would be able to activate some of its abilities without you telling me to."

"Anticipating my needs so we can work more efficiently," I state.

"Correct. I will make assumptions based on your past decisions, though the more experience I have with you, the more accurate they will be."

I look at Cayla quietly for a moment.

"Marc says that she will not regain consciousness again, not without major repairs to her body."

I sigh. "It's time, then."

Sada comes in and looks at Cayla sadly. I note a tear in her eye as she starts to remove the nutrient patches.

She then helps me pick up Cayla and I reposition her in the tube. Before I put the mask back on her, I gently rub her cheek. "I'll be back for you, and I'll be prepared then. You'll be okay." Sada reaches in and rubs her cheek.

Once I have her mask back in place, I hook up the breathing tube. After it clicks, I close the door and lock it.

Sada leans on me while we watch the cryotube fill. Cayla begins to float as the air is pushed from the tank. After a few minutes, a green light comes on, signaling that she is in full cryo-stasis. With nothing more to do, we quietly pick up and leave the room.

*   *   *

With no further reason to stay and a destination to find, I have Aime download everything she can on this planet. I set up my pack and start pulling items out of boxes that are going to be the most use. Having been unable to locate any form of working transportation, we plan on walking to the dig site. Aime assures that this will take several months, so we try to pack accordingly.

Sada opens a long box and pulls out a meter-long, thick silver pole. I grin as I watch her turn it around, trying to figure out what it is.

"It's a tent," I state. Her reaction is a somewhat unique mix of surprise and disbelief. "Here, let me show you."

She hands over the pole as I step to the center of the room. Holding it upright, I turn a dial near the bottom and it extends downward to the floor. I then press a small button on the dial and several arms release from the upper section.

I easily open these like an umbrella and then use a dial on the collar adjusts the length of the arms, increasing or decreasing the overall diameter. Keeping it small, I press the button on the collar and thin poles drop down to the floor from the ends of each arm. With it now able to stand freely on its own, I press another button on the shaft and the top starts to fill itself in with fabric.

I step over to Sada, chuckling again at her new expression of awe. Putting my arm around her, I look back at the tent. "What do you think?"

She walks under the roof and touches the fabric. After a moment of wonder, she turns back to me. 'Nice, but where's the walls?'

"I didn't set them up," I confess, walking up to her, "there's too much stuff in the way right now."

Reversing the process, I quickly collapse the tent back to its pole form and put two of them into my pack. I also pack the pair of portable mini-converters we found, a pair of collapsing chairs, and several canteens, which aren't much more than a micro converter that produces water through a small nozzle. Using a small compression bag, I pack a few outfits. As I seal up the compression bag, it automatically shrinks down, squeezing the air out.

Marveling for a moment at how much smaller it got, I realize that I can pack more than I had originally planned. I grab another couple of compression bags and quickly pack several blankets in one and several towel sets in another.

Sada comes out with a compression bag of her own. I notice that it looks like there's nothing in it. "Packed?" I ask, curiously looking at the bag.

She tosses it to me. 'Not much I want.'

I frown a little but stuff it in my pack. As I pick up the other three to put them in the pack, I tell her what's in them. "My clothes, towels, blankets."

I put a few spare compression bags in as well. Sada hands me several flashlights, a couple of extra pocket blades, and the medical kit we put together from all the salvaged kits. I think for a moment and grab the AI updates I've gathered and tuck those in the medical pack.

Sada holds up a tablet. 'This?'

Thinking, I take it from her, "Aime, can you interface with these directly?"

"Yes, I can also use their memory to store additional information."

"Okay, good," I comment. Sada hands me the other four tablets and I put them all in my pack. With less than half the pack's space taken up, I look around at the other stuff that's in the boxes. I find one box labeled light armor. I pull out a two-piece outfit that looks like long underwear. Offering a pair to Sada, she simply shakes her head and curls her lip at them.

Chuckling at her reaction, I stuff a pair in my pack and keep looking around. Sada opens a box and hands me two black poles from it. I notice that they look just like the chairs I've already packed. "We already have two chairs," I comment to her.

She gives me an odd look and double checks the box. 'Tables,' she signs, still looking at the box.

"Ah," I exclaim and stuff them in the pack.

After several more minutes of looking and not finding anything perceivably useful on a walking trip, I decide on a shower. "I'm going to get cleaned up," I sigh. Sada nods to me and I notice that she is not as white as she could be. "You may want to also. It may be a while before we have the opportunity again."

She gives me an odd look and then looks herself over. I chuckle lightly as I head to the shower.

Once in, I rinse my clothes and hang them up over the door. I step into the shower and wet myself down. Before I can reach for the body wash, I feel a hand start rubbing my back with soap.

Knowing that she knows me better than I know myself, I hesitantly turn around and ask, "Just how well do we know each other?"

She looks curiously at me and then touches her nose to mine, purring.

"That well, huh?"

She smiles and nods slightly and then gives me a sign to turn around. I do and she starts to soap up my back and shoulders. I find myself enjoying her touch, relaxing as she rubs my back. After a few moments, she reaches across my shoulder and points to the showerhead. I hand it back to her and she turns the water on and rinses my back off.

She then pushes gently down on my shoulders, and I kneel. She then gently pulls my head back and wets my hair thoroughly as she pulls out the ponytail holders. She then sticks the showerhead to the wall while she reaches for my shampoo and lathers up my hair. As she does, I realize that it hear her purring, apparently happy with what she is doing.

After she rinses my hair, she taps me on the shoulders. Turning to look at her, I see that she is now standing with her back to me, holding out her bottle of shampoo.

Knowing what she wants, I take the showerhead from the wall and start to wet her down. I quickly notice that the normal setting does not get through her fur, so I adjust it to a slightly higher pressure massage setting and try again.

Feeling the pulsing water jets, she straightens and arches her back, obviously enjoying the sensations. I thoroughly wet her back and stick the showerhead to the wall. Starting from her shoulders, I start massaging the shampoo in. She again stretches and arches her back.

Working my way down, following her spine, she begins to purr arches her back towards me, her eyes closed. As I reach the base of her spine, I switch to her tail and gently work the shampoo in. She reaches out to the walls to steady herself as I finish with her tail.

After I rinse her off, she turns to me and signs, 'You're mean.'

I kiss her on the nose. "And you walked in on me in the shower."

She gives me a pouting look. 'But you liked it.'

I grin at her and give her another kiss. "I liked it a lot, and it seems you did too."

She averts her gaze for a moment, seemingly embarrassed. As she looks back at me, she suddenly turns away, ashamed, and darts from the room, leaving me standing, wondering what just happened.

After I redress, I set the body washes down by the pack and sit next to Sada. Not really knowing what to say, I just wrap my arm around her and pull her close to me. She sighs heavily and relaxes into me.

We sit in silence for a few minutes, until she gets up and retrieves the brushes and combs from the bathroom. I help her pack the few remaining items in silence.

Now fully packed, we head out the door and descend several levels. Finding the ground floor, we find a skeleton of a very large creature blocking the door to the main corridor.

"How did a karnesh get this far in?" Aime asks as I start to crawl through the skeleton.

"We both saw the video," I state.

"That is not what I mean," she chides. "There are several security doors that are supposed to be closed to prevent creatures from getting in."

Trying to slip through a broken rib, I offer, "I seem to recall some ocean liners sinking because their crew bypassed safeties." I pull the pack through the gap I just barely fit through. "Or this thing may have just simply smashed through them all."

Sada, being much more flexible, simply crawls through and easily slides between the ribs. "Show-off," I chuckle as I brush off some dust and put the pack back on.

She lightly shakes her fur and hands me something. As I take it, I realize that it's a large scale, almost as large as my hand, and a dull silver-green.

"That scale has a high metal content and is still very strong," Aime states.

I stuff it in my pack and look at the opening, noticing that the surrounding walls buckle both outward. "I think it got stuck in the door frame."

Aime seems to pause for a moment. "I believe you are correct, which would suggest that the other doors should all be passable."

I shine my light down the corridor ahead. "Well, if this is the way it came in, we'll find our way out."

Sada takes my hand as we start walking down the extra-wide corridor. I seem to know without looking at her that she is nervous. Glancing back at her, I realize that I'm right. Her ears are laid back, she has her light on, but is shining it behind her, and she is trying to stay as close to me as possible as we walk. I tighten my grip on her hand slightly, trying to convey some form of security to her.

We come upon a set of heavy-duty double doors that have clearly been forced open. Both have been severely bent and smashed into the walls with enough force to bind them in place. Looking closely at one, I realize that this is one of the sets of security doors that Aime mentioned.

We continue, in the silence, hearing only our breathing and footsteps. Passing a few more sets of smashed doors, we get to a Y in the corridor, with both halls leading off at similar angles. I shine my light down one and then the other, uncertain for a moment which corridor to take.

Sada points to the right.

"Are you sure?" I ask.

She nods and shines her light on a scrape on the wall to our left, on the near side of the corner, before the corridor splits. I check the opposing wall; there are no marks there.

Realizing her logic, I say, "All right, to our right it is."

We proceed down the right hall, and I quickly realize she was correct. When the corridor turns again, we find more scrapes on a wall. Around the corner, we find a pair of doors smashed open, leading into a smaller hall, away from the main hall. Shining my light down the main hall, we see a pair of intact doors. With them being closed, we decide to follow the path of destruction the karnesh left on its way in.

We turn and walk down the hall. After passing the second set of doors, the hall opens into a large room. Looking around, we find that the room has been thoroughly destroyed.

I realize that this room looks familiar. "Oh no," I groan, realizing that this is where the nanite-virus was kept. "Aime, is there anything left here?"

"I am not detecting any traces," she responds.

"Good," I sigh. Sada gives me an odd look, unsure of what I'm concerned about. "Come on," I say, taking her hand again. "Let's get out of here."

We carefully make our way through the room and out the other side. Coming out the other side into the other corridor, we continue to follow the trail of destruction. Making our way through several more sets of doors, we finally find dirt and sand on the floor. As we approach the last set of doors, I realize that there is no light shining in from outside.

We step out under a high, cave-like opening, and Sada and I both breathe deeply the cool, dry night air. We walk away from the facility, into the field, but Aime suddenly interrupts with a warning, "I would not recommend traveling at night. There are several nocturnal predators."

As if to reinforce her statement, we hear a loud shrieking from the field in front of us. Sada ducks in fear as I start backing us up under the overhang.

"Set up the tent," Aime quickly suggests.

"What good will that do?" I hesitantly ask.

"It can dampen your heat signatures, smells, and sounds once you're inside it."

"Yeah, okay." I quickly get the tent out and set it up, making it about four meters across. Once the walls and floor are in place, Sada and I quickly enter and close the door behind us. I drop my pack beside the door and turn around. I see Sada staring at a full-sized bed in the middle of the tent.

"Where'd the bed come from?" I curiously ask as Sada turns to me with a similarly curious look.

"I have taken the liberty of having the tent raise part of the floor to be used as a mattress."

'Why is there only one?' Sada asks curiously.

After a moment of silence, I repeat her question. "I could make it into two, but given your sleep habits, I assumed that one was more appropriate."

Sada leans against me, as if in thought, but something else bothers me. "Aime, why didn't you answer her question?"

"As an AI, my programming forbids me from responding to anyone but my host, you. It is a safety to prevent undesired actions."

"You've answered them before."

"Not directly. Till then, you have repeated or restated her question in some way."

"Can you respond to her, like you do me?"

"If you name her as your executor, I can, though I must caution you to make sure you trust her with your life, as she will have nearly the same control over me you have."

I look at Sada for a moment; she is looking back at me curiously. "I name Sada as my executor," I state, smiling. "I may not yet understand why yet, but I know I can trust her with my life."

"Very well, Sada is your executor." I watch Sada's jaw drop in surprise, as Aime asks, "Sada, would you still like me to separate the bed?"

Sada looks at me, then at the bed and shakes her head no. I wrap her in a hug. "I'm sorry if I overstepped my bounds earlier," I confess.

She sighs and starts to purr lightly. 'It was my fault too,' she admits.

I lie down on the bed and breathe a heavy sigh. Sada crawls across the bed and lies down on my left, her favored place. I start gently rubbing her back. "Aime, wake us when the sun rises."

"Certainly."

With it now morning, we use our mini converters to make us some breakfast. After packing up our gear, we head out from under the overhang and get a good look at our surroundings for the first time.

CHAPTER 4

The cavern opens out into a field that extends as far as the eye can see. There are occasional trees or mounds scattered around, but they are fairly distant from each other. Most of the plants are typically green or brown, though there are occasionally red, yellow, and even some blue and purple plants scattered throughout. Among everything, several dozen hammer-tails wander, grazing on the grasses and ferns.

"Aime, I expected it to look more . . . different. It looks more like . . . home."

We stand gawking as she begins to explain, "When this planet was discovered, its ecosystem was collapsing. Because of that, the researchers did not have to abide by the planetary conservation laws. They imported countless plants, reptiles, insects, and various other life to try to save it. You will find a lot of life from Earth, and even some other planets here."

"Other planets?" I ask, curiously.

"Yes, there have been several planets discovered that have Earth-like conditions, but none, that I am aware of, have had sentient life."

"Maybe that's what they were trying to do here, create some non-human sentient life to interact with."

"Possibly, the records for the founding were sealed; however, you both were transported here before the evolution research's beginning."

We start walking toward the rising sun, and I stop suddenly when a thought hits me. "Does the sunrise in the east here?"

"Yes, the dig site should be nearly due east of here."

Feeling more assured, we start walking again, clearing the cavern overhang. I notice that the ground starts to change from nearly level to a more uneven, naturally rolling terrain. I realize that this area is the quarantine area that I saw in one of the security videos. This is where everything started that day, long ago. I push those thoughts from my mind, trying to make them as gone as the fences and cages that once stood here.

Nearly an hour into our walk, Aime interrupts us, "I would like to point out something that you will find most non-Earth-like."

Stopping, I curiously look around. "And what would that be?"

"Turn around and look up."

I look at Sada and we both turn to face west and look up. I stand in awe as I hear Sada gasp.

"Rings!" I blurt out. "This planet has *rings!*"

"Yes."

I stand in disbelief as I look at the rings, seeing their subtle colors. Reds, browns, yellows, and even some grays. I notice that they follow an east-west plane but are hard to see against the bright morning sky to the east. I feel Sada's hand thump on my shoulder a little and I notice that she is pointing slightly higher in the sky. A moon, a large one it seems, like Earth's.

"There's another, look above you."

We look almost straight up and see the second moon. It's considerably smaller like it's farther away.

As if reading my mind, Aime chimes in, "The larger moon is actually much farther away than the smaller, and they orbit in opposite directions."

As we continue to look, I notice that the moons are following the same plane that the rings follow and that we are north of that plane. I also notice that the facility was not a large building, but inside a mountain, which is why there were no windows and everything was a constant temperature.

"They carved it out of a mountain?"

"Yes, it took construction bots a few months to carve out the halls and rooms, as others installed the geothermal and MHD generators on the far side. They then spent about a year setting up the equipment inside."

"Well, as much as I'd like to hear about that, we really should be moving," I comment looking at Sada, who nods in agreement.

Setting my sights on the east again, we start walking. The hammer tails ignore us as we walk, but we nervously keep our distance from them as we head for a group of mounds. As we get closer, I begin to realize that the mounds are actually structures, covered with plants.

Coming up to the first of them, I see that they are, or were, storage containers, exposure to the elements have taken their toll on them.

"From the condition of the containers, they have been without maintenance for at least two hundred years," Aime advises.

"I'm beginning to think it's not going to make much difference how long it's been."

"You may be right, but I will still keep track," Aime retorts.

"Well, unless it's profound, keep it to yourself."

Sada turns and gives me a dirty look and a few stern motions. 'Shut up, I can't hear over you two.'

I put up my hands in a mock surrender motion and continue walking in silence.

After several minutes, Sada stops abruptly and tilts her head slightly with her ears perked straight ahead. I reflexively stop walking, letting only the sounds of nature surround us.

'I hear . . . whistle,' she signs and then points straight ahead.

"I am picking up a faint power signature in the same direction," Aime indicates.

I pull a pair of binoculars out of my pack and look in the indicated direction. After a few moments, I find a large mound of vegetation.

"That should be it," Aime indicates, "about five kilometers away."

"Whatever it is, it's buried under foliage. I wonder why it's so far from the facility."

"I would need to know what it is to answer that," Aime chides.

"Yeah, no sense guessing about it right now," I agree. I look at Sada; she's listening intently. "Come on."

I start to walk, but Sada grabs my hand and stops me. I look back at her and her ears have slanted back, and she is starting to snarl.

"What?"

"Something is approaching, moving fast," Aime warns.

Sada turns suddenly, scowls and hisses. I turn to where she is looking and pull one of my blades. I hear another hiss, this one from the grasses. Suddenly, something leaps from the grass at Sada. She ducks and rolls to her left, leaving me standing in the path. I close my eyes and swing. I hit nothing but my spin apparently takes me out of its path.

"Open your eyes!" Aime commands.

I open my eyes and see a tan dinosaur-like lizard, about half my size. It's standing on its hind legs, and its mouth is lined with sharp teeth. As I look at it, the thing squats, preparing to jump again. This time I keep my eyes open, turning so it is to my left. Seeing Sada sneak up from its left, I back up a little to keep its attention. In response, it takes a few steps forward to close the distance. Sada crouches and pounces as it hisses and jumps right at me, mouth open. Sada lands where it was just the moment before.

I swing the blade like a bat and connect, slicing the lizard open. Unfortunately, by stepping into the swing, I have no time to dodge, and its dead body slams into my chest, mouth open. I feel teeth tear into my left shoulder, and I fall back from the impact, landing on my pack and hitting my head on the ground.

Feeling dazed, I lie there for a moment, until Sada's worried face appears, this brings me back to my senses. I groan and put my hand on my left shoulder. A sharp pain runs through my arm as I touch torn flesh.

"Aime," I weakly call. Sada starts pulling things out of the pack I'm laying on.

No response.

"Aime!" I call again with a little more energy. Sada finds a towel and presses it firmly on the wound. The pain is intense. I let out a scream and Sada cringes.

"Sorry, I am back now. Please remove the towel from the wound. It will only slow the repair process."

Sada reluctantly, but gently removes the towel. I see my own pain reflected in her eyes as she takes my right hand. Suddenly, the pain starts to diminish and Sada lets out a gasp. She looks from the wound to my eyes, puzzled. Letting go of my hand she starts signing, 'Shrinking, how.'

Aime states, "My nanites are accelerating your healing process."

After a couple of minutes, Aime lets me know she's done, and Sada helps me sit up. I take off the pack and we start putting the things back in it. Despite being healed, I'm hesitant to use my left, doing things more with my right arm.

I pull the cloak over me as Sada puts the pack on. I retrieve my blade and we walk on in silence, Sada listening carefully for any odd noises in the grass.

After nearly an hour, we near the source of the power signature. Being closer, it looks less domed and more triangular, with the nearest end having a sharp point and the farthest end, the widest part, having the highest point. Overall it's huge, being slightly longer than a football field, almost as wide.

"I cannot determine what it is. The vines completely obscure what is under them."

I pull out a blade and take a swing to cut some vines. A shower of sparks nearly blind me, and as I turn away, I manage to see Sada jump clear, her fur standing on end.

"What the?" I stagger back a few steps, blinking my eyes.

I look at the edge of the blade and see fresh scorch marks on it. Sada shakes off the surprise and steps over behind me, her tail still puffed from being startled.

"Sorry about that," I say to her. I put the blade up and take off the pack, setting it on the ground by Sada. I step back to the vines and examine the cut ends. They look like electrical wires, with green insulation.

"Wire vine, not Earth's kind either. These have unusually high metal content," Aime reports.

I look back to see that Sada's still by the pack. I pull the blade and finish cutting an opening in the vines, being careful to shield my eyes from the sparks. I examine the blade again and see no damage other than some more scorch marks. As I part the vines and step inside, several small creatures scurrying quickly away. The ones I manage to see look like small dragons.

"What were those?"

"Dragons, not the mythical ones, but they are similar in appearance. They are some of the few native creatures that can fly. Some can also spit a mild toxin or adhesive to catch the bugs they eat. They will normally flee from larger creatures."

"So they're harmless?" I ask.

"Correct."

As my eyes begin to adjust, I see several vines hanging throughout. Among them, several three-meter tall posts hold up the entire structure. After another step, I begin to recognize some features.

"It's a ship!" I gasp.

"A Black Hole class rescue ship. These are reserved for the most dangerous or most sensitive rescue missions."

In the dim light, I can make out some of its features: wide hull, wings folded forward, from the aft, meeting the smaller canard wings in front. All the vine-covered posts are the landing gear.

"Sada, come on," I call out, and she pokes through the vines, carrying the pack. She looks around and her gaze stops suddenly, and then her ears droop, noticeably sad. I look where she is looking and see that there are three identical stones under the aft section of the ship.

"Oh, no," I groan, knowing what they are. We walk over to the stones and see that they each have an engraving. "Graves."

The stones are labeled "LT Commander Geres," "LT Commander Ines," and "Commander Crowl." There are no dates.

"The captain is missing," Aime concludes.

"Well, someone had to put the stones here." I sigh, turning to look along the length of the ship. Seeing no ramps or ladders, I ask, "How do we get in?"

"I cannot establish communication with the ship's computer, so we will need to enter manually. Go to the foremost landing strut. There should be a manual release ring one and a half meters up."

Once there, I pull aside the vines and find a large D ring.

"Pull the ring down and turn clockwise, one-quarter turn, and that will lower the loading ramp."

I find the top of the handle and, with some effort, pull it down. Turning it, however, is out of the question. "It's stuck."

"It seems that the vines have grown into the structure of the ship. You will need to force it."

I look around for something to pry with but see nothing. Opening the pack, I look for something to use. I pull out the chairs, a table, and the tent; each time Aime tells me that they're not strong enough. I put the things back and think for a moment. I pull out a blade and insert it into the release.

"Don't. That will cut the handle," Aime warns.

I pull the blade out and put it away; this time I pull out the sheath too. I put the sheath into the release; Aime indicates that this may work, so I push down on the handle of the blade. The release starts to turn, slowly. We hear some screeching, metal on metal, and then stops. Sada takes the other blade off of my belt and inserts it into the other side of the release. She tries to lift as I push down. It turns a little more but again stops.

"We're going to need more leverage."

After a brief moment, Aime says, "I found something that may work. Check the converter."

Putting the blades back into my belt, I turn to the pack and pull out the converter. In it, I find a short, round bar, maybe a quarter meter long. "What's this?"

"It is a pocket staff, similar to the pocket blades. There is a release that will open it. I have preset its length to fit you."

I press the release and both ends extend outward, stopping just shy of two meters long. "Nice," I find myself saying.

I insert one end into the release, sliding it through to center it. Sada and I again try to turn the release. With the increased leverage, it turns, making terrible screeching sounds in the process.

Once we complete the quarter turn, we hear a loud clunk. Looking up we see a loading ramp start to open, slowly at first, but a sudden screech, it drops freely. We reflexively turn away as the ramp falls to the ground, hitting with a loud bang.

Waiting for a moment, to let the dust clear, I collect the staff and we slowly proceed up the ramp. At the top, we find a door with a similar release ring. This one turns easily, but the door does not open.

"It slides to your left," Aime indicates.

I grab the handle and slide the door open. Looking beyond, there is only darkness. I get out the flashlights and proceed in. Sada follows close behind me.

Looking around, we see that the room we entered is filled with cargo containers, all are still closed and neatly stowed, save for a large one that's out and left open. A quick look inside reveals three devices that look similar to high-performance street motorcycles, without wheels. It's obvious that there was a fourth inside, but it's been taken.

Continuing aft to the next door, I turn the release, the door slides open on its own. "The interior doors are designed to open if manually released during a power failure. They will reclose if exposed to vacuum though," Aime states.

I step through the door into a small hall with four more doors. Looking at the doors, they are labeled Gym, Lift, Stairs, and Aft Hold. I open the door to the aft hold and step through. The room is lined with several rows of cryotubes, similar to the ones in at the facility. Sada and I walked the length of the bay looking for any occupied tubes but they are all empty.

Returning to the smaller room, I turn to the door that says Gym and open it. I look in and see only exercise equipment, so I turn back to the last two doors. I open the door labeled Stairs, figuring the Lift won't work without power. We walk up to the next level.

Opening the door, we step out into a long hallway; a diagram on the opposite wall indicates that there are several crew cabins and a galley forward, with a medical bay, science lab, and engine room aft.

"We may be able to get some power restored in engineering," Aime suggests.

"This way," I say to Sada and we head aft.

When we get there, I open the door and instantly feel like gagging.

"What's that smell?" I ask, using my hand to plug my nose.

Sada covers hers, turns, and heads back to the stairwell to get away from the smell.

"Coolants, mostly. Harmless to breathe but do not smell very good. The air has not been filtered for years. I should have warned you. I will before you open any more doors."

I turn to Sada, noticing that she is too far away to have heard Aime. "It's harmless, just smells bad."

She signs back, 'Really bad.'

"Wait out here, unless you want to check the crew quarters. Careful, you may find more smells." She nods and starts forward.

I turn and walk into the engine room. Aime directs me over to the auxiliary power panel, and after turning the appropriate breakers, the lights come on, dimly.

"There is not much power left," Aime states. "You should see if you can clear the solar panels."

"Where would those be?" I ask, regretting the answer.

"They are on the dorsal hull."

"That figures," I retort.

I leave engineering and walk forward. Seeing Sada come out of a room, I ask, "Found anything interesting?" She shakes her head and steps inside the room.

I stop at the nearest cabin and go in. In the dim light, I see a single bed, a dresser, a chair, and two doors labeled Bathroom and Closet. There is barely a bit more light coming through the small windows than from the overhead lights. There is nothing on the dresser and the bed is neatly made. "Unused room?" I ask.

"This class of ship is usually crewed by four to six, but can easily carry more, " Aime responds.

"But there are only five cabins," I respond.

"The captain's cabin is on the top deck, aft of the bridge. It is also the largest."

I exit the room and find Sada looking curiously at a door. I read the door and it shows Galley. I look at her and she signs, 'I smell something bad.'

I put my hands flat on the door. "Aime, can you tell me what she smells?"

After a moment, Aime responds, "There is something in there, decaying. The emergency food stores would have gone bad so long ago that it would not be them. It would be best to wait until I can start the ventilation system to open that door."

"Yeah, okay, power first," I agree. "Up to the top then."

We proceed to the stairwell and up to the top deck. When we open the door, we immediately see two heavy doors, labeled Air Lock.

I pull the release on the door to the left and it opens. The room is small and does not have another door. Looking up, I see that the top is domed slightly and has several lines spiraling out from the center.

"The top hatch is opened by a crank. The handle is located behind the panel marked Emergency. Just push on the panel to open."

I find the panel and open it. Inside it, I find the folded crank handle, as well as some tubes, marked flares.

"Unfold it and insert the flat end into the notch inside the circular arrow. Turn it clockwise to open."

I insert the handle into the slot and start cranking. The hatch, at the top, starts to open like an iris. As the light pours in it brings with it a cascade of sand and dirt, which falls on my head and back. I shake my head to get the grit out of my hair, pull the hood over my head and start cranking again. More dirt and sand falls, but I keep cranking. After a few dozen turns, it stops. Looking up I see that the hatch is completely open and blocked by a mesh of vines.

I pull the cloak off and toss it into the hallway. Pulling out a blade, I climb up the ladder and start cutting the vines that block the opening. Sparks fly as before but the vines pull away from the opening when cut. I climb up through the opening, coming out into the sunlight.

Looking around, I see that the ship is thickly covered by vines. "Will my blades cut through the hull?"

"Not easily. The hull is a much tougher material."

"Where are the solar panels at?"

"There are some both fore and aft, both sides of the centerline."

Still standing on the ladder, I chop on some vines next to the hatch. Sparks fly, some cut, and they pull apart. After a few more, harder swings, the remaining vines separate suddenly, making an odd whoosh sound. I start chuckling as Sada pokes her head into the airlock to see what it was.

When she sees me laughing at the puzzled look on her face, her ears sweep back, telling me she's getting annoyed.

I stand up and help her onto the hull, and kneel in the cleared area. "Watch this." I take a hard swing at the vines, sparks fly and the vines part violently, snapping free of the roots and even breaking some of the smaller vines.

"Their roots are not strong enough to hold this much weight," Aime volunteers.

I continue chopping vines, heading aft from the hatch, and Sada takes a blade and works her way forward, both of us being careful to not stand on the vines as we cut.

Once we have the vines cleared from the solar panels, which ends up being most of the ship, we head back inside, closing the top hatch behind us.

"Now we should let the ship charge for a while, then we can restart life support and get the air cleaned."

With the lights noticeably brighter, we head aft. We open the door at the end of the short hall and enter a lounge. There is a large screen next to the door with two smaller desks on the opposite side. Further in, there's a rectangular booth style table to the left and another table to the right that's round with six chairs around it. The table in the booth is clear but the smaller round table has cards and colored chips on it at four of the chairs.

With the vines mostly gone, the small windows let in the sunlight for the first time in nearly two centuries.

We continue aft, opening the next door. Stepping inside the captain's cabin, we are awestruck, there is a king-sized bed, two dressers, and two reading chairs. Though there is still one bathroom, the closet has two doors. The room is over twice the size of one of the crew cabins and there are four windows allowing a lot of light in.

"Captains are the only ones allowed to bring their spouse along," Aime interjects, "though not all do as a lot of them have children."

I look at the dressers and only one has things on it. I walk over to the dresser and look at some of the things: a framed collection of medals, a few very faded still pictures of people, and a small collection of figurines.

Sada walks over to the bed and cautiously sits down. She smiles, apparently satisfied with its comfort. She looks at me and pats the bed, feeling the softness of the blanket.

Something suddenly strikes me as odd, not at what Sada did, but at what didn't happen. "Aime, where's all the dust?" I ask, running my hand across the dresser, leaving no trail and picking up no dust. Hearing my question, Sada gives the bed a couple of hard thumps and also looks puzzled at the lack of dust.

"The ship's life support would have been the last system to go offline. Air would have kept circulating through filters until the power failed, leaving the air thoroughly cleaned."

Sada lies back suddenly, flopping on the bed. She stretches and then curls up on the covers. I watch her eyes close and wonder how it is she can easily get that comfortable, that quickly in a new place.

"I'll check out more of the ship," I say. Getting no reaction from Sada, I figure she is either already asleep or too comfortable to respond.

Retrieving my pack, I place it in a chair in the lounge. I fold the cloak and put it away and change into a fresh shirt. Looking at the ripped and blood-stained shirt, I get my first look at what happened to my shoulder.

"Aime, what was that creature that attacked us?"

"The researchers called them vipers because of how fast they can come upon you. As you discovered, they can be deadly, but easily killed."

"So I should expect to find more out there?"

"Yes, there are other predators, some larger, more dangerous too," she offers.

Tossing the shirt into a converter, I pull out the light armor suit. Looking at the thin material, I find it hard to believe that it's really armor. "This will protect me?" I ask.

"It will protect you from most cuts and can even absorb some light impacts. Small animals will not be able to bite through it, but it will not be able to protect you from heavy impacts, or attacks from a large animal."

I sigh, draping the armor across the back of the chair. I remove the blades and the staff from my belt and set them on the table. I won't need them while on the ship.

I leave the lounge and head back down to the cargo bay. I check out the remaining bikes in the open crate. Aime tells me that they will not work, time having depleted their power cells. I start checking other crates, looking for anything that may be of use that still works. Several crates and numerous pieces of equipment later I find a small crate labeled Emergency Power Cells.

Aime informs me that one can run the backup systems on the ship. I quickly open the crate, hoping that one still works. Inside, I find four cylinders. All currently seem to be powerless.

As Aime tells me how to activate them, I take out one of the cells, pull up the top ring, turn it ninety degrees, and then push it back down. Nothing happens, so I try again with another and it starts to hum and give off a gentle glow. Aime announces that this one works, but has a slightly reduced power output.

I try to activate the other two and one of them works, and its power output is even less than the other.

With two working cells, I head up to engineering. Following Aime's instructions, I hook the cells up to the backup power system. Almost immediately I hear a quiet hum and then feel air moving.

"Between the solar panels and the power cells, life support is back on, and the ship's computer is coming back online. I have set it to low power mode to try to conserve energy, but we can interact with it from the lounge or bridge."

I return to the cargo bay and finish looking through the containers. Finding nothing else of use, I exit the cargo bay and notice a small locker next to the exit hatch. Opening it up, I find that it's a weapon locker. Inside hang six sets of pistols in holsters. I pick up a pistol. It is light, well balanced, and has a comfortable grip.

Aime starts running through the weapons specks, range, accuracy, and things like that. I find that I'm not really paying attention to her until she says, 'Fires several kinds of projectiles.'

"What kinds of projectiles?" I ask, interrupting her.

"Popular loads are explosive, flair, scatter, homing, and armor-piercing. Others can be added at the user's discretion."

"Does it work?"

"I cannot tell. This type of weapon can only be activated by an AI with a military package."

I put the pistol back in its holster and head back up to the lounge. I sit down at the table and dig into the pack for the box of AI updates. Finding it I pull out the bottle with the military packages.

"You said that these had combat programs too?"

"Correct. The military nanites have the ability to increase your strength, stamina, enhance your senses. There are also some components that can increase my scanning and healing abilities."

"How long will it take to set up?"

"If you take one capsule, eight hours, two capsules, four hours, and I can increase my processing capacity with the extra materials. Taking more than two would be counter-productive."

I see a flash from the farther converter and reflexively glance at the closer. "Let me guess, this one's broke."

"Under stable conditions, most devices will last about one hundred years. Ship systems should last over two hundred years without maintenance, but for a ship, ideal conditions are deep space, constant temperature, and humidity. With the ship being planet-side for so long, it allows the ship to heat up and cool off. That expansions and contractions are bad for a ship's internal systems."

I retrieve the drink and ask, "One at a time?"

"Yes."

Like before, I take the capsules one at a time when prompted and then finish drinking the juice. Putting the glass back in the converter, I look out the window and realize that it's getting late.

I walk into the captain's cabin and see that Sada is still sleeping in the same position she was when I walked out. I change into a pair of shorts, lower the shades, then dim the remaining light. With the life support working, the ship has warmed up comfortably and I lay down on the bed, on top of the covers.

Sada rolls over and puts her head on my left shoulder, so I wrap my arm around her. She starts to purr and we drift off to sleep.

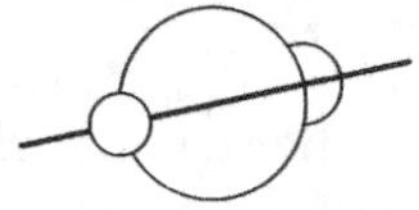

The light shining through the windows wakes me, and I quickly realize I'm alone. Hearing sounds, I get out of bed and walk out to the lounge.

Sada is sitting in a chair facing the large screen, watching some kind of video. Around the perimeter of the screen, there's a rolling time stamp and various other displays. Aime informs me that it's sensor video footage, from landing.

The image in the center is an aerial pass over a forest. When a new feature passes by, a still image shows of it, off to the side. As we watch, the forest gives way to grasslands; a river passes by, a rocky outcropping, another river, and then several round objects appear.

"What are those?"

The aerial pass pauses, then the still of the round objects enlarges to full screen. The data around the edges changes as the main image focuses.

"Huts? A village."

Sada stands up and takes a step closer.

Looking around the edge of the screen, I find a section with "Life Signs" as a heading. Looking under that, I see various types listed: human, avian, reptile, and mammal. Most have a zero but reptile has 23 and mammal has 1347.

"It appears to be uninhabited," Aime concludes.

I think for a moment and then ask, "Would Sada show up as human or mammal?"

After a moment of silence, Aime replies, "Mammal."

"So if the research people were working on evolving animals to humanoid, would they show up as mammal also?"

Aime seems to consider for a moment, then answers, "Most likely they would still register as mammals."

"It could be possible, then that the village is inhabited with," I look back at the screen, "1347 evolved mammals."

She again pauses before answering. "A reasonable assumption. I would like to point out that the researchers started with only one hundred specimens of each animal they were trying to evolve. If this village is one of those products, they were prospering well, most likely still are."

"And most likely not seen a human in two centuries," I add.

"Safe assumption."

I sit in a chair, still looking at the screen. "Did the sensors log what types of mammals were in that village?"

"No, they did not," Aime responds.

Suddenly, Sada goes to the screen and starts repeatedly zooming in on the huts. Each time she adjusts the zoom the picture enhances and shows more detail. Soon the image is zoomed so there is only one hut in the middle, showing enough detail to see individual sticks in its roof.

She starts sliding the image around looking for something. It doesn't take her long to find it, a figure standing outside a hut. She starts zooming in again on the figure, and once the image clears again, we see it. There in the middle of the screen, we see a leopardess, walking upright, not too dissimilar from Sada. She walks with a staff and is wearing a wrap-style dress.

"Cats!" I gasp, standing up.

Sada takes a step back, her jaw dropped open in surprise. 'Like me?' she signs after a moment.

"Yeah, some may be like you."

'No!' she signs, getting upset. 'I don't want to go there.' She then wraps her arms around herself as if cold.

Looking at her, I see that she is afraid. "What's wrong?" I ask, putting a hand on her shoulder to comfort her.

She looks at me, then back at the screen and walks over to the booth and sits down. I glance at the screen. *Aime, scan the sensor footage for any other settlements or signs of intelligent life.* The video changes back to the aerial video as I follow Sada to the booth and sit across from her.

As I look at her, she tries to look away. I sigh and gently ask, "What is it?"

She sighs, heavily. 'You want to go there,' she signs, slowly.

"Yes, they may be able to help me find other humans."

'Are you going to leave me there?' she asks, a tear forming in her eye.

"Wha–No. Why would you think I want to leave you?"

'You don't love me like you used to.'

I sigh, wishing that I knew what I had felt for her before I lost my memory. "Sada, I may not remember what I—*we* used to do together, or how we felt for each other, but I do know we are supposed to be together. It's difficult to explain, but it feels right. Just because I don't remember right now doesn't mean I won't remember. I don't want to jeopardize what we had just because I don't remember yet."

She squeezes my hands and nods. I reach with the intent of wiping the tear from her eye but she puts her cheek in my hand and closes her eyes. I find myself gently working my fingers through the fur, massaging the side of her face, as if she was still a house cat.

Seeing her enjoy the sensation and hearing her purr, I find myself saying, "Maybe you can help me remember the little things that we used to do." I work my fingers around under her chin, prompting her to extend her face forward. I lean forward to meet her and kiss her on her nose.

Surprised, she opens her eyes and pulls back a little. Then realizing what I did, she smiles and then frowns a little.

"What?" I ask gently.

'We can't do . . . that,' she signs. 'I bite.'

Puzzled by her statement, I ask, "What do you mean you bite?"

She gets up, pulling me with her, and leads me to the cabin. Once near the closet, she has me stand in front of the door and she opens it, revealing a full-length mirror. Then she gestures for me to look in the mirror while she traces out a series of scars on the right side of my neck and collar.

I look at her and then take a step closer to the mirror. The scars are a series of dashes in a U shape that crosses over my collar bone and jugular. There are two larger round scars near the bottom. The overall shape matches the shape of Sada's teeth. I look back at her and she hangs her head a little and slants her ears, clearly ashamed. Turning back to the mirror, I turn to get a look at the back of my collar, the scars continue in a similar pattern.

"You . . . bit me?" I curiously ask.

She slowly nods. 'We tried to . . . mate. I became so excited I blacked out. I don't remember what happened, but you said I became . . . feral. I didn't know I bit you. It was a good thing a doctor was close. You would have . . . died.'

"Oh." I run my hand over the scars, feeling the small bumps, wondering what it felt like to be bit while being glad that I don't remember. Looking back at her, she is genuinely ashamed of what happened. I step to her and wrap my arms around her, pulling her in close. She wraps her arms around me and starts to subtly cry.

"It's okay," I find myself saying and kissing the top of her head.

She pulls back a little and signs, 'You're not mad?'

"Why would I be mad? The fact that we tried, tells me just how much we care for each other. Besides, you didn't mean to do it."

She looks at me curiously, nods, and then gives me a short hug. 'Hungry?'

"Yes, yes I am," I admit and she grabs my hand and leads me back to the lounge.

After we've finished breakfast, Aime informs me that the scans do not contain any other villages or other structures other than the village and the facility. Having her add all the new information to our existing map, Sada and I head for the galley, where the air was fouled.

Looking at Sada, I ask, "Smell anything?"

She shakes her head and then steps into another room. Inside we see several booths, each with seating for four.

"Why are there both a galley and a lounge?" I ask, suddenly realizing that the ship has more places to eat than sleep.

"The galley is more for rescued people than for the actual crew. It can also serve as an auxiliary medical bay or science lab. There is also a kitchen, which allows crew members, who want to, to actually cook."

"I suppose that makes some sense." I look around. "Now, what could have fouled the air?"

"The source is in the kitchen."

We walk to the right and slowly open the door. On the cooktop, we find what looks like a small black volcano. I put my hands up so Aime can scan and ask, "What is this?"

"It is basically a rock now, all carbon anyway. It was one of the heating elements. It appears to have decomposed, a process that should take centuries. I would surmise that this was what fouled the air."

I poke at the black rock and it doesn't move. "Well, I don't see me using the stove anyway." I look at Sada and she shakes her head no. "I wonder if there's anything useful in here."

We start looking through the cabinets, finding all sorts of pots, skillets, and serving dishes. None are very fancy but seem made to take a beating. Coming up empty on useful items, we head to the medical bay.

Once there, Sada sniffs, nodding that it's okay to open. Inside we find an exam room at one end, with places for two cryo-pods at the other end. Sada walks to the exam room end so I turn my attention to the other end of the room. Where the pods would be, there are tracks along each side that seems to extend down below the floor; there is also a hatch in the floor, apparently for a cryo-pod to pass through. I start going through the cabinets, finding much the same items that were in the cabinets back at the facility. Not finding anything significant, I head to the other end of the room.

Turning, I see Sada looking closely at a small bottle of familiar design. I walk over to her, and she turns and hands me the bottle. I look at it and the label shows Medical Package. "Well, these could come in handy if we're attacked again. I assume that these are similar to the military package."

"Yes, but with different abilities. These would give us micro tractors, healing enhancers, and various other medical tools that can be used to perform a large number of medical procedures."

"So, say, if Sada got hurt and her nanites weren't able to heal the wound, I . . . you . . . uhm, *we* would be able to heal her wound?"

"Yes, but within the limits of our energy reserves," Aime states. "In her case, I would be coordinating with her nanites to heal the wound. If she had no nanites, I would be doing all the work, and that would consume more of our own energy."

"Is this safe to use with the other updates I already have?"

"Yes, quite safe. If you were to take the medical package, it would classify us as a combat medic."

"Would it be enough to save Cayla?"

"Unfortunately no, she needs regenerative surgery. A surgeon's package has that ability."

"How many expansions are there?"

"More than you'll be able to physically carry."

Sada looks at me curiously, so I ask, "What do you mean?"

"Even with skeletal enhancements, there is only so much mass that can be added to the soft tissue of your body. If you were to add too many updates, your soft tissue would be stripped from your skeleton by the mass of the nanites. It would not be a pleasant death, but I would not permit you to do that to yourself anyway."

"Good to know you watch out for me," I admit. Sada gives me a mockingly sad look. "You both look out for me, just in different ways," I say and reach around her and pull her in for a hug. I feel her smile as I kiss the top of her head.

We finish searching the med bay, coming up with enough supplies to put together another medkit, this one mostly complete with various bandages, nanite salves, wound cleaner, and even a self-setting, adjustable splint.

We return to the lounge for lunch, putting our new found supplies on the table near the pack. I keep the bottle in hand and follow Sada over to the booth. She starts pressing buttons on the converter and produces a plate of food.

'You used to love this,' she signs and hands me a plate of pasta. Taking the plate, I'm flooded with its aroma and a memory.

"Spaghetti, extra marinara, garlic, and parmesan, with a side of soft garlic bread with shredded mozzarella melted on it," I find myself saying, smiling.

Sada smiles. 'You remember?' she signs hopefully.

I find myself happily confessing, "Yes, that was a memory." I set down the plate and scoop Sada up in a hug, planting a kiss firmly on her muzzle. Her eyes go wide with surprise but she recovers quickly and wraps her arm around me. We hold each other for a moment and she pulls away, puts a hand to my cheek, and then taps the plate. I get the hint and sit down and start to eat.

While I do, I mentally conspire with Aime, giving her a recipe of my own. When it appears in the converter, its aroma immediately catches Sada's attention. She starts sniffing the air and licking her chops. I take the dish out of the converter and put it across from me on the table. Hearing the plate slide on the table gets her attention and she turns around. Taking a single hop back to the table she sits down, glances at me, then dives into the food, not bothering with using a utensil or her fingers.

When she finishes, she licks the plate clean. Then realizing what she did, she subtly puts her plate in the converter and quietly slinks off to the captain's cabin. I chuckle and finish my spaghetti.

Once done, Aime produces a fresh glass of milk and I take two of the medical packages, like before, one at a time. With lunch done, I clean up and walk into the cabin. Sada is curled up on the bed, staring out a window, her tail flicking restlessly.

"What's wrong?" I ask gently.

She looks at me, then back out the window. Her tail twitches a mild agitation.

"Are you mad at me?"

She shakes her head no.

Looking at the action of her tail, I see that she is still mad. "Are you mad at yourself?"

She looks back at me for a moment, sits up so she's cross-legged, then nods. I sit next to her, putting my arm around her and pull her close.

"I knew that you would like the fish, but I didn't realize that you liked it that much."

She gives me a playful slap and pushes me down on the bed and lays down, her back to me, with her head on my chest and sighs. I pull a pillow under my head and gently grab her tail. Getting no reaction I slowly bring her tail up and start tickling her ears with the tip, making them flick and move about.

When she realizes what I'm doing she pulls her tail out of my hand. "Aww, I was playing with that," I pout playfully.

She rolls over gives me an annoyed look with her head still on my chest, and sighs.

"Tired?"

'No,' she signs.

"There's still more rooms to explore."

'Later, we just ate.'

"Okay, so what are we going to do now?"

'Nothing.'

"Okay, but were going to look through at least one of the rooms later."

She gives me a lazy 'whatever' and rolls back over, this time careful to keep her tail out of my reach. So I just start rubbing the fur on the back of her head, which makes her purr. We lay there enjoying each other's company until Sada stops purring. Aime confirms for me that she is asleep, so I put the pillow under her head as I gently slide out from under her.

I quietly collect the pistols from the locker and head down to the ramp. Having a seat on the ramp, I start testing them. Most of them I set aside, either having no charge or next to no charge, but I find one that has enough charge for a few shots. I put on the holster and walk out from under the ship through a gap in the vines. Looking around, I see a large triangular rock, about forty meters away.

Following Aime's instructions, I select the standard ammo. As I aim the weapon, I see a crosshair track across my vision.

"What the...Where'd that crosshair come from?" I lower the weapon and the crosshair disappears from my vision. "Where'd it go?"

"It only appears when the weapon is pointed close to where you're looking. I would recommend keeping it until you are used to handling the weapon. With this type of weapon and the sensors that I have available, the crosshair will correct for wind, rain, and even some movement."

I raise the pistol again, seeing the crosshair come into view. I adjust my aim to have the crosshair fall on the rock. Once it does, I pull the trigger. I watch as a puff of dust appears in front of the rock, the round having fallen short of hitting its target. I find that the pistol is surprisingly quiet, so I line up for a second shot. Again putting the crosshairs on the target, I pull the trigger.

This time, instead of falling short, the round lands wide to the left. "Why am I missing?"

"It seems there is a problem with the micro converter in the weapon. It is not making the ammo correctly."

"Can it be fixed or do I need to find a different weapon?"

"I cannot correct this problem. We should charge the others to see if they operate correctly. There is a charging station in engineering."

I scoop up the other pistols and head to engineering. Aime directs me to the charging station and how to put the pistols in it to charge. Leaving the already bad pistol aside, I start hooking them up to charge. Of the remaining five, two generate an error message when connected to the charger and one doesn't respond to charging at all, leaving just two to charge.

I head back up to the lounge. Peeking through the door to the cabin, I see that Sada is still asleep, so I collect the chips from the round table and put them in the broken converter. I pick up the deck of cards and fan through looking at the face side. I'm pleased to find that it's a standard deck of fifty-two, though several break in the process.

"Brittle," I mutter and walk over to the converter. I set the deck in the opening. "New deck."

I watch as the old deck of cards disappears in a flash of light, then a moment later, another flash and a new deck appears. I have a seat at the round table and start shuffling. Without thinking much about it, I deal out the cards and start playing solitaire.

Feeling myself being shaken, I awake to find myself face down on the table, so I sit up and Sada pulls a card off my face.

"What's up?" I ask groggily, rubbing my face where the card was.

'I found something,' she signs and pulls me from my seat.

She leads me to the bridge and points to the chair in the middle. I walk around front and see a human skeleton that looks like is made of a silver metallic mesh. There are also several small metallic objects scattered around on the chair and the floor right in front of it.

"What is this?" I ask and squat down for a closer look.

"It is an AI matrix and all its peripherals. I detect several expansions, the most visibly prominent, being skeletal reinforcements."

"An AI matrix? From a person? Shouldn't there still be bones?"

"Yes, there should, but I am not detecting any kind of biological material or nanites in the area. It is possible that he was infected and only the artificial systems were left behind."

"Is the AI still active?"

"Not at a sentient level, but I can establish a link and access her memories."

I stand up and sigh. "All right, but don't catch anything."

"Understood."

While we wait for her to sift through the other's memories, I take a good look around the bridge. Around the outside, there are five stations, the foremost and center being the pilot's station. To the pilot's right, appears navigation and then sensors. To the pilot's left, there's communications and engineering. Several screens are arranged overhead.

Sada slowly walks around the bridge, looking at all the screens. She sits down in the pilot's chair and turns to face forward. Her hands trace over the controls without actually touching anything. I find myself momentarily entranced by her graceful movements when Aime interrupts.

"I found something you should hear."

Startled, I sit in the navigator's seat as an audio recording starts playing. We hear a man's voice, gravely, very weak, his breath is ragged.

"Captain's final log: I'm dying . . . My crew is already dead. Whatever the . . . contamination, it got through their . . . suits, and it didn't even . . . leave their bodies . . . I'm not sure how it got in . . . the ship, but it did . . . I've launched the . . . quarantine buoy . . . Planet should be . . . off-limits . . . forever."

We hear some coughing and wheezing, and then he concludes, "To my wife . . . my love." Then silence.

Sada creeps over to me and cowers into my lap, trembling. I wrap my arms around her and hold her. After a few minutes, she calms enough to sit up and sign a few words.

'What if that happens to us?'

I pull her close and explain what Aime had discovered about the "contamination" and how it was released. I also explain to her that it only affects humans so I would be the only one affected, but I have Aime on guard against the nanites that cause it and that she hasn't detected anything. Sada seems somewhat comforted by that, but she stays curled on my lap for a while longer.

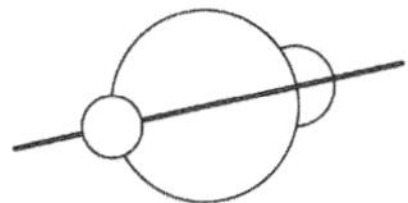

Continuing our exploration, I open the door to the science lab. Aside from replacing the beds with workbenches and tables, it looks a lot like the medical bay. The first thing I notice is the portable converter on a table. I look around and, seeing nothing of major interest, walk over to the converter.

"Why is this portable here, when there are two others in the room?"

Aime seems to consider possibilities, then answers, "I cannot say. The ship's logs do not show any specific reason for it being here. The converter itself is powerless, so I cannot interface with it for its logs."

I pick up the unit and start for engineering. As it walks down the hall the converter suddenly expands, almost doubling in length. The shift in weight almost makes me drop it. "What the—It's longer."

"It is an expandable unit?" Aime asks, apparently shocked. "That is not supposed to be possible."

"What do you mean?"

"Changing the distance between the two matter-energy plates would require changing the plates and several other components," she explains. "It is complicated, but think of it like a magnifying lens, one focal point.

I adjust the unit for balance and continue walking. "Well, they seem to have found a way. Let's see if it still works."

I put the unit on a workbench near the charging station. Aime tells me how to connect it to charge. I also check the pistols, and with their charging complete, I holster them and return to the lounge, leaving the converter to charge.

I set the pistols with the blades and staff and have a seat at the table. I watch Sada for a moment, sitting at a terminal, looking through images of different types of outfits. Seeing some of her selections makes me wonder if she actually likes the outfits or is just trying to humor me, having asked her to find something to wear that can offer some bodily protection, at least more than the bikini-style outfit she has been wearing. When she selects an Arabian-style outfit to look at, I conclude that she has a taste for more unusual, loose-fitting styles.

Aime interrupts, "We really should do some sword training. You have good reflexes but that baseball swing of yours will not always work."

Annoyed at her for interrupting my observations and for being right, I sigh. "Yeah, all right, where do you want to do this?"

"Right here," she answers. "I will be training you through an advanced form of deep hypnosis, so get comfortable."

I situate myself a little. "Okay, now what?"

"Just close your eyes and relax." Closing my eyes, I see a series of flashes followed by different colors of light and then darkness.

I awaken in a training dojo. A figure approaches and helps me stand. "Aime?" I gasp, recognizing the face of my first friend from back at the facility.

"Yes," she confirms, taking a few steps back. I can see now that she is still wearing the white lab coat, just like in the images, though now I can see black dress pants and pumps. She stands a little taller than Sada, but not quite as athletic in her build.

I look at myself and see that I'm still wearing the same clothes. "Where are we?"

"Welcome to my dream," she responds, giving me a welcoming bow. "Dream?"

"For you, it is like a dream. For me, it is a VR simulation. This is a new ability courtesy of the military package. Let us change into more suitable clothes, shall we?"

Before I can respond, our clothes change to martial arts training uniforms, I in white, with a white belt, and her in black with a black-and-red banded belt.

"Martial arts?" I ask, puzzled.

"To fight well with a sword, it is best to know how to fight without a sword. I will begin by teaching you a combination of karate and judo. Once I am confident with your ability, we will begin kendo."

I think for a moment, apparently with an odd look on my face. "What is it?" she asks, puzzled.

"I know what karate and judo are, but what is kendo?"

She nods. "It means 'way of the sword' and was used by the samurai. It has been adopted by almost all Earth's military personnel for close quarters blade combat."

I think for another moment. "For some reason, that sounds familiar."

"It could be that your memory may be trying to return already. Please let me know if anything else seems familiar."

"I'll try."

"Good," she says with a nod. "Now back to the task at hand. Are you ready to learn?"

I stand at attention and bow to her. "I am your student, sensei."

She smiles. "Good, but there are some things about this environment that you should know. You will feel pain, you will feel exhausted, you will be bound by all the laws of physics. Those are *my* rules." She pauses to let that sink in. "I will, however, allow you to shrug off the pain and exhaustion quickly. After all, these will all be part of the simulation and are not real. The only thing here that is real is the training. You will not feel hungry, thirsty, or anything else that can distract you. We are here to train, and that is what we are going to do."

"I understand."

"Then let us begin."

She begins teaching me moves and counter moves, attacks, and defenses. We spar. Sometimes she attacks, and sometimes I attack. We continue for what seems like hours before Aime announces that the session is over as she is running low on power. Like before, she has me close my eyes and after a series of flashes, I awake at the table.

When I open my eyes, I find myself looking right into Sada's blue eyes. "Hi."

She smiles and presses her nose to mine, her version of a kiss. 'You're awake.'

"Yeah. How long was I out?"

'About an hour.' Then she stands up and signs, 'Wait here,' then she happily bounces out to the cabin carrying something.

She returns a minute later wearing a new outfit, much like the Arabic dance outfit I saw earlier but with this one is light blue, like her eyes, with gold thread accents and jewelry. She even has a few gold bands on her tail. Her legs and arms are covered with white mesh-like fabric, allowing air to pass easily through. She has on a tiara, though there is no veil attached. The look seems to increase her already graceful actions. She does a dance-like spin and flows into a chair across from me. 'What do you think?'

Finding myself at a loss for verbal words, I simply sign, 'Beautiful.'

'Thank you,' she signs as she blushes.

"How'd you find this?"

'I looked through the styles of clothes.'

"I can't imagine anything that could make you more beautiful."

She blushes again and then bounces back into the cabin.

She comes back out in a moment, wearing a light blue wrap-style dress. 'For walking,' she signs and gives a light spin, her tail flowing smoothly around like a ribbon, from a gap in the back of the dress.

"Nice. Looks comfortable on you," I compliment.

'It doesn't irritate my fur,' she states, then adds, 'It's also light armor, just in case we get attacked again.'

"That's my girl, beautiful and smart." I reach out and touch her cheek, prompting her to nuzzle my hand and purr.

'I have something else.' She gets up and heads back to the cabin. After a few moments, she comes back wearing only a really long white T-shirt with pink trim.

"And what's that for?" I ask, suspect of the answer.

'Sleeping.'

"Aww, but I like the feel of your fur," I pout.

She gives me a small mocking pout and goes back into the cabin, coming out a moment later wearing a light blue pajama shirt, which actually looks more like a sports bra, with cartoon kittens on it, and matching shorts, apparently with an opening for her tail since it's waving happily behind her.

I chuckle. "That's really cute on you," I admit.

'Thank you,' she signs again. 'Come on, time for bed,' and she walks into the cabin.

I look out the window and seeing the sun low in the sky, I sigh. The longer days here on this planet are starting to wear on me. I walk over to the converter and get a glass of warm chamomile tea, hoping that it will help. After I slowly sip it down, I head to bed.

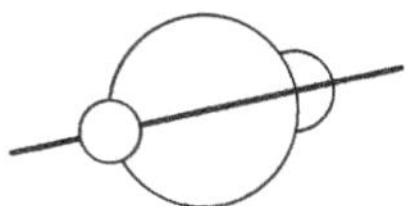

In the morning, after breakfast, I start looking over the map, noting the location and distance of the village that the shuttle detected on its landing pass. The exterior maps from the facility were corrupted and largely unusable.

"Aime, what's the distance from here to the village?"

"Close to two hundred and sixty kilometers."

'Long walk,' Sada points out.

"Six or seven days at the speed you walk, barring distractions."

"Maybe we should shoot for seven or eight days, in case the terrain changed since then." I glance at Sada, who looks back with a mischievous grin, so I smile back and add, "And distractions."

"Agreed."

"How well can you keep track of where we are while we walk?"

"Using the length of each stride, compared with magnetic north, not counting the terrain map, I should be able to maintain 99 percent accuracy."

"So after a kilometer, you could be ten meters off."

"Correct."

"And counting the terrain map?"

"Uncertain, here in the plains area, it offers little assistance with landmarks, but along a river, for example, erosion will alter the features, making accuracy dependant on the amount of erosion."

"Are there any satellites that we could use to get a new map from?" I ask, rubbing my face with mild frustration.

"To scan for a working satellite, I will need to activate the ship's sensors and communications. I will need to reroute some energy from life support. The lights and air conditioning will both lose power for a while. I have already disabled the charger in engineering."

"For how long?"

"A scan will take, at most, twenty minutes."

"All right, do it."

With that statement, the screens blink off, as do the lights. The air coming out of the vents still blows gently but it is no longer cooled.

Sada gets up and opens the shades on the four windows for more light. I grab the deck of cards and sit down at the booth. Sada sits across from me, takes the cards from me, and starts shuffling.

I watch as she deals out ten cards apiece and sets the deck in between us, turning the top card over for a discard pile. I give her a curious look, and she signs out, 'Gin rummy.'

I smile back and start arranging my cards accordingly. We play until the lights come back on, me losing most of the games.

"I could not find an active satellite. There are still several in orbit, but none responded to data requests. I did, however, get a limited scan of the surrounding area with the ship's sensors, and I have factored that information into our current map."

"Limited?"

"Since some of the sensors don't work, ground-based scans are currently limited by line of sight."

"Does the ship have anything that can be launched for a surface scan, or is there anything that we could make in the converter that we could use?"

"While the ship's deployable drone is dead, I could have the engineering converter make a smaller, more portable version. It will be limited in range and flight time, but it should be able to allow us to keep an accurate localized surface map. It will not have any life form scanners, as it will not be large enough to hold them."

"While that would be handy, I'll take what I can get."

"The drone is waiting in engineering."

Sada follows me down to engineering. I find a liter bottle-sized cylinder in the converter. The first thing I notice is that one end is slightly larger than the other.

"Is this the drone?" I ask, giving it a suspicious look.

"It is inside. What you are looking at is the launch canister."

"Launch canister?"

"When you place it on the ground, I can have the canister launch the drone into the air, then the drone's engine will take over for the powered flight."

"Ah, I get it."

I hand the drone to Sada and I take the, now charged, collapsible converter and collapse it down. Making sure it's locked in place, I heft it over my shoulder and we head back up to the lounge.

After setting it on the table, I take the drone from Sada and climb out a top hatch. Following Aime's instructions, I place the wide end of the launch canister on a level spot of the ship's hull, take a few steps back.

"Launching," Aime announces. The top of the canister pops open, and then the drone is flung skyward from the canister. As its wings take form, I realize that it looks like a glider, as the main wing is oversized.

I watch as it flies straight away, shrinking until it's no more than a dot. It then turns and flies in a clockwise circle around me. After it overlaps its starting point, it returns, coming in for a slow landing on the hull. Once the wings retract, I pick it up and reinsert it into the canister, nose up, per Aime's directions. I take it back to the lounge and set it on the table while Sada looks through more clothing selections.

"Aime, how long before a new map is ready?"

"About an hour. I am having the ship's computer compile the data."

"Do you have enough energy for more training?"

"Yes, I do. Get comfortable."

Like before, I sit and close my eyes so Aime can pull me into a training session. We review some of the more advanced techniques that she taught me in the last session, and then we continue.

When I awaken, I open my eyes to see Sada, nose to nose with me again. She bumps my nose with hers and signs, 'Your turn.'

"My turn, for what?"

She takes my hand and leads me into the cabin. Immediately I see an outfit laid out on the bed. At first glance, I'm reminded of motorcycle gear, but Aime tells me it's Ranger Class reactive armor, designed for snipers, infiltrators, and light scouts. It's almost entirely black with red piping for accents.

"For me?" I ask in disbelief.

She gets a bashful look for a moment but recovers quickly by reaching up and touching her pinkened nose to mine, and then, with a smile and a flick of her tail, she bounces out of the room, leaving me to change.

Aime quickly advises me that I should also wear the set of light armor underneath, to increase its effectiveness. I retrieve the two-piece armor and change into them. I then start pulling on pieces of the armor, noticing that they seem to adjust themselves for the correct fit, making it incredibly comfortable to wear. After pulling on the boots, I finish with the gloves, finding it odd that there is no headpiece.

The first thing that I notice is that moving is a lot easier than I thought. Aime reminds me that this was designed for the troops who sometimes needed to move fast and retain their agility. As I walk out to the lounge, I notice that the boots make no sound. Aime fills me in on the passive stealth abilities of the suit; it dampens any sound that it makes and that most holsters will automatically attach.

Sada gasps when she sees me, I turn around, nowhere as gracefully as she did, and then hold my arms out in a "what do you think" style pose.

She puts her hands over her muzzle and I can see her eyes water a little. 'Wow, you look great,' she manages to sign and then reaches for a bag next to her. She walks over to me and pulls out a long black cloak with red trim and puts it around me, fastening it in front with my signet. Then she pulls out a wide-brimmed black safari-like hat and puts it on my head, looks at it for a moment, then curls the right side up a little, and tilts the hat slightly so the curl is a little higher than the other.

She stands back and looks me over. 'Something's missing.'

I look down at myself and then back at her. "What's missing?"

'These.' She reaches into the bag again, this time pulling out two short, slightly curved swords and hands one of them to me. I pull it from the sheath, discovering that, like the survival blades, the sword is longer than the sheath. Unlike the survival blades, these are much thinner, styled for fighting. One word comes to mind.

"Katana."

"Correct," Aime states. "The hat and cloak are also armor class."

"Nice," I comment. I look at Sada curiously. "You didn't make these with the converter, did you?"

She smiles. 'I made the hat and cloak, but found the rest in the captain's closet.'

I look at the sword. "Captain, you had good taste in weapons."

With the new local map ready, I sit down and relax. With the drone's short sensor range, Aime was only able to update a few square kilometers of land with the first flight. I also begin to realize that, at the current rate, the drone will need to stay in constant flight, ahead of us, as we walk to keep the map of use.

"Aime, can any of the converters create any upgrades for you?"

"Sorry, only nanite-class converter can do that. The ones at the facility were inaccessible, and there are not any onboard this ship."

"That figures," I comment, as Sada walks in.

'What does?' she asks, curiously.

"No way to make upgrades for Aime."

'Oh,' she sighs and sits down next to me. 'What do we do now?'

I close my eyes for a moment, thinking, "Well, there's not much more we can do here, so . . ." I rub my face with my hands. "I suppose we should get moving in the morning." I look at her. "What do you think?"

'If I'm with you, I'm happy.' She then leans into me, purring.

I happily wrap my arm around her and kiss her on her head. "Me too."

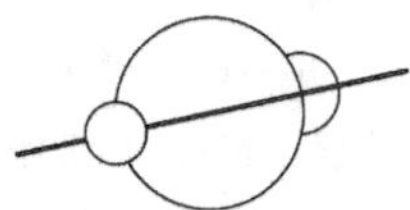

Dressing for the walk, I put on the light armor suit, followed with the medium armor sections. I then put the pistols on my hips and the swords I stick to the back of my forearms, a surprisingly convenient place to draw them from.

As I start packing everything back in my pack, I realize that it's a tight fit. I repack, adjusting where I put some of the smaller items and manage to come up with some extra room.

Sada comes out of the cabin wearing her light blue two-piece outfit. I heft the pack onto my shoulders, and at Aime's suggestion, we head to engineering. She has me pull out the emergency power cell that has more charge. I carefully pack it into the little remaining space. Before we leave, I have Aime create one last thing. I pick the stone up out of the converter as we head to the ramp to exit the ship.

Once on the ground, we head aft and approach the three marker stones. Feeling somber, I carefully position the fourth marker with the other three. As I do, Sada brushes some of the dust off of the other three markers.

"I know none of you are actually buried here, but at least you will be remembered together," I say. Sada stands up beside me, puts her hand in mine, and we stand in silence for a few moments.

As we turn to leave, I grab several of the vines, coil them up, and tuck them in a pouch on my pack. Sada keeps her ears open as we walk in silence.

We make camp early for the second night, having learned quickly the night before not to be outside past dusk.

CHAPTER 5

After we eat, I sit and review the map. I'm somewhat surprised when Sada puts her foot-paws on my lap and wiggles her toes. I set aside my tablet and start gently massaging them. Noticing that they have picked up some burrs and other debris, I start picking them out as I find them.

Hearing Sada start to purr, I realize that she is enjoying this, so after I have one clean I start on the other. After only a moment, however, she jerks her foot-paw away.

"What?" I ask, unsure as to why she just jerked.

'That hurt.'

"Where?" I curiously ask as she puts her foot-paw back on my lap. I carefully start spreading her toes and find a thorn suck in the side of a pad. I carefully pull it out, making her flinch a little.

"Aime," I say as I start gently massaging the pad.

"Done," she comments.

Sada flexes her toes a few times and sighs.

I lean back in the chair and look to the sky. I watch as the sky darkens and the moons start to overlap.

"Oh, you will like this. It is called Moonstorm," Aime states.

Sada turns to watch the moons overlap. As the sky darkens further, I notice that I'm not hearing any of the calls and sounds that I heard last night when night came. I glance at Sada and she seems aware of this also, as her ears are flicking about, responding to any slight sound she hears.

Suddenly the larger moon lightens. "It has begun," Aime states.

We continue to watch in silence, the moons slowly converging, the larger getting brighter, and the smaller getting dimmer. With the sun finally set, the effect seems to intensify a little, the overall effect is still washed out by the evening light.

The larger moon darkens as the moons start to diverge, their orbits carrying them apart. With the last traces of light quickly diminishing, we suddenly hear the calls and sounds of night returning. We quickly move the gear inside the tent and call it a day.

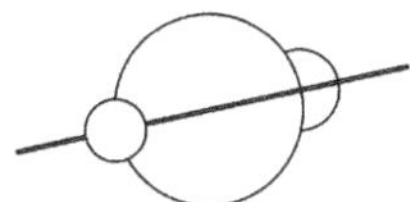

Still being a couple days out from the cat's village, we come across a clearing. In the clearing stands a well-worn, patched tent. Looking around, we see no one, but Sada stats sniffing the air, apparently smelling something.

"Hello?" I call out.

A gravely voice calls out from beyond the edge of the clearing, "Hello! I'll be there in a moment." Sada and I look at each other, unsure of what to make of the response.

After a brief moment, a cloaked, hooded figure steps out of the taller grasses. "Welcome," it says, waving its gloved hand in a welcoming gesture. "I am Moku." He steps over closer to us. "You made it here in time. I have a special offer for the both of you." Sada hides behind me and hisses quietly.

Suspicious, I ask, "What kind of offer?"

"Nothing you need to do anything to get. It's yours if you want it, or you can leave it all behind, your choice," it says, bowing. I find myself unable to figure out if this creature is male or female, but with the gravely sounding voice, I hesitantly settle on male.

"Why are you offering this to us?" I ask curiously.

He sighs, also dropping his rather showy way of presenting. "Because you're the first to come this way, and the last I'll see. I'm dying," he says sadly.

"But in Moku tradition," he continues with all the bravado he can muster, "I will give you all that you see, if you camp with me." He pauses for a moment, either to catch his breath or for drama. "You would do well to take me up on the offer. I have wares to trade, a tent to sleep in, and supplies you'll need. Young female, would you like some jewelry? I have some. Young male, how would you like a weapon? I have that too." He pauses again. This time I notice, it's to catch his breath.

"Sold," I find myself saying, if for no other reason to get him to rest a little. Sada, to her credit, comes around from behind me and nods her agreement.

"Well then, let's sit and I'll show you my wares, let you know just what you've got." He goes into the tent and comes out with his sizable pack. He pulls out a worn and tattered blanket and lays it on the ground.

He starts pulling various bowls and plates from his pack, explaining who made it, how to tell, and what he feels it's worth. When he starts pulling out the jewelry, Sada takes particular interest. As he sets them on the plates, she'll pick up a piece and look at it carefully. This continues for a few minutes, until he collects the items and sets them aside. Then he starts pulling out a few blankets and lays them out as he talks about who made them and with what kind of fur or grasses.

Finally he gets to the weapons. He pulls them out one at a time, talking about what village it came from, who may have used it, and why it looks the way it does. I listen carefully, knowing that Aime is remembering every word he says, learning everything she can from what he says. When he finishes, he carefully starts to repack everything. He then slides the pack to me with a nod.

He then reaches into a pocket. "We Moku rarely accept these. We prefer things we can trade, but they occasionally come in handy when one needs supplies." He reaches out his closed hand, so I hold out mine to accept what he's offering. He lets a handful of coins fall into my hand. "Use them wisely."

I look at the coins, most are copper, some have a hole, and others have bands of silver or gold around them. "Thank you," I say, not knowing what else to say.

The Moku looks at me curiously for a moment, then says, "You're not from any of the villages, are you."

Smiling, I say, "That obvious, huh?"

He looks back at me, then at Sada. "Your face is shaped wrong, but other than that," he pulls off his hood, revealing a scaled, barely furred, rodent-like face, "I'd say you look all right."

I hide my reaction, but Sada doesn't do so well. He chuckles and puts his hood back on. "Don't worry, as a Moku, I'm used to people wanting to avoid me."

Sada makes some signs and I translate for her, "She says, 'Sorry, I was expecting you to look more like Kyle or me.'"

He nods and then looks at me again. "What are you, anyway?" he asks, honestly curious.

"I'm a human . . ."

He holds up a hand to stop me. "Are you a lab coat or a caretaker?"

I look at him blankly for a moment, trying to figure out what he just asked. "I'm not sure I follow. We were, up until a month ago, frozen."

"That makes you a project, like the rest of us. Sorry, most of us Moku hate the lab coats. They made us like we are—all of us—not just the Moku. There are cats, dogs, deer, otters, rabbits, and a lot of others. None but the Moku remember the lab coats. Some may remember the caretakers since they were the nice ones. They gave us places to live, taught us how to take care of ourselves. They kept in touch, trying to help us any way they could. Up until they all just vanished."

He looks at me, thinking for a moment. "I'm going to tell you some things that only the Moku know. Starting with, we are smarter than a lot of people think. We know what our parents knew, remember what they learned."

"You have a genetic memory?" I find myself saying.

He nods. "You know what that is. Good." He continues on, explaining how his people prefer their nomadic ways and why they'd rather be alone as they wander. We listen intently to his stories, breaking only to eat supper and prepare for the night.

He chuckles as I set up the tent. "Have yourself some of their toys, I see."

"Yeah," I admit. "They were left for us by our caretakers. She tried to save herself, but that didn't work out too well." I glance at Sada and notice her look of sorrow.

He frowns. "What happened to them anyway?"

I think for a moment, trying to decide how to tell him. "Well, they liked to invent things, and one of the things they made killed them."

He sighs, looking at the ground in silence for a moment. "They didn't deserve that. They deserved something for what they did to us, but not that," he states, obviously meaning every word.

We sit in silence for a while, letting him process the news. He straightens up and asks, "Could you do me a favor? I'd do it myself, but I don't have much time left."

I look at Sada; she shrugs, so I turn back to him. "If I can."

He smiles. "Thank you, all I ask is for you to tell some of the other Moku what you just told me about the caretakers and lab coats."

I nod. "I should be able to do that."

He nods his appreciation. "I'd be happy to answer any questions you have."

We spend the next hour asking him questions about the villages, the cats, and anything else we can think of.

With the fading light, he announces, "We better get inside. There are many things out there that hunt at night. They will not go through a wall, though, no matter how thin."

I reach out to shake his hand. "See you in the morning."

He looks at my hand, as if considering his words, then shakes it. "Not likely. Take care of each other. Good luck to you."

Realizing his meaning, I simply say, "Thank you."

Once in our tent, Sada wrinkles her nose. 'He smells bad.'

"I know," I concede, "but he had a lot of useful information." I drop my armor and climb into bed and roll to my back. Sada changes into her pajamas and crawls up on me, purring. Sighing, I start rubbing her cheeks, and she stretches out her chin and neck. I start scratching her chin and she purrs harder.

Hearing her sigh heavily while still purring, I move around to the back of her neck. She suddenly raises her shoulders and arches her back, then lies down and relaxes onto me. I give her a kiss, smooth out her fur, and let sleep take me.

Stepping out of the tent in the morning, I find a small bundle positioned in front of the door. I look around for the Moku's tent, and not seeing anything, I look back at the bundle and quickly realize that the bundle is the Moku's tent and cloak.

As Sada comes out, she almost trips over the bundle. She looks down at it, then at me, 'What's this?'

"The rest of his stuff," I quietly answer.

'Where did he go?'

I slowly look around and not seeing any sign of him, I sadly state, "To die."

She sighs heavily as she looks at the bundle. 'What do we do with that?'

I think for a moment. "I have an idea," I state, starting to smile.

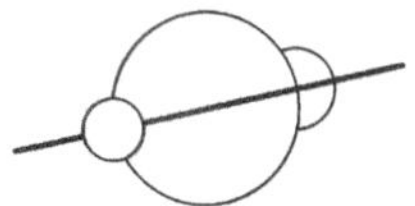

Working with the information the Moku gave us, we follow the crude path through the trees and ferns until come across a decent-sized sandy clearing. Sada points over at an arranged rock pile across the clearing near another lightly used path and looks back to me.

"Yep, looks like this is the place."

I look around the clearing while taking the pack off of my back. Selecting a suitable location for the tent, I set it up so the door faces both paths. I open the door and toss my pack just inside to the left. I turn to see that Sada has removed the trader pack she was carrying and is now looking around, checking the area for anything interesting. I pick up the trader pack and enter the tent. Inside, I grab my pack and start pulling out gear. I put a couple of blankets on the bed, and start setting aside various other items. The converter though, I set by the wall.

"Do you have the disguise ready?" I ask Aime.

I see a flash from the converter as she answers, "I have completed it. The mask will alter your natural voice, and you will look and smell similar to the Moku we met."

"Good." I take off my cloak and hat and set it aside as Sada enters the tent.

'Ready?' she signs.

"Almost," I answer as she retrieves a mask and a simple copy of my signet from the converter. I remove the pistol and holster from my hip. I pull the two swords from my arms and reposition them on my back with handles down, so I'm able to pull one with each hand. Seeing me do this, Sada gives me a disapproving look.

"Only for protection," I insist. She frowns a little, but accepts my reason.

She puts her hand to my cheek as a worried look crosses her face, so I put my hand to her cheek and work my fingers into her fur. "I will be careful, I promise," I softly reassure, and I pull her close and kiss her muzzle. She returns the kiss for a moment, before wrapping me in a hug.

Sighing, I admit, "I know, I'm nervous too."

Breaking the hug, she hands me the mask. I look at it and see that it will cover only my nose and mouth, giving my face some semblance of a muzzle. Sada opens the trader pack and pulls out the tattered cloak that we got from the Moku. I see her nose wrinkle at its smell, but she pulls it around me and pins it in place with the signet-copy.

"All right, Aime, let's finish the disguise," I say as I put the mask on. I watch the gloves on my hands change to look like that of the Moku trader's. I look down to try to see my feet, but discover that the cloak covers them, so I swing a foot forward and see that my boots now also resemble the Moku's.

I look at Sada, and to my surprise, she does not look pleased to see my like this. I see the fur on her neck is standing up and her ears are laid back, with a scowl on her face. It reminds me of her reaction when we first met the Moku.

"I take it the disguise is working well?" The new sound of my voice startles me. It's lower pitched and has a growl type rumble to it. Sada responds by hissing at me, obviously not happy with my disguise. I almost chuckle at her reaction.

"I'll be back before nightfall, as we agreed," I reassure, then pick up the trader pack and step out of the tent.

I put a strap over my shoulder and start walking to the path to the village. I pause for a moment, turning to see Sada standing just outside the tent door, looking a little sad. I sign to her, 'I love you.'

She signs back, 'I love you too,' then steps back into the tent. I turn back to the path and walk into the foliage.

As I follow the path, I notice that the few trees and ferns quickly give way to grasses, making the path gets harder to follow. Thankfully there are more arranged stone piles indicating where the path goes. I pause a moment to scan the area, seeing that there is a hill ahead, I head for it.

Topping the hill, I am relieved by what I see. I've arrived at Pridewyn, and it's larger that the overhead view that I last saw. At this distance, I see several of the larger huts set up along the near side of the river, with many slightly smaller scattered among them. Set back from the river, there are numerous small huts, with a large round central hut at the heart of them. Across the river is mostly vacant, save for some odd-looking structures leading up to and up the side of a nearby cliff.

"The village is much larger than I expected, and that looks like an obstacle course across the river," Aime offers. "That was not on any of the scans"

And the Moku indicated that the larger huts near the river are where the markets are.

"The large round one toward the center should be the council hut."

I walk down to the hill to the village, heading for the council hut. I need to get their permission to set up in a stand.

As I near, I start passing fenced-in fields with small reptiles in them. I try not to stare at them as I walk by, but my curiosity has me wanting to look. In one smaller field, I notice that the farmer is an evolved bobcat. He looks curiously at me for a moment but continues feeding some reptiles in a pen. These must be the ma'pai farms that the Moku mentioned.

I also notice that everyone I pass is wearing clothing that is either wrapped around or tied-on. I suddenly remember Sada choosing similar styles of clothes, not wanting to irritate her fur.

I have to stop momentarily for a group of the ma'pai being herded across the road. I get a chance to look closely at them; they look much like chickens, having beaked faces and walking on 2 legs, but they have scales instead of feathers, long tails and no wings or forelegs. The two young lynx that are herding them barely even look at me as they pass by.

Reaching the village, I find that it's much more crowded than I expected. Some of the species I recognize easily: cheetahs, tigers, lions, panthers, and bobcats. I also begin to notice that cats are not the only evolved creatures in this village, as I find a small scattering of evolved rabbits, deer, raccoons, and a few I don't readily recognize.

As I make my way through the busy dirt streets, I occasionally pass carts pulled by either very large eight-legged reptiles or ostrich-sized versions of a ma'pai. I try to stay casual, but find it difficult when everything is so new and different.

Finding my way through the village, I arrive at the council hut. Like the other huts, it appears to be made of mud brick, but instead of a stick or thatch roof, it has wooden shingles. Inside I find a counter and a few chairs.

Having seen me enter, the leopardess behind the counter approaches me. I see that she's wearing a simple medallion etched with a symbol, identifying her as a mediator. "Would you like a kiosk?" I find her voice surprisingly pleasant.

"Yes, please."

"How long will you need it?"

"Five days."

She looks at something behind the counter and then retrieves a card and writes some numbers on it. "Keep this with you. You can use kiosk four. Please leave it clean when you are done." She gives me a slight bow as she hands me the card.

"Thank you," I state, returning the bow.

She returns to her seat so I turn to leave. I don't get but a step when I hear, "Please be alert. The Trials will be starting next week. Some cubs have been extra mischievous lately."

"Thank you, Mediator." I find myself suddenly wondering what the "Trials" are.

I head toward the river and locate my assigned kiosk. I find that it's fully open to the public in the front, with a counter separating the front area from the back. I circle around to the back and enter through the door.

Now on the backside of the counter, I start unloading the pack, setting up the tableware together to my right, then the jewelry to my left, blankets in front, and finally the few weapons on the wall racks behind me. I leave the mini converter I brought in the pack right behind the counter on the floor so it's not visible.

I find it a good thing that the Moku walked me through how he handled his daily business. I spend the day talking with the few customers who browse through. I manage to trade a blanket for a small hanging basket woven out of vine.

Nearing suppertime, I pack up my wares and close up the kiosk. On my way out of the village, a young lion cub runs by me, nearly hitting me as he passes. I pay him no mind and keep walking.

It takes me nearly an hour to get back to camp. Thankfully Sada sees me coming and makes us supper. As I enter the tent, I set down the pack and drop the cloak and armor. As I come back out, Sada ushers me to my chair and sits hers next to me. We sit in silence as we eat, Sada purring the whole time, happy that I'm back.

After we finish, she insists on my staying put while she puts things away. I get the feeling that she has something planned, but she just sits down next to me and gives me a curious look.

Understanding her expression, I start telling her about all the different cats I've seen today and how they all walk like she does, similarly shaped. I also explained that, aside from looking like cats, they were all civilized people, relaying the types of work I saw them doing and how they dressed. She listens intently as I ramble on about anything I can remember.

When the sun starts to set, we move inside and I gladly flop onto the bed. Sada happily lies down next to me and purrs. Letting the day slip away, I fall asleep to the rhythm of her purring.

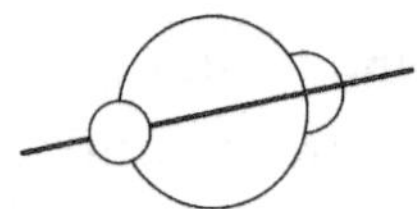

After breakfast, I spend some time having the converter learn about the basket, the better blankets, and the jewelry. Afterward, I then have Aime come up with some similar designs of the baskets and jewelry, increasing the number of things I can trade. Sada still refuses to go into the village despite my reassurances.

I pack my new wares and then get dressed in my armor. As Sada helps me with the cloak she notices that my signet-copy is missing. Not too concerned, I make another in the converter and put it on. I give her a kiss and put my mask on and then head out to the village.

I spend some time browsing through some of the other kiosks. When I see items similar to mine, I inquire about the prices. After picking up some jerked fish, I make my way to my own kiosk and prepare for another day.

After setting up, I add the few hanging baskets to the display and then settle onto a chair to wait for the afternoon crowd. To my surprise, a dusty pink-furred lioness quietly comes in. She looks around and eyes the baskets for a moment. As she turns to leave, I take the initiative. "Is there something I can help you find?"

She looks back at me for a moment. "Do you have a basket that this will fit in?" she asks, holding up a decent-sized ball of rice.

I look carefully at it. "I do have some baskets I haven't put out. Let me check." I squat down behind the counter and start rustling through my pack. *Aime, make a basket slightly larger than the rice ball.*

My rustling muffles the slight sound and the pack itself hides the light from the converter as the basket appears. I pull it out and stand up. "How would this work for you?" I offer her the basket.

She takes it and carefully places the rice ball in it. Eyeing it carefully, she thinks for a moment. "What would you take for this?"

Looking at her, I see she has nothing more than the rice ball and the red toga-style wrap she is wearing. "I don't normally take coin, but for you, fifteen."

She looks again at the basket, then cautiously back at me. "Five."

I expected some haggling. "Oh, come now, it's in excellent condition, ten."

She looks again at it and concedes, "All right, ten." She reaches in a pocket and hands me a ten coin.

I give her a light bow as I accept the coin. "Thank you."

She departs as quickly as she came in, leaving me alone once again. I have a seat and wait for my next customer.

After a few hours, I see a group of cats looking around. I can't help but notice that they are wearing the same type of green, scale armor, and short swords. After they look through some of the other kiosks, two of them approach mine and enter.

I stand, ready to show them my wares, or barter trade, but one of them, a male panther, holds his hand out, "Is this yours?"

I notice that in his hand, he has my other signet-copy. "Yes," I answer. "I thought I'd lost it while walking back to camp." I look from one of them to the other, puzzled as to why a guard would be worried with returning it.

"Would you please come with me? The council would like to see you. You can leave your things here. Anon will guard them for you." He gestures to the other, an ocelot, who stands at attention at the door.

Unsure of what else to do, I say, "I will follow." I slide my pack against a wall with my foot and exit the kiosk, following the panther.

He quickly assigns a second guard to the kiosk, and the other two follow us to the council hut. Once there, the mediator ushers me and the panther inside as the other guards wait outside the hut.

The panther escorts me to the center of the room and then hands the signet to the center councilor, a cheetess. After bowing to her, he then turns and leaves the room.

Not knowing what else to do and feeling nervous, I stand still, looking around at the council members, waiting for them to speak.

"Is this your signet?" The question comes from the cheetess.

"Yes, it is," I nervously answer.

"Do you know why you are here, now, before us?" she asks.

"No, I do not."

She sighs and motions to a mediator standing by the door. He turns, opens the door, and motions to someone outside. A moment later a lion cub comes through the door looking very defeated, ears back, head down and dragging his tail. I realize that he is the same cub that ran past me last evening and must have stolen the signet as he did. He's short, not yet old enough to have a mane, but his tail has the dark brown tuft at the tip. As I look at him, he fidgets with his gray toga, apparently not happy to be in it.

Aime, keep alert for pickpockets from now on.

Aime gives me a green thumbs-up symbol in my vision. We had agreed that her speaking to me may not be a good thing since, if Sada can hear her, the other cats probably can too.

"We have summoned you here because this cub entered you into the Trials. Were you aware of this?" she asks.

"No, I was not."

She looks at me curiously for a moment, then at the signet. "Mediator, please take the boy out. Wait in the foyer."

With a bow, they leave and the door closes behind them. She sits back in thought, the other council members looking between me and her, curious of what is to come. Sensing this, she suddenly stands, "Council, please excuse me. I must continue part of this conversation without the rest of you." She walks around the other members and approaches me.

"Walk with me," she commands.

Unsure of what else to do, I follow her.

As we exit into the foyer, she looks at the cub sulking on a stool. "Kotu, we'll get to you when we return. Sit and behave yourself."

He looks sorrowfully at her but nods. "Yes, ma'am."

As she leads me out of the hut, she pulls her robe's hood over her head.

After a few steps, she stops and looks curiously at me for a moment, "*You* are not a Moku, so who are you?" she asks, her tone of voice not changing.

Considering my words carefully, I answer, "I am a traveler, heading east, to a place I only know as the Dig. Two days ago I met a dying Moku, and he passed on to me his belongings and his wares. We talked for several hours and he guided me here for supplies and hopefully some information."

"Why the disguise?" she asks as she starts walking.

Sighing, I answer, "Forgive me, but I was unsure how someone like me would be received."

She stops walking and turns to me. "What is it you feel you need to hide?"

I think for a moment. "What do you know of humans?"

She tilts her head slightly, then starts walking again. "Not much, I'm afraid, beyond that they're a myth now." She again looks at me curiously. "Why do you ask?"

We walk a few steps before I answer her, "That is why I'm going to the Dig, to see if any remain."

She stops walking and faces me. "Tell me, why would you want to go to a place of myth, looking for another myth?"

"To fulfill a promise to someone who may not even survive to know if there's anyone left."

She looks at me carefully. "You would do that?"

"If it means finding lost people and helping them find their way back home, then yes." My desire to find my own home again surfaces and I quickly push it away.

Thinking for a moment, she gently scratches the fur of her cheek. Suddenly she looks around. "This way." She leads me between a couple of huts, away from the foot traffic, and out of sight. Once secluded, she turns back to me. "Why do you have a fascination with humans? They are gone, let them be gone."

I look carefully at her and seeing the worry in her eyes, I decide it's the only way to let her know. I take off the hood and remove my mask. "Because I'm human."

Her reaction, or rather lack thereof, surprises me. She simply raises her hand to my cheek and feels my skin. "I see why you choose to hide your face," she gently says. "But you should not be afraid of us, only the oldest of us remember humans, and then only in stories."

I marvel for a moment at how similarly structured her hands are to Sada's, though her pads are rough, showing her age. "So now that you know, what should I do?"

She perks her ears at the sound of my unaltered voice and seems to smile. She pulls my hood up and points to my mask. "Now, you need to put that back on. We have a boy to talk about."

I put my mask back on and follow her back out to the street.

"What do you think we should do with him, since he stole your signet?"

I give her a curious look. "What did he do with it, enter me in something?"

"Yes," she states. "He entered you in the Trials. It's a series of tests, of sorts, that earns you prestige, grants you permissions, and allows you to offer, or be offered, a contract."

"Contract?"

"Yes, it can be for almost anything. It allows the person offering to select who they want to offer it to. They can, in turn accept, refuse, or challenge if they like."

"Can anyone enter?" I ask, suddenly curious.

She looks at me skeptically. "Only cats can enter; however, a cat *can* enter someone who's not. Other than that, we hold no disparity. Every part of the Trials is a test of skills, abilities, and strengths. Truthfully, we could let others freely join, but some feel that it would dilute our tradition."

She again stops walking and looks at me, surprised. "You want to go through the Trials."

"I am considering it," I admit, starting to wonder if she can read my mind. "Honestly, I could use some help as I travel, from someone who knows the area."

She smiles and starts walking again. "If you choose to accept entry, you would need to do well to be able to offer a contract."

"If I choose?"

"Since Kotu entered you without your consent, you can stay in or bow out." She sighs as she continues. "The cubs have taken a liking to entering outsiders and watching them stumble through the Trials. I would warn you, if you join, you will be treated like a cat."

I look at her, noting her expression of concern. "I understand. How old do you need to be to enter?"

She thinks for a moment. "Sixteen. Kotu wants to enter, but he's only twelve."

I suddenly realize that we have circled back around to the council hut. She smiles at me. "Ready to determine his punishment?"

Grinning behind my mask, I answer, "I have an idea."

She smiles back. "I thought you might."

As we pass through the foyer, she motions for him to follow. He sighs and reluctantly follows. Once back in the council chamber, she circles around behind and takes her seat. I return to the middle of the room and Kotu joins me, refusing to make eye contact with anyone.

"Council, we will continue with the cub's punishment," she announces.

A male snow leopard to my right speaks up, "Kotu, you have stolen property and entered someone into the Trials without their consent.

This is the second time you've done this. What have you to say for yourself?"

Beside me, the cub squirms uncomfortably. "Uhm, sorry?"

The leopard sighs heavily, shaking his head. "Cub, this is serious, with your record, if you weren't already a ward of this council, you would be made one now. If you keep this up, you will be exiled before you're old enough for the Trials."

"Kotu, I have an offer for you," the cheetess says.

He looks up at her, his curiosity momentarily overwhelming his shame.

Seeing her glance at me, I give a slight nod. "You will spend the next week teaching this male all about the Trials. If he scores high enough, we will let you off the hook. If he fails to perform, you will spend the next year cleaning out the jata stables."

I see his eyes dilate in shock and his posture slumps further. "No, not the stables," he whines, truly meaning it.

"What is your decision, cub?" the leopard asks.

He looks back at the floor, then at me. He sighs heavily. "All right, I'll do it," he concedes. He looks again at me. "I hope you're better than the last Moku that was entered."

I look back at him. "Remember whose fate your hands are in. If you don't do well teaching me, maybe I'll do terribly on purpose," I growl at him.

His eyes dilate again as he backs up a step. "You wouldn't," he manages to gulp.

"Try me." I give him a cold stare. Kotu dons a defeated look, ears slanted back, realizing just how correct I am.

"Mediator," the cheetess calls, "a Trials pack, please. I will put your signet in the Trials. Good luck." She looks briefly at me and I nod again. "Kotu, it will be more productive if you stay with him for the week, collect your belongings."

I bow to the council. "Thank you for your time." I turn to Kotu and put my hand on his shoulder. "You have much to learn, cub." His puzzled reaction makes me chuckle.

After showing us out, the mediator hands me a small booklet as Kotu retrieves his things. "This is a list of rules, the equipment you will need, keep with you, and the things you should and shouldn't wear during the Trials."

Taking the booklet I nod to the mediator. "Thank you."

While waiting for Kotu, I flip through the booklet, giving Aime the chance to scan the pages. Kotu quickly returns with his things, so I make my way back to my kiosk with Kotu in tow.

There, I thank the guards for watching my wares. Kotu sets his pack in a corner and sits next to it on the floor, unsure of what else to do at the moment. I let him sit in silence as I start reading through the rules.

> First: You cannot seek help from anyone not entered in the Trials; your aide(s) are considered entered as long as they bare your symbol.
>
> Second: A warrior can use any and all of their abilities during the Trials as long as they stay within the course.
>
> Third: All weapons and equipment must be worn or carried, even if they are not needed for the current course.

Leaning back in the chair, I realize that it's pretty straight forward.

Interrupting my reading, a young white tiger male comes in. "I'm looking for something for . . . a female."

"Hmm." I size him up; he's a little taller than Kotu, slightly bigger build. While not wearing armor, he has on a white toga, with a light blue-colored signet that matches his eyes. Over his toga, he wears a pack and carries a short sword at his hip. I decide on a complement as the best approach. "To win your favor, she must be quite special." I pull over the jewelry display to help him look.

"What's this female look like?" I casually ask.

Suddenly a shout from the street draws our attention, "Flutter bug!"

He turns suddenly to look. Beyond him, in the street, I see a young, orange tigress, wearing a light blue wrap, bouncing around like she's chasing something. He sighs happily. "That's her."

"Well, quite energetic, and lovely if I may add." I turn the display, looking for a certain piece, "Ah, here we are." I pick off a necklace, a simple leather string with a crystal pendant. The crystal is clear, but there is a reddish-orange object within giving it a fiery appearance. "I believe this would flatter her well."

He takes the necklace and looks closely at it. His eyes sparkle as he speaks. "Yeah, it would," he manages to agree. He looks back at her for a moment, then at me. "How much?"

I look at him, then at the tigress, still chasing the flutter bug. Finding a soft spot in my heart and a wide smile on my face that I'm glad no one can see, I nod to him and close his hand around the pendant. "For you, I will make my first exception. It's my gift to you."

He gives me a look of disbelief but is smart enough not to argue. "Thank you."

I give him another bow. "Good luck to you both."

Thanking me again, he heads out to the tigress. When she sees him approach, she turns and happily wraps him in a hug. He returns her hug, with equal affection and gently puts the necklace on her. She looks curiously at it for a moment, then happily hugs him again. They nuzzle each other for a moment, then slowly stroll off, hand in hand.

I sigh happily as they disappear from view. "Another happy customer."

A voice from beside me interrupts my inner joy with a single word. "Gross." I turn and see Kotu with his tongue sticking out, obviously not enjoying the moment.

Chuckling, I sit down and open the booklet again, finding the section on required equipment. "Required weapons: staff, I have, sword, I have, bow, I need, throwing weapon, I also need."

I glance up at Kotu, noticing that he's looking at me curiously. I take a moment from my reading. "Is there something wrong?"

He sits. "You're taking this seriously, aren't you?"

"Yes, why shouldn't I?"

He looks at me with a look I can't identify. "You're a Moku."

I set the booklet aside and lean forward. "And what would that have to do with anything? Just because I dress like a Moku does not mean I am a Moku. Don't judge someone solely by the way they dress. They will surprise you."

He slouches back against the wall. "Whatever, when do we eat?"

I sigh. "After we get back to my camp."

"When's that?"

"Later, before dark." He slumps, sighing, as I turn back to reading the booklet, aloud this time. "Items to make: tokens with my symbol and a dozen arrows."

"You will wear your armor and equipment at all times, as you would for combat, however, we would recommend that you not wear anything that will prevent you from being able to swim, jump, run, crawl, climb, see, hear or smell."

"Hmm, pretty straight forward." I further look down the page. "There will be four courses. They could be focused on any of these: speed, agility, strength, stamina, archery, stealth, and block. Prepare accordingly. There are other attributes that will be tested, like resilience, acuity, restraint, cunning, and compassion. These tests will not be announced."

Dropping the booklet in my bag, I lean back in the chair. "Some tests are announced, some aren't." I look at Kotu. "What can you tell me about the courses?"

He looks at me and shrugs. "They usually have ten parts, but they're different every time to keep the repeat entrants on their toes. They're even behind walls, to keep prying eyes out."

I lean back again. "Keeping it fair for all."

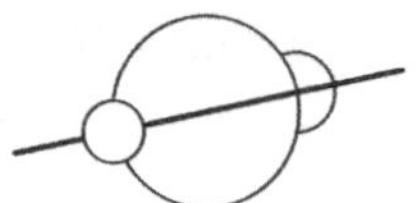

Kotu helps me pack up as I close the kiosk for the evening. I head to my camp and he follows close behind, with his own pack on his shoulder. Once outside the village, though, he starts to fall behind, easily distracted by the sights. Apparently he doesn't get out of the village much.

Approaching the tent, I notice that Sada has not come out to greet me. Looking around, I see her tail waving in the taller grasses. It takes me a moment, but I realize that she's stalking Kotu. Finding myself suddenly torn between concern for the cub and curiosity as to what will happen, I watch for a moment before deciding to warn him.

"Kotu!" I call out.

He looks up at me, totally unaware of Sada's presence. "What?"

Watching the tip of Sada's tail twitch, I call, "Duck!" His expression tells me that he doesn't understand why I just told him to duck, but before I can do anything, Sada pounces.

In a blur of white fur, she leaps from the tall grass. He doesn't even see her until she's right on top of him. She lands on him, claws first, driving him to the ground. I drop my pack and run back to him as she does a flip and lands on the other side, facing him, hissing.

I slide up to his side and put my hands on his fresh wounds, knowing Aime will start healing them. "Sada!" I scold her. "He's a friend." Her demeanor changes suddenly from aggressive to apologetic as she slinks around alongside me. Aime gives me a visual indicating that the boy is healed.

As he blinks his eyes a few times, then he looks at me. "What happened?"

I chuckle. "Next time you're told to duck, duck. You just met my companion."

"You have a companion?" he asks as I help him stand.

"Yes. Kotu, this is Sada, she's my companion." I turn to Sada. "Sada, this is Kotu. He'll be with us for the week."

Sada looks at me, obviously upset. "It's complicated. I'll explain as we eat." She frowns, but starts back to the tent. I turn to Kotu. "You will not tell anyone of anything you see here, understood?"

He gives me an odd look but nods.

"Now, the councilor that I talked to, the cheetess, she knows this already but no one else," I tell him.

"Knows what?"

I pull back the hood and remove my mask. "I'm not a Moku." The sudden change in my voice startles him more than seeing my face does.

He looks curiously at me for a moment and then shrugs. "Okay." He then turns to follow Sada. "What's for supper?"

I stand in disbelief as he casually walks toward the tent.

I spend much of supper recounting the day's events. Sada asks several questions and makes it clear that she's not too happy with me bringing the cub out to camp without warning her first.

Kotu, simply not able to understand half of the conversation, sits quietly as he eats. To my surprise, he handled seeing the converter produce food quite well, simply shrugging it off like he did when he saw my face. With supper and conversations aside, Kotu takes out a short dagger and starts whittling on a short branch he found.

I adjust the tent, making it a little larger, and set up a bed for Kotu. I also set up interior walls, making two bedrooms and a common area. Aime reminds me that we will now have need of a restroom since he has no nanites to consume his waste. She walks me through setting that up and even produces a waste converter to put in the camp toilet. I also set up an area in the tent for a shower, using one of the shower heads we took from the facility.

With night setting in, I tell Kotu how to use both and show him to his room. He sets his pack down and, with a large yawn and a stretch, falls asleep quickly. I retire to my room and find Sada waiting for me.

'Is he asleep?'

"Yeah."

'Sorry I pounced on him.'

I sit on the bed and start to take off my clothes. "Don't feel too bad, no harm done. Besides, the boy wants to be a warrior, and he seems to be able to take a hit. He needs to learn how to pay attention and duck though." I turn and crawl into bed. After a yawn of her own, she curls up against me and we drift off.

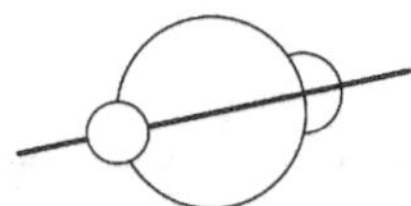

The next morning, Kotu and I head off after breakfast. I spend most of the morning looking for a suitable bow, arrow parts, a throwing weapon, and the wooden disks for the tokens. The tokens were easily found, though not having the coin for them, I trade a necklace for them.

At the weaponsmith, I also found several fletches. While not real feathers due to the lack of birds on this planet, they are actually from something called a Fletch Fern. Kotu explained that the fern grow leaves perfect for making fletches from. When pressed and dried they will retain that flattened shape for months.

Not finding any arrowheads to my liking, I decide on making them. After settling on a simple broadhead design, with a reinforced center, I spend the afternoon running the kiosk and carving the shape, repeatedly, into a flat chunk of sandstone, making the molds. As evening approaches, we close up and head off to camp.

Nearing camp, I notice that Sada is once again stalking Kotu. As I turn to watch her, Kotu seems unaware of her presence. She circles around behind him, and when she pokes her head up, I find myself fighting the urge to laugh. With a smile on her face, ears laid back, and tail twitching, she sneaks up behind him on the path.

He keeps walking, oblivious of her presence. Instead of pouncing on him, she starts putting flowers on his head. When he finally notices the flowers, Sada has ducked back into the brush and circled around to the tent. He looks around, puzzled, and I start laughing. Apparently this is going to be a game.

After supper, Aime creates a small melting pot for me. Heating it in the fire, I manage to melt small amounts of wire vine in it, extracting the natural metals and binders from the plant. I then pour the molten metal into the molds. Aime helps, making sure I get the right amount of in each.

Aime has selected some bow designs for me; from them, I selected a reflex design, as it combines power with a small size. To my surprise, Sada has offered to paint my tokens. Having easily found the wooden disks and paint needed at another vendor, I hand them to her and she happily starts painting, using another copy of my signet as reference.

In the morning, we set out to find the right kind of reeds for arrow shafts. With the vendors sold out of them, I have to harvest my own. According to Kotu, they only grow in certain wet areas where the soil has a high metal content. We find area after area, where there are reeds that are too short or too young to be used. After several hours walk upstream, we finally find a patch of usable reeds.

Kotu tells me that as long as they're damp, they'll be flexible, but when they're dry, they'll become rigid and waterproof. I harvest as many as I can and pack them in a watertight bag to keep them moist until back at camp. Once there, I smooth some bare ground and carefully make some straight grooves to lay the reeds in.

While those dry, I meet with the smith in town, a rather burly jaguar. Without the funds to have him make the bow, I trade him some things for permission to use one of his bow jigs. I adjust the positions of a number of pegs to create the desired shape of the unstrung bow. Aime helps me keep things balanced while forming its shape, but I seem to already know what I'm doing.

With his curiosity peaked by the strange shape I've planned out and a couple more trades, he lets me use the shorter strips of bow wood, the ones too short for most of the longbows he makes. I bend the wet wooden strips and place them in the jig. With the core and several layers in place, I add several clamps to hold things in place and put the jig up to dry. The smith curiously studies the design and seems doubtful of its functionality.

We head back to my kiosk to finish out the day. Once back at camp, we check to see how dry the reeds are, and I make another set of arrowheads. Sada, having finished painting the tokens, secretly works on something else.

After a hearty breakfast, Kotu and I set out to find some lacrylic to glue and seal the bow with. Fortunately, the palm-like trees that produce it aren't too far. Once there, Kotu advises me not to touch the fluid itself, as it will quickly seal my fingers together. To encourage the tree to weep the lacrylic, I cut off a branch-sized leaf and hold a bottle under the cut to catch the thick fluid.

With nearly a half-liter of lacrylic in the bottle, Kotu pours in some water. The water floats on the lacrylic, keeping it from drying. I put a cap on the bottle and we head back to the smith. With the wooden strips dry, I start carefully gluing the laminate pieces together with the lacrylic. Fortunately, once applied in a thin coat, the lacrylic does not take long to dry, so I assemble the bow quickly while at the smiths. I notice that not only is Kotu and the smith overly interested, but there are a few others watching me as well. With the bow assembled, I give it a final overcoat of lacrylic.

Finishing the day out in the kiosk, I start working on the bowstring, using more of the wire vine. I find myself suddenly pleased that I collected so much of it back at the ship. We collect the bow from the smith before he closes and head back at camp. I tie a light string to the grip of the bow and hang it from a tree nearby to finish curing overnight.

The following morning, I begin the final assembly. With the bow cured, I hook the bowstring on one limb's bow nocks, then I hook the bow through my legs and bend the bow against its curve. When bent far enough, I set the string into the other limb's bow nock, turning it from a C shape into a shallow M. Getting to see the working shape of the bow for the first time, Kotu's jaw drops. "Wow, I never thought it'd look like that!"

I give the bow a test pull, allowing Aime to calculate the draw weight. "The bow has exceeded my initial estimate. Draw weight is one hundred ten pounds," she states.

"Can I try?" Kotu eagerly asks.

I look carefully at him for a moment. "Don't let go of the string."

He takes the bow and tries to pull. Unable to pull it more than a few centimeters, he hands it back. "That has some power."

"Yes, it does."

I put the bow away in the tent and turn my attention to the reeds. After checking each one for straightness, I collect most of them, discarding the few that dried with a curve or dent. Selecting the best dozen of those, I carefully cut them to length and set them aside. I then dissect a few lengths of thinner wire vine to get to the individual strands of wire, carefully unweaving the fine wire strands, I set them aside also.

Once I have enough, I pick up a reed and nock the end. I pick two matching and one colored fletch and arrange them carefully at one end of the shaft. Holding them with one hand, I wrap a strand of the fine wire tightly around the shaft and the fletch's lead end to secure them in place. I continue a spaced winding through the fletches, then resume the tight dense winding until I reach the nock. I finish off the wire and coat the knock end and wire lightly with the lacrylic.

Kotu sits and eagerly watches me as I work. As I wind the wire around the third arrow's fletches, he asks, "What's the wire for?"

I give him a curious look. "It holds the fletches in place."

"We usually just use lacrylic," he states.

"The wire will also strengthen this part of the shaft, reducing the possibility of the nock splitting out, help the arrow last longer."

He thinks for a moment and then says "We should do that. Our arrows usually split after a few uses."

As I finish this arrow's fletches, I hand it to him so he can get a closer look, and I start on the next. He looks at it for a moment, then sets it with the others. Satisfied for the moment, he pulls out his dagger and resumes whittling on his whistle flute.

I smile but continue on with the arrows. As I set the last one down, I flip them over so the empty end is up. I pick up an arrow, nock the end, and grab an arrowhead, give it a light coat of the lacrylic and insert it into the nock. Using more wire, I tightly wind the wire around the end, binding the head in place. I give the wire wrap at this end a coat of lacrylic to seal it and set it aside to dry. I finish the remaining arrows this way.

Kotu stops whittling for a moment and picks up an arrow, "How'd you learn how to do this?"

I think for a moment, suddenly realizing that Aime hasn't really helped me that much with the process. Aside from the quality and accuracy of design, the rest of the process I just seemed to know. "Where I come from, this is how they made the arrows. The materials were a little different, but the method was about the same."

Sada comes over holding two items both wrapped in scrap pieces of cloth. She hands one to me and nods. I unwrap it and find a long, small-diameter quiver. It's a typical brown, with a reinforced bottom and a shoulder strap. I also notice that she has painted my signet on it.

Smiling happily, I give her a kiss. "It's beautiful, thank you." I pick up the arrows and insert them into it. I am pleased to see that it leaves the fletches sticking out.

She then turns to Kotu and hands him the other wrap. He looks skeptically at me, then curiously at her.

"Open it," I encourage him.

He unrolls it. His jaw drops in surprise at what she made. "You . . . ," he gasps, looking at his gift. It's a ceremonial sash, black with red trim, and my signet embroidered near one end. "You want me to be your aide?" He looks curiously at me for a moment and then at Sada.

I figure this is Sada's revenge for bringing him into camp unannounced, so I roll with it. "Why not?" I ask, smiling.

He looks at me for a moment. "If you score low, I share the humility."

I give him a stern look. "Sounds only fair, since you entered me."

He hangs his head, a little. "Sorry, I thought it'd be funny, but now . . ."

I give him a moment to think before I speak, "What if I do well?"

He thinks for a moment, looking at the signet on the sash. "If you do well, I get to share a little of the prestige." He sits up and looks at me. "I haven't even seen you practice . . . anything."

I pick up the bow and an arrow. "Pick me a target."

He looks around. "The tree branch, where you hung the bow from."

Turning to look at the branch, I realize that it's almost thirty meters from me, "Okay." I nock an arrow, as I raise the bow I draw the arrow to me. I'm pleased that the draw is silent, telling me that nothing is slipping or breaking. Taking careful aim, I let loose the arrow. With a quiet *thwip*, it quickly finds its mark. The branch cracks and leaves fall from the impact of the broad-head arrow.

I look at Kotu. He stands in awe, staring wide-eyed at the arrow stuck in the branch. Sada smiles and applauds, bouncing happily.

Kotu looks at me. "How . . . ?"

"I used to make bows," I confess. "Making this one brought some of those memories back." I look at the bow in my hand, appreciating its design.

"Memories?" he asks, suddenly curious. "What happened to your memories?"

"Oh, I never told you. I lost them, but they're slowly coming back. If something familiar happens, some of them come back quicker."

I find myself holding back a chuckle at his sudden displeasure, sinking back down to his chair, groaning.

"If it helps, I learned to fight after losing my memories."

He turns his head, looking at me curiously. "You know how to fight?" he asks skeptically, sitting up a little.

"Yeah," I answer. "Can't walk for a day in this place and not be attacked by something. Sada and I walked for more than a week before we got to Pridewyn."

He looks at Sada and she nods her head. Sighing, he concedes, "I'll be your aide." He gets up and heads over to the arrow in the tree. After a little effort he manages to get the arrow out. After looking at it for a few moments he brings it back and puts it in the quiver. "Didn't split," he states, somewhat surprised.

He then picks up the sash, wraps it around his waist, and then ties it, making sure that the emblem is easily visible.

"Since the Trials start in two days, as your aide, I'll need to make sure your tokens are in and your board is correct."

As Sada fetches the tokens, I ask, "The board?"

"The board is where the judges keep your scores."

Sada hands him a pouch with the tokens in it. He dumps some into his hand and looks at them carefully. "What's this symbol mean?"

"Truthfully, I have no idea. I have been told that it has to do with something mysterious or unknown," I scowl, realizing the circle of that logic.

He puts the tokens back in the bag. "I know you're not a Moku, but what do you want as your name on the board?"

I sit back in thought, looking absently toward Sada. She tilts her head curiously, as in thought. 'Why not you?' she signs.

"Why not me?" I repeat curiously, misunderstanding her meaning.

'Not *you*.' She waves. 'You, K-Y-L-E,' she spells out my name, making sure I understand.

"Why not me." With understanding I turn to Kotu, who looks a little lost. "Kyle, my name is Kyle."

"Kyle?" he asks. "What kind of name is Kyle?"

"You should learn not to ask such questions aloud," I chide. "Someone may take offence to it."

His ears slant back as he looks down, ashamed. "Sorry."

I sigh and lean to him. "Are you going to spend the rest of your life apologizing for your mistakes, or are you going to start learning from them?"

He thinks for a moment and I see his ears droop back a little as he starts to speak. "Ss . . ." He stops abruptly, his ears perking up. "Learning."

I smile and sit back. "That's a good start. Now, what else do you need to know?"

He thinks for a moment. "If you score high enough, will you be offering or looking for a contract?"

I look up to the sky for a moment, then to Sada, who shrugs. "I think I will offer."

He gives me a questioning look. "Do you know what for?"

I think for a moment. "How far east have people been?"

He sits up, thinking. "Uhm, maybe a week's walk past Three Lands. After that, you're in the Wilds."

"What kind of person would I need to get us there?"

"Uhm, a scout, no, most of the way is known. Uhh, a guide then, or an escort."

I think for a moment. "Guide."

"Okay, I'll go to the judges and update your board."

As he stands, Sada pushes him back down into the chair.

"Now?" I ask.

"Yeah, it's my job as aide to take care of this for you."

"Can it wait until morning?" I ask. "You only have a couple hours till dark, and we still have to eat supper."

He thinks for a moment, lightly rubbing his stomach, then smiles at the thought of food. "Uhm, yeah sure, it can wait."

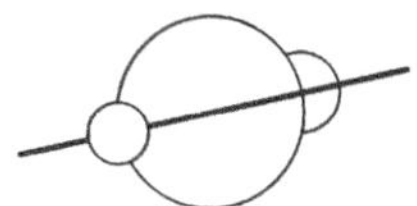

After breakfast, Kotu heads off to the village to update the board. While he's gone, I sit and figure out what I want to use for a throwing weapon. Aime comes up with several selections, but without being able to handle it, I'm unable to make a selection.

"Aime, can you set up a training session with all those weapons available?'

"I can."

I get comfortable and relax. "Let's do it."

I spend the next several "virtual" hours picking through thousands of hand throw-able knives, shurikens, darts, chakrams, axes, and a large number of things that I can't identify. I eventually settle on a simple hand-sized throwing knife.

After a half-hour of practice, I still haven't learned to control its rotation. Aime thinks for a moment, then produces a similar, but double-ended throwing knife. Throwing this one, I find that I don't have to worry as much about its rotation since both ends are equally shaped and sharp.

Waking up from training, I find a pair of throwing knives in the converter. I take them out and stick them to the underside of my left forearm. Like the swords and pistol holsters, they stick automatically.

When Kotu finally returns, he's carrying a card. As he approaches, I watch as Sada sneaks out of the taller grass and quietly starts to follow him. After a few steps, he turns and looks at her. She smiles and wraps him a hug.

Taken off guard by her actions, he struggles to get free. "What was that for?" he stammers, confused.

"For paying attention," I offer. "You're learning to stay alert. As a warrior, you want to be aware of your surrounding at all times."

He looks at me, his eyes wide, slightly surprised that I'm now standing right next to him. "All the time?" he asks, then looking a little confused, he adds, "Why?"

I hold up his dagger. "Because you never know when someone, whether you know them or not, will do something."

His eyes go wide again with surprise. "How'd you get that?" he snaps, reaching for it.

"Right after you turned around," I state, handing him back his dagger.

He puts the dagger back in its sheath. "How'd you do that? You were too far away."

"Another thing you need to learn," I offer, looking at the card he was carrying. "Never underestimate anyone. That's something you taught me when you stole my signet."

Noticing that I have the card, he looks at his hand and finds a leaf. His jaw drops in surprise, but he says nothing, instead just sits in a chair and stares at the leaf, apparently trying to figure out how I got the card from him and put the leaf in its place.

"You're easily distracted," I offer while I sit, still reading the card. "So I'm one of sixteen, seven males and nine females. Hmm, there's a wolf, cheetah, lion, panther, cougar, snow leopard . . . a question mark?" I pause, looking at the name. "Oh, that's me." I continue, "Another lion, jaguar, bobcat, serval, Bengal tiger, Siberian tiger, a liger, lynx, and a caracal. Quite a diverse group."

Kotu drops the leaf. "Yeah, when the village heard there was a Moku in the Trials, it seems everyone wanted in. The council had to limit the number of participants. The ones who were already in were kept as is, but for the ones who joined after you, they drew lots to see who would participate. Judging by the spread there, I think they drew lots from each group."

"How many people normally enter?"

"Last Trials had eight, before that, uhm, five."

"How many were there when the last Moku was entered?" I curiously ask.

He thinks for a moment. "Uh, I think there were sixteen then too."

I chuckle. "Everyone wants to show up the Moku." I think again for a moment then ask, "Do you know who had joined before me?"

"The judges put them in the order they joined, so everyone before you," he states, curious again. "Why?"

"Come over here. Tell me what you can about the others."

As he slides his chair over to mine, Sada sits next to me. We listen carefully as he goes down the list, telling me what he can about the other entrants. For the cub not being able to participate in the Trials yet, he's surprisingly knowledgeable about the ones that entered before me. However, for the newer entrants, he knows they are all young and their first time in the Trials, but not much more than that.

After we eat lunch, I finish the bow by wrapping a leather pad around the grip, gluing it in place with lacrylic. I also sharpen the arrowheads, being careful to keep the angle balanced so it doesn't affect flight. Sada takes initiative and paints my signet on the widest part of the upper limb of the bow, just like she did with the tokens. I can't help but wonder if I taught her how to paint or if she learned it on her own. I asked her once, but she just grinned.

Kotu picks up a piece of a small tree branch and starts whittling on it. I find myself thinking about his situation. Being a ward is somehow familiar, but unable to recall my own life, I can't figure out why. Hoping to jog my memory, I ask him, "Kotu, why are you a ward of the council?"

He stops whittling for a moment and sighs. "My parents died when it was little. With no aunts or uncles, I became a ward of the council. Been working for them ever since."

Seeing the sadness in his eyes, I say, "I'm sorry."

He pokes his knife at the stick. "You didn't know," he groans.

I look at him, trying to figure out his buried emotions. "Well, I do now, and I am sorry to hear about your parents. No child should grow up without a parent."

"Well," he sadly confesses, "I grew up with the council, so . . ."

Before he can finish, Sada wraps him in a hug. This time he doesn't squirm, he just sits quietly, head hung slightly. After a moment, though, he drops his dagger and wraps his arms around her. Hearing him sniffle, I step over and kneel down next to him.

He tries to sit up, but I put my hand on his back to offer my comfort. With this simple action, he lets go. Tears roll down his face as he breaks down, sobbing hard. He tucks his chin, burying his face as he cries. Sada looks at me, confused, obviously unsure of what's happening.

'Never got to properly let it out,' I sign, somehow understanding his feelings.

She gives me a look of understanding and hugs him a little tighter. I gently scrub the fur on his back, letting him cry.

After a few minutes, he starts to compose himself. "Sorry, I—"

"Don't apologize, not for this," I softly interrupt. "Everyone cries sometimes."

He looks at Sada and she nods her agreement. He takes a heavy ragged breath, trying to regain a little more control.

Running my hand over his head, I say, "I bet, without that headache, you'll feel a lot better." Aime takes my statement literally and relieves his headache.

He sighs, sinking back in his chair. As I stand, he looks up at me. "Thanks."

I nod. "You're welcome."

I return to my seat and resume sharpening the arrowheads. Sada gives him a light bump with her nose. He smiles and gently pushes her away. Sada and I both smile at his reaction. Apparently feeling much better, he picks up his dagger and starts whittling again.

CHAPTER 6

Kotu leads me across the bridge to the course head. He's wearing his sash over his usual loincloth and bandolier. I'm in my armor, swords on my lower arms, throwing knives under the left. On top of that, I have the Moku's cloak, with its hood up and my mask on. Over the top cloak, on my back, I have the quiver, with my bow hanging on it, and my staff tucked in the strap.

Sada follows, now dressed in a similarly tattered cloak, with the hood up. I had advised her that she didn't need to hide, but she nervously insisted. I had Aime humor her with the cloak, leaving out the smell. She hangs back in the crowd, trying to be just another spectator.

"Over there, where your signet is," Kotu instructs, pointing to a currently vacant canopy. As we approach, I notice that few of the contestants have an aide or two, but most have none. I also notice that I'm getting plenty of stares. I try not to let this affect me as I claim my spot.

I slowly look around at the others, allowing myself to be curious about them like they are of me. Suddenly the crowd parts, a snow leopardess warrior walks through the opening, ignoring everyone. I see a few people point and cover their mouths and quickly realize that they're laughing at her.

As she gets nearer, I can easily see that she's athletic, slightly taller than most of the other cats, and carries herself with honor, despite the crowd's treatment. She takes the canopy to my right as I face the gathered crowd. Given her species, I conclude that this must be Larrah, as she was the only snow leopard listed as an entrant. I find myself wondering what she, a warrior who shows no shame, could have done to deserve some people's ridicule.

As I wait patiently the last few find their places. Kotu stands at my left, trying to hide his nervousness, but his tail and ears both keep twitching, giving him away.

"Entrants," a male voice booms, "welcome to the Trials."

This gets everyone's attention, and silence takes over as we all turn to look at the announcer, a lion, standing in an elevated tower.

"For this Trials, we have sixteen entrants." He turns and motions to the board Kotu was talking about as the crowd cheers.

He holds up his hands and the crowd quiets down. "For those new here today, we randomly select the order of the events. The first event is archery. Entrants, please find your marks."

Kotu points me to the targets. I turn and see a row of targets, large disks of wood with painted circles, currently set at thirty meters. They are arranged with two archers per target. Finding my mark, I discover I share mine with a lion, who stands to my right. I remember his name from the card as Roush.

"Archers, ready!" the announcers calls.

I ready my bow and pull an arrow from my quiver. I intentionally fumble nocking the arrow while watching the lion work his longbow like a pro. I hear him chuckle, having noticed that I fumbled the arrow.

"Thirty-meter target, three arrows, draw and fire at will."

I let him lead me in the draw. I watch as his arrow scores in the outer red ring. I take aim and score in the inner red.

Roush chuckles. "Lucky."

I pull another arrow and decide to lead him. To show him I'm not lucky, I score in the outer gold ring.

He lets a subtle hiss escape his teeth as he lets loose the arrow. It scores inner blue.

Smiling behind my mask, I loosen my third arrow to the center gold. He looks at me, a mix of curiosity and contempt in his eyes. He lets loose his third arrow and scores outer red.

After a moment, the announcer calls, "Score and collect your arrows."

Kotu runs out and meets the scorer, who removes the arrows as she tallies the score. She hands Kotu all six arrows, and he jogs back. He quickly sorts the arrows and hands Roush's to him and me, mine. I give mine a quick once-over and put them back in my quiver. The lion puts one of his in his quiver and drops the other two on the ground, apparently broken.

"Targets at fifty meters," the announcer calls, "three arrows, draw and fire."

Deciding to skip with any more teasing, I loosen my three arrows in sequence, scoring an inner red, outer gold, and another inner red. Roush scores an outer blue and two inner blues.

With the seventy-meter target, the lion tries to show me up. He loosens his three in succession, not giving me a chance to take a turn. I watch as he manages to score two inner red and an outer gold. I draw and loosen my three, intentionally having each land one ring inside his.

When the targets are moved to ninety meters, Roush looks at me and growls, "Quit playing around. Show me what you got."

I knock my first arrow and draw; I give the lion a glance. He stands watching, grinning. Unsure of what he's thinking, I decide to show him. I let loose the arrow. It flies the shallow arc to the target, scoring, in the center gold. I nock my second arrow and draw. The arrow scores right next to the first, still inside the center gold. I let loose my last arrow. It sticks just below the first two, creating a small triangle in the center gold.

He stands agape at my shots. It takes him a moment to shake it off, and when he does, he takes his three shots. Each gets progressively closer to the gold but none make it in.

The other archers finish their final shots and the announcer calls for scores. Kotu comes back with the arrows and I check mine and put them in my quiver. He hands the lion his three, and he in turn drops them on the ground with the other broken arrows, leaving him two in his quiver. The scorer comes by on her return trip and counts our remaining arrows.

We return to our tent for lunch. Some vendors come by, and since I'm an entrant, they give me and my aide, Kotu, our meals for free. We sit and enjoy our meals, waiting for the judges to tally the scores. Before the scores are posted, however, the next event is announced and I follow Kotu to the next section and find my place.

This time I'm next to a young female serval. As with a typical serval, she's tan with dark spots and oversized ears. She wears light leather armor that does little to hide her slender figure. Remembering her name as Aria, I see why Kotu was so interested in her.

On the other side of me stands a rather large gray wolf named Garra. He stands tall, slightly taller than me, wearing little armor. Like the rest of us, he still carries his bow and remaining arrows, as required by the rules of the Trials.

We all stand patiently, waiting for the announcer. The lion climbs on the platform. "Welcome to the second event. This is the agility course."

I hear the wolf groan, leading me to think that he's going to have problems with this event.

"Inside this course, there is one target that you will need to hit with your throwing weapon. You will run one at a time. First up, Tayla. Good luck."

We all turn to watch the first entrant head to the entrance. In the short time I get to see her, I see she's a cheetah. I find myself intrigued by how she carries herself with confidence, but some of her motions belie her youth and inexperience as she enters the course cautiously.

Being later in line, I have a seat, as do many of the other entrants, and wait for our turn. I occasionally look to the other entrants, seeing what they are doing. Aria does some practicing with her staff, working on some of the more difficult moves she knows. Garra, on the other hand, seems to fall asleep. I begin to wonder why he entered.

After waiting a while, I notice that the entrant in front of the wolf, a bobcat named Farol, is starting to gear up. I conclude that she is up next as she starts stretching. A short time later, her name is called and she heads to the entrance. I look at Garra, expecting him to start warming up. Instead, he remains seated, casually waiting for his turn. Looking at Aria, she is now meditating. I find her dedication reassuring.

When Garra's name gets called, he grumbles and sets off for the entrance. I figure that he's not doing this willingly, given his disregard for preparation. I stand and make sure all my gear is in place. I see Aria nod to me, so I politely nod back as I begin to stretch and limber up. After a minute, I see Farol return to her area. She looks wet, ragged, and sore, nursing her lower left arm like she took a hit.

Hearing my name, I make final adjustments and look at Farol. She gives me a nod, apparently wishing me luck. I nod back and with a glance at Aria, who stands and starts her stretches. I set off to the entrance.

I follow the entrance hall as it turns left and then back to the right, the corners hiding what is to come. Stepping out into a wider corridor, I find the floor abruptly stops, replaced by a shallow pit of black liquid. Over that runs a single wooden beam, no wider than my hand. It extends straight forward, then zigzagging through some swinging weights. I pull my staff and hold it crossways to help balance. I start walking across the beam, fairly easy, even when it comes to avoiding the swinging weights.

As the beam ends, I find two vertical walls three stories tall, each barely a meter wide and a little farther apart. Looking around, I quickly see the only way forward is up. Sighing, I realize that this is more than just a test of physical agility.

Aime, camo off. I won't need it here.

Stepping up between the walls, I run my hands across the wood, feeling the surface. The walls are rough, allowing enough texture for grip. Spying several claw marks in them, I realize that it's a wall climb. Pressing outward on both walls with my hands, I lift my feet to the walls and start working my way up.

Reaching the top, I discover that the walls now run parallel forward over more of the black liquid. I edge forward, reaching the end. Instead of finding a floor where the walls end, I find overhead bars.

Switching to the overhead bars, I continue, swinging from bar to bar. Interrupting my rhythm is a corner, swinging myself around the corner I continue straight for a short distance and then turn another corner. Now at the end of the overhead bars and surrounded by walls, I am without a direction to go. Looking down, I see a hole big enough to fit through. Not seeing any other way to continue, I drop from the bars, through the hole, to the floor below.

I now notice that one of the walls is now rock. Looking across that wall, I find a small opening. Bits of fur around the opening tells me that this is the way everyone else has gone. Looking into the hole, I see nothing. With no source of light, I slide headfirst into the opening.

As I feel around, I discover a small divot in the floor. I use it to pull myself forward. Feeling around again I find another. Pulling myself to it, I start repeating this process, making small slides forward until I see a light. As I pull toward it, I realize that by following the handholds, they will lead me away from the light. I look at the opening and realize that it may be another test.

I slowly slide toward the opening and cautiously look out. I discover that I'm looking through the waterfall at a target, a small red disk with a white center. Unable to even kneel, I reposition myself to maximize my throwing angle. Now lying on my back with my right arm out the hole, I pull one of my throwing knives and line up the shot. After taking a couple of practice swings, I throw the knife through the falling water. I'm pleasantly surprised to hit the red ring. Rolling back over to my belly, I slide over and continue following the handholds.

Emerging into a narrow crevasse, I quickly see that the only way to go is a few meters up. I start climbing, something made slightly more difficult by the fact that my staff keeps hitting rocky outcroppings. Repositioning it slightly, I continue climbing.

Emerging into the light, I find a series of short posts with wires strung from post to post at knee level. With walls around, I start sliding on my stomach under the wire, this time with my staff in hand. Turning my head, I get a close look at the wire. There are tufts of fur clinging to spots all over the wire. I carefully touch a strand; it's sharp.

"Razor vine," Aime states, "similar to the wire vine, but naturally sharp."

"Great." I continue sliding along on my stomach until I get to the other end. Picking myself up, I put my staff back under the quiver and follow a narrow rocky path to the river's edge.

A series of hanging ropes point me to a platform in the middle of the falls. I swing easily out, landing on the platform. Looking around, I see that it's easily another ten meters to the other side. With the current up here too strong to swim, I turn to look over the falls. There's a pool below, surprisingly deep. From here I can see where the path goes.

Being a short distance up and the water below being clear, I make up my mind. I pull a cinch strap on my quiver to keep the arrows in. With one hand, I hold my mask and with the other I grip my staff and bow, holding them to my hip. I jump forward off the platform. As I fall, feet first, I cross my legs just before hitting the water.

After splashing into the cool water, I swim back to the surface and over to the path.

Climbing out of the water, I head over to the narrow path and notice that there are a dozen more swinging weights. Timing my sprint, I start down the walled path, dodging the weights as I go. After a few meters, I round a corner, with no obstacles; I sprint to the other end and round another corner.

I find myself looking at a pair of slanted rails. They run downhill to the end of this course. Looking down between them, I see another pit of black fluid; I also notice that the rails end before the pit does. With it too far to jump, I again pull my staff, holding it crosswise above the bars. I slide down, hanging from the staff as it rides down the rails. As I near the end of the rails I swing my feet up, launching me upward off the rails. I clear the pit and land hard on the ground and then roll to a kneeling position. I plant my staff and stand up.

Being at the end, I take the last few steps through the exit, emerging to be handed my throwing knife. I hear Aria's name get called, signaling her to begin the course I just finished.

I follow the path back to where I began to find Kotu waiting for me. He helps me out of the quiver and sets aside the bow, quiver, and staff to dry. Looking to my left, I see Garra and realize that he must have had a difficult time. He has several patches of fur missing; his tail is bloodied. None of it really seems to bother him as he sits. I also notice that from his footpads to his knees are black, apparently from falling into, at least one of, the pits.

Looking past him, I see that Farol now has her arm wrapped. I wonder for a moment if it broke, but when she uses it, I realize that it's not.

I look at Kotu. I realize that it's starting to get late in the day. "Have you eaten yet?"

"They brought some snacks around while you were running the course. I had some fish jerky."

I nod, knowing he wouldn't pass up some food. "Have you heard anything about the others yet?"

He looks down the row of entrants. "Well, I heard Tayla did well, no surprise there. She may be young, but she's still good. Uhm, Roush, broke his arm, he's out. I heard someone say that Larrah broke the female's record, again. Krat finished without falling but scored low. Farol did better, but her arm is heavily bruised. Garra, well, you can see the razor wire really tore him up. He almost lost his tail and fell in the muck a few times." He takes a breath, looking me up and down. "You seem to have done well, no muck, no obvious injuries."

I think about what I went through. For me, it didn't seem that difficult. I quickly realize that I have an advantage, because of my nanites hold off fatigue. They also increase my reflexes and overall strength. I wonder if this means that I'm cheating. Thinking for a moment, I concede that possibility, but argue that I've been relying solely on my body's abilities and not the armor's or weapons'.

Mentally reviewing the course, at the beginning, the biggest problems were falling off or being knocked off the beams. Later, though, falling from the walls or hand-over-hand bars would have easily been a painful drop. Crawling through the cave, I could have become lost.

I'm beginning to think the trials are more than fun and games. "Kotu, has anyone died in the Trials?"

He thinks for a moment. "No, but broken bones and nasty cuts are common. Sometimes someone gets injured worse, but no deaths that I know of."

Sighing, I sit back. "Great." The Trials are also a test of courage or stupidity.

When Aria comes back to her station, she's wet and limping badly, using her staff as a crutch. When she sits, I see that her entire foot is obviously deformed. I would guess that a few bones are dislocated.

Kotu looks at her foot and cringes, "Oww, that looks painful."

As she tries to lift her foot-paw within reach of her hands, she winces in pain. Seeing everyone else occupied with their own wounds, I look at Kotu. "I know that if you see someone outside the Trials for medical help, you're out. Do the rules mention anything about getting help from another entrant?"

An odd look crosses his face as he thinks. "Not that I'm aware of," he slowly states.

"Do you know who you can ask to find out?"

"Yeah, I do."

"Well, go find out, quickly," I insist. He quickly jogs off, following my instructions. I turn to her, watching once again as she tries to pull her foot-paw to her. She manages to get it a little closer but still flinches in pain and stops.

Kotu quickly returns. "The judge says it's okay to help another entrant. Why?"

"Wait here, and watch." I get up and walk over to Aria. Approaching slowly, I bow to her. "May I offer some assistance? It is permissible under the rules."

She gives me a look of both curiosity and skepticism. After glancing at her foot-paw, she nods. "Please."

I kneel and gently taking her foot-paw in hand. *Aime, let's fix this, painlessly, if possible.* As I slowly start massaging just below her ankle, I strike up a conversation, "You landed hard, didn't you?"

She sighs, a little disgusted with herself. "Yeah, that last landing got me."

"May I offer some advice?" I ask, now working down her upper foot.

She thinks a moment, then shrugs. "Sure."

Moving my hands down to her foot-paw, I say, "As you land, tuck and roll with the momentum. If you do it right, it'll keep injury to a minimum."

She gives me an oddly curious look. "Why help me?"

I sigh, working her toes. "Because I do not believe that the Trials are, for example, me against you, but rather me against me, or you against you. Do you understand?"

She gives me a thoughtful look. "I think I do. You're saying that it's to prove to yourself what you're capable of." I nod my agreement as she continues, "Then why be able to earn contracts?"

I run a finger from her ankle to her pads. Her toes flair and her claws extend, making her giggle. "Perks," I state, "for doing well."

I stand as she flexes her toes and ankle. "How'd you do that?"

I bow. "Knowing how to heal is as important as knowing how to hurt."

As I turn, she stands and gives me a slight bow. "Thank you."

I bow back in kind. "You're welcome."

While we all walk back to camp, the sun starts to set. Sada, tired from the day's events, holds my hand and wearily leans on me. She's still wearing the cloak, but with the hood down.

Kotu lets out a large yawn and shakes his head. "Tired?" I ask, putting my hand on his shoulder to steady him.

"Yeah, been a long day."

"Tomorrow, we pack something to eat, okay? Don't need to sit and be hungry between meals."

He muffles another yawn. "Dagger and flute too."

"Making another one? What'd you do with the last one?"

"Sold it. I got six coins for it."

"Is that good?"

He shrugs. "It's okay, but I'd like to get a little more."

"Well, what if you painted it or carved design on it?"

"Paint costs coin," he admits. "I never thought about a design."

"What about a natural stain then, and covering with lacrylic?"

"I guess I could do that, find some berries, make some wood stain. Collect some lacrylic." He scratches his head in thought. "Without chores, that'd take me a day. They'd last for months." He smiles. "I could do that."

I chuckle, patting him on the back. "That you could."

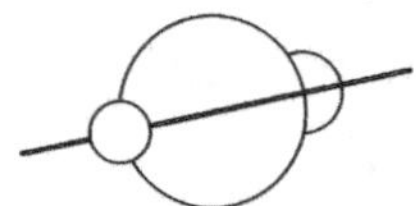

The next morning after breakfast, I empty the trader's pack. I put back in one of the better blankets and the weapons. I use the converter to make several kinds of jerked fish and put them in the basket. I also pack one of the mini converters if I need to make more. After putting a bladder of water in the pack, I put the basket of jerky on top.

Sada dons her cloak as I redress in my armor, Moku cloak, and weapons. Kotu packs his dagger and puts on the sash.

All packed and dressed, we set out for the village. As we get close, Sada separates from us and enters the village on her own, mixing into the crowd just like she did yesterday.

Kotu and I approach the staging area and see that the board has been updated with the current scores. Looking across the board, I find my score and start comparing it to the others. For archery, they range from as low as forty-seven to my high score of one hundred thirteen.

That is twelve points over the actual score. Why is it different? This appears floating in my vision, a question from Aime.

"Kotu, what do they add for the scores? The booklet didn't have a lot on the scoring."

He looks up at the board. "Uhh, well, there are the target scores," he states, thinking. "Oh, they add the number of good arrows you had left."

"Ah, that's the extra twelve points." I'm beginning to see that the Trials test you in any way that they can think of, craftsmanship included.

I start comparing the other score, for the agility course. I find that I'm again the one with the high score. The lowest I see is a zero, for Roush, who broke his arm.

Noticing an additional number on my board, I look at the rest and see that no one else has one. "What's that extra number on my board mean?"

Kotu looks up at my board again. He looks at it for a moment. "I'm not sure."

"Well, we need to find out." I see him nod his head in agreement.

Finding our way to our area, I set down the pack and have a seat. Kotu roots in his pack and comes out with his flute-to-be and starts whittling on it.

After a few minutes, the announcer makes his appearance. "Welcome to day two of the Trials. Our first event of the day is strength. Entrants, please find your marks."

Kotu leads me past the archery field to another course head. Just like the agility course, it has a wall around it to prevent us from seeing inside. I find myself between a Bengal Tiger named Krat and a jaguar named Cheen.

Krat wears plate scale armor that covers most of his body; it's heavier than most others I've seen. He also has a helmet, with bulges for his ears. He stands my height and, in addition to the longbow, staff, and quiver, has a two-handed long sword on his back. With all that added weight, I find myself amazed that he made it through the agility course at all.

Cheen, on the other hand, wears lighter armor that also covers most of his body. He has a similar longbow, apparently the favored type here, but his sword is a single-handed short sword. He also wears a bandolier with several throwing knives in it.

In both their cases, they wear no protection over their foot-paws. Of course, now that I've noticed that, I realize that no one wears any shoes or boots or any kind of foot-paw covering like the Moku and I do.

The closest thing I've seen to foot coverings were some various types of wraps between the footpad and ankle.

The announcer interrupts my thoughts. "Welcome to the strength course. First up, Faru. Good luck."

We all turn to watch Faru enter the course. The lioness walks with pride and confidence as she approaches the entrance. Without a second thought, or care, she enters. I risk a glance at Krat. He stands tall and ready, apparently eager for his turn. After several minutes, his name gets called, and he heads to the entrance.

I stand up, and after making sure my gear is in place, I start doing some simple stretches.

Kotu watches for a moment and then asks, "Is that going to help?"

"Can't hurt," I counter.

A few minutes later, I hear my name get called. Giving Kotu a nod, I head across the sand to the entrance. Walking through the opening, I make a quick right and then left. The hall narrows and a barrel blocks the way. It's on its side and has "100" printed on it. It looks like I need to roll it.

As I roll the barrel, I see ropes wrap around each end. When I get to the end of the hall, I find a passage to my left. I step through and let the barrel roll back down the hall. I turn and find another barrel, this one marked "150." I start rolling it, and like the other, it rolls, but not as easily. This time the hall is longer. Reaching the end of this hall, I find yet another barrel to push.

With this third barrel marked "200," I feel my muscles actually starting to tire a little. As I push, I also notice that the ground bears several claw marks. Because of this, I occasionally slip, losing traction. When the barrel runs out of the hall, I step into the next hall and let it roll back to its place.

Without another wall to push, I take a short breather and slowly proceed forward. Walking around a corner, I find a rope hanging through a hole in the ground, from the hole, I hear running water. Since the rope has a large knot spaced every half meter, I can't slide down the rope. It's a controlled decent, then.

Taking the rope in hand, I start climbing down the rope. After several meters and immersion in darkness, I reach the floor. Without being able to see, I reach out, but don't find anything but the rope.

"Aime, I could use some light," I say, wishing I brought a flashlight.

Unexpectedly my vision brightens. "I have no way to produce light, so I have enhanced your ability to see with the ambient light. Will this suffice?"

Looking around, I say, "Yes, thank you, just remember to turn it off when I get real light back. I don't want to go blind."

"Understood."

Now that I can see, I notice I'm in a cavern, with only one way out. Following the cave, I exit right under the falls. To my right is the pool I jumped into as part of the agility course, to my left is the cliff wall behind the falls. On the other side of the falling water, I see that the cave continues. Tightening my quiver strap, I start walking the narrow rock ledge directly under the falling water. The water batters me, trying to knock me from the path and making it hard to see. Holding onto parts of the wall for balance, I continue the remaining distance to the far side.

Entering the cave, I find another rope, this one, with no knots to climb up. I start climbing, pulling myself up with my arms first, then with the rope wrapped around one leg, pinching it between my boots to hold me in place while I move my hands.

Reaching the top outside, I step over to a platform that leads me to another hall. I start down the hall, turning a corner; I again see a movable wall. This one is marked "10," and it has a series of handles. Lift walls.

I grab a set of handles and lift. The wall moves easily, straight up. I try ducking under as I hold it up by my staff snags. Lifting it a little higher and ducking a little lower, I try again. Making it underneath, I let the wall fall behind me. It lands with a loud *whump*, and I proceed to the next wall, just a couple meters away. After adjusting my staff, I lift the second wall, marked "20."

Getting under that one easily, I continue through the next several walls, their weight increasing by ten kilograms each time. Ducking under the one hundred kilo wall, I'm pleased to discover no more walls. I am, however, not happy to discover a ten-meter tall tower with no obvious way up to the platform near the top. I walk up to the base of the tower and notice that two of the massive legs have a row of angled pegs running them.

"I know this." I gasp, realizing that I've seen this before. Pulling my staff, I place is crosswise on the pegs. Then grabbing it like a chin-up bar, I pull myself up off the ground. With my body raised, I quickly jump the staff up to another set of pegs and start pulling myself up again. Repeating this process up the tower is quickly exhausting. When I land on the platform, I put the staff on my back and take a moment to catch my breath.

Feeling better, I start forward again, heading down a ramp to the ground. Once there, I find another barrel. This one is marked "200" and it's not round. The sides have flat spots to keep it from rolling easily. I try rolling it and all I do is slide. My boots are unable to grip the ground.

I suddenly realize that cats have claws, increasing their traction. So despite the nanites enhancing my strength, stamina, and agility, I've still been doing this with disadvantages. Taking a step back, I recall the rules to the Trials. "A warrior can use any and all of their abilities during the Trials as long as they stay within the course."

"I haven't been using all my abilities," I state quietly, then in a determined voice say, "Aime, don't let me slip."

"Understood."

I lean into the barrel and push. I feel my boots start to slip, but quickly stop, like they locked to the ground. As the barrel starts to roll, I take a step. Feeling the boots again seem to lock to the ground, I push harder. Reaching my limit, the barrel seems to hit something and stop.

"I need more strength," I gasp.

"Acknowledged."

The armor seems to get tighter as I start to push again. The barrel starts to roll again, easier than before. I keep rolling the barrel as it bounces along, putting dents in the packed ground. After several steps, the barrel abruptly stops and I hear a board crack. I stand up and see that I've moved it past the exit.

As I turn and pass through, four big males rush through to move the barrel back. I walk back to the trailhead as my strength returns to normal and the armor loosens slightly.

Reaching my spot, I sit on a stool and reach for the basket of fish jerky. Kotu notices and slides it to me. "You okay?"

Pulling my hood forward to hide my face better, I pull off the mask and take a bite of jerky. "That was not easy."

"Which part?"

"The last barrel."

He gives me an odd look. "The last barrel, you moved the last barrel?" His voice changes from astonishment to intense curiosity. "How far?"

He's leaning forward to me, eager to hear my answer. "All the way to the exit."

His jaw drops. "No, you couldn't have. No one has."

I take a bite of another piece of jerky. "Really?"

He nods. "I'm sure, the only other to move it even halfway was...uhm, Xander."

I finish the piece of jerky. "Who's Xander?"

"He was a really good warrior, set the record score for males last time he was in, died earlier this year, though. Ambushed or something." He looks down, apparently saddened by that revelation.

Seeing his posture droop, I let the subject go. I hold up the water bladder and take a long drink. After putting my mask back on, I try to relax and wait for lunch.

The announcer calls us back to the staging area and I wait at our canopy for the other entrants to arrive. Kotu, though, heads out to find out about the extra score on my board.

As he returns the announcer speaks up, "Last event, folks. Entrants, please report to the speed course."

Kotu leads me to the far side of the archery area, which is now cleared of targets. The field now has lines marking out several lanes. Just over a hundred meters away, I see the first of several hurdles. I look at the other entrants and realize that there are twelve of us left.

"Entrants," the announcer calls, "welcome to the speed course."

Aime, be ready to anticipate my needs based on what lies ahead.

A green thumbs-up signals her readiness.

"Find your marks and stand ready."

I quickly adjust my gear, making sure straps are tight. Standing on my mark, I put my toes on the line, ready to run.

"Get set!"

I feel my pulse quicken, my armor tightens. I loosen my cloak, so it can flow behind me, staying clear of my legs.

"Go!"

Bolting from the line, I run all out. Seeing a hint of yellow fur to my left, I risk a glance. It's Tayla, the cheetess. The hurdles quickly near and I adjust my stride, preparing for the jumps.

I clear the first hurdle easily. Taking two steps I jump again, clearing the second. As I reach the third, I hear hurdles hit the ground behind me. Clearing the third, I don't bother to look back, focusing instead on what's in front of me. With Tayla still visible to my left, we clear the last jumps.

With the path obvious on the other side of the river, I pull the cinch strap on the quiver to hold in the arrows as I run. Nearing the water, I again adjust my stride. Tayla disappears from my vision as I dive in, one hand over my mask.

With the added resistance of my cloak and weapons, my speed slows quickly. I surface and start swimming, an action that comes naturally. Reaching the other side, I risk a look back. I see Tayla standing on the shore, with a few others, apparently hesitant to get into the water. I raise my arm and encourage them to follow. "Come on. Swim it." I turn back to the course and hear several splashes. They're entering the water.

I run down the corridor toward a cliff wall, suddenly a weighted bag swings at me and I spin to avoid being hit. Avoiding a second bag, I dive for the ground and start crawling under the weights.

Reaching the cliff wall, I see a flag marker above. Up it is. With there being plenty of handholds, I start climbing the wall. As I near the top, I hear an "*oof*" from below. Risking a look back, I see the wolf lying on his back, apparently having been hit by a weight. I roll onto the top and climb to my feet. Seeing the marked corridor, I take off at a run again, crossing the one-hundred meters quickly.

Reaching the end, I find a series of small platforms leading across a small chasm. I start jumping from one to another, trying to time my jumps and steps to keep my balance. Reaching the other side, I find several ropes strung across the river.

Climbing onto one, I hook my legs over and start dragging myself along the rope headfirst. Easily looking back, I see that Tayla has passed the wolf again, as she's starting across the platforms, followed closely by Larrah and Aria. Reaching the end of the rope, I drop to the ground.

I turn to find a large cargo net. I start climbing up the net, risking another look behind. Tayla is catching up, with Larrah and Aria close behind. Reaching the top of the net, I find a long rope leading down to the course end. Not finding anything to slide down it with, I pull my staff out and hook it over the rope and lift my legs, letting myself slide down the rope.

Reaching the far end, the rope levels out and I quickly realize that slowing down isn't happening quickly enough. Dropping to the ground, I tuck and do a summersault to absorb the momentum.

I stand and jog through the exit, ending my run. I turn around and watch the others. Tayla comes in followed closely by both Larrah and Aria, but instead of using their staffs, they're using heavy straps, which slows them down faster. Tayla lands first and sprints out the exit directly at me.

As she approaches, I get my first good look at her. She stands as tall at Larrah, being slightly shorter than me. Despite her obvious athletic ability, she still has an overall softness to her build, something I would not have expected of a cheetah. She wears a two-piece, lizard skin armor set, upper foot wraps, and lower arm guards, all brown. Like everyone else, she has a bow and staff hanging from her quiver. She, though, has two short swords hanging from her belt, apparently one for each hand.

Walking right up to me, she asks curiously, "Why did you encourage us to follow?"

I give her a curious look of my own. "If you went to battle, would you leave behind a fellow warrior?"

"No, I would not," she states. Not picking up the connection, she asks, "What does that have to do with the Trials?"

"I've learned that the Trials are not 'me against you' but more 'us against the course,' do you understand?"

She seems to think for a moment. "What leads you to that?"

I notice that several of the other entrants have gathered around, also listening to my explanation. "The rules tell you, 'no help from outside the Trials.' I checked. That allows us to help each other."

"As you did with me?" Aria asks.

"Yes. Just like in a battle, we help each other. Why do you think we are called entrants and not contestants? Or why it's always called the Trials and not a competition?" I look around at the faces, realizing that several are beginning to nod, agreeing with me.

To my surprise, the head Councilor comes up to us with her hood pulled up. "It's been a while since anyone's realized the truth behind the Trials."

I step back a little, turning to her as I bow. "Ma'am." I notice several others also bowing.

"Please." She holds up her hand to stop us. "Here, on this side of the river, I should be bowing to all of you."

"Why should you be bowing to us?" Aria asks, hesitantly curious.

"Here, you are warriors proving yourselves." Having almost all the remaining entrants' attention, she sighs and changes the subject. "Do any of you know how the Trials came about?"

Most shake their heads while others look at her curiously.

"The Trials were originally a training course for our warriors when we thought we were going to fight the dogs. The council came up with several ways to test abilities, then they combined them into courses. The courses were generically named for what they challenge the most, but they test more than that one skill. For instance, in the strength course, when you climb the tower, how did you do it?"

"Clawed up a leg," Aria answers.

"Climbed up the pegs," another states.

"How many of you noticed that there were pegs up two of the legs?" she asks.

"I did," I admit.

"So did I," Krat states.

"And yet only one of you climbed the tower the correct way." Krat and I exchange glances, obviously wondering who that was. "The way you perform the obstacle is sometimes more important than overcoming it. They are all designed to test more than just one skill. Some tests are not part of the regular courses." She looks at me. "You found a few of them already."

Remembering the rules, I say, "The unannounced tests."

"You showed me compassion," Aria states, absently, "when you healed my foot."

I look at her, realizing what the extra scores are from and nod to her. "And when I told you how to land to avoid doing it again."

"You also showed both restraint and compassion by encouraging them," the councilor states, looking at me. "You could have easily left them behind and yet you chose to spur them on." She gives me an odd look. "Interesting," and then bows and turns to leave.

"I'm going to reread the rules," Tayla states, giving me a long, curious look as she turns to leave.

"Me too," Aria agrees.

I smile behind my mask and return to my staging area. Kotu gives me a curious look. "What was that all about?"

"Learning experience, for everyone." Remembering that Garra was not down there with us, I add, "Well, almost everyone."

When all the entrants have returned to their tents, the announcer takes his stand, "Entrants, thank you for your participation. Tomorrow begins the contracts, so prepare accordingly."

With the day over early, I spend some time browsing the various tent games and other attractions. At a weapons booth, I find the smith. "Hey! I've been waiting for you to wander by."

Finding myself curious, I ask, "Why's that?"

He picks up a bow that he obviously made after I removed mine from the jig I used. It's unfinished, not having a handle or any coloring yet. "How do you string this thing?"

Chuckling, I take the bow, and he hands me a string with several loops along it. "It's called a recurve bow. This is how you have to bend it to string it." Just like I did with the one I made, I have a seat and hook it on one leg, then prying against my other leg, bending it against its curve. With the innermost loop on the string longer than the one I made, I don't have to bend it as far to hook the string on.

With the bow now correctly strung, I run my hands over it, feeling the smoothness of the wood laminates. I draw the string, getting a feel for the power. Since the string is longer, it's not as powerful as mine. Aime gives me an in-vision message of eighty pounds. "Good job on the bow," I compliment the smith, handing it back to him. "I would recommend no shorter a string than that loop. It'd be too difficult for most to draw."

He gives the bow a test draw. "I see what you mean." He makes some notes on the bow itself and then turns to me, "Since this is your design, I'll offer . . . ten coin per bow I sell. I'll be selling them for about a hundred each."

I look at him in thought. "Ten percent, I can accept that, but for that type of bow, normal arrows won't work well." Pulling an arrow from my quiver, I say, "You'll need to reinforce them just like this one."

The smith sets the bow aside and takes the arrow. "Wire wrap to strengthen the nocks and shaft ends." He makes a few more notes on the bow. "I can give you a coin per arrow I sell, but it won't take long before people start doing this themselves."

"That's fine," I admit as he hands the arrow back. "For the bows, make sure that you use good quality wood or it won't hold up for long."

He nods, so I continue, "And don't make it any narrower than that. If you do, the bow can easily reverse itself when strung."

He makes more notes on the bow. "That's good to know." Setting the bow aside again, he reaches out to take my hand. "I'm Mang."

"Mang," I repeat. "I'm Kyle."

"Kyle, thank you. I'll hold your share aside for you. You can come by and collect it anytime."

"Thank you."

As Mang goes about his business, I resume my browsing. With evening quickly upon us, we make our way back to camp. Sada happily greets us as we approach.

After supper, I take a shower. When I come out of the tent wearing only shorts and a T-shirt, Kotu's jaw drops. "Where's your fur?"

"I don't have any."

"But earlier you had black fur."

"What you saw was my clothes, a tight-fitting shirt, and pants that I wear under my armor."

He gives me an oddly curious look. "I could have sworn that was fur."

Sada gives him a series of motions, prompting him to turn to me. "What?"

"She said, see what you see and you will see what it is."

He gives me a confused look. "What does that mean?"

"If you don't pay attention to what you see, you assume what it is, but if you pay attention to what you see, you see the truth of what it is. Understand?"

"Now I do," he states. He lets out a yawn, signaling his fatigue.

I look up to the sky, seeing both moons and the rings in the fading light of the sun. "Bedtime."

He puts his things away and heads to bed. Sada and I follow after making sure all our gear is put up for the night.

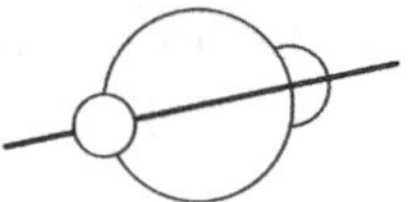

Entering the village in the morning, I am met by the cheetess councilor. "Kyle, before you begin today, I must tell you the etiquette of offering contract."

I bow to her. "I'm your student." Turning to Kotu, I say, "I'll meet you at the tent." He nods and heads off to the tent with the pack.

She leads me as we walk. I listen intently as she explains the wording that should be used during various times when offering a contract. She also explains about offerings of thanks and the purpose of challenges. I soak it all in, not wanting to offend the people who I've come to respect. After an hour, she finishes. I thank her for her time and head off to my tent.

Catching up to Kotu, who sits under the canopy chewing on some jerky, I quickly root through the pack. I start removing the weapons, repacking it with them on top. I find myself pleased that I brought the big converter today. I place a few of the daggers in it and give Aime the command to scan them in case I want to make variations. I then repack so the converter is empty and close up the pack. I quickly teach Kotu a series of simple hand signs in case I need him to do something.

Suddenly the announcer makes his presence known. "Entrants, welcome to the Offering of Contracts. Will those entrants seeking contracts please report to the south line and find your mark. For those of you offering contracts, please find your mark at the north line."

Kotu points to line just off the tents. I find my mark near my tent, just like it was for the archery event. As I look along the line, I see that only two others stand on this side with me, Cheen the jaguar and Terro the panther. The rest of the entrants stand on the other side, ready to receive an invite into a contract. A glance at the board tells me that they all scored high enough to accept contracts. I also note that there are now titles under each name, mine shows Pendekar.

Silat? They know Silat? Aime flashes in my vision.

The announcer again interrupts, "With a new record high score, Kyle, you get the honor of offering the first contracts."

Taking a deep breath, I step forward and approach the opposing line. Looking carefully at all the entrants, I say, "I require a guide to Three Lands ."

With a bow, Aria steps forward. Larrah steps forward with her but does not bow or even look at Aria. As I look down the line of entrants, I notice that most are looking between Larrah, Aria, and I. All with exception of Tayla, her ears are slanted back and she's nervously looking away, avoiding eye contact with me.

"I offer food and shelter as long as you are with me. Once we reach Three Lands, you will be free to return." Suddenly Tayla steps forward, still not looking at me.

Curious, I step over toward her and quietly ask, "Is there something wrong?"

She glances curiously at me. "No. Nothing."

Nodding to her, I step back toward the center. "Anyone else?" After a moment, I nod again, and all three girls kneel to me. I suddenly feel embarrassed by what I need to say next.

Addressing them in a superior manner and using the ranks posted on the board, I state, "Chegu Aria, Pendekars Larrah, and Tayla, I stand above you as your superior. I require a guide. I will see to all the food and shelter for the journey as well as other necessities. You will in turn provide me with your wisdom and experience. Do you accept or do you stand and challenge?"

All three stand, but Aria is the first to answer, "Challenge."

Since she spoke first, I step over to her and bow. "I accept your challenge. What is your choice of combat?"

She thinks for a moment. "As we are."

I realize that by her choosing that way, we can fight with anything we have on right now, basically a no-holds-barred kind of way. "Are you certain you want this way?" I cautiously ask.

"I am."

I glance at Tayla and Larrah and they back up to the line, giving us the field. Bowing to Aria, I say, "Challenge accepted."

As soon as I speak the words, she pulls one of her daggers and starts lunging at me, trying to poke at me. I easily start dodging the thrusts, scooting back a little with each of her thrusts. I hear the crowd start to gasp and awe, but I tune them out, focusing on my opponent.

She suddenly switches tactics, drawing a second dagger. She starts altering between slashes and lunges, keeping me moving. As she progresses, I start needing to block her attacks, using my hands to swat away her daggers.

Getting angry, she quickly tucks her daggers and pulls her staff. As she starts to swing it at me, I do a backflip, evading her swing. Coming to rest, I pull my staff and start parrying her swings, meeting her swing for swing.

After a few dozen blocks, I switch tactics and go on the offense. I start with a sweep, making her jump. I follow that with a lunge that she blocks with her staff. As she lands, she tries an overhead swing. I duck in close and spin with an upward swing. Her staff goes flying and lands in the sand behind me.

She backs up, giving me a look of disbelief and anger. I toss my staff back toward hers, keeping the match even. She comes at me, barehanded. I start dodging and blocking as she sends attack after attack my way. She quickly starts adding an occasional kick that I either evade or block.

With one of her kicks, I spin to dodge and her claws snag in my cloak. As I hear fabric tear, I suddenly reverse my spin, releasing her claws, and she falls to the ground. I take a step back, recovering my balance as she does a flip-up to a standing position and pulls her daggers again.

I reach up my sleeve and pull out one of my swords. I see her eyes go wide and I wonder for a moment if she thought I didn't have a blade of some kind. She takes a stance and makes an attack. I lift my blade in defense and block her first attack. Taking advantage of an opening, I make a sudden attack. She manages to block it with one of her daggers.

Pulling my sword back, she makes a quick overhead attack with both her daggers. I make an upward swing to block the attack. I feel my sword hit her daggers and then suddenly continue upward without resistance. Aria hits the ground behind me as I stumble away.

As I turn around, she gets up and readies for another attack. I see her holding her daggers, or what's left of them, As she sees her now blade-less weapons, she drops them to the ground and falls to her knees.

I slowly sheath my sword and approach her.

"I am beaten," she gasps in disbelief, her fatigue showing heavily as she breathes.

I squat down, careful not to let my knees or hands touch the ground. "You are only beaten if you believe you are."

"But how could you have beaten me?" she asks, picking up one of the severed blades to her daggers.

I put my hand on her shoulder. "The weapon does not make the warrior. The weapon knows no skill, no heart. Both, you have much of."

She shakes her head. "I cannot be your guide. I should not have taken the offer."

Picking up the pieces of her daggers, I turn and sign to Kotu. "I accept your withdrawal, but not your reason." Kotu reaches my side, and I put the pieces of the daggers into the converter. "I want you to keep practicing, keep working on your skills. Regain your confidence."

She stands and nods. "I will."

With a hidden flash, her daggers are repaired. I pull them out of the pack. "Here, your weapons." As she takes them, she gives me a look of disbelief. "As I have fixed your weapons, you can fix your confidence."

She looks at them curiously and then slowly sheathes them, then nods. Kotu hands us our staffs and retreats to the tent. I bow slightly to her, wishing I could say more.

She bows and walks quietly back to the line, and I suddenly feel that the rules of this arena prevent us from telling each other how we really feel.

I put my staff back under my quiver strap and step back over to Larrah and Tayla. They both re-approach and kneel. "My offer still stands. Do you accept, or stand and challenge?"

Larrah stands slowly, a determined look on her face. "I challenge." Tayla once again retreats to the line.

"What is your choice of combat?"

"Tokens," she answers.

I bow to her. "Very well, I accept your challenge."

Kotu comes running out, as do two others, both carrying straps. Larrah and I hand our staffs, bows, and quivers to Kotu as the other two put the straps on us. They are simple bandolier type straps with our tokens on them, a dozen for each person.

With them in place, we each adjust the position and tightness slightly and bow to each other. The rule of tokens is simple: take all the other's tokens before they take yours. Kotu and the others retreat as we take our fighting stances.

As Larrah assumes an attack posture, I assume a more neutral stance. We both hold our positions for a moment, waiting to see what the other does.

She lets loose a snarl, baring her teeth and claws as she lunges at me. The type of attack narrows my options. Not having the proper stance for blocking it, I flip back and put a foot up to keep her away from me, using her momentum to propel her over and beyond. I continue my backflip, landing on my feet, and quickly turn to face her.

I assume a hunched stance and make a quick lunge. She raises her arms to intercept me and I quickly feign a spin, reaching for a token as I do. She sees through the spin and blocks me from her token.

She turns and sweeps at my feet. I jump to avoid being tripped and dive to her side. She takes advantage of my maneuver and reaches for a token. I manage to block her grab as I land and flip to my feet. She turns to me and makes a second attempt at a token. I spin to block and reach out with both hands for her tokens. She blocks my leading hand but I snag a token with my trailing hand.

She gives me a quick look of disbelief, but quickly recovers, hiding her emotions again. She starts relentlessly attacking, using her feral style of Silat to try to wear me down. I find myself switching between judo and karate, trying to keep her at bay. During this I somehow manage to snag another token from her, and she, one from me.

After a few more minutes, I see her start to tire. She does a good job of hiding it, but I manage to snag two more of her tokens to her one of mine. After several more minutes pass, I begin to think she has found her second wind. She has managed to snag two more of my tokens, but I have also managed to snag two more of hers.

We continue our hand-to-hand exchange. As we do, I start using some of her own moves, surprising her. Apparently she did not expect me to learn from her as we fought.

As I pick the tenth token from her, she holds up her hands. "Hold!" She drops to her knees, gasping for breath. "I yield."

"Do you accept the contract to be my guide?" I ask, slowly approaching her.

"Yes," she manages to say between breaths.

I squat down by her, again careful not to let my knees touch the ground. "Are you okay?" I softly ask, noting how hard she is breathing.

"Yeah," she gasps, then with a slight smile, adds, "It's been too long since I've gone up against someone that could outlast me."

I signal to Kotu as I rise and speak to her, "You are now under my contract." I reach out my hand to help her to her feet. She looks at it skeptically but takes it and stands.

I reach into the pack, pull out a signet copy, and carefully put it on her armor. She bows to me and slowly walks over to her tent. I see Kotu help her collect her things and they return to my tent as I approach Tayla. Noticing my cloak is in shreds, apparently from Larrah's claws, I remove the token strap, and pull off the remains of the cloak, revealing my armor to her and the crowd. It's sand-covered at this point, so it appears aged and brown, not the dull black that it normally is.

She stands and approaches for the third time. "My offer still stands. What is your choice?"

She looks down, avoiding eye contact. "I . . ." She pauses, then looks back at me, her golden eyes quiver like she's seen a ghost. She slowly bows to her knee. "I . . ."

I squat down to her. "What is it?" I gently ask.

She looks up at me, and meeting my curious gaze, her eyes calm a little. "I need to see your face, please," she whispers to me. I see a tear run down one of the black stripes along her nose.

I pull off my mask. Her eyes go wide and she quickly looks away. Unable to figure out that look, I add, "You don't have to accept if you don't want to."

She shakes her head slightly. "I claim my right of reserve."

"Right of reserve." This means she will do the contract but may request to change her title or position at any time. The Councilor had told me about this. It's rarely used, and when it was used last, a teacher was looking for students, and the student later became his mate.

A brief thought comes to mind. Could she want to be my mate? I look at her, realizing that she is rather attractive, built similarly to Sada. I push that thought aside, concluding that since we just met a few days ago, that would be a very unlikely possibility. Summoning Kotu again, I stand and put my mask back on. "I accept your reserve." I pull another signet copy from the pack and pin it to her armor. She stands and bows to me, and Kotu follows her to her tent.

I turn to the remaining entrants and with a slight bow, I say, "Good luck to you all." I pick up my things and depart the field. "How about that folks! Two successful contracts already! Cheen, offer your contracts," the announcer calls.

Before I sit down at my tent, Larrah curiously asks me a question, "Doesn't it bother you that I was not able to complete my last contract?"

I drop my shredded cloak in the pack. "Should it?"

She gets a puzzled look. "It bothers everyone else."

Sighing, I ask, "Did your last contract have anything to do with being a guide?"

She tilts her head slightly. "No."

"Then whether or not you completed that contract is irrelevant to me. I'm interested in your ability to lead me safely east."

"You seem to have safety covered," Tayla states.

"I'm not the only one traveling," I state, signing to Sada.

She comes over and takes off her hood. "Tayla, Larrah, this is my companion Sada. Sada, our guides, Larrah and Tayla."

Larrah stands and bows lightly to Sada. "Nice to meet you."

Sada bows back to her as Tayla rises and bows lightly. "You're not from this village, are you?"

Sada shakes her head and makes a series of signs. I translate for her, "No, we come from the mountains, far to the west."

Tayla looks at me and then back at Sada. "What was that?"

"She can't speak, so she uses her hands."

She nods, and then Larrah asks, "Why Three Lands?"

Sitting down, I start to explain, "I need to find a place called the Dig. Kotu told me that Three Lands is the eastern-most village. I don't expect you to lead me beyond that point."

"That makes sense, but why do you need to go out into the wilds?"

"I don't know how far I need to go past there. Regrettably, I just know that it's far to the east. There was a team sent long ago to explore something and I need to find them."

"A rescue?" Tayla asks. "Just you two on a rescue mission."

"Well, I don't know if it's really a rescue. It's been so long that they may not be there anymore."

"Then why go at all?" Tayla asks.

"If you knew someone who went somewhere and didn't come back, wouldn't you want to know why?"

She gets an apologetically sad look on her face. "When you put it that way, yeah."

Larrah nods. "Not to take away the significance of your goals, but what do we get out of this?"

"Yes, payment. As I said, I will also provide food and shelter for the duration," I reach into the pack and pull out two of the pocket blades. "But these will also be yours."

Larrah takes one and looks it over. "This is a rather thick dagger."

"It's not a dagger, pull it."

She pulls the blade out of the sheath. Her eyes widen in amazement as the blade nears a meter long before ending.

Tayla pull hers too, then tries to look into the sheath. I chuckle. "I tried that too. I didn't see anything. The blades are stronger and sharper than the ones you're used to."

Larrah gives the blade a practice swing, checking its balance. "It's a nice weapon. I will accept this as payment." Tayla nods in agreement and they tuck their new blades into their belts.

"Kyle, may I speak with you, all of you, in private?"

"Ma'am," I hear both Tayla and Larrah say as they bow slightly.

I turn to see the familiar cloak of the councilor cheetess. "Of course."

"Please come with me."

We quickly pack our things and follow her to the council hut. As we pass a mediator, this one a tiger, in the foyer, the council member looks at him. "Please make sure we are not disturbed."

"Yes, ma'am," he replies, bowing.

Entering the main room, we see that the rest of the council is out. She takes down her hood and turns to us. "I would like to congratulate you on your performances, Pendekars."

Tayla and Larrah both bow, as do I, but I politely ask, "Surely you didn't want us here just for that?"

She sighs. "Yes, I wanted to talk with you before you left. Tayla, Larrah, you are the first to accept a contract from someone who's not a cat." I take the cue and remove my mask, placing it over my left shoulder; I then turn to face them.

"I apologize if I misled you in any way," I confess, bowing to them. "I meant no disrespect or harm."

"I believe him," she continues, "as should you. He has told his reasons to me, and I am satisfied with them."

"His reasons are his own. I am pleased to have the chance to regain some respect," Larrah confesses.

She puts her hand gently against Larrah's cheek and looks at her for a moment. "My dear, you will find more than that on this journey."

Larrah nods but says nothing.

"And you," she moves to Tayla, who interrupts her.

"I already know, ma'am," she softly states.

She pauses for a moment with her hand on Tayla's cheek. "Your grandmother did not tell you."

"She did not have to."

After a moment's thought, she smiles at Tayla. "May you find it . . . agreeable."

Tayla smiles back as she nods.

She moves to Kotu, touching his cheek like she did the others. "You have done well, learned some things too I see."

He shifts his weight uncomfortably and looks to the ground. To my surprise, he recovers quickly, looking back up to her. "Thank you, ma'am."

"Manners too. My, you have matured." To his surprise, she gives him a gentle hug. To his credit, he manages to awkwardly hug her back.

Turning to Sada, she gives her an odd look. "You are feeling out of place, lost." She takes her hands and holds them gently. "You have no reason to fear. It is still there, and we are all the same, so relax and enjoy."

Sada smiles and starts to purr and bumps the councilor's nose lightly.

The cheetess nods. "You are welcome." She then turns to me. "You have been busy, teaching a cub, helping young love, teaching other entrants things they should have already known, and even brought us a new type of bow." She pauses, putting her hand alongside my face. "It seems your destiny to have an impact on all you meet."

"Good or bad?" I hesitantly ask.

"Good, even if you do not see it." I give a light sigh of relief as she continues, "I am proud of you, all of you, willing to look for something better." She takes her seat as she continues, "Your next destination should be Arroketh." From under her desk, she produces an envelope. "Kyle, when you're at Three Lands, someone will need this information."

Taking it from her, I look at it curiously. She smiles. "You can read it if you like. It won't make much sense now, but it will, when the moment is right." I flip it around, looking at it, and then put it in my pack.

"Arroketh? Why Arroketh?" Larrah asks. "Lorholt would be quicker."

She nods. "Sometimes, the straightest path is not the right path."

"Why are we really here?" I politely ask. "You could have told us this in public."

"You are correct. I have you here for a different reason. Over a month ago, four canids were standing where you are, all looking for the Dig just like you. While I don't remember all that was said, I have a friend that does." She glances around at each of us. "What I'm about to share with you is not to be said to anyone without your complete trust." She looks at Kotu, Tayla, and Larrah. Getting nods from them, she then looks at me. Both Sada and I nod. "Sage, will you please."

"Yes, ma'am," a male voice speaks from nowhere, or everywhere. I find myself confused and looking around for the source. As I do, I notice that the others are doing the same. "My apologies if I have startled you."

Aime, do you know who Sage is?

[Yes,] she visually replies.

Tell me.

"Sage is a non-symbiotic AI-series designed for governmental installations, such as this. Their primary function is to assist with day-to-day activities, though they can also be used for advice and long-term strategy management."

"Correct," Sage replies.

"There's an AI here?" I ask skeptically.

"Correct," both Sage and Aime answer in unison.

I suddenly realize that everyone is looking at me and that I had instructed Aime to *tell* me, something she took literally. Suddenly embarrassed, I have a seat next to the councilor and sigh heavily.

She turns to me. "I am used to Sage, so hearing a voice without a body is something I'm accustomed to, but for the others here, would you mind explaining about yours?"

"Aime, please talk with Sage while I try to explain."

"Certainly."

I rub my face with my hands. "You're bound to learn sooner or later, so I'll start at the beginning."

I take a deep breath and sigh. "Let's see. I awoke about a month and a half ago with no memories of who I was, where I was, how I had got there, things like that. What I did remember was how to do things and what things were called."

"One of the first things I found out is that I have another life form living inside me. She, Aime, can talk to me, help me, heal me, things like that. Sada woke up a week later and, thankfully, was able to show me my name. After another week, a third person, another human, woke up . . . dying."

"I did what I could to try to save her, and she told me where some people—humans—might still be. I had to put her back to sleep to save her life." Sada wraps her arms around me from behind and starts purring. I gently rub her cheek, trying to comfort her.

"Sada and I left the mountain where we were and found our way here. The rest, you already know."

Larrah looks curiously at me. "How do you know how to fight?"

"Aime taught me. She taught me how to do a lot of things. Occasionally, things trigger memories, but right now, they're small memories, no big personal revelations yet." I look around at their faces, some concerned, some indifferent.

Tayla looks at Sada for a moment. "Is she your mate?"

"Not really. I love her, don't misunderstand that, but it's difficult for me to explain how or why. I know that I loved her before we went to sleep." In response, Sada nuzzles her nose into my neck, prompting me to nuzzle back. I notice that this makes Tayla smile slightly.

"Why do you want to do this, for people you don't remember?" Larrah asks.

"I guess because when we were asleep, they watched after us, made sure we were safe, and had things when we woke up."

The councilor shifts her weight. "Tell us, how long were you asleep?"

"Not sure exactly, but somewhere around a thousand years."

"How could you sleep for so long?" Kotu asks.

I smile, realizing that "sleep"' probably wasn't the best word. "Well, for us, it was like we were asleep, but in truth, I suppose it was more like frozen."

As the others sit in silence, absorbing the information, Aime interrupts, "Sage and I have had a rather prolific conversation."

"What do you mean?"

"Perhaps I should let Sage explain as he was already prepared to do so."

"Thank you. Kyle, I understand you are from the facility to the west. What little I know about the dig site is that it was discovered shortly before humans stopped visiting the village. Thanks to Aime, I now know why they stopped visiting, so I hope your quest is fruitful.

"I have provided Aime with a copy of all the topographical data I know. I have also taken the liberty of giving you a copy of our historical accounts. My apologies, Councilor, if I have overstepped my bounds."

"No apology needed, I trust your reasons." She then turns to me. "That was shorter than I expected."

"Aime and Sage can talk faster than we can. She'll go through what Sage gave her and present it to me later."

"Tell me more about this Aime."

"Well, much like Sage is a part of this hut, Aime is a part of me. She goes where I go, experiences what I do, and senses what I do, though she can notice more details than I can."

"Seems to me we should be calling you a shaman too."

"No, no, no, I'm not a shaman," I stammer, suddenly embarrassed.

"You healed Aria. That's one of the many things that shamans do. You also have someone with you at all times that no one can see. She talks to you, teaches you, guides you if you will. These are all traits of a shaman."

"I am not a shaman," I repeat.

"Believe what you want, but be prepared, people will most likely see you this way."

"Even with the armor?"

"We've seen warrior shamans before, though none as good as you."

Sighing, I change the subject. "So what next?"

She stands, prompting those of us who also sat to stand. "Now, enjoy the festival, then, prepare for your journey."

We bow and as the others start to leave, she touches my cheek again. "You will find what *you* are looking for." She then puts her finger to my lips, keeping me from asking any questions.

I can't help but to wonder what she meant as I catch up to the others, and we head back across the river. Before parting, we agree to meet on the road to Arroketh at noon in two days. Kotu takes off on his own while Sada and I spend much of the afternoon wandering around, visiting game booths, even occasionally playing them.

To my pleasant surprise, we are received warmly by many of the vendors. This makes it easier for me to sell most of the items from the Moku's pack. Then we return to our tent in the early evening, allowing time for us to relax and eat.

Sada hears something as we near our camp and sprints toward it. As I catch up to her, I see Kotu sitting on the ground, crying softly. Sada scoops him up into her arms, frantically trying to find out what's wrong.

Kneeling next to them, I try to help her check him over. "Kotu? Are you okay?"

"Yeah," he sniffles.

"What's wrong?"

He sits up a little, and we get to see that he's holding the sash.

Sighing, I realize what's wrong. "You're upset because we're leaving, aren't you?"

Still crying, he nods.

Behind him, Sada's expression changes. Her eyes get big and her whiskers and ears droop. I quickly realize what she is after, which happens to be the same thing he wants, to stay with us. As I look at Sada, I realize that the Councilor was right. I have impacted his life in more ways than I was aware of, and I have a feeling I'm not done.

I sit down on the ground next to him. "So what do you want to do?"

As Sada sits down, he fidgets with the sash. "I want you to stay."

I hang my head slightly. "You know why we can't do that."

This time, he sighs. "I know. It's just . . ."

I look at him for a moment, sitting there with tears in his fur and find myself understanding his feelings. "I know," I softly confess. He sighs heavily again, so I start to get up. "Come on, let's get something to eat." I take his hand and help him stand. "Maybe we can work something out with the council in the morning."

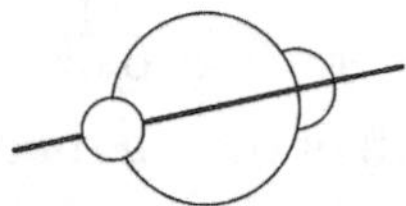

Walking into the foyer of the council hut, we find a mediator waiting. "Please. They're expecting you."

As she moves to the door, I ask, "Expecting us? Were we summoned?"

"No, just expected." She opens the door and ushers us in.

Walking to the center of the room, Sada waits behind us as Kotu and I stand side by side.

The snow leopard speaks up, "Kotu, with the conclusion of the Trials, you were to return to us last night."

To my surprise, he bows. "My apologies, Council, I needed . . ." He swallows hard, suppressing emotions. "I wanted to say good-bye."

The leopard sits back, obviously noticing the sincerity of Kotu's emotion. "I understand."

"Thank you," Kotu states, breathing a small sigh of relief.

The cheetess looks at him curiously. "You have something to say, don't you?"

He looks up to them, then nods. "Yes, ma'am." He takes a deep breath, calming his nerves. "Council, I would like to thank you for the learning experience." He swallows hard again, and I notice that the leopard leans forward to speak, but the cheetess holds up her hand, stopping him. "I also apologize for my behavior. I have been . . . disrespectful. You did not deserve to be the ones to receive it."

I find myself staring at the cub, surprised at his sudden change of character. As I turn back to the council, I see several expressions reflecting my own feelings.

The leopard slowly leans forward, stunned, and speechless.

"Kotu, you have changed for the better," the cheetess states. "I wonder if your coming back to us would be a good thing."

He looks up at her, puzzled. "Ma'am?"

She looks at me and having understood her statement to him, I nod to her. She looks back at Kotu. "Kotu, I'm assigning you to Kyle, as his ward. You will continue to learn at his direction. Understood?"

His mouth drops in surprise, but he manages to pull himself together enough to answer, "Yes, ma'am."

Sada happily wraps him in a hug, lifting him off the ground like a rag doll.

I quickly sign to her, 'Put him down.' Embarrassed, she suddenly sets him down but doesn't let him go, keeping him in a hug.

Smiling, the cheetess continues, "I see that he is in good hands."

"Yes, he is," I admit.

"Thank you, ma'am," Kotu states, as Sada puts her chin on his head and purrs.

"Don't thank me," she counters. "You're at their mercy now."

I turn to him and give my best evil chuckle. He instantly cowers, and I can't help but laugh at how his expression contrasts with Sada's blissful one sitting on top his head. *Aime, remember that image.*

"I believe that concludes our business this morning," the cheetess states.

"Council, thank you for your time." I bow to them as does Kotu and Sada, and we exit the council hut.

Once in the street, Kotu wraps me in a hug. I wrap my arms around him, finding myself inexplicably happy. After a few moments, he manages to let go, and I get to see that he has tears in his eyes and a smile on his face.

"Come on, let's get you ready for our journey." We set off for Mang's shop to see if he has anything for me.

As we approach, we see several bow-jigs setup, drying, all are of my design. "You're not going to believe this," Mang states, walking up to me. "I don't even believe it."

I look around, seeing a few new apprentices behind him, working on arrows and bowstrings. I venture a guess, "You're busier than ever?"

"I've hired four and I still need more." He smiles. "I've taken nearly forty orders for your bow. I've lost track of the arrows, selling them faster than I can make them." He reaches under the counter and checks a card. He then counts out coins and put them in a pouch and hand it to me. "Heard you were leaving. Here's your cut."

He turns and looks at his workers. "I expect everyone will have a new bow in a month or two. I am going to be busy till then."

I pat him on the shoulder. "Hope you don't run out of supplies before then."

He chuckles. "I already have, and so have my usual suppliers." He turns back to me, extending his hand to me. "Best of luck to you on your journey. I'll hold your future cut till you get back."

Shaking his hand, I state. "If I'm not back in a year, put it to good use."

"Wouldn't seem right, but okay."

With plenty of coin in hand and most of our business concluded, the rest of the day is ours to enjoy.

After packing up the gear in the morning, we set out to meet Larrah and Tayla. Kotu seems to have an excess of energy, being eager to travel, I try to warn him to save some of that energy. By the time we reach the girls, he seems to have settled.

CHAPTER 7

Larrah takes lead as we start our journey to Arroketh. Tayla stays close behind me, as Sada and Kotu walk alongside. Kotu's curiosity gets the better of him and he starts asking all sorts of questions. Having not been far outside the village, I quickly realize that he has a lot to learn. Tayla politely answers his questions, and Sada and I listen intently, learning about this world alongside him.

The week-long trip is largely uneventful as most of the day predators are solitary hunters and normally won't attack a group. With the cats unwilling to enter Arroketh, we make camp to the south, about an hour's walk away.

Tayla and Larrah sit down with me and tell me all they know about the dogs and how they live. From what the girls tell me, they seem to have a pack mentality, and because of their tendency to alpha others, I won't find a lot of non-canids in this village. Despite the contrast in their behavior, the village layout is nearly the same, with exception of the Trials and river.

Wondering what I could possibly find here that will help me, I set off to the village about noon. Since Larrah shredded the Moku cloak, I now wear my own over my armor. I also wear the hat and mask, as well as my swords on my forearms, my quiver and bow over the cloak, and my staff in its shortened length, stuck to my right thigh where I would normally have the pistol.

Walking into the village, I see that the dogs tend to keep to groups. Some are just standing around while others walk the streets like groups of teenagers, laughing and pointing at others. I walk down the center of the street, keeping my wits about me and my senses alert.

As I walk to the council hut, I mentally note the wide variety of canids I see. Aside from the many mixed breeds that I can't identify, I see foxes, wolves, coyotes, dingoes, hyenas, and many other breeds of large dogs. Part of me wonders how many breeds are in this village.

While passing a rather large hut that I'm sure was an inn at Pridewyn, I see a rather proud-looking brown-and-black female sheltie, wearing a matching kimono, watching me carefully from the doorway. To see if she's really paying attention to me, I give her a courteous nod. To my surprise, she politely nods back.

Nearing the council hut, two guards run by me, toward the hut. One of them shouts, "Captain!"

A rather athletic gray fox comes out of the council hut and faces them. She has on typical leather armor, hers being a reinforced jerkin and skirt. Her markings, though, are more typical of a red fox, with her lower legs having black socks. Oddly, it's her upper arms that are black and her lower arms and hands are gray. She also has a white stripe down her neck that disappears under her jerkin, but her most prominent feature surprises me; she has a bigger bust than any female I've seen so far. After a brief exchange of words she grabs a halberd and runs after them down the road.

I cross the street to the hut, and as I reach the door, I hear a howl and a yelp from down the street. Curious, I step back and look. I see the crowd part and the two guards come through, followed by the fox captain. She's single-handedly dragging a wolf by his scruff and dumps him on a cart. The other two guards haul him away.

Remind me to stay on her good side.

Definitely, Aime replies in my vision.

Going through the door, I find a mediator, this one a mixed breed collie, standing behind the counter. I step up to her as she asks, "May I help you?"

"I hope so. I'm looking for information on a place called the Dig. Who could I talk to about it?"

She thinks for a moment. "Someone came in several months ago asking about that. I had to send him to the archives."

"Where would those be?"

She points. "Next door."

"Thank you." I exit the hut and walk next door in the direction she indicated. Entering this hut, I find it looking like a library with several scrolls and a few books. I look around and see a couple people studying some papers, and a third one browsing through a stack of scrolls.

A young female golden retriever comes up. "May I help you?"

"I'm looking for information on a place called the Dig."

"You'll want to look through the myths and legends. This way, please."

She leads me past several rows of shelves toward the back of the hut. Directing me to a table, she says, "The myths are all right here, within reach of the table. Please take your time and leave things like you found them."

"Thank you." She leaves as I start looking through the scrolls. While the writing is sometimes difficult to read, I eventually find some that mention "a place far to the east" or "the land of the humans." Despite the very limited information on those two, I keep looking for almost an hour.

Finding nothing more, I put the last scroll back in its place and return to the front counter. Seeing a bottle labeled Donations, I scoop a few copper coins out of my pocket and drop them in.

"Thank you," the retriever happily says with a bow. "I hope you found what you were looking for."

"I was told that someone else was here looking for information on the Dig. You wouldn't happen to know where I could find them."

She thinks for a moment. "I don't know. I think they may have left." She turns to look at the others at a table. "Molly, you were here that day. Do you remember what happened to him?"

Molly, a rather attractive red fox, turns to us and thinks for a moment, then her face lights up. "Oh yeah! He got a group together and headed off. One of them left his mate behind. If you could find her, I bet she'd help."

"What was her name though?" the retriever asks.

Molly skews her face for a moment. "Uhh, Rai . . . something."

One of the others at the table suggests, "Railu?"

"Yeah! That's her name, Railu. She's a red fox, like me."

"How long have they been gone?" I ask curiously.

"Almost a year, I think."

I drop a couple more coins in the bottle and flip a ten coin to Molly. "Thank you."

Heading for the markets, I work out a plan to find Railu. I start by browsing the various vendor kiosks, casually asking about her. I spend over an hour trying, but either no one knows her or no one wants to admit that they know her.

Feeling like giving up for the day, I head back the way I came. After passing the council hut, I again see the sheltie. This time she's standing in the street, with a couple huskies standing nearby, keeping guard. She sees me coming and calls to me, "Traveler, I need a moment of your time, please."

Surprised with the direct invitation and relieved by the total lack of threat from her guards, I nod. She quickly leads me into the hut; the guards follow but stay outside the door.

Inside, I can clearly see that she is a female of wealth, as most of the furniture is intricately carved and well maintained. As I follow her, I notice that she walks with poise, holding herself properly. I quickly settle on her being raised by someone who instilled manners and etiquette into her. Once in an office-like room, she sits in a chair and motions for me to do the same.

"I am Arru. Please sit. No doubt you have some questions for me, but I would like to know something from you first. What are you? You don't walk right for any kind I know about."

I sit, trying to hold myself properly like she does, but her question makes me uncomfortable. "My name is Kyle. I am a traveler, looking to go far to the east."

"Just how far east? Arindell? Garrent? Dendros? Three Lands?"

"Beyond Three Lands."

She smiles slightly. "You seek the myth? Many have tried and none have returned."

"There can be many reasons why no one has returned."

"True, but you still haven't answered my initial question."

Realizing that there's no bluffing her, I slowly remove my hat and mask. "Does this answer your question?"

She looks at me curiously for a moment. "I've been to every village I know, and no one has looked like you."

I slowly fidget with the mask. "I'm a human, apparently the first to be here in two centuries." I lean forward a little. "I've been told that there should be more humans at the Dig but I need to get there to find out."

She sits in silent thought for a while, then suddenly leans forward. "May I come with you, at least to Three Lands?" she asks eagerly.

Taken by surprise, I nearly drop my mask. "Why?"

She leans back again, a sad look on her face. "I want to travel again. I miss it. My mother was an ambassador. We would travel to 'whatever' village, working on trade agreements, carrying news and even letters." She sighs. "It's been years since I've traveled like that. I can pay my way, and I can council you on proper etiquette, teach you about the villages that you visit."

I hold up my hand, stopping her. "I will need to talk to my companions, but first, how do you feel about traveling with cats?"

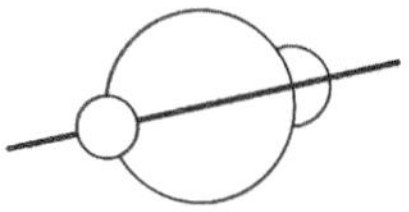

Back at the campsite, I recount my day to the others as we eat, carefully leaving out the sheltie for now.

Seemingly disappointed, Larrah asks, "Why would the councilor send us here if there was nothing to learn?"

Tayla speaks up, "She obviously thought that there was something here worth finding."

"Well, I did find out about the previous group, and if I can find Railu, maybe she can be of help."

We fall silent for a moment, all of us in thought. Sada watches us carefully while Kotu seems oblivious to the conversation, having started on a new whittling project. Taking advantage of the moment of silence, I speak up, "I was also approached by someone who want to travel with us."

"What!" Larrah blurts.

"Why didn't you tell us this first?" Tayla scowls, giving me a light punch.

"Sorry, I was trying to figure out how. She's an ambassador's daughter. She's offered to provide council and what she knows about the villages we might come to."

"How far does she want to go?"

"As far as Three Lands."

Larrah leans forward. "Is she a dog?"

I sigh. "Yes, she's a sheltie, but as I said, her mother's an ambassador. She grew up traveling and wants to travel again. I spent a while talking with her. She's educated, can afford her own way, and not afraid of getting dirty."

"How does she feel about cats?" Larrah asks dryly.

"She told me that as long as you're willing to try so is she. When she called on me, she had her own guards. After being on the streets for a while, I saw why."

"Not a pleasant way to live, afraid of your own neighbor," Tayla admits.

"Not wanting to walk into the street without a guard." Larrah shakes her head in disbelief. "If she is willing, I will try."

"Having someone who's been there before is always helpful," Tayla nods. "I will also try."

Larrah suddenly gets an odd look on her face. "Why ask us? We are under your contract."

"I know, but I also value your opinion, as well as your state of mind. I don't want to do something that'll make you mad at me." I turn and look at Sada. "What do you think?"

She tilts her head in thought for a moment. 'Is she nice?'

For the benefit of the others I repeat her question, "Is she nice? Well yes, she's polite . . . educated . . . mature."

'Is she nice looking?'

Chuckling, I sign back, 'You would ask that, wouldn't you?' Sighing, I say, 'Well, she has long brown-and-black fur and was wearing a full-length kimono wrap. Believe it or not, my attention was not on her body, but on her brown eyes, but she seemed to have a full figure. Satisfied?'

She looks at me, curiously, apparently waiting for more from me.

'She's not my type, okay?'

'You don't know your type,' she jokes.

Getting upset, I stand and sign, "Look, I'm more interested in . . . Tayla than I am in her."

Kotu falls out of his chair in surprise, and Larrah turns to Tayla, shocked. Tayla looks at me, eyes wide and mouth agape in complete surprise.

Realizing that I said that aloud as I signed it, I sit and bury my face in my hands, embarrassed. "And there's nothing I can say that will make that right."

I give Sada a scowl and look back at Tayla. "Tayla, I . . ." Not getting a reaction, I curiously ask, "Tayla?"

Sada waves her hand in front of Tayla's eyes, breaking her surprised stare. "Huh?"

"Tayla? Are you okay?" I ask.

"Uhm?" Bewildered, she looks around at all of us. "I'm...just gonna...go to bed." As if in a trance, she gets up and walks slowly to the tent.

Larrah looks at me, shaking her head. "What were you thinking?"

Sinking down in my chair, I say, "I have no idea."

Waking up early, I quietly walk outside to find Tayla looking through the dense fog to the early morning sun. Seeing her ears twitch toward me, I slowly walk up alongside her. "I'm sorry about last night."

She shifts her weight and looks down at the ground in thought.

"If I hurt your feelings in any way, I'm sorry. That was not what I wanted."

"What *do* you want?" she quietly asks, surprising me.

"I would like to at least be friends."

She turns and looks at me, her ears perking up. "Friends?"

I look into her eyes, seeing them quiver like they did when I offered her the contract. "Yeah, friends, you know, someone you care about and trust, and they feel the same way about you."

"I've never really had a real friend, not since I was little anyway," she confesses.

I give her a curious look. "What about Larrah? You both seem to get along well."

She sighs. "She was my mentor for almost four years, before . . ." She looks down again, apparently ashamed. "You hold our contract. Why be our friend too?"

"Well, I'd rather be out here with someone I know and trust than just someone I just know."

She looks back up at me, a glint of hope in her eyes and a smile spreading across her face. "I'd like that."

We both turn back to watch the sunrise. I gently put my arm around her shoulders. "I'd like that too."

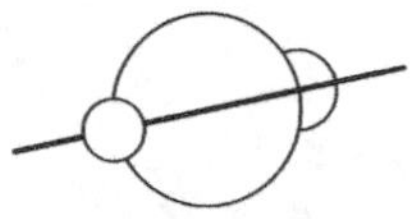

Walking into the Arroketh, I get the feeling of being watched. Keeping my eyes and ears open, I slowly make my way to the sheltie's hut. Seeing the guards outside her door, I approach.

"She's been waiting for you," one of them states, opening the door for me.

I quickly step inside and indeed, find her waiting for me.

"Well, what did they say?"

"If you are willing to try, so are they."

"Oh good. I'll pack my things. Do I need a tent?"

"I have a tent big enough for us all. Were on foot too, so we carry our own."

She starts jotting down some things, apparently updating a list she made. "Okay, I'll adjust my pack."

"I have some things I'd like to check on. I can meet you here in an hour."

"That would be perfect." She heads off to another room as I set out for the markets.

I get about halfway there when I'm approached by a rather large wolf. "I heard you're looking for someone," he growls.

Being careful not to show any fear, I answer, "Yes, I am."

"Why are you looking for a scout that never finished her training when you could have the best." He grins, puffing out his chest, obviously trying to show off.

I laugh, intentionally showing contempt. "What made you think I needed a scout?"

"Why else would you be looking for that mangy fox?"

Hearing the distain in his voice, I decide not to tell him. "That is no business of yours."

This time, he laughs. "No one hires a scout without my say so." With that statement, he takes a quick swing at me.

I dodge left and he misses. "Nice, you can dodge. Good for you," he taunts.

He follows with a scooping left, trying to claw me. I lean back out of his reach.

"What, are you afraid of getting hurt?" he taunts again.

If he wants to play that way, fine. *Aime, strength.* As he tries another swing, I brace myself and catch his hand. Shocked, he tries to pull back, but I hold fast. He growls and tries to hit with his other hand. Catching that too, it becomes a battle of strength. He tries to push, twist, and pull his way out of the hold.

Having little success, and his anger brewing, he growls loudly in my face. Noticing that we're drawing a small crowd, I decide to let him go. Spinning to my left, I release both his hands and he sprawls to the ground. I step back to see what he'll do next.

As he gets up, two guards grab him, attempting to restrain him. The wolf throws them off into the crowd. He stands up fully and howls, getting everyone's attention. As he charges at me, I hear someone call for more guards. I quickly take a defensive stance as he closes the distance. He swings at me and I punch his hand.

He yelps and falls to the ground. After a roll he gets back up and comes at me again. This time he charges at me with his mouth wide open, obviously trying to bite me.

In a blocking motion, I shove my armored forearm crosswise into his mouth, jamming it open.

With his mouth stuck on my arm and one of his hands broke, he panics and tries to pull his mouth off. After a few hard yanks and no progress, he falls to his knees, defeated. With the arrival of two more guards, I pull my arm out of the wolf's mouth.

"Are you okay?" a female voice asks.

I turn and see who it is. "Yes, Captain, I'm fine."

She looks skeptically at me. "What started that?"

I sigh, looking down at the wolf. "He insisted I hire him for a job I wasn't offering."

"That again?" She looks down at the wolf. "Haven't you learned your lesson yet, Trag?" He cowers as she grabs him by the scruff and drags him to his feet. "You're getting more than a week this time." She turns and looks at me with a nod. "Thank you for not making a mess."

I simply nod back to her.

With him now in custody, I continue on my way to the markets, and I once again get the feeling I'm being followed. *Aime, can you find who's shadowing me?*

"Not yet."

I scowl a bit but keep my eyes open, looking casually around, taking in the sights as I walk. Coming to an intersection, I abruptly turn. "Got him, rooftop, left side."

Scanning casually, I see a pair of ears poking above the roofline. They quickly flatten, trying to avoid my gaze. Chuckling, I continue on to the weaponsmith.

Once there, I sell the last two daggers I received from the Moku. Pocketing the coins, I make my back to meet with the sheltie. Aime keeps tabs on the person tailing me, as best she can. I try my best not to let on that I know he's there, remaining casual with my walk.

As I approach, the sheltie gives some instructions to the guards. They both bow to her and retreat into the hut. She adjusts her pack, grabs a staff, and joins me. Together, we head out to the campsite.

Stepping into the clearing, she looks around at the four cats. "I'm suddenly nervous."

"This is Arru. Arru, my friends and guides Tayla and Larrah, my companion Sada, and my charge Kotu."

After she bows to the girls, she turns to me. "They're *your* guides?" She turns back to them and they both nod. She apparently notices the signet pinned on their armor and looks back at me. Seeing my signet, she says, "They're under your contract. How did you get into the Trials?"

"I stole his signet and entered him," Kotu states, cringing a little.

"So they let you stay in," she states, shifting her weight. "I would have loved to have been there for that."

I take off my mask and hat off and have a seat. "I broke records."

She sets down her pack as Tayla speaks up, "And taught us all a lesson about our own history."

Sada puts another chair out, and Arru sits. We spend the rest of the evening talking, getting to know Arru and letting her get to know us. By the end of the day, everyone is comfortable, and we enjoy a hearty supper.

The whole time, Aime keeps track of my follower, keeping me apprised of his location. By dusk though, Aime has lost track, concluding that he has retreated back to town for the night. I have her set an alarm to wake me up before sunrise and head to bed.

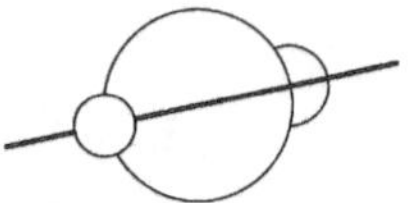

I stand in the shadows against a larger tree, waiting near the road halfway to the village. Not knowing what to expect, I'm in full armor with all my weapons. As the sun begins to light up the sky, Aime activates the armor's camo, rendering me invisible to normal vision.

I keep my eyes moving, watching for any activity on the road. After a while, a small clutch of ma'pai scurry by, and not long thereafter a young viper lizard follows, its nose to the ground, apparently tracking them by scent.

Several minutes later a lone fox slowly makes her way down the path, sticking to the shadows, heading in the direction of my camp. I wait for a moment after she passes to make sure she's the one I'm after and then start to follow her. With the camo on, the armor absorbs any noise I make, but I still try to avoid stepping on anything that could make a sound.

I follow her until she gets to the outskirts of my camp. Seeing her find a suitable place to watch from, I need no further proof. I walk up behind her and draw a sword. Deactivating my camo, I put the point to her back. "Keep walking to the tent."

She sighs, hanging her head. Holding up her hands in surrender, she stands and walks out to the clearing. Larrah and Tayla come out from the other side and take her weapons. Kotu and Sada come out of the tent, followed by Arru.

Suddenly out of the shadows, I see that she's a red fox. "Railu?"

She turns around angrily. "How do you know who I am?"

I put my sword away. "We mean you no harm. I was hoping you could help me."

"Help you, how?"

Sighing, I say, "I was told that you may have some information about the Dig."

"Why do you want that?"

I take off my mask. "Because I'm going there."

Her eyes widen. "Who are you?"

"My name is Kyle. I'm a human."

She gasps, covering her mouth. "Amsel was right. He was right. That means—oh no." She turns away, a look of fear crossing her face. "He's been gone too long. I need—" she abruptly turn back to me, her face calms, her eyes settle on me. "I need to go with you," she states.

"Why should we let you come with us when you've been stalking us?" Larrah scolds.

Railu hangs her head. "I am sorry. I wanted to know why you were looking for me." She swallows hard. "And I was afraid."

"Afraid? Of what?" Larrah demands.

"Of everyone, okay? Y-you don't know what it's like, finding the one you love, only to have him demand that you stay behind while he goes off on some quest." She pauses, trying to regain some composure. "We were together almost a year. We wanted to have kits. Amsel came to him, wanted him to go. Roen made me stay. HE MADE ME STAY! I would have gone with, in an instant."

She turns back to me. "I have to find him. Please." She starts to cry, letting out her pent up emotions. "Please let me find him." She collapses to her knees, her words disappearing into her sobs.

Unsure of what else to do, I kneel down next to her. "So you are the reason the councilor sent us here." *Aime, what can you do for her.* I place one hand on her forehead and the other on her cheek.

"She's suffered massive emotional trauma. I can only do so much to help her. The best thing for her may be to find her mate."

Do what you can. We'll work on the rest. "Railu, relax. In a moment you'll feel better, but I need you to focus for me, okay?" When her breathing becomes regular again, she slowly nods and Aime indicates that she's done.

I put my hands on Railu's cheeks, holding her face to me. "Listen to me," I calmly state. "You can find your mate. I will help you. Okay?"

"I can find him," she repeats, her eyes focusing on me. "I feel better."

I stand up and help her up. She takes a deep breath and scratches her head. "I really feel better." She looks curiously at me. "What did you do?"

"I helped you be yourself again, something you needed."

"I never expected the help of a shaman."

"I'm not a shaman," I politely counter.

"Well, whatever, I haven't felt this focused in almost a year." She looks around at the others. "I'm sorry. After my mate left, I kinda lost it."

To my surprise, Kotu and Sada get chairs out, and we all sit as she continues, "A friend of his, Amsel, heard the myth of the Dig and became obsessed. He convinced Roen and a couple of others to follow him on his quest to find it.

"Part of me can't believe that he actually went. The rest of me can't believe he wouldn't let me come with them. After they left, I got so mad, then I felt so alone. Some of the villagers started making fun of me. I couldn't take it. I'd lost everything. I just lost it."

She falls silent for a moment, holding back some emotions. I take the moment to try to distract her. "What direction did they go?"

"Arindell," she states. "Amsel planned on visiting all the villages, gathering all the information he could before heading east. When they left, they had four jata worth of gear."

"Pulling or carrying?" Larrah asks.

"Carrying, they didn't want to have to deal with a cart."

"Smart, but while jata can carry anything, they are incredibly slow," Larrah comments.

"It would have taken them two weeks just to reach Arindell," Arru adds.

"Longer. Jata aren't allowed on the river bridges," Railu adds. "They're too heavy."

"Well, that's a benefit to us then," Tayla states. "We'll be moving twice as fast as they are."

Larrah gives her an annoyed look. "At least until they eat their last jata."

Railu groans. "They'll only do that if they run out of food."

Trying to keep her from dwelling on negative outcomes, I say, "Tell us about the members of his party."

She sits up a little. "Well, there's Amsel, a rather wealthy black-and-white border collie. He's usually hired to prepare people for travel. He told Roen that he found the story of the Dig one day and figured it'd be a good thing to find.

"Then there's Rami, a shepherd. He likes to travel and adventure. Amsel's set up a number of caravans for him in the past, so when he was asked, he jumped right in.

"Sarn's a wolf, likes to fight. I'm guessing Amsel got him by offering to let him hunt anything he wanted."

"And there's Roen." She sighs, as a tear rolls down her muzzle. "My mate. He's a scout, and a good one. He was teaching me before he left."

I lean back in my chair, slowly looking at the others. Larrah seems indifferent, but every now and then, her throat tightens as if she choking something back. Tayla has some tears in her eyes, obviously sympathizing with Railu in some way. Arru seems deep in thought, and Sada is looking at me, sad.

"How soon can you be ready to leave?" I ask Railu.

"I'm ready now. I don't have anything left but what I have on," she sadly confesses.

As the girls hand her back her weapons, I give her a quick look-over. She's petite, dressed in the rags of two different dresses, bandolier, and armed with two simple daggers. While her fur still looks healthy and thick, I can tell she hasn't eaten properly for a while, being able to see the outline of her rib cage around her stomach.

"Well, we'll need to go back into the village, get you outfitted properly."

"I'll go with you," Arru states, grabbing a pouch from her pack.

Kotu suddenly pouts. "Can it wait till after breakfast?"

Hearing Tayla chuckle, I agree, "Yeah, after breakfast."

Railu's ears perk up. "Breakfast?"

After a light, vitamin-filled breakfast, Arru, Railu, and I venture into town. I find myself glad that Arru came with us when we start looking for clothes. I wait patiently as they browse the selections, picking out some things that both flatter her colors and fit her figure. To my relief, Arru pays for the clothes, and we head off to find the smith.

Railu sprints ahead as we approach, getting to the counter ahead of us. "Please tell me that you haven't sold them," she pleads to him.

The burley smith, a rottweiler, smiles at her. "Back to your old self now, I see."

She glances back at me. "I . . . had some help with that."

He looks to me. "I see you found her. Sorry 'bout lying to you, never know who you can trust."

Railu starts bouncing. "Come on, come on, do you have 'em or not?"

"All right, calm down." He chuckles, reaching into a chest. "I didn't sell 'em." He pulls out a pair of nicely engraved daggers, studded with some red jewels. "If you'd been anyone else, I would've," he insists.

She dumps the cheep daggers on the counter and puts the good ones in their place. She then wraps him in a hug. "Thanks."

"You're welcome, but now that you have them, what are you going to do with them?"

"I'm going after Roen."

"Then you'll need this too." He reaches into the chest again and pulls out a set of red leather armor and sets it on the counter.

She slowly picks it up. "For me?"

He smiles. "I made it for you when you swore to go after him."

She picks it up the armor, tears coming to her eyes. "It's beautiful."

"Take it, find your mate."

"This is too much, I can't—"

He grabs her shoulders. "Railu, this is something you've wanted to do since he left. I made this for you to do just that, so don't argue with me."

She sighs heavily, defeated. "Thanks, Dad." She bumps his nose with hers lightly. With all her needed gear, we head back out to the others.

On our way out of town, I look at her. "Dad?"

She smiles. "He's not my real father. I never met him. Behri helped my mom raise me."

Meeting the others back at camp, I provide Railu with a pack, and then set up her and Arru with a table, chair, flashlight, and a water nozzle to use as a canteen, just like I did over a week ago with the others.

Now ready to travel, we set out to the east, following Railu and Larrah on the road to Arindell.

CHAPTER 8

A couple of days out, while walking the road through a brush-filled meadow, Tayla suddenly stops walking and starts sniffing the air.

Turning to face her, I ask, "What is it?"

She doesn't even acknowledge that I spoke.

"Tayla?" I ask again, with no response. I watch as she sniffs the air like she's searching for something. Suddenly, her eyes dilate and she drops her staff and starts walking off toward a large, but distant, group of green bushes.

"Tayla!" I call again, as Sada bumps into me, walking on as if I wasn't there. "Sada?"

I watch them as they walk, being happily led by their nose. "Arru, do you smell anything?"

"I smell something, but I don't know what it is," she replies, looking between Sada and Tayla.

"Aime, what is it?" I ask.

"The only new scent I am detecting has trace amounts of nepetalactone, but my database does not contain a list of what on this planet produces it."

I turn and look to Larrah, who is still walking toward us. "Aime, I need to smell it."

As Aime enhances my sense of smell, I watch Kotu stop walking and start smelling the air. I start to pick up traces of the foul scent, as I watch Kotu's eyes dilate and he follows Sada and Tayla. The aroma gets potent enough for me to smell.

"I know this." I look at Larrah, who's now bringing up the rear, and call out, "Larrah, stay there."

She stops in her tracks. She looks at me for a moment, puzzled, and then starts smelling the air. Soon she's following the other three cats.

"Great. Come on." I grab Tayla's staff and start following them.

Arru walks up beside me and asks, "What is it?"

Railu sprints over and joins us as we follow the cats.

"I think I know, but I need to see the plant first," I respond.

We follow the cats for a few minutes, before arriving at a group of similar bushes. They literally dive into the bushes, rolling in it, rubbing it on their fur, and even eating it.

"Great. Remember that smell. We will need to avoid it from now on."

Railu watches the cats as they rub themselves with the bushes, rolling and twisting around. "What is that stuff?" she finally asks.

"Catnip," I say dryly.

"What is 'catnip'?" Arru asks.

"It's a plant that makes cats really happy." We watch for a moment as Kotu starts trying to play with something that nobody else sees. While he bounces around, he bumps Tayla, who springs to her feet, hissing, ready to attack. Seeing Kotu bounce away, she sinks back into the catnip. "Effects can be extreme playfulness, aggression, hallucinations, and lethargy."

"Is it harmful?" Railu asks.

"Not to them, but they may be to anyone who gets too close right now. They'll be done with it soon."

We wait as we watch the cats. After several minutes, Kotu is the first to stagger over to us. He tries to look at me, eyes dilated, fur ruffled with green stains smeared throughout. His mouth moves as if trying to say something but no sound comes out. He licks his lips and then collapses on the ground.

I sigh and take his pack off him. It too is heavily stained with catnip. I check his vitals, confirming that he is asleep and roll him to his side so he can rest.

Larrah is the next to try to join us. With some help from Arru, she manages to stagger over and sit on the ground; her pack had come off while rolling in the nip. Portions of her spotted white fur are now green.

Sada is almost completely green, curled up and purring while asleep in the now matted cluster of catnip. Having rolled out of her pack early, it's still relatively clean.

Tayla walks over as if in a trance, puts her arms around me, and gives me a lick across my face as she purrs. I stand in mild shock and surprise, as Railu snickers.

"Iys shlicks shu," Tayla manages to slur, looking right into my eyes, and then she giggles a little, puts her head on my chest, and collapses into my arms. Reflexively I catch and hold her in my arms for a moment before gently lowering her to the ground.

"I lick you," Railu mockingly repeats while laughing and walks over to retrieve the abandoned packs.

I roll my eyes and follow. "You're going to need a bath," I mutter as I pick Sada up and carry her back to the others.

We wait a while for them to awaken. When they do, Kotu has a migraine; Sada throws up, having eaten too much catnip; Larrah, embarrassed by her lack of control, doesn't look at anyone. Tayla has the side of her face matted from drooling on herself, and won't look at me, apparently somewhat embarrassed by giving me a lick.

Aime and I help each with the physical after-effects, and we move on, looking for somewhere to get them cleaned up.

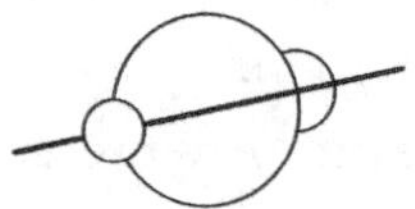

Nearly halfway to Arindell, we come upon the crossing for Pride River. Railu stands between a pair of stone pillars at the edge as the rest of us approach. I quickly realize that there *was* a bridge anchored to the pillars. Looking across the river, I see a matching set of pillars on the other side, almost fifty meters away. Remnants of rope hang from either set of anchors.

"It's gone," Railu points out.

I peak over the cliff-like edge, looking down at the rushing water below. With as steep as the sides are, as far down as the water is, and as fast as the water is flowing, there's no way to cross here.

"There's a secondary crossing almost a day's walk downstream," she adds. "This way."

"Why is it so large here and less than a third this size when it gets to Pridewyn?"

"There's a large branch that goes underground a few days south of here."

We follow the river downstream, walking along a rough cut path. The path follows the bank in most places, though most of the view is blocked by the plants that grow along the bank.

Where there is a view of the water, I find myself checking the features of the river. I discover that the river is getting wider as we go downhill towards to water level. I also notice that Sada keeps glancing at the water. While she does a good job of hiding her facial expressions, her tail tells me she is agitated.

'What's wrong?'

'Water.'

'We've crossed several creeks and streams.'

She gives me an odd look, then realizes something. 'River.'

'Okay, what's wrong with a river?'

She gives me a slightly defeated look. 'I can't swim.'

'I didn't teach you?'

'Didn't have a way.'

'Well, we do now. We'll make some time.' I put my arm around her and pull her close to me. She purrs in response, putting her head against mine.

We make the river crossing by late day. I look out across the river and Aime quickly tells me that it's over a kilometer wide.

"We should cross tonight. The river is rising," Railu observes.

"How much time do you think we have?" Larrah asks.

She looks out across the water. "An hour, maybe two, before it's too deep to walk across."

"Let's get going then," I state, taking Sada's hand. I start walking toward the water and she abruptly stops. I turn and see the fear in her eyes, so I take off my pack and pull out a length of wire vine. I tie one end around Sada's waist and the other around me. She gives me a skeptical look, so I think for a moment. "Aime, I need a flotation device."

"I have a life vest waiting for her. With this current, I would not recommend anything larger."

I reach into my pack. Opening the cover on the converter, I find a roll of fabric. I pull it out and unroll it. Noticing its vest-like shape, I suddenly realize what it is and how to use it.

I gently put it on Sada, clipping the straps to hold it on her securely. "If you slip and can't stand up, pull this cord. The vest will inflate and you will start to float, okay?"

She grabs at the pull cord a couple of times to get a feel for where it is and then nervously nods at me.

I get ready to put my pack back on when Kotu taps on my shoulder. I turn and look at him, curiously.

"Could, I, uhm," he stammers, nervously, pointing at the vest.

"No one will understand you if you don't ask," I instruct, already knowing what he wants.

He sighs heavily. "Could I get one of those?"

"Anyone else want a life vest?" I ask looking around.

Arru steps over. "Please. I don't mind the water, but I'm not a very good swimmer," she politely confesses.

I take the two freshly made vests out of the converter. I hand one to Arru as I unroll the other and put it on Kotu. Arru mimics my actions with the other as she watches me fit it to Kotu. Once I finish with Kotu, I double-check Arru, making sure she got it right. "Like I told Sada, don't pull the cord unless you can't get back up. If you pull it too soon, you'll have trouble walking in the deeper water." They both nod their understanding, and I get out more wire vine and we all tie together.

Sada takes my hand as we start into the water. Railu leads, keeping us in the shallowest areas as we cross. I decide to have Aime let the water flow through my armor for a while. The cool water feels very refreshing.

With the water reaching a half-meter deep, the current gets a little stronger, giving Kotu a little trouble keeping his balance.

Larrah notices this. "Kotu, lean into the current a little. Use your staff to steady yourself if you need to," she coaches. I smile, glad that she has taken him in as a student to teach.

Railu abruptly stops as we near waist-deep water. "Kyle!"

I wade to her and notice the problem. A few meters ahead, there's a noticeable increase in the current.

She points. "That's going to be a problem."

"Aime?"

"The current is 68 percent stronger. Given this increase, I would conclude that we have arrived at the main channel."

"And that would make it deeper," I conclude.

"Correct," Aime confirms.

"There's not supposed to be a deep channel here," Railu interjects.

"The bridge out and a new channel cut in the river bed. What happened?" Larrah asks.

"That's a puzzle for later. The water's rising. Aime, what's the underwater capabilities of this armor?"

"I could quote statistics, but if you plan on walking through that, the suit can easily handle it."

"I'm cold," Kotu complains.

I turn and see him trying to ruffle his fur to keep warm. I put my hand to his chest and Aime gives me a display of his vitals. He's starting to suffer from mild hypothermia.

"We need to hurry up and get across this," I state, my mind racing for ideas. "Everyone tie to me. I'm going to walk us across. Aime, vests." I reach into my pack, into the converter and pull out three more vests and hand them out. "Put them on," I instruct. "It'll be easier for me to pull you across if you're floating.

With everyone secured to me and wearing a vest, I ask, "Ready?" Several nod, nervously, so I add, "When you lose your footing, pull the cord and then relax. Let yourself float on your back."

They nod again. "Aime, let's get this over with." With my next few steps, I feel the armor shrink around me, closing out the water. Then I feel myself starting to sink a little into the soft riverbed as its density increases. With the heavy current just a few steps away, I double-check my mask and hat strap to make sure that they are secure.

The river bottom drops suddenly, and I drop into it like a rock. As I land, I hear several pop-hiss sounds. I look up and see that the others have all inflated there vests. I'm now their anchor. I also realize that, for being underwater, I can see clearly. Aime must have altered my eyes to compensate. With the mask acting like a rebreather, I start walking; the river bottom here is rocky, providing my boots something to adhere to as I fight the current.

After a dozen steps, the river starts to shallow slowly. As it does the current also starts to diminish, making it easier to walk. I pick up my pace, but it's still slow when I'm still over a meter underwater with six people anchored to me, all trying to drag me downstream.

After a few minutes, the river gets shallow enough for my head to rise above the surface. I turn back to look at the others, Kotu is shivering hard and both Sada and Tayla are shivering noticeably. I press on, trying to walk as fast as I can through the water.

When it gets waist-deep, Larrah, Arru, and Railu quickly regain their footing. We grab the others and help them to their feet. Kotu trips and I scoop him up and carry him to shore.

We quickly run up the bank to a clearing. I set Kotu down in the waning sun and take off his pack and vest. I untie the vine, drop my pack, and get out several towels. I throw one to each of the girls and then quickly dry Kotu off. I then pull out my blanket and wrap him up in it.

"Armor off," I command, and my armor drops off. As it falls, I reach for the hat and realize that it's gone, apparently swept away in the water. I then pull the converter out of my pack.

"Aime, what . . . ?" I start to ask but the converter flashes and a drinking bowl with dark liquid appears.

"Warm ma'pai broth and medicine. Do not let him drink too fast."

I sit Kotu up in my chair. "Sip this, *slowly*," I tell him. I look and see that both Sada and Tayla are also seated, wrapped in blankets. Aime produces two more bowels of broth and I give them to Sada and Tayla, also telling them to sip it slowly.

Railu starts collecting firewood as Arru and Larrah set up a fire ring. I get out the tent and find a suitable place for it. By the time I'm finished setting it up, Railu has a fire going, and Kotu, Sada, and Tayla are gathered around, warming up.

I walk over and put my hand on Kotu's back to check his vitals. Aime lets me know that he is warming up nicely. I check both Sada and Tayla and they too are recovering nicely. I pull up my own chair and sit near the girls, letting the warmth of the fire flow through me.

Sada puts her foot-paws on my lap and spreads her toes. I start gently massaging them, carefully picking out the rocks and other debris from between her pads and claws. After a few minutes, I switch to her other foot-paw.

When I finish, she wiggles and flexes her toes. Apparently happy with my work, she puts them down. I take a moment to check on Kotu. Satisfied that he's doing well, I sit back down and a different set of foot-paws get placed on my lap. I look over and see a tentative but hopeful look on Tayla's face. I chuckle and start massaging and cleaning her toes like I did Sada's. She smiles and, to my surprise, starts purring.

With a good fire going, Railu and Larrah start cooking some fish that they speared. Arru slowly works a converter to get some drinks and sides. Kotu, having warmed up, helps Sada set up some tables.

We eat in relative silence, no one having the desire or energy for conversation. Afterward, I help Sada brush the sand and other water debris out of her fur. I notice that the others are doing the same, except Arru, who always seems to look like she just finished brushing herself. She's stretched out a length of vine between two trees and is hanging up some of her clothes to dry.

When nighttime falls, I crawl into bed, and Sada curls up tightly to me, purring, apparently still feeling cold. I listen to her purr for a while before I drift off.

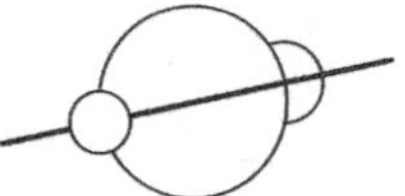

Still nearly a day away from Arindell, we come across a large field, bordered with a waist-high rock wall. On the other side of the wall, we find grain, instead of the typical grasses, planted in rows, this is clearly farmland. I try to take some of the plants in hand, but they simply crumble, unable to withstand my touch.

"These are old crops. Why weren't they harvested?" Railu wonders.

Larrah thumps the ground with her staff. "Grounds hard, drought maybe?"

Looking across the field, there are several trails where small animals have wandered through. As we walk, we too leave similar trails. The plants are so dry; they do not bend, but simply break off, crumbling at the slightest touch.

"There's a farmhouse over there," Arru indicates, pointing to what looks to be a small building, some distance ahead of us.

Railu arrives first and knocks on the door. Not hearing a response, she calls out, "Anyone about?"

I look around, seeing the lack of belongings. "I don't think anyone's been here for a while."

Railu tries the door. It's unlocked, but as she pulls it open. Its hinges give, letting the door simply fall outward. She dodges it easily, avoiding injury, then pokes her head inside but does not go in. "It's empty. Whoever lived here moved out long ago."

Hearing Kotu suddenly yelp, we all turn, drawing our weapons. Kotu freezes, seeing all of us ready to attack. His ears slowly droop and he starts to look ashamed.

"What happened?" I ask, seeing that he is holding the end of his tail in both hands.

"Sorry," he meekly says. "I thought something was behind me. When I snapped at it, I bit my tail."

I start a light chuckle, Larrah scowls at him, Tayla just sighs, but Arru walks over, wraps his tail around him, and tucks it under the shoulder strap of his pack. "Don't worry. Sometimes I forget that it's there too."

He sighs, heavily, not looking very comforted by her words. "Can we just go?"

"Yeah, let's go." I chuckle.

We continue our journey to the village, taking a path that we found near the abandoned farmhouse.

We walk on for several more minutes before hearing a deafening roar, followed by a girl's blood-curdling scream, "Daddy!"

I reflexively drop my pack and charge to the sound. As I clear a small rise, I see a frighteningly familiar sight. "Isn't that one of the things that wrecked the facility?" I ask.

"Yes a karnesh," Aime offers.

I draw my pistol and jump on top of a rock wall; with a clear shot, I fire several shots at its head, with no visible results. "Aime?" I call as it sweeps its head from side to side, looking for something.

"They were direct hits. It appears to be heavily armored."

"Armor-piercing," I call and fire several more shots, with a similar lack of results, aside from the creature finally taking notice of me standing on the wall. Even though it's still about fifty meters away, I can hear it breathing as it looks toward me.

"The pistol is not powerful enough to pierce its armor," Aime calls.

"Explosive."

"That will kill the girl," Aime quickly corrects.

"Girl? Where's—?" I start, but notice a small brown spotted creature curled up this side the wall in front of the karnesh. "Great."

Thinking quickly, I say, "Homing." I focus directly on its left eye. Pointing my pistol at it, I wait until Aime indicates a lock and fire. The micro-rocket travels the distance in less than a second, curving slightly to compensate for the creature's head movement. I watch as its eye pops, the pain causing the creature to let out another ear-shattering roar.

I drop from the wall to find myself facing Tayla, Larrah, and Railu. "We need to get that girl out of there." I think for a moment and Sada arrives, then an idea hits me. "I want you three to go that way and distract it, keep your distance but get it to follow you. Sada, when it turns toward them, you get the girl. I'll lead you right to her, but I'm going to get on top of it, to see if I can find a way through that armor."

I get nods from the girls and I turn back to watch the beast as Tayla, Larrah, and Railu swing wide to my left. I jump back up on the rock wall, watching for the girls to distract the beast.

When they make themselves visible, I realize Tayla is very hard to see with her coloring and armor matching the dried grains. Fortunately, Railu and Larrah both stand out.

The karnesh sees them and turns to its right, leaving its blind eye to me and the girl. I break into a sprint and see Sada quickly follow as I move toward the girl. As I jump to the last wall, I point down at the girl. When my foot hits the wall, I jump again, launching to the beast's back.

Landing on the creature's back is easier than I thought it would be. My boots stick to the creature easily. I try stabbing it, but my sword just glances off the scales, throwing sparks.

"Jab between the scales," Aime offers.

Taking her advice I drop to my knees. Thankfully my armor sticks to the scales just like my boots do so I don't slide, but with the karnesh now walking, trying to follow the girls as they distract it, it is not easy to line up my sword to get underneath a scale. After a few misses, I finally get my sword up underneath and shove it all the way in.

The karnesh breaks into a run, roaring again at the pain. It thrashes, but thankfully it's unable to reach me. I pull out my sword and crawl up to the creature's neck. I jam the sword up under another scale. This time I start moving it side to side, trying to cut the creature's insides with the tip. This causes it to thrash some more, but it's not slowing or showing any signs that I'm causing much damage.

Getting an idea, I wave the girls away for their safety. I make sure that they are indeed retreating before I twist the sword, prying the scale up. I then jam my pistol under the raised scale and pull out the sword. Pulling the trigger several times gets me some blood squirting out from under the scale, and some more thrashing from the beast, but not much else.

"Explosive," I call and pull the trigger again. The creature raises its head as the round detonates, causing fire to gush from its mouth. Some of it even comes back at me, from under the lifted scale. I quickly pull the pistol out as I lay back, dodging the small spout of flame that comes back at me.

Beneath me, the creature collapses roughly onto its belly, dead, from the explosion in its neck. I stay lying on its back for a moment, breathing heavily, crashing from the adrenaline rush.

"Are you okay?" I hear a voice call.

Looking, I see Tayla rushing to me. Finding the strength, I turn and allow myself to slide down to her, landing on my feet. "Yeah," I admit as I put up my weapons.

"That's the first time I've seen someone kill something this big," she admits. "You're either incredibly brave or crazy."

I sigh heavily and pull my mask off. "Probably both," I answer. "How's the girl?"

She puts her arm around me, encouraging me to come with her. "Let's find out."

It takes us a few minutes to cover the distance that the karnesh ran while I was on its back, making me wonder how something so large can move so fast. Once there I see Sada, sitting by the rock pile, a young doe curled up in her lap, crying. As Sada looks at me, I see tears in her eyes. Kneeling next to her, I get a close look at the girl; she's wearing a tan-spotted wrap-style dress, but I also notice that she still has white spots on her back, a clear indication of her youth.

"Are you okay?" I gently ask.

"Is it gone?" she sobs.

"Yes, it's gone," I gently reassure her.

"Where's my daddy?" she asks, turning her head to look at me.

"I'm sorry, I don't know. Was he nearby?"

"No." She wipes her eyes. "I was collecting berries. He was across the field when it showed up. I hid behind the wall."

"Which way across the field?" Larrah asks.

The fawn sits up and looks around, then points to the far end of the field.

Larrah taps both Tayla and Railu on the shoulders; all three then set off to look for her father.

I look back at the girl. "My name's Kyle. This is Sada, Arru, and Kotu." Each nods in turn as I say their name. "What's your name?"

She looks at me suspiciously, but answers, "Fey."

"Fey, if you and your dad get separated, what do you do?" I ask gently.

"I go back home and wait," she explains. "Why?"

Arru takes her hand, helping her to her feet, or rather hooves. "While the others look," Arru explains, "let's go see if he is there waiting for you."

Fey hesitates, showing some obvious signs of worry. "Uhm."

"I promise, we won't hurt you," Arru gently insists.

"We just want you to be safe," I continue.

Somewhat consoled by our words, she relents, "Okay."

She leads us back toward the path but turns onto a smaller path. We soon arrive at a small, semi-rundown double hut. Fey slowly opens the door and leads us in. "Dad?" she calls but getting no answer, she sighs with disappointment.

Arru sets her pack down just inside the door against the wall and asks, "Why do you live so far from the village?"

Fey sits on a stool at the small table in the middle of the room and starts to absently play with a bowl. "After Mom died, Dad and I moved out here. Dad said it was because the crops were better, but I knew better."

"What's your dad's name?" I ask.

"Tarrow, why?"

"I'm going to help the others look for him. I'll be back. Sada, Arru, and Kotu will stay with you."

I nod to Arru as Sada pulls another stool up by Fey and sits next to her. Before I can turn to leave, Fey tugs on my armor, so I kneel by her.

"Please be back before dark. There are big mean creatures that fly at night."

"I know," I softly state as I rub her head, hoping to reassure her. As I walk out of the hut, I hear Arru ask Fey if she would like something to eat. "Aime, did you get a DNA scan of Fey?"

"Yes, I did."

"Thank you." I break into a sprint to quickly get back to the field where the karnesh lay. Stopping, I say, "Aime, let's see what we can learn about this thing, and see if there's an easier way to kill it." She sets up the overlay to direct me where she wants to scan, starting at its nose.

"Olfactory sense is almost nonexistent."

I continue, moving up to its still good eye. "Completely near-sighted."

I climb up on its front leg to get to the upper part of its head. After trying in several locations, she states, "I cannot locate any auditory senses."

"No ears?"

"None," she confirms.

"How did this get to be an apex predator?" I wonder out loud.

"The armor may have something to do with that."

"Possibly." Having an idea, I hop down from its leg and get a close look at the bottom of its foot. "What do you see on its foot?" I ask. Aime brings up the overlay again, and I follow her lead.

"The feet are covered with millions of neuromasts, vibration detectors. There is also a bladder-like structure in each footpad, apparently to quiet its own vibrations." The visual has me move up along the creature's side. "There are several arrangements of neurons, something like lateral lines."

"Lateral lines . . . that's a fish thing, right?"

"Yes, and with as many as this creature has, it can feel its surroundings in three dimensions. I would also speculate that when it roars, it can use the echo to see things that don't move."

"That's what would make it an apex predator." I put my hand on its back. "Can you come up with something that can penetrate these scales?"

"The pistol lacks the power needed to be able to penetrate the scales with an armor-piercing round. As you witnessed, the explosive did not even penetrate the armor, instead, it contained it within the neck. I would also like to note that the back does not have any neuromasts. When you jumped on its back, you entered its blind spot."

"That's good to know."

"Kyle!" Railu shouts. I look to the far end of the field and see her waving an arm in the air to get my attention.

As I approach I see an area of heavily trampled plants, mostly green, apparently this end of the field is still worked. I also notice that there are a few baskets strewn about, the grains that they contained now covering the ground. Looking at Tayla, I realize that she has some tears in her eyes. Without a word, she points to a patch of ground near the edge of the trampled area. Looking, I see spatters and a small pool of blood. Upon closer inspection, I also find an antler just outside the trampled area.

I hold my hand over the blood pool for Aime to scan. "Regrettably, the blood is a male, parental DNA match for Fey," she reports.

"Could he have survived this?" I ask, fearing the answer.

"Possibly, but he would not last long without medical attention."

Sighing, I stand, looking at the path that the karnesh left as it walked through, coming from afar, almost directly to where Fey's dad was standing, and then directly to where we found Fey.

I look at Railu. "Are there any signs that he may have gotten away?"

She sadly shakes her head. "His trail ends here."

I run my fingers through my hair, scanning the visible horizon, hoping to see a way out of telling Fey that her father died. "I'll tell her." I turn and head back to the hut. As I pass by the beast, I kick it angrily, trying to vent some of my frustration.

I stop just outside the door, thinking about how I'm going to do this. How do I tell a little girl that her dad's gone? Not yet having an answer, I open the door. Finding myself unable to look at her, I start taking off my armor, dropping it on my pack.

Fey notices my apprehension and takes the initiative. "You didn't find him, did you."

It was not a question.

Sighing, I drop my last piece of armor and walk over to the rocking chair that she is sitting in. I can't help but notice just how small and fragile she looks in the chair. I sit next to her in the chair and pull her into my lap, hugging her. She starts to cry, and the only thing I can think to say is "I'm sorry."

She starts sobbing uncontrollably. Sada walks over and puts her head on the girl's back. She, too, starts crying while trying to purr. Arru stops cleaning up the food she had made and sits down on a stool next to me and starts rubbing Fey's cheek. I feel the little girl's tears soaking my shirt. I then realize that my own tears are running down my face, dripping onto her fur. Kotu quietly stands, walks out the door, and sits on the rock wall just outside, his head in his hands.

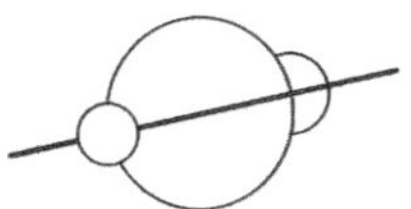

The others return just before nightfall. With Fey still curled up on my lap, having cried herself to sleep, I simply watch them come in.

Larrah hands me a large scale. "A trophy," she quietly says. I quickly realize that it's one of the karnesh's scales; this one is a little larger than my hand. I look at it, turning it over in my hand, realizing that the scale from the one in the facility was still just as strong as this one, the time has had no effect on it.

I set the scale aside and watch Sada help Arru with supper. Kotu keeps looking at Fey with a mix of concern and wonder. I can't quite tell if he might be thinking of her as a potential friend or feeling sorry for her now that she is an orphan like him or both. Larrah stands by the door, looking out its small window, as if on guard. From what I can see of her expression, she seems to be focusing on the distance, but I can tell that she is really lost in thought.

Tayla and Railu have similar expressions, looking at Fey and me with an interesting mix of sadness and curiosity. Tayla looks like she has a slight smile for a moment but quickly turns her head when Sada hands her a plate of food.

The smell wakes Fey. "Daddy?" she asks groggily.

Without thinking, I answer, "What, hun?"

Not bothering to open her eyes, she takes a big sniff of the air. "That smells good."

"Hungry?" I ask, suddenly realizing that everyone is staring at me with a strange mix of expressions on all their faces.

"Yeah," she answers weakly, still mostly asleep.

Sada quickly recovers and brings a plate of food to me and sets a drinking bowl of water on a small table next to the chair. Without leaving my lap, Fey sleepily sits up and starts eating, savoring the flavor as she slowly chews.

I find myself smiling as I watch her eat and get an odd sense of déjà vu as I gently rub the back of her head and neck. I hand her the water, and she takes a long slow drink.

"I had a bad dream," she says after handing me back the water. "There was this big monster that came in the field while I was picking berries." She then turns and looks at me, her sleepy eyes open in surprise. "Oh." She looks down at her hands, sadly realizing that it wasn't a dream.

"It's all right," I comfort. "I understand."

She slides out of my lap and starts wandering slowly around the small hut. Sada brings me another plate, and I slowly start eating while I watch Fey walk around. She eventually sits on a small stool in front of the fireplace and hangs her head. Kotu grabs a stool and quietly sits next to her.

He visibly thinks for a moment and then softly speaks, "I lost both my parents too. I was just a few years old when it happened. I was put in the orphanage with a few other children and worked for the council."

"What are you trying to say?" she asks, a little confused.

He sighs, takes her hands, and gently puts his forehead to hers. "You are not alone," he whispers to her.

They sit and talk for a while, Kotu talking more than she does, but it seems to do her some good to talk to someone her age. I find myself smiling at how the boy can try to be so macho and still have a sensitive heart.

After supper, Fey insists we rearrange the furniture to allow for us all to lie down inside, the cramped quarters making the usual sleeping arrangements impossible. Fey curls up on her own bed but doesn't fall asleep.

At her request, I lay down on her dad's bed and roll to my side to keep an eye on her. I watch her lay there awake, seeing her eyes shining in the otherwise-dark room, watching her ears twitch toward the door whenever she hears a noise. I wonder whether it's fear or hope that's keeping her awake.

After a while, she notices that I'm watching over her and smiles slightly. With a heavy sigh, she closes her eyes, I wait until I'm sure she is asleep before I close my eyes.

CHAPTER 9

Before breakfast, Fey warily comes up to me. "Are you going to the village?"

"Yes," I answer. "You should come with us. I don't really expect you to stay out here by yourself."

"I don't want to stay here," she answers, hanging her head slightly. "I didn't want to move out here anyway. The council made us."

"Why'd the council make you move out here?"

"Cause dad knew how to harvest the grains. Not many others know how, anymore."

"Why is that?" Tayla asks.

Fey sighs. "Dad used to tell me stories of how people were happy, farms stretched for a day's walk. Then people started disappearing, harvesters and traders mostly. People got hungry, traders stopped traveling. The harvesters that remained refused to leave the village to work. The council had to force us back into the fields to collect food. That's how we wound up out here. That was after Mom . . ." She stops talking as tears well up in her eyes.

Tayla puts her hand on Fey's cheek and gently rubs her muzzle alongside Fey's. "I'm sorry."

Fey takes a deep breath, trying to control her tears. "I'm okay," she sniffs, wiping at her eyes to remove her tears.

"How long have people been disappearing?"

She thinks for a moment. "We moved out here . . . a year ago, I think . . . so, maybe, two years."

"Have you seen that big creature before?" Railu asks.

"Once, a few months ago, I was up in a tree, playing when it showed up. I never heard it, but it seemed to know I was near, but couldn't find me. I stayed in the tree until it left."

"I wonder if it's the reason people have gone missing," Larrah comments.

"Possible, if it can walk quietly, it can easily sneak up on someone while they're working," Railu adds.

"Well, let's not get to into that line of thinking while were eating breakfast," Arru chides as she and Sada hand out plates of food.

"Agreed," Tayla states.

Except for Fey's occasional question, which we happily answer, breakfast is relatively quiet. Afterward, we pack, and I give Fey a small pack to put her things in. She starts walking around the hut picking up various small knickknacks and trinkets. She pauses when she picks up a small, painted, stone carving. I walk over to her and see that it's of a white-tailed doe.

"Dad got this for me, to remember Mom," she comments absently.

"She was pretty," I admit, putting my arm around her to gently rub her back.

She sighs and kisses the carving, then wraps it in a rag, and puts it in one of the small pouches on her pack. She continues looking through the few possessions, picking out a few more things that she sees as of value.

"I'm ready," she sadly announces.

"Fey, do you mind if we collect some things from the house, to trade for what you might need?" Larrah asks.

"I don't care," she shrugs, "most of it was already here. Some we took from other huts nearby."

Fey and I step outside while Larrah and Tayla start looking for items to trade.

Arru, Railu, and Kotu come up, each carrying a bag or two. "We brought in the grains that were harvested," Arru indicates, putting her bags down next to several others.

Fey goes around the far end of the hut and returns pulling a wooden, wheeled cart. It looks like a horse-drawn wagon but, the cargo area is half as wide, the wheels are larger, and the tongue has two arms with a crossbar and straps at the end. I quickly realize that the crossbar and straps were added later, apparently to make it easier for a person to pull it instead of a nakku.

"We can use this to take the harvest into town," Fey says sullenly. "Dad and I usually take turns pulling it." She then walks over to a door on the smaller section of the hut and pulls out another bag of grain and loads it on the wagon.

Kotu gently stops her from getting another. "I'll get them," he insists, and he gets the remaining bags out of the hut, giving us about a dozen to load on the cart.

As we load the bags, I notice that there are three bags by the hut's main door. When Larrah and Tayla come out carrying a bag of things to trade, they also pick up the bags by the door and put them on top of the grains. I take first turn at pulling the cart, Fey takes Sada's hand, and we start toward the village.

Arru spends much of the walk bringing me up to speed on the protocols I will need to speak with the council and not offend them. She also lets me know that each member represents a branch of control. There will most likely be someone representing the interests of the military, trade, agriculture, family, and finance, though there may be more. Each will handle things specific to their area or will voice concerns their group would have, but final decisions are usually made by the senior member, who represents the village as a whole.

We continue talking as we clear a stand of trees and finally see the village. Unlike the others, Arindell has a small, crudely made wood-and-stone wall around it, with several gates. Fey leads us to the nearest, where the gatekeeper, a rather large impala buck with long antlers wearing a brown sarong and holding a staff, waves and opens the gate to allow us in.

"Fey, nice t' see ya," he calls, greeting her openly. Noticing her company, his voice changes to one of concern, "Where's yer pa?"

She hangs her head, and I see tears come to her eyes, but she says nothing, so I answer, "He's gone."

He looks at me. "Please don' tell me that thing got 'im."

"I'm afraid so."

He sighs heavily and kneels to hug Fey. "I'm sorry 'bout yer pa. We'll certainly miss 'im."

"Thanks, Marl," she whispers as she hugs him back.

"I'll take care of the load ya brought, and I'll make sure t' credit yer pa's account." I notice a tear in his eye, noting his sincerity. "I'm sorry, but since yer not of age, an' I know yer ma's gone, I'm gonna 'ave t' send ya t' the council."

She nods to him. "I know," she sniffs, rubbing more tears from her eyes.

He stands and turns his attention to the rest of us. "'Fore I can let the rest of ya in, I need t' know yer business."

"I have council business. Railu and Arru have trades."

"What kind of council business?"

"It's about the beast."

"Are ya one of them fools who want t' kill it?" he asks, skeptically sizing me up.

Arru and I had already decided on a subtle approach to its death. "Well, I do have important information about it."

He thinks for a moment. "All right, ya can come in. Be careful though, been a while since we 'ad any outside traders."

We take our things from the cart, leaving the bags of grains, and head our separate ways. Railu goes looking for information about Roen while Arru and Kotu go to the markets to trade for supplies. The rest of us head to the council hut.

On our way, I notice that the people are mostly types of deer. As we pass more people, I realize that everyone is wearing clothes that wrap around, whether it is something like a toga, or an elegant gown or dress. It doesn't take me long to realize why all the clothes wrap, aside from a few species of females and almost all of the children; deer have antlers.

Can't pull things on over antlers. It comes to mind that antlers are also the reason that the doors are all extra wide and tall here.

The guards, a pair of imposing sambar bucks, let us in the outer chamber. There we are met by a white-tailed doe in a lavender shawl and skirt outfit, and around her neck, she wears a pendant identifying her as the lead mediator.

I bow to her. "I need to speak to the council."

"Please tell me the purpose of your request," she asks.

"I have news, and many things to discuss with the council, starting with the creature that plagues this village."

She looks at me hesitantly. "Many others have come before you, intending to kill it."

"You misunderstand," I correct. "I did not offer to kill it."

"You dress as, and travel with warriors, and you do not offer to kill it. What kind of warrior are you?"

"Killing the creature was not my original intent."

"The council may not hear you if you cannot offer to kill it."

"Then you should tell the council that it has already been killed and that they have lost another harvester."

She looks blankly at me for a moment, trying to decide how best to respond. After a moment, she says, "Wait here" and disappears into the main chamber.

"Aime, has Sage responded to you yet?"

"Yes, I am currently bringing him up to speed."

"Good."

Fey looks up at me and asks, "Who's Aime?"

I kneel to her and whisper, "She's a very special friend that's with me all the time, but no one can see her." Then I get an idea. "Put your ear to mine."

She gets a very skeptical look but puts her ear up to mine.

"Hello, Fey, my name is Aime."

Fey pulls away and looks at me, eyes wide with surprise. I smile and put my finger to my lips. "Shh."

As I stand, the mediator comes back in. "The council will see you, but they request that you have proof of its death."

Larrah holds up a bag, stating, "We have proof."

The mediator looks at the bag, then at the ones also being held by Tayla and Sada. I pull out the scale that Larrah had handed me and show it to her.

"This way." She opens the door and ushers us in and waits just inside the door. We walk into the middle of the room and wait to be addressed. There are seven members all dressed in matching gray robes. Each is a different species of deer.

"You are here about the beast?" the senior member asks, his voice sounding very old and gravely.

"Yes, how many beasts plague your village?"

My answer comes from the member second from the left. "Our scouts have only spotted one."

"Then I have solved your problem," I announce. "The beast is dead."

"Show us proof," one from the right side, this time, says.

I hold up a large scale.

"One scale is not proof of the creature's death."

I step back. Tayla, Larrah, and Sada all step forward and drop the bags. "Then perhaps three bags of them is enough proof." The girls open the bags, displaying the contents; all are full of the large scales.

The council members all gasp and start talking among themselves for a moment. The senior member waits a few seconds, then holds his hands up. The others immediately fall silent. "How do we know that these are from the beast?" he asks.

The girls step back, and I step forward again. "The beast is a karnesh. I have only seen one other, and it was already dead," I explain. "It had died over two hundred years ago in a place far to the west."

"So you know what it is called. How are to know that you speak the truth?" from a new voice on the left.

I smile under my mask. "Sage?"

"He speaks the truth," a new voice announces from above, drawing several gasps and another round of murmurs from the council members.

The senior member again quiets the others. "Sage, it is forbidden for you to speak to anyone not part of this council."

"My apologies, senior council member, but his authority is greater than this council's. I must speak to him if he asks," Sage comments.

"Who are you to have such authority?"

I remove my mask, revealing my face to the council, spurring yet another round of murmurs, which the senior member again quiets. "Who are you?"

"My name is Kyle. I am a human," I admit, trusting Aime to have filled Sage in on the details. "Sage can answer all your questions, but I assure you that I have killed the beast."

"He has indeed killed the karnesh," Sage confirms.

The council starts to murmur again, but the senior member quiets them. "If Sage believes him, then we believe him," he announces, pausing for a moment. "What news did you have of the harvester?"

I look at Fey, and she walks up to stand by me. Her ears lay back and she takes my hand as I speak. "Harvester Tarrow was the creature's last victim." I feel her squeeze my hand, so I gently squeeze hers in kind.

Several of the council members sigh, obviously disheartened by the news. "Harvester Tarrow was one of our most productive farmers," the member immediately left of the senior member states. "His service will be sorely missed." He pauses for a brief moment. "Not wanting to sound callous, but did his crops get brought in?"

"We brought in the twelve bags that he had collected. Gatekeeper Marl has seen to them," I answer.

"Was he made aware of Tarrow's death?"

"He was. He told Tarrow's daughter that he would credit Tarrow's account."

"Thank you," he responds. "I'm certain his family will appreciate that."

Taking that as my queue to change the topic, I ask, "Council, what will become of his daughter, Fey?"

A completely new voice, female this time, from the right speaks, "Is this Fey?"

Fey nods as I answer, "Yes."

"Fey, where is your mother?" the doe gently asks, looking down at her.

Fey starts to sniffle softly, so I answer for her, "She was a victim of the beast last year." I notice that Fey nods in agreement.

"Did your parents have any brothers or sisters?"

Fey shakes her head.

Frowning, she looks back at me. "If no one can claim her, she will stay at the orphanage as a ward of the council," the doe explains.

Fey pulls on my hand, getting my attention. I kneel and she whispers in my ear. I look at her for a moment, "Are you sure?"

She nods, and I see a hint of fear in her eyes. I nod, then stand and address the council, "What is required of the person who claims her?"

"Since you are obviously not family, it would require proof that you care for her," she answers. Noticing that Fey is holding my hand and I hers, she continues, "but in your case, I can see that it's already there." She pauses for a moment, looking at the senior council member, who just nods to her. "Kyle, do you claim responsibility for Fey?" she asks.

Following protocol, I state, "I claim Fey as my daughter."

"What is your proof of love?" she continues.

"I have killed a karnesh to protect her."

"Are there witnesses to this act?"

Without looking, I know that the girls have all raised their hands. Seeing a motion beside me, I look to see that Fey has also raised her hand.

"Very well, I accept your claim," she announces and turns to the senior member.

"Are there any objections?" he asks, waiting a moment. When none come, he continues, "Then it is decided. Kyle, Fey is your daughter."

The councilor on the right end, speaks up, "As Fey's parent, you have the right to Tarrow's possessions and access to his account. I will have that settled and brought to you in the morning."

"Thank you, council members," I say as I bow to them.

"It is we who should be thanking you," the senior council member says and bows slightly to me. The rest of the councilors follow suit.

The mediator opens the door. "This way please, and bring your proof." We follow her through to the outer chamber where we find Railu, Arru, and Kotu waiting for us.

"How'd it go?" Arru asks.

"It took a little convincing, but they took the news well, and Fey will be staying with us, as my daughter."

Arru kneels and gives her a gentle hug. "Welcome to the group, young lady." Kotu follows, also giving her a warm hug, and Fey warmly hugs him back. Railu simply scrubs the girl's head, apparently not sure how else to welcome her to the group.

The mediator comes up to me. "You and your group are welcome to stay at the council inn for five days. Your stay will be free, as part of the reward for ridding us of the creature."

"*Part* of the reward?" Tayla asks.

"Yes, there will be a banquet in your honor, and afterward the vendors will give you discounts. We will let you know when that will be."

We all look around at each other, mildly shocked. Railu, though, manages to say, "Wow."

"Please follow me," the mediator says and leads us across the street to the inn.

Once inside, the innkeeper, a reindeer, jumps up when she sees the mediator. "The room is ready, Mediator," she says, bowing slightly.

"Thank you." She returns the light bow, then she turns to us. "This is Tita. She will be your hostess. She and her staff will see to your needs while you are here." She bows to us and then walks back to the council hut.

Tita bows to us. "At your service. Please follow me." As she steps out from behind the counter we get to see she is wearing an orange and yellow two-piece wrap that shows her midriff. We follow her down the hallway to our room. To our surprise, the room is almost as big as the council hut but divided into sections.

"This is our ambassadorial suite," Tita announces warmly. "This is the common room." She walks over to a door to the side. "Here's the ambassador's sleeping chamber, and one for your children," she explains as she leads us around the outside of the common area, gesturing to several other doors. "These are for your staff." As she finishes, she turns to us and waits. I scan the rooms, seeing that everything is arranged circularly around a fireplace in the middle. Most of the benches and chairs are padded, and there are several pillows at each bed.

"This is excellent. Thank you," I find myself saying. Several others just nod in agreement.

Tita bows to us. "Supper will be served in about an hour. Would you like to eat here or in the dining hall?"

"Here," I state, realizing that the stress of the day is wearing on me.

"I will send servants to take care of you." She again bows to us and leaves the room.

Suddenly I hear several deep sighs and bags start dropping to the floor as people start sitting at the nearest bench or chair.

"What did you get us into?" Larrah asks, looking accusingly at me.

"I didn't know there was a reward for killing that thing." I drop my pack and sit down.

"I get the impression that she thinks we're ambassadors," Arru states.

Larrah shrugs then leans back in the chair and rubs her head. We sit in silence for a few minutes until a knock at the door gets our attention. Fey, being the closest to the door, gets up and opens it.

Standing outside the door are two people, one is a short golden tan female rabbit with a series of white spots down her forehead and nose, and long ears draped back like long hair. The other is a sambar buck with subtle markings and a modest rack. Both are wearing orange and yellow wraps, similar to Tita's. They bow slightly and step in, the male starts handing out menus as the female speaks.

"My name is Megai," the girl explains as she looks around at everyone, "and this is Janik. We will be your servants for your stay. If you wish to call on one of us, please ring this bell." She sets a small golden bell on a table next to the door. "Supper will be soon, and if there is anything not on the menu that you would like, please let us know. We have a large library of recipes at our disposal."

"Shall we return in a few minutes to take your orders?" Janik asks.

"Please," Arru says as she looks at the menu.

They bow and leave the room, closing the door behind them. Tayla sits back, looking at her menu, and comments, "I could get used to this," causing Railu to agree.

"But how long would it last," I ask her, "before their hospitality wears out?" She smiles but says nothing more, so I ask Railu, "How'd you do?"

"I found out who Amsel was after here." Railu adds, "I'll talk to him in the morning and find out where they went next."

"Will you want some company?" Larrah asks.

"Regrettably no, he's only agreed to meet with me because my mate is in that group." She pauses for a moment, flipping the page of her menu. "And I offered him a scale."

"Treat it like it's your only one. Best he has no idea we have more of them," Arru offers.

"I was planning on it."

"Are we ready to order yet?" Kotu gripes. "I'm hungry."

"When aren't you?" Arru chuckles. "Everyone know what they want?"

Everybody agrees, so Kotu rings the bell and both servers promptly return to the room. Janik waits by the door as Megai starts with Fey, taking her order for supper. She proceeds to Kotu, who knows exactly what he wants and how he wants it fixed. The others are easy and I translate for Sada, an experience that she obviously has not had before. As she takes my order, I can't help but notice that she subtly leans against me as I speak.

When done, she winks at me. "Please, let me know if there is *any-thing* else you would like." As she walks out the door, she twitches her tail and puts a little extra sway in her hips, reinforcing the offer she just made.

Turning my attention back to the others, I see that I'm not the only one who recognized her invitation. Railu and Arru seem indifferent but stare at the door for a moment while Larrah looks at the door with a bit of disgust. Fey and Kotu look confused, apparently not understanding what happened, while Sada just scowls. Tayla looks upset like Megai could have just stolen something from her. All of them turn to look at me for my reaction. Not sure how I should react, I just shrug, causing some of them to chuckle.

We get comfortable and relax while waiting for the food. At one point, Kotu starts to complain about being hungry but Larrah shuts him up quickly with a stern look, something I have yet to be able to do. Sada moves and sits next to me as supper shows up. Janik and Megai quickly set the round center table, evenly spacing the eight place settings and chairs around the table.

Once they are done, we quickly find ourselves places to sit. I find myself with Fey to my right and Kotu on my left. Megai sets out the plates with food as Janik pours drinks. Once everyone is served, we start eating. Right away, Kotu gets a light head slap from Sada.

"Kotu, use your manners," I reflexively say, then noticing where Sada is pointing, I add, "and your utensils."

He sighs but does as he is told, prompting Sada to give him a smile and a gentle pat on the back. "Thank you," I say to him as I cut my steak.

The rest of the meal is relatively uneventful, Megai keeping the bread, crackers, and various sauces available while Janik keeps all our various drinks full. Talk is light, and we settle on enjoying the meal.

After we finish, Janik takes the dirty dishes away while Megai serves us a spiced cake. Fey finds this dessert particularly enjoyable, saying her mom used to fix it. As everyone finishes that, they slowly adjourn from the table.

I pull the stone figurine out of Fey's pack and interrupt Megai as she cleans the table. "Do you know who made this?"

She sits next to me, gently takes the carving, and carefully looks it over. "There's a stand in the market with them, but this one looks like it was custom made."

She hands it back to me, and I return it to Fey's pack. "Thank you."

"I don't think that they're open this late, but should be in the morning," she adds.

She starts to stand but I stop her. "Megai."

She looks at me curiously. "Yes?"

"Please don't take this question the wrong way, but . . . your offer to me... is that part of your job here, or . . ."

She bows her head a little, looking slightly ashamed. "I'm sorry if I offended you," she says, starting to turn away.

"No, you didn't offend me, but I'm curious as to why you did it."

She sighs. "Sometimes I can't help myself. When I meet a male I find attractive, I want him. I become very preoccupied with him until I have him, or at least offer myself to him. Tita doesn't care, as long as I don't charge for it, or let it interfere with my work."

"It doesn't bother you that I'm a different species?"

She smiles for the first time, revealing her teeth. "Actually, that's part of what I find attractive."

Seeing the truth and genuine interest in her eyes, I ask, "How do you know we are even compatible?"

She leans in close, softly rubbing her cheek along mine. "That's the fun part," she whispers and then nibbles my ear a little, before scooping up the rest of the dishes and putting them on the cart.

She turns back to me, giving me a warm smile. "Let me know what you want to do." She then pushes the cart out of the room, again wiggling her hips and tail as she does.

I sit and think about her for a while, wondering if I want to take her up on her offer or not when Arru quietly sits next to me.

"Well, are you?" she asks, obviously aware of my thoughts.

"I'm not sure," I find myself saying, still looking at the door.

"No one would think less of you if you did."

Curious, I turn to face her. "What do you mean?"

She leans forward, resting her arms on the table. "In our society, mates usually stay together long enough to raise their children, sometimes not even that long. It is unusual to find a couple who stay together out of love alone. Usually, those couples work together or something like that."

She pauses for a moment to let that sink in. "Another thing is that most females have only a few days each month that they can mate while most males can be ready almost anytime. Combine that with the fact that females outnumber males four to one, it's not uncommon for a male to have a few mates at once."

I lean back, finding what she just explained both odd and normal at the same time. "Where I come from, we would usually stay with our chosen mate out of love, children or not. It was unusual or even forbidden to have more than one wife."

She looks at me puzzled. "Wife?"

Realizing what I said, I say, "Oh, do you know what a marriage is?"

"No."

"Marriage is where a male and female agree to spend the rest of their lives with each other, sharing everything they have. Once they agree, usually in a ceremony, the male becomes the female's husband, and she, his wife."

"Ahh, what you are talking about is a life mate," she says. "Those are rare, and even then the male may sometimes have a second mate."

I sit back and absorb what she said. "There are so many differences between what I know and the way it is here," I say, burying my face in my hands for a moment. "So many differences to learn and get used to."

She puts her hand on my shoulder. "You seem to have already gotten over some of the physical differences, and that's something that everyone else is used to. Don't expect to get over your learned behavior as quickly. Give yourself some time."

I sigh, putting my head down on the table. In the near three months I've been awake, I've only seen one other human, and she was dying.

Now I find myself surrounded by fur-covered people, and now one of them wants a one-night stand with me. For some reason, I'm both interested and bothered by this.

Seeming to read my mind, Arru lightly chuckles and rubs my back. "You'll figure it out," she says and gets up and walks to her bed-chamber.

I sit there, with my head on the table for several minutes. I feel a hand gently rub my back, so I slowly sit up and see Sada sitting next to me, looking concerned.

'What's wrong?' she signs.

"I'm really not sure anymore," I confess.

'Come to bed,' she urges.

Noticing that there is no sunlight from the window, I follow her into the ambassador's chamber and go to bed.

I lay there thinking about what Arru told me while gently rubbing Sada's back. I begin to realize that the problem I'm having is not with the fact that Megai came on to me. It's with the fact that she is not human. I also realize that for more than two months, I have been sharing a bed with a humanoid cat and it hasn't bothered me past the first few days.

This hits me as hypocritical until I realize that Sada just sleeps with me and Megai wants to do more than that. I then remember that back on the ship, Sada had informed me that we had tried. I move my hand to the base of my neck where Sada had bit me, wishing I could remember just what had moved us to try.

Feeling Sada sit up, I look at her.

'Tell me what's wrong,' she insists, giving me a stern look.

I sit up 'I'm not really sure.' I sign back.

'What are you thinking about?'

I sigh, wishing I didn't have to ask. 'Why did we try to mate?'

She looks at me, curiously, for a moment. 'We will not try again. I don't want to hurt you.'

'I understand you don't want to try again, and I will not force you to. I just want to know *why* we tried. I don't yet remember.'

She tilts her head, apparently trying to figure out something, then answers, 'Love.'

I smile, realizing that I had overlooked the one thing that I knew from the time I first remember seeing her—I love her. I sigh and hug her, feeling both reassured and embarrassed at the same time. To my relief, she warmly returns the hug, purring.

She pulls back after a moment. 'Do you want a new mate?' she asks.

'I would not replace you,' I insist.

'No, a *mate*. You had one before.'

'You don't consider yourself a mate?' I ask, a little confused.

'We are more like—companions. No, more than that. Like mates, but not mates.' She gets a little flustered trying to explain it to me, apparently not able to think of the correct words.

'I understand what you mean. I have trouble describing it too. You would not be mad if I took a mate alongside you?'

She gives me an odd look. 'I would not deny you that.'

I think for a moment. 'What about Megai?' I ask, curious about her response.

She gives me a skeptical look, which changes after she thinks for a moment. 'You want her?'

'I'm not sure. Would it bother you if I did?'

She smiles. 'No, have a mate if you want. I will still love you.'

'And I will always love you,' I insist and flop back on the bed. She lies down against me and starts to purr again as I rub her back. Feeling a lot more at ease, I soon fall asleep.

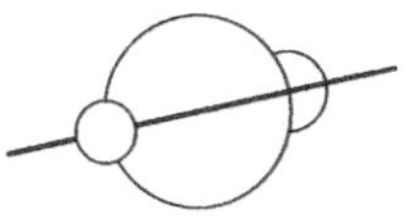

In the morning, we get cleaned up and head to the dining room for breakfast. There we find a rather large breakfast buffet. After I select a couple of double-yoked ma'pai eggs, a biscuit, and some type of sausage, I find the others at a large table and join them, sitting down between

Tayla and Fey. I notice that Fey has a stack of pancakes, covered with an orange-colored jam, and is enjoying them thoroughly. As I start to eat I notice that Tayla's plate has a few slender strips of meat covered with gravy that I did not see in the buffet.

Tayla notices me looking at her plate and says, "Gray fish with gravy. Want some?"

"No, thanks. I was just wondering what it was."

After breakfast, we return to our room. A mediator delivers Tarrow's account as promised. It's a small decorative wooden chest. As I look it over, I see it has Tarrow, Nina, and Fey's names engraved on the lid.

"Fey, come here, please."

She joins me at the center table, looking curiously at the chest. "That was dad's," she says solemnly.

I put my arm around her. "Let's open it." Together, we open the small chest. Inside we find a rather large collection of many different coins. I pick out a wooden one to look at. One side has the council logo burned on it, and the other, the village name.

"What are those?" Arru asks, curiously.

"That's a voucher," Fey explains. "Dad uses them for supplies and stuff."

I run my hand through the chest, moving the vouchers and coins aside to see if there's anything else in it. When I feel my fingers hit a couple wrapped items near the bottom, I pull one out and carefully unroll the cloth and find a stone figurine of a whitetail buck, complete with antlers, and fully painted, very similar to the one Fey already has of her mother. I realize that this one is most likely of Tarrow himself.

Turning to Fey, I gently hand her the figurine. Tears swell up in her eyes as she takes it. "It's my dad," she manages to whisper as she looks at it.

I gently pull her close in a hug, realizing that this is how Tarrow had prepared for his death. "Your dad loved you very much," I gently say, trying to comfort her. "He wanted to make sure you were taken care of."

As she hugs the figurine, I reach into the chest and find another wrapped figurine. Unrolling this one, I discover that it's of Fey. I hold it up to her, "It's you."

She takes it, holding each in a hand as she looks at them. I see Sada offer the figurine of her mother. Fey gently takes it, putting the figure of her mother, Nina, with the one of Tarrow.

She sinks in her chair, looking at the figurines of her parents. "Why did you leave me?" she wonders aloud, still softly crying.

I scoop her up into my lap and she leans into my chest. Wrapping my arms around her I say, "I'm certain that if they had the choice, they would both be here with you now."

"How do you know?" she asks skeptically.

I pause for a moment, planning my words carefully. "As parents, we put our children first in a lot of things. We give up things we want so that you have clothes, food, and shelter. We try to get you something on special days." I see by her expression she is thinking of times when they did all that for her. "As parents, we love our children unconditionally. I can tell by looking at you, by the way you act, that both your parents loved you very much."

"But I miss them," she insists.

"No one expects you not to. Your dad got these to help you remember, and as long as you remember them, they will always be with you, here." I gently point to her heart. She nods and gives me a one-armed hug, keeping the figurines held close to her with the other.

As I sit there hugging Fey, I notice that Larrah is removing all the coins from the chest and is neatly counting them out, placing similar coins in stacks of ten. I watch as she soon has more than seven stacks of vouchers lined up, as well as several stacks of other coins.

"Seventy-four vouchers, twelve thousand five hundred in coin," she points out.

"How did he manage to save up so much coin?" Arru asks, surprised.

Fey shrugs. "Dad never bought anything he didn't need."

A knock at the door interrupts us and Larrah quickly scoops the money back into the chest before Kotu opens the door.

Megai stands at the door, looking slightly ashamed, but noticing the door was opened, she bows. "I do not mean to interrupt, but I have a message for Kyle from the council." Seeing me sitting with Fey on my lap, she walks over to me and hands me a card and bows again, turning to leave.

Fey gets down off my lap as I take the card. "Megai?" I ask before she gets too far.

She stops walking and hangs her head again. "I did not mean to overhear. I will not tell anyone."

"About?" Arru asks, curiously.

She slowly turns around, still hanging her head. "About the money. I did not mean to eavesdrop on your conversation. I have excellent hearing, so I can hear the bell from almost anywhere."

Larrah sets a chair down behind her and nudges it forward to sit her in it. When seated, her shame changes to fear, and she starts trembling, trying to shrink into the chair.

"Relax, we won't hurt you. I would like to ask you a few questions." She suddenly looks more puzzled than afraid. She starts looking from face to face, trying to figure out what's going on.

"How do you know we can trust her?" Larrah asks.

I smile. "Because she's not interested in the money."

"How can you be sure?" Tayla asks.

"She apologized for overhearing. She has other ways to make a lot of money and doesn't, and besides, I know what really interests her," I confess, still looking at Megai.

"And what would that be?" Tayla asks with a slight scowl on her face.

I look at Tayla and smile. "Me."

Tayla curiously looks at me, as if trying to figure something out as I turn back to Megai. "Megai, please tell us how the council vouchers came about."

She swallows hard, still very nervous and confused but starts talking. "About two years ago . . . when that . . . *thing* . . . showed up, there were . . . well over a hundred harvesters . . . that worked on the farms." She takes a breath as if telling the story is helping her relax, and continues, "Almost thirty went missing as did two groups of traders before our scouts sighted it.

"We lost another twenty or so harvesters over the first year. Our scouts started to notice that it didn't go through the stone fences, but around them, so we built the wall to keep it out of the village. Soon after we built the wall, we lost a group of scouts, so the military went after it. We lost thirty warriors, and they didn't even hurt it.

"The council started assigning areas to harvesters, offering them vouchers, good for extra food, supplies, whatever they needed to do their job. They were given out based on how much food they brought in."

I lean back in the chair. "I bet now that I killed the beast, these things are going to drop in value."

Megai looks at me, shocked. "You *killed* it?"

"We thought you knew already since the council set us up here," Tayla says, a little confused.

"We thought you were ambassadors."

Sensing the mix of tension and mild confusion, I think for a moment. "Until the council announces otherwise, we are ambassadors. There may be a reason that they haven't announced its death yet." Looking at Megai, I add, "This goes for you too."

She nods her understanding and then suddenly remembers. "The message," she says, pointing to the card.

As I look at the card, Railu comes through the door, back from her meeting. She stops abruptly, looking at all of us gathered around Megai. "What did I miss?" she asks suspiciously.

"History lesson," Arru says.

"And we *are* ambassadors," Tayla adds. "I fill you in later."

Railu looks surprised and a little confused but says nothing more.

I break the wax seal and open the folds of the card, and read it to myself once before reading it aloud: "There will be a banquet held in your honor in the village center, midday tomorrow."

"Decrypting," Aime announces to me. Tayla looks at me, puzzled, apparently having heard Aime.

"Megai, who gave you this message?" Arru asks.

"One of the mediators."

"Why didn't they deliver it themselves?" Arru wonders. "Protocol would mandate that they deliver a message from the council personally."

She shrugs as Aime announces. "Decryption complete, imbedded code translation: You created quite a stir. Council worried about how you will use your authority. I tried to advise them that you were friendly. They seemed to believe that you have a hidden agenda. Please take care and exercise caution as you conduct your business." She pauses for a moment, then adds, "I do not like what this implies."

"Who was that?" Megai asks, looking around, puzzled.

"That's Aime," I say. "She's my conscience." Quickly changing the subject, I say, "It looks like Sage sent us a hidden message in the invite. He wants us to be careful while we're here. He thinks the council doesn't trust me."

"You know who Sage is?" Megai asks, surprised.

I give her a curious look. "Yes, we do. How do you know of him?"

"I can hear him talking with the council a lot, but the council has been pretty thick-headed lately and they tend not to take his advice."

I look at her, noting the sincerity and some disappointment in her voice "Why are you telling us this?"

She looks down, sighing. "I've heard Sage ever since I came here. No one else can hear him. I could never figure out why. You already knew about him, so I knew you'd believe me."

Railu pulls up another chair and sits down. "I know some of the people I spoke with aren't happy with the way the council's been acting lately. What do the people you know think about that?" she asks.

"I know Tita's not too happy. The last ambassadors we had didn't leave a tip or anything and the council didn't even cover the bill like they usually do. Janik, I'm not sure, he doesn't talk a lot while at work. The few merchants I've dealt with all seem upset with them too, 'cause they keep changing the value of the vouchers."

"What are they worth?" Arru asks.

"I think they're two fifty apiece. It's the highest they've been."

"At that exchange rate, Tarrow was very wealthy," Larrah comments.

"Yes, he was," I agree absently.

I see Sada lean forward, looking at my expression. She waves her hand in front of my face, but being deep in thought, I don't react right away. After a moment, I look at Sada and she signs, 'What's wrong?'

"I'm not sure," I confess. Turning to the chest, I pull out a handful of the vouchers and start to hand out three per person. "I would like everyone to make a few purchases, trades, have some fun. While you're doing that, try to get an idea of what the people think about the council and their recent actions. I also want you to find out what they've been told about the event tomorrow, and if they've heard about the beast's death. If they've not heard, let them know. Spread it like a rumor. "

I give Kotu a couple vouchers. "You just get to have fun. If someone asks you about it, just do your 'I don't know' shrug. Okay?"

"I got it." He nods.

I hand three to Fey, kneeling so I'm eye level with her. "I want you to find yourself something, whatever you want, just be smart about it, okay? Don't worry about anything else, okay?" I say as I gently rub her cheek.

"Okay," she says, pressing her head gently to my hand, then sets her "family" of figurines on the table, taking care to place hers in the middle, with her mom and dad facing her.

I stand up. "As far as anyone is concerned, you are all travelers or traders. Don't let on that you are in any way partially responsible for the beast's death."

"What can I do to help?" Megai asks eagerly.

I, and most of the others, look at her, surprised. "Don't you have duties here at the inn?" Arru asks.

"As I am currently assigned as your servant, anything you would have me do is part of my job," she reminds.

After thinking for a moment, I say, "I don't want to put you in a position, but I do have a personal errand for you." I pick up four of the vouchers and hand them to her. "Do you remember what we talked about last night?"

"I cannot charge for —"

"The other thing." I interrupt, glancing over at the three figurines.

She catches my hint. "Oh, that thing," she says, embarrassed.

I smile, but continue, "Can you find one of each of us, or as close as possible?"

"I will do my best," she says, bowing.

Tayla looks at me curiously. "And what will you be doing?"

"I have business with Sage." I start pulling on my armor.

'How do you plan on doing that?' Sada asks.

"I'm not sure yet."

She walks up to me and gives me a nuzzle, with her hand to my cheek to hold me close, so I return the affection in kind.

"Come, let's find you something nice," Arru states, taking Fey's hand. She then leads her out, and the rest follow.

Finding myself alone in the room, I sigh heavily, wondering what I'm doing. I could leave the village, continue on my journey to find the humans, and let the village sort things out for itself. I then realize that it would not be fair to anyone in this village, and I would be no better than the council if I did that. Recommitted to my self-assigned mission, I finish putting on my armor.

Activating the camouflage, I walk out of the room and right past Janik, unnoticed. Hearing him knock on the door to my room, I turn and watch. When he opens the door, I follow him in, wondering what he is doing. I watch him check the sleeping rooms before turning his attention to the center table and the chest that still sits on it.

He circles the table a couple of times, before finally deciding to approach it. Before he can, I purposely nudge a chair with my foot so it slides across the wooden floor, making a rumbling sound.

He jumps, looking around for the source. Not finding anything, he waits a few moments in silence, regaining his confidence. When he reaches for the chest again, I give the chair a small kick, moving it farther across the floor. This time, he sees the chair move. He looks around again, but not being able to see me, he gets rattled and rushes from the room.

I shake my head in disappointment, deactivating the camouflage. I pick up the chest and slide it under Fey's bed. With it safely out of view, I reactivate the camouflage and leave the room.

Walking across the street is easier than I thought it would be, the foot and cart traffic being relatively light this morning. Instead of going inside, I circle to the back of the large hut, following the wall.

Aime, can he hear you yet?

"I have made contact. He has sent details of his concerns but the council does a good job of concealing their real intent, occasionally having meetings outside the hut."

Does he know where?

"No."

Does he know who might?

"He has a few possibilities."

Is the council in right now?

"No. He indicates that they are most likely in a private meeting somewhere."

Okay, does he know which direction they went?

"No."

I sigh, wondering what to ask next. *Is there a mediator?*

"Yes, the same one who saw us yesterday."

Good. Being in a secluded spot I deactivate the camouflage and walk around to the front of the hut.

Entering the main door, I am immediately greeted by the mediator. She bows to me. "May I help you?"

Returning her bow, I say, "I have more information about the beast that the council should know about. May I see them, please."

"The council is not in right now."

"Can you tell me where I may find them?"

A look of confusion crosses her face, obviously unsure what to do. Trying to help her decide, I gently press, "Please, it's important."

She starts breathing hard, putting her hand to her chest. Apparently having a conflict between duty and loyalty. Her panic escalates; she starts frothing at the mouth as she gasps for air.

"She's aspirating!" Aime alerts.

I quickly put my hand to her chest and catch her with the other. I help her sit as Aime starts removing the excess fluid from her lungs.

"Calm down. Calm down, breathe," I coach, helping to calm her panic as Aime administers a mild sedative. She starts to breathe slower, and her pulse slows down as her panic subsides.

"Are you okay?" I gently ask.

She takes a few slow deep breaths. "Yeah, thank you." After another few deep breaths, she asks, "How did you do that?"

"It's a long story. Please, what's going on?"

"The council told me to handle things while they adjourned," she says nervously. "They've done this a few times in the last year, but never before. They're the council. They *live* here," she admits, confused.

"Do you know where they go?"

"The Northern View Café."

"Thank you," I say. "You should rest for a while."

She nods, leaning back in the chair as I get up and head north to find the Northern View Café. It takes me several minutes to get there, but when I find it, I see that it's a series of oval huts, with open walls, situated at the top of a small hill at the edge of the village. I find the council seated at a larger table at the far end of the dining area. So I pick a table near the middle, a few tables away, and sit sideways to them, looking out over the farmland.

After ordering a sweetened tea and a cinnamon cake dessert from the waitress, I have Aime listen in on the council's conversations. Rather than partake of the eavesdropping, I just sit and look out over the green fields. Remembering that Fey said they reach for nearly a day's walk, I can't believe that there aren't many people working in these fields, being as it's so close to the village.

The waitress brings me my tea and cake. I pay her for the food and give her a generous tip, encouraging her to refill my drink often. I eat slowly, enjoying both the view and the food, giving the council plenty of time to finish their conversations.

After the council leaves, I wait a few minutes and nonchalantly finish my drink. Leaving another tip for my waitress as thanks for keeping my drink fresh, I stroll out and work my way through the markets, picking up some fruit to try, and a few other small items that I find interesting. I hear people talking about the event planned for tomorrow and to my relief, they are mentioning the beast's death and being happy about it, so I slowly work my way back to the inn.

Once there, I find that the others aren't back yet. I take off my armor as Aime fills me in on the highlights of the conversation the council had. I quickly realize that their concerns are about people wanting to leave and that they think that there are not enough harvesters left to continue feeding the populace and still have some to trade. These are worries I had expected them to voice in the presence of Sage.

Aime surprises me by saving the worst for last. She replays the conversation they had over me, each member voicing their concerns about me being able to speak with Sage and that I have more authority with him than they do. I also realize that their other major concern is that the council is nearly broke, having increased the value of the vouchers several times for incentive to get people to harvest.

I sit at the center table for a while, thinking of how to help the council, when Arru and Fey come in. I immediately see that Fey has changed into some new clothes. She is now wearing a two-piece wrap, much like the other females of the village. Hers is a deep blue with golden highlights. I can't help but smile at her.

She sees me and spins around, making the dress flair a bit. "What do you think?"

I give a light chuckle. "You look beautiful," I compliment and kiss her on the nose.

She gets a funny look on her face and touches her nose. "What was that?" she asks, not sure what to make of the kiss.

"I gave you a kiss," I explain warmly. "It's a way of showing I care about you."

"Oh," she says and after thinking a moment, she lightly licks my nose, obviously trying to imitate the kiss.

I chuckle. "Close enough." I rub her head, making her smile. "Could you bring me the chest, please. I put it under your bed earlier." She nods and happily heads to her room, returning promptly with the chest. "Thank you."

Before I can open the chest, we hear a knock at the door. "I'll get it," Fey calls and opens the door.

Megai bows, noticing Fey's new outfit. "Well, you certainly look nice."

"Thanks," Fey says, smiling back as she closes the door behind Megai. Seeing me at the table she smiles as she walks over and places a package on the table.

"How many did you find?" I ask, reaching for the package, eager to know the answer.

"One of each of you," she offers.

"Really?" I exclaim, removing the wrapping to find a small box. Feeling like a child at Christmas, I open the box and carefully pull out one of the cloth-wrapped items. I unroll it, finding a small look-a-like of Tayla. I look it over. "Beautiful," I comment. Standing it on the table, I open the next one. It's of Arru. I hold it up and compare it to her. "Good likeness," I confess.

Arru picks it out of my fingers and examines it for herself. I notice that she is grinning at it, apparently impressed at the likeness. "Nice," she says, carefully placing it next to the one of Tayla.

I continue opening the rolls until I have all the figures lined up and everyone in the room gawking at them. There on the table stand figures of Tayla, Arru, Larrah, Kotu, Sada, and Railu.

"These are great. Thank you, Megai," I say and kiss her on the nose.

Her jaw drops in surprise, though she quickly recovers and smiles.

"Fey," I gently call.

She comes over and looks at the line of figurines. "They're of you," she says, looking around at the others.

I hug her. "These are for you."

She looks at them, then at me. "But there's not one of you."

Megai smiles and reaches in her pocket, as she says, "I've got that covered." She pulls out two more rolled cloths and hands them to her.

Fey unrolls the first and smiles happily. "It's you," she exclaims, looking at me, and carefully stands it with the others. Then she unrolls the other and giggles. "This is you, Megai, even has your spots," and she quickly hugs Megai. "Thank you."

"You're welcome," Megai says, returning the hug.

I dump all the coins from the chest into the smaller box and put all the cloth wraps in the chest. "You can keep them safe in here," I tell her, sliding it close to the figurines.

She wraps me in a hug. "Thank you."

I hug her back. "You're welcome. I want you to remember that we can all be part of your family, just like your mom and dad."

"I know," she says, looking at the figure of me.

"Smart girl."

"I know that too," she insists.

I chuckle and she puts the figure with the others on the table, sits down, and starts looking closely at the new figurines.

Turning back to Megai, I ask, "How did you find one of me?"

"You got lucky. The carver got a good look at you when you entered town yesterday and made a carving from memory," she explains. "I helped him with some of the colors when I showed up, and he repainted carvings for Arru and Sada to get their colors right." She then pulls out a small pouch and hands it to me. "The rest of your money," she says, bowing slightly.

I take advantage of her bow and kiss her on top of her head. "Thank you very much." She sits up, looking at me, shocked. "What?"

"No one's been this nice to me before."

Not having noticed when Tayla walked in, I'm slightly startled when she says, "He can't help himself. If you know him long enough, he gets even nicer."

She skeptically looks up at Tayla. "Really?"

"Yep," she answers as several others nod in agreement.

She thinks for a moment as if trying to figure out what to make of that when a knock at the door interrupts us. Megai jumps up and quickly answers it.

Tita stands in the doorway, looking slightly distraught. "Megai, good, have you seen Janik this morning?"

"He was here when I delivered the council's message," Megai explains. "I was sent on an errand right after that. I just got back."

"Can you take their orders for lunch then? I'll keep looking for him."

"Certainly," Megai answers, bowing.

"Thank you," Tita says and with a slight bow, turns and walks down the hall.

Megai closes the door, picks up the menus from the small table, and starts passing them out. "I will be serving lunch today. Please let me know if you would like anything that's not on the menu." She returns to the door. "I'll return in a few minutes to take your orders." With a bow, she steps out.

A moment of silence follows, interrupted by Railu, saying, "I wonder what happened to Janik."

"I bet he thinks this room is haunted," I confess.

"And why is that?" Tayla asks, giving me a suspicious look.

"After I activated the camo on my armor, he came in, tried to take some of the money. I moved a chair to have him think again. I think it worked too well."

Several chuckle, but Arru chastises me, "That was mean."

"Would you rather I have hurt him, or let him steal the money?" I ask, knowing the answer.

"No," she concedes, turning back to the menu still a little upset.

"All I did was move a chair. I didn't expect him to get that scared."

She sighs, realizing that I was as subtle as I could have been without letting him get away with it. We sit in silence and Megai comes back a few minutes later, looking a little flustered.

"Did you find him?" Tayla asks.

A little taken off guard, Megai thinks for a moment. "Yes, he was hiding in a closet mumbling something about ghosts and not doing it again."

Feeling a bit embarrassed, I ask, "Is he going to be okay?"

She gives me a funny look, but answers, "I hope so. Tita gave him the rest of the day off." She looks puzzled for a moment, then looks around. "Is everyone ready to order?"

Everybody nods, so she takes turns with each of us, taking our orders. She leaves and conversation becomes light while everyone takes turns examining the figures Megai picked up for me.

Lunch comes, and we all eat. Megai keeps busy filling drinks and serving the various foods to the correct people. Fortunately for her, we are all patient and keep the mood light, despite her occasional mistake, understanding that she is doing two jobs at once.

After lunch, we review how the morning went. I share what Aime overheard with everyone, and they in turn share the versions of the rumors that they heard about as they shopped. The general consensus is that the council does plan on celebrating the creature's death, but the people did not know much more than that. Railu also shares the information that she got from her contact. Our next destination will be Dendros, nearly fifteen days away by pack animal.

Afterward, I sit back in one of the lounge chairs to relax. I watch Fey sit at the center table and play with the figurines. Tayla and Railu grab a few more vouchers and set out for the shops again. Sada however sits at a table and tries to put together a shaped wooden puzzle she found. Larrah coaches Kotu, both having nice new wooden staffs, while Arru quietly reads one of the books she picked up at the market. Megai comes and goes, checking on us periodically to see if we need anything.

I catch her during one of her visits. "Megai, do you know of any masseuses?"

She thinks for a moment, then kneeling next to me, says, "We don't have anyone here in town that does massages."

"Do you know anyone who I could get a back rub from?" I ask, smiling at her.

Apparently catching my hint, she smiles a little and asks, "Are you asking me for a rubdown?"

"Yes, I am."

She nervously thinks for a moment. "Would it lead to . . . other things?"

"Possibly."

She smiles, thinking for a moment. "We have a grooming room we could use."

"Grooming room?" I ask, not having heard the term before.

"Yes . . . Oh, come with me. I'll show you." She gently takes my hand and leads me down the open hall to the door at the end. She opens the door and shows me in. Looking around, I see a bed in the middle of the room. The walls have shelves with various towels, sheets, and even shampoos and perfumes. I also notice that the room has windows, but they are high enough that no one could see in. Apparently this room was designed with a certain amount of privacy in mind.

"How do we know we won't be disturbed?"

"You are the only guests here at the inn." She gently presses herself to me. "And the door has a lock."

I smile down at her, realizing for the first time just how much shorter she is than me. Pulling her in close to me, I ask, "When do you have a couple hours free?"

"My duties end at sundown."

"I will meet you here, then." I run my fingers down her arms, feeling her soft fur.

She smiles as she bows to me, then turns and steps happily out of the grooming room. I can't help but notice that there is a lot more bounce and wiggle in her walk.

Hoping that Aime predicted my request, I ask, *Aime, what did you learn?*

Her words display in my vision, so Megai does not overhear. *Without a proper DNA breakdown, I hesitantly estimate a 10 percent chance of pregnancy.*

Ten? Did the researchers plan on humans reproducing with the evolved species?

If they did, they made no record.

I sigh, leaning against the bed to think for a moment. *If you make me sterile, you can reverse it, right?*

Yes.

Do it.

Done.

I return to my room and have a seat at the center table. I notice that Fey had left her figurines set up with Megai, Tayla, and Sada standing right behind mine, while mine faces Fey from her figure's right, and to the left stand Tarrow and Nina. Behind Fey stand the rest of the group, almost perfectly spaced apart. All the figures face Fey while Fey's figure faces the door. I can't help wondering what she was thinking when she arranged them.

Sada interrupts my musings by happily showing me that she solved her wooden puzzle. I smile and scratch her head, complimenting her, "Nicely done. How do you take it apart?"

Her smile quickly changes as she tries removing a piece, but realizes that since she turned it around, showing me, she's lost track of the last piece she put in. Letting out a huff, she returns to her seat, glaring intently at it while turning it slowly, trying to find the correct piece to pull out.

I smile, turning my attention back to the figurines. I see that I never opened the pouch containing the rest of the money that Megai handed me after she got the figurines. I dump its contents onto the table, a voucher and various coppers. I pick them up and grab a handful of vouchers from the box and head to the market.

Wandering around the markets, I casually glance over the various wares at each stand. Finding the stand where Sada picked up the puzzle, I purchase a couple of different ones and then continue browsing, looking over anything from dishes to weapons. I round a corner and find a bookseller.

Looking through the display, I find a slightly worn book labeled *The Myths of Arcania*. Suddenly curious, I open the leather-bound book and flip through a few pages. I can't help but notice that it's all hand-printed and even has some drawings of what someone thought things would look like. Aime advises me that many myths were born of facts, so I buy the book and put it in the pouch with the puzzles.

I turn to leave and notice Railu talking with a vendor. I walk over to see what she wants and see from his wares that the vendor is with the carver Megai had purchased the figurines from. Getting closer, I hear Railu asking if he has a gray wolf, Border Collie, and a German shepherd. I see that she has already picked out a Red Fox, and only has one voucher in her hand. I look across the display, most of the prices are between seventy and ninety coin, making the purchase of all four more than she appears to have. While the vendor is occupied looking through his inventory, I take a voucher and subtly push it in her hand, giving her two. She closes her hand around it but doesn't look at me.

I casually look over the wide variety of figurines, occasionally picking one up to get a close look at it. Railu completes her purchase, apparently happy with the appearance of the figurines. As she turns to leave, she sees me and smiles, giving me a slight nod of thanks as she continues through the marketplace. I continue browsing the figurines for a while looking for characters of interest. Realizing that Railu and Megai have everyone covered, I move on and continue browsing the market.

After more than an hour, I finally wander back to the inn. As I enter my room, I'm assaulted by the smell of supper.

Megai turns to me and bows. "Your friends took the liberty of ordering for you." She smiles at me. "I hope you find it to your liking."

I sit as Megai brings over the tray. It's a type of steak, with a sauce, some vegetables, and a few breadsticks. I take a bite of the steak; it has a rich herbal flavor. "Very good, thank you," I compliment.

Megai keeps busy with drinks and the dishes, but still finds time to glance at me, smiling each time she does. I find that I can't help but smile back when I catch her looking at me. After supper, Megai clears the table and heads off for her other duties.

I put the book of myths on the table for anyone who would like to read it. I also give the two puzzles to Sada, who smiles and hugs me as thanks. I notice that Railu has given the four figurines she purchased to Fey and is currently telling her about them. To her credit, Fey is an attentive listener, soaking up the information like a sponge. Kotu sits with her, but having heard about the four already, is paying more attention to the figurines instead.

As the sun starts to descend, I get out a towel and change out of my armor and under-armor and put on a simple T-shirt and shorts. As I walk out the door I hear Railu joke, "Showing a lot of skin tonight."

"Leave him be," Arru chides. "He is a male. He travels with all of us females, and none of us are interested in him that way. It can't be all that easy for him."

As I close the door, I hear Tayla softly sigh and agree, "No, it can't."

Entering the grooming room, I find myself alone. I lay my towel out across the bed and take off my shirt. As I start browsing through the various oils, conditioners, and even some candles, Megai comes in.

Upon seeing me, she puts her hands to her mouth and gasps, "Where's your fur?"

I gently take her hands in mine. "I don't have fur. What you saw me wearing was a bodysuit, clothes."

She looks at me for a moment, then cautiously reaches out and gently runs her fingers across my chest. "No fur. Are you a Moku?" she asks, noticing other differences.

Smiling, I softly say, "No, I'm human. I wear the bodysuit to avoid awkward moments with people I meet."

She shyly giggles. "Like this one?"

"This isn't awkward," I admit, surprising myself. "Do you still want to do this?"

She looks up at me, smiling, and nods nervously.

I tilt my head and give her a curious look.

"Yes," she softly reassures. "I get nervous when I'm with a male."

"Well, if it's any help, you'll be my first female with fur," I confess, running my fingers through the soft fur on her cheek.

She looks at me, curious. "But you have so many with you and you even sleep with Sada."

I lean on the bed, and as Megai comes up next to me, I gently run my fingers down her arms and take her hands as I explain, "I hired Tayla and Larrah as guides. Arru came along because she wanted to travel and see other villages again, and Railu's looking for her mate." I tell her, "Sada and I tried to mate long ago, but she defended herself and bit me."

"Oh. Was she in heat?"

"Honestly, I don't know."

She runs her fingers across my chin. "Fortunately for us, as a rabbit, I am always ready." She coos, "But I remember someone asking for a backrub."

Smiling, I say, "Yes, I did, how do you want me?"

She grins, giving me a hungry look, but puts a small pillow on the near end of the bed. "Clothes off, face down." She then hands me a towel and turns to the shelves, looking for something.

I drop my shorts, wrap the towel around me, and lie down on my stomach. Turning my head to watch her as she browses the shelves, I can't help but notice that the height of the bed puts me at eye-level with her very fluffy white tail.

She turns around holding a bottle and notices that I'm watching her tail. She smiles and twitches it teasingly. She then moves a small table over next to the bed and puts the bottle on it. Without a word, she removes a pin from her top and one from her dress, setting them on the table. She looks at me and then gracefully spins. Both parts of her dress fall loose to the floor, leaving only a golden tan string bikini to cover her.

Picking up the bottle again, she coos, "You'll love this. It's Keema oil." She pours some of the liquid down the middle of my back. The first thing I notice is that the oil immediately feels warm despite having been sitting on the shelf in the slightly cooler air.

Finding the aroma soothing, I close my eyes. My mind starts to wander as her small hands start to work the oil over my back, gently caressing it into my skin, all the way from my neck and shoulders down to the towel around my waist. I occasionally feel her lightly scratch my back with her claws as she works.

After a few minutes, she shifts position and starts pressing her fingers firmly into my muscles, working out any perceived stiffness she can find. Unfortunately, the nanites keep me from having stiff muscles, but that doesn't stop Megai. I let out the occasional sigh or moan, letting her know that I'm enjoying her work.

After several more minutes of treatment, she nibbles my ear a little. "Would you like some more?"

I roll over and look her in the eyes, smiling. "I would *love* some more."

She pours a little more oil on my chest. Instead of massaging, though, she starts caressing, gently pushing the oil around, making sure to feel every part of my chest and shoulders. I can't help but notice that her posture has changed, instead of the unassuming servant girl, she now stands more sensually, seductively, and her expression reflects both her curiosity and desire.

Following her lead, I start rubbing her sides as she leans forward over me. She looks into my eyes, squinting seductively as I rub, so I reach up and start rubbing the back of her neck, starting just below her ears, and working down to her mid-back. I notice that her eyes narrow as my fingers rub between her shoulder blades.

Starting again, I gently rake my fingers through her fur; she quivers slightly and starts to purr. I reach up and grab the strings to her top and untie them as I again run my fingers across her back. Her top drops to the floor, revealing her small, fur-covered breasts.

She bends down and starts rubbing her hands and chin gently over my chest. She starts working her way up my body, and when she gets to my ear, I notice that her purring is really her working her jaw rapidly. I reach up under her and feel her breasts, making her gasp softly. She grabs both sides of the bed and easily hops from the floor to the bed, straddling me at my hips.

She slinks down and rubs her chin across me as she works her way back up, this time dragging her breasts along my stomach. As she reaches my neck, I rake my nails down from between her ears to her back. She nearly collapses on me, pressing her chest firmly to mine as her legs quiver, seemingly unable to support her.

"Oooh!" she manages to weakly gasp, interrupting her purr.

I bring my hands back up and scrub again. She lays her head on my chest with her fluffy tail up in the air, twitching. I find myself enjoying the view and eager to continue.

"Yessss," she hisses, as I do it again. This time, I follow her spine down to her waist and untie her bottoms and drop them to the side. She rises slightly and reaches down to remove my towel. I raise my hips to let it slide out from under me. She sits up and gives me a hungry look.

I nod slightly, understanding her desire. She takes me in hand and slowly sinks down on me. Her intense heat envelops me as she descends, taking as much in as she can stand while letting out a gentle moan.

I let out a subtle moan, letting her know I'm enjoying what she's doing. I slide my hands up her ribs to her breasts, and she grabs my shoulders for balance as she raises up, stopping with just my tip inside, then sinks down again, farther than before, but still not all the way. Finding her nipples with my thumbs, I start gently circling them, slowly bringing them to a point.

She rises up again and then descends. This time, she takes all of me, letting out a long quivering moan. I feel her body tense up for a moment, then as she relaxes. She lets go of my arms and braces herself on my chest, gasping, as she looks into my eyes.

Realizing what just happened, I give her a look of understanding and put my hand to her cheek. She gives me a weak smile and nuzzles into my hand.

Not letting her off my lap, I sit up and wrap my arms around her, and she wraps her arms and legs around me. I run my fingers down her back, and she inhales sharply, clutching me tightly. Feeling her quiver, I decide to go easy on her. Instead, we sit like this for a moment, letting her catch her breath as we gently nibble on each other's ears and necks, keeping the mood alive.

After a few moments, she pulls her legs back under her and she begins to set a steady rhythm. Not wanting to push her as hard this time, I start gently caressing her breasts, kneading them just enough to get a reaction out of her. She hangs her head back, moaning to the ceiling while she steadily works on me. I pull her close and start licking at her nipples. She gasps and stops her action for a moment. I feel her grab my head and hold me to her as she lets out a long moan. I move on to nibbling her neck and ears, and she slowly resumes her rhythm.

I lean back as she starts to increase her pace. I slowly give in to the urge to rise to meet her. She leans forward, bracing herself up on her arms, as I continue to caress her body. As I look into her eyes, seeing the amount of pleasure on her face, I notice that she is starting to pant. I run my hands down her legs and feel them starting to quiver with every movement. I sit up and put my hand against her back, holding her to me. Realizing my intent, she wraps her legs and arms around me and tucks her tail. I roll forward onto her, letting my legs fall from the bed and swing them up behind me.

Now being the one in control, I set a rhythm close to the one she had. With her in a more passive role, she closes her eyes and starts letting out small squeaks and moans with every thrust. Feeling her body start to tense with each thrust, I pick up my pace slightly. She tightens her legs around my hips and holds onto me, urgently meeting my every thrust. I happily speed up, adding a little more force to my thrust, my own body starting to call for release.

Megai starts to squeeze hard with her legs, demanding more from me. I push harder, faster. Suddenly her body tenses up, her back arches, her insides grip me tightly. Managing one more thrust, I explode inside her, my own body tensing up. Her entire body seems to squeeze me tighter, reacting to the added presence inside her. Her legs locked, holding me in place. She lets out a nearly silent scream and I feel her whole body tense, locking herself to me.

As her scream dies off, her body falls limp, and I almost collapse on top of her, exhausted. After a brief moment, we manage to shift ourselves slightly and lay side by side on the narrow bed. I hug her to me and she puts her hand on my chest and sighs heavily. We lay there for a while, enjoying each other's company.

Starting to feel the chill of the night air on my sweaty skin, I gently climb out of her embrace and sit up. Noticing that she didn't move, I put my hand on Megai's chest, the other on her forehead, and Aime tells me that she is asleep, so I give her a gentle kiss.

I quickly dry myself off, put on my shorts, and gently wrap her in a sheet. First picking up our clothes and the pins for her dress, I scoop her up in my arms and carry her back to my room. Noticing my bed is empty, I gently lay Megai down on it, making sure her head is on a pillow.

I lay down with her and cover us up with a blanket. After wrapping my arm around her, I let myself fall asleep.

CHAPTER 10

Feeling the bed move, I awaken to find Megai inching up to my neck, getting more comfortable. Without thinking, I start gently rubbing the back of her head, right between her ears. Hearing her lightly murr, I realize that she's awake.

"Did I wake you?" she gently asks.

"Not really."

"Where are we?"

"In my room."

She thinks for a moment. "How...?"

"You fell asleep, so I carried you."

"Thank you." She stretches, then gently rubs her head against my neck. "You're a lot for me to handle," she confesses. "You made sure I enjoyed myself as much as I enjoyed you. No one has done that for me before."

"Maybe you should pick your partners a little more carefully."

"After what you did, I've not got much choice."

We lay there in silence for a while, as the room slowly gets brighter.

"It's morning."

She sighs heavily. "Yeah, it is. Time for me to get up."

As she sits up, I follow, wrapping my arms around her from behind and pulling her to me. I put my nose in her fur at the base of her neck and slowly inhale, smelling her natural musk.

She giggles lightly. "What are you doing?"

"Remembering your smell."

She hands me Sada's brush. "Well, here's something else to remember," she says slyly. "Brush my back."

I take the brush and start at her head, slowly working my way down her back. She subtly leans or stretches her body, encouraging me to brush longer in some areas. As I get to her tail, she leans forward, lifting her tail slightly off the bed. I take my time, making sure that it's tangle-free and fluffy again.

Finishing, I sigh. "Oh well."

She turns, looking at me puzzled.

I shrug. "Still beautiful."

She smiles at me as she stands to get dressed. "Flirt," she chuckles. Finding her bikini, she says, "Help me tie these."

I help her get dressed, and once she's ready to go, I give her another hug, making her giggle. "See you at breakfast," she says and quietly heads out the door.

Not feeling like sleeping anymore, I dress and have a seat at the center table. Seeing the book of myths, I open it and find the table of contents. I notice that there appear to be several myths in the book and wonder to myself how a young culture could have so many.

As I skim down the page, I see names I'm already familiar with: "The Moku," "The Karnesh," "Humans," "Sage," "Moonstorm," and "The Dig." Looking at some of the other titles, I see "The Sleeper," "The Wilds," "The Ghost of Garrent," "Our Ancestors," "Swimmer People," and "The Great White Dragon, with eyewitness accounts."

Thoroughly curious, I start reading "Humans." As I do, I realize that it is surprisingly accurate and appears to be written by someone with first-hand knowledge of, at least, the scientists that worked at the facility. I turn to the section about "Sage" and as I read, Tayla sits down next to me, folds her arms on the table, and puts her head down on them.

I continue to read, as I ask, "Still tired?"

"No," she says into the table. "I have a headache."

"Come here." She leans on me. I put my hand on her forehead. Aime understands my unsaid command and takes care of Tayla's headache.

She slouches onto my shoulder with a sigh. "Ohhh, thank you."

In response, I lean my head on hers for a moment but continue reading about Sage. From the way it's written, the author had no idea that Sage was technology, but treated him like a spirit, trapped in the council hut, that only the council could speak to. Despite that error, I'm pleased to find it's surprisingly accurate.

Tayla finally notices that I'm reading. "What's that?" she asks.

I playfully answer, "A book," earning me an equally playful jab in the ribs.

"I know it's a book," she snorts. "What's it about?"

"Myths," I answer, "and the ones I've read are surprisingly accurate."

She picks her head up off my shoulder and gives the book a good look. "May I?" she asks, reaching for the book.

"Sure," I answer and hand her the book.

She closes the book to look at the cover, then opens it and skims the first couple pages. With a scowl, she then flips to the back of the book, apparently looking for something.

"What is it?" I ask, suddenly curious.

"Several years ago, when I was little, a red panda came to my grandmother's home and spoke with her at length. She told him all sorts of stories, and he wrote most of them down. She kept insisting that they were just stories, but he seemed to think that they were real and that she knew more than she was telling." She flips a page and suddenly points. "That's him! That's the one that she talked to," she exclaims, pointing to the name, "Terador."

"Can you tell when he wrote this?"

She scans the page again, then flips a page and continues looking. "I don't see a date here, but it can't be more than ten years old. I was almost eight when he visited."

I give her a funny look. "You're eighteen?"

"Yes," she answers, returning my odd look. "I'm an adult, have been for two years now." Her head tilts, giving me a curious look. "How old are you?"

I think for a moment. "Well, if I go with how many years I've been awake, I think I'm close to thirty, but if you add the time I spent sleeping, I'm over a thousand."

Her jaw drops and her eyes widen in surprise.

"What?" I ask, suddenly concerned.

She fumbles with the book, flipping pages. When she hands it back to me, I see "The Sleeper" on top of the page. She points to it, so I start reading. I don't get too far into it when I realize "It's me!"

She nods. "When she told the stories, my brothers and I thought that they were just that, stories."

"What are you two shouting about?" Railu asks, staggering out of her room, holding her hands over her ears.

I look at her, finding something oddly familiar about her behavior. I look back at Tayla suspiciously. When she notices that I'm looking at her, her ears lay back, ashamed. "What did you two do last night?" I find myself asking.

"I picked up a bottle of something called Baijiu," Railu confesses.

"How much did you drink?" I ask, fearing the answer.

Tayla looks down, more ashamed. "About half the bottle."

Railu picks up the bottle from one of the smaller tables and shows me.

"Did you know it has alcohol?" I ask, putting my hand on Railu's head.

Tayla's ears droop. "No."

Railu gives a heavy sigh of relief as Aime takes care of her headache.

"Congratulations, you both had a hangover," I chastise as I take the bottle from Railu.

I pop the cork and get a whiff. "Whew, that's strong," I comment as I pull it away and put the cork back.

"It is white liqueur, 70 percent alcohol," Aime states.

I set the bottle in the middle of the table. "Don't let the kids get a hold of that."

"We won't," Railu states as she sits next to me. "What's the book about?" she asks.

"Myths, and apparently I'm one of them," I offer, showing her the page about "The Sleeper."

She takes the book and starts reading, her eyes going wide in surprise as she notices similarities. "Oh, wow," she says, looking up at me. "You weren't kidding when you told me that, were you?"

"No, I wasn't. I have a feeling that the myths in that book are all based on real facts. I've already read the ones about humans and Sage and they're relatively correct."

"How can you assume that they're all true, from just three of them?" she asks.

"Because they're all from the same storyteller," I comment.

"How can you be sure?" she asks again.

"Because my grandmother never told the stories any other way. I've heard them dozens of times and it was like she was reading from a book. They never changed."

"How did she learn them?" Railu urges.

"She never told anyone."

"Could we go ask her?"

Tayla looks down, sullen. "She passed, several months ago. She had been getting interviewed by the council. I think they wanted her to become one."

I think for a moment, then I have a revelation. "*Now* it makes sense," I interject.

"What does?" Railu asks, puzzled.

"When I first met with the head councilor in Pridewyn, I got the impression that she knew I was coming, and what I was going to do." I look at Tayla. "Your grandmother must have told the elders her stories, and since they had Sage to confirm most of them, they must have believed the rest of them."

"Is that why they allowed you in the Trials?" Tayla asks.

"Not really. Kotu stole my signet and entered me. The head councilor saw through my disguise and then gave me the option to bow out, but I chose to stay in."

"What better way to learn about a people than to join in the activities," Arru offers, joining the conversation.

"That's kind of what I was thinking at the time," I admit, "but it was mostly just curiosity of my own abilities."

"And what better way to test your own abilities than the Trials," Larrah comments, also joining us.

I look out a window, noticing how bright it's getting. "I better wake the kids. Breakfast will be soon."

Before I can get up out of my chair, Fey groggily walks out of her room, followed by an equally groggy Kotu. Sada follows them, looking fresh and ready to face the day.

"Good morning," Tayla teases, getting groans in response.

"Better get ready for breakfast," I call to the kids. "Megai's walking down the hall."

Kotu focuses on the door for a moment, then says, "No, she's not."

Megai opens the door and giggles. "That's because I'm already here."

Getting a mix of looks, I hold my hands up in surrender. "What? It was a lucky guess."

Megai graciously takes the heat off me by announcing, "As you have *guessed*, breakfast is ready." She smiles again as she bows and closes the door behind her.

During breakfast, the lead mediator enters the dining hall. "Kyle," she says, trying not to be distracted by the food, "the council would like to see you at your earliest convenience."

Swallowing a mouthful of pastry, I manage to croak, "My convenience?"

"Correct."

We all look back at her, confused, for a moment before Arru comments, "That's unusual."

The mediator catches herself looking at the food and turns her attention back to us. "Yes, it is. I was not privy to the nature of the request, but I heard some arguing from within the chamber before the request was made." She glances back at the buffet table again.

I see that she's unable to keep her eyes off the food. "Are you hungry?"

"I was called to the council before I could get breakfast," she explains.

"I won't tell if you don't." I make a gesture to the food. "Grab something."

She bows. "Oh, thank you" and darts over to the buffet table.

I look at Megai, who nods and whispers, "She is telling the truth. I couldn't make out anything specific as everyone, including Sage, was trying to talk at once. No one sounded happy."

"Thank you," I whisper back to her, turning back to the others. "This could be good, or this could be really bad." Fearing the latter, I add, "Keep your eyes and ears open."

I finish my juice and stand to leave when I notice the mediator stuffing the last piece of a pastry into her mouth. "Don't choke on it," I lightly chide.

She covers her mouth, embarrassed, and finishes chewing. "Sorry, I needed that." She then downs the last of her juice and hands the dish to Megai, bowing. "Thank you."

Megai bows back. "You're welcome, Mediator."

I follow the mediator across the street, and she ushers me inside the council chamber. I walk to the middle of the room and wait to be addressed.

The senior council member sighs. "Master Kyle, thank you for seeing us on such short notice. It is the unanimous decision of this council that you, having the most authority, are to take charge of this village."

Realizing just how desperate they are to have their problems solved for them, I skip protocol. "What? Why?"

He sighs and looks to his right. "Financier, if you please."

The council member he looked at nods. "Two years ago, the karnesh showed up. The harvesters started disappearing. Some were . . . eaten. Others, we think, left to other villages. At Sage's advice, we issued vouchers to the harvesters, to encourage them to keep working. More disappeared, so we increased the value of the vouchers. Last year we had to take more drastic measures to keep food production going so people wouldn't starve. We had to order harvesters to work and again increased the value of the vouchers."

"Needless to say," the senior councilor takes over, "we are at a point where we are in debt to our people, with no foreseeable way out."

Picking up the hint, I ask, "So you want me to take over and get you out of this mess?"

He looks down, ashamed. "We would not put it so bluntly, but you are correct."

I sigh heavily, looking around the room at the various members. "What advice did Sage give you on how to deal with this?"

He sighs again. "We felt that Sage was the cause of this problem, so we did not discuss it in his presence."

"That was your mistake," I scold. "I have almost three months of practical memory. I don't remember much before then. Fortunately, I have an advisor of my own, Aime, who I listen to a lot. She has saved my life quite a few times, earning my complete trust.

"You have an advisor too," I continue. "Sage has all the learned knowledge of thousands of leaders. He was set up here to help you through any type of problem. I seriously doubt that he would start you on a path, dealing with a major problem, without having a way out."

"If he had a plan to get us out of this, he never shared it with us," the senior council member argues.

"Did you ask?" I retort, knowing that AIs will not normally volunteer information without being asked. The council members all shake their heads, so I ask, "Sage?"

"Now that I'm fully aware of your concerns, council members, I can tell you that the best way out of debt will take about two years and will require establishing a bank."

I stop him before he gets too far into his description. "See, he has a plan. Are you willing to heed his advice?"

Most of the councilors look shocked at first but then shamefully nod. The senior member speaks up, "We are."

"Good, I want you to keep in mind that Sage is here for the village's well-being. If needed, he will tell you exactly what to do, but he can't do it for you, and if you don't talk to him about a problem, he won't be able to help you with it."

The senior member sighs. "You seem to be wiser than us."

"No, I'm not," I correct. "I was put in a situation where I had to rely on someone I didn't know to survive. I simply *chose* to trust her, just as you must choose to trust Sage."

He bows his head slightly. "Thank you, Master Kyle, for your help." The rest of the council bows in kind, so I return the bow and head back to the inn. Stopping by the dining hall, I manage to snag another pastry and juice before the kitchen staff puts them away and head to my room.

When I open the door, everyone stops what they were doing and looks at me. I look around the room. Tayla and Larrah are polishing there armors, Railu is lacing up one of her leggings, Megai brushes Sada's back while Sada works on her own tail. Kotu just sits with an unhappy look on his face while Arru works on some of the knots in his tangled tail tuft as Fey watches.

"That was unexpected," I comment.

"But you handled it well," Arru compliments, pulling a knot of fur out of Kotu's tail.

Slightly puzzled, I look at Megai.

"I narrated what I heard," she says with a slight bow and turns her attention back to brushing Sada's back.

"You did tell us to keep our eyes and *ears* open," Larrah points out.

"I did, didn't I?" I admit, "Well, I guess it saves me the trouble of repeating it."

"It seems like you managed to get the council mess sorted out without much effort," Tayla commends.

"Leaving us with a celebration in our honor," Railu adds.

"I don't do parties," Larrah states.

"Then why are you polishing your armor?" Arru skeptically asks.

Larrah looks at her dryly. "I'm oiling it so it lasts longer."

Railu and Tayla both chuckle, but I offer, "Then you can attend as a guard. Enjoying yourself is optional."

"I might be able to handle that."

I turn to Megai. "Would you be able to join us?"

"I'll be there," she replies, "but I won't be able to join you at your table. I have my own invite from the council."

We spend at least a few hours just getting ourselves cleaned up and dressed. Megai spends a good amount of time helping, either brushing fur or helping with the small details of our outfits. I am pleased to see that most of the girls had picked up new outfits from the market.

Tayla's wearing a two-piece wrap; the top covers her right shoulder while still showing her midriff, the skirt dips just below her knees. The whole thing is a mid-toned brown, matching her spots, but with golden thread inlay throughout to accent. She's also wearing a pair of brown leather straps, wrapped in a crisscross style, from just above her foot-pads to her ankles.

Sada's outfit is almost the same, but in a light blue, matching her eyes, with her left shoulder covered instead. Her upper feet are wrapped with black leather crisscrossed straps. Both girls have bracelets, matching their dresses.

Larrah has donned a flowing black one-piece wrap with white accents throughout. I notice that the lower part of her dress has several splits, allowing her to move freely. She does not wear any wraps on her feet but is wearing a set of black bracelets.

Railu's outfit is more unusual. Its top is a pleated strip of fabric that wraps around her neck from behind, crossing in front, covering her breasts, then wraps her ribs and joins her dress near her tail, leaving her upper back and stomach exposed. The skirt is a spiral wrap, starting in front of her left knee and getting shorter as it wraps behind her, leaving her right leg almost completely exposed. Both pieces are black with muted red trim, allowing her red fur to stand out. She too wears leather straps crisscrossed around her upper feet, but against her black fur, they are difficult to see.

Kotu is wearing a simple light brown toga while Fey is wearing the same blue two-piece I saw her in yesterday, though now it fits her properly, having had help from Megai putting it on.

Arru has somehow managed to find a rather elegant one-piece dress. It's a black open-back design, with a single strap across her right shoulder, and a split from her left hip down. She has a reddish-brown belt around her waist, matching her fur. Like Sada, she wears black leather straps wrapped around her upper feet. I stare for a moment, admiring how she makes it work, even with all of her fur fluffed.

I'm wearing my armor, per Arru's instructions. She has told me that it's proper for warriors to wear their armor at events. I've also attached some of the new scales to the armor, putting them along the arms, legs, and some other areas, to give it a more native appearance. Aime indicates that the addition of the scale actually increases the defense rating of my armor.

With just over an hour till midday and everyone finally ready, I give Megai a kiss for all her help this morning as we depart for the village center. On our way, we meet several people heading to the banquet. This is the busiest I've seen this village since I've arrived.

As we approach the village center, I notice that the pavilion looks like a greatly oversized oval hut without walls. Getting closer, I see several dozen dining tables set up with several chairs at each. Across one end, there is a pair of long head tables, with chairs on one side, so the occupants can see everyone under the pavilion. Between those two tables is a podium.

Seeing us approach, the lead mediator comes out to meet us. She ushers us to one of the head tables and promptly seats us. Servers bring drinks as we wait for the banquet to start. I find myself sitting toward the middle of the table with Sada on my left and Tayla on my right. Beyond Sada sits Fey, Arru, and Railu and beyond Tayla sits Kotu and Larrah. I notice that there is an empty chair at each end of our table, as well as three extra chairs at the council's table.

As we wait, the villagers fill in the available seats. Apparently the planners didn't expect so many people, as the servers quickly start setting up more tables, trying to keep up with the growing crowd. It doesn't take long for these to fill either.

Now with seating taken up, people start lining the outside of the pavilion. The four other mediators try to keep people organized while the lead mediator occasionally talks with the service staff or inspects various things at the other head table. I figure she's playing the part of hostess.

The council arrives via a long open-top carriage pulled by a jata. The crowd settles as the mediators gather at the carriage step. The first few councilors exit without needing much help but the others, including the senior councilor rely on the mediators for stability until they're on the flat ground. Once out, they slowly walk to their table, as the crowd watches in silence.

With everyone seated, a large group of servers come out of the kitchen carrying large trays of food. I find myself pleased to see that Megai is one of our table's servers. It soon becomes obvious that she is in charge of our table when she starts directing the other two servers where to put various dishes. When she sees that I'm watching her, she smiles but continues her work.

"I thought you had an invite?" I ask as she works.

"I do! I was invited to be the lead server for the guest of honor. Aside from where you're sitting, it's the best place to be during one of these events." As she explains she helps set out various bowls and makes sure that they all have serving tools.

Looking around, I notice that Janik seems to be in charge of the council's table, also having two servers to direct. All around, the servers place large platters and bowls of all sorts of food on the tables. I also notice that everyone seems to be waiting for something as the servers work, not yet touching the food. The mediators sit in the remaining chairs at each end of both head tables.

As the servers finish, the senior councilor stands, looks to the podium like he wants to walk there, but changes his mind and raises his hands, the crowd quickly hushes. "Let us thank our farmers and our hunters, for bringing in this food. Let us thank Master Kyle and his companions for ridding us of the beast. May we all rejoice in our re-gained freedom."

As the councilman sits, the crowd erupts in a surprisingly calm ova-tion and Arru turns and suspiciously looks at me. The servers then start pulling lids off the various dishes, so people can start eating. Megai pulls the cover off the largest dish at our table and I see that it's a pair of baked ma'pai, with several types of dipping sauces around them. The other dishes contain various vegetables, fruits, and fresh breads.

As we eat, some of the villagers make their way to our table. They po-litely, yet enthusiastically, introduce themselves and give their personal thanks, a gesture that I find more meaningful than that of the senior councilmen's. We graciously accept their thanks and I often find my-self complimenting the farmers for having the guts to still get out in the fields to work when they knew that the beast could be nearby. I notice that several of them often agree, even expressing earnest gratitude for the return compliment.

After the council has finished, the lead mediator gives a signal and the food and dishes are cleared from all the tables, but the servers soon return with serving trays loaded with dessert. I find myself surprised at the dish that Megai places before me, vanilla ice cream. Megai notices my shocked expression. "Is there something wrong?" she asks.

"I haven't had ice cream in almost three months," I admit.

She smiles. "Glad we can surprise you."

I scoop some up and almost put it in my mouth when I realize some-thing that makes me abruptly stop. The only mammals on this planet are all evolved species; reptiles don't produce milk. With that thought stuck in my head, I put the spoon down and quickly realize that every-one at the table is looking at me, both curious and confused.

Trying to act calm about my sudden thought, I curiously ask, "What do you use for the milk?"

Megai smiles. "We have both soy and rice styles for everyone else," she explains, "but they aren't very good. I brought up the good stuff for you from the inn. It's coconut ice cream. Tita imports it."

Fears allayed, I take a bite. Aside from the hint of coconut flavor, it's very much like the dairy ice cream I remember. "Thank you," I say, giving her a slight nod.

She bows as one of the other servers sets a few small pitchers of various syrups on the table. I notice that one of the pitchers of chocolate at the other end of the table quickly disappears, and I use the other to periodically drizzle a little over my ice cream to hide the taste of the coconut.

After dessert, the council retreats to the carriage, returning to the council hall. The lead mediator announces that a street fair has been organized that will last until twilight. She encourages every to enjoy themselves and be safe.

As we get up from the table, I personally thank Megai for getting the coconut ice cream. She says she needs to stay and help clean up the pavilion but will see us later at the inn. Larrah promptly informs us that she will return to our room, not wanting to partake in the festivities. Railu quickly disappears into the crowded streets. We wander around for a while before Arru sees something of interest and breaks from the group.

Down to just Tayla, Sada, the kids, and I, we start browsing some of the game booths, letting the kids play to their hearts' content. I find that Kotu is trying to show off at some of the games involving skill, though he quickly learns that he still needs some practice.

We spend over an hour at the various games when Larrah comes running up. "Kyle! Something's wrong with Railu!"

"What!"

"She came back, hunched over holding her stomach. She said she felt sick, and then she started twitching and fell to the floor."

I turn to Sada and Tayla. "Stay with the kids," I shout as I break into a full run back to the inn.

Arriving quickly, I duck inside my room to find Megai trying to calm a convulsing Railu. I jump over a couch to get to them and quickly put my hands on Railu's stomach and head.

Aime does a quick scan and reports, "Theobromine poisoning. She's had too much chocolate. We need to empty her stomach."

"Megai, I hope you don't have a weak stomach," I say, rolling Railu on her side.

"No, I don't, why?" she asks, as I move my hand down to Railu's stomach.

Before I can answer her, Railu wretches, puking on the floor. Reflexively, Megai and I both turn our heads away, not wanting to see what came out.

Megai recovers quickly, retrieving several towels from the washroom as I slide Railu away from the expanding chocolate-vomit puddle.

"Keep her airway open. She's seizing," Aime commands.

Megai throws a couple towels over the puddle and turns to me to help. "I need you to grab her tongue and pull it out and to the side." I use three fingers to wedge Railu's mouth open. Fortunately, Megai's hand is small enough to reach undermine into Railu's mouth and grab her tongue.

After several seconds, her seizures start to diminish. "I have given her an anti-seizure medicine, but she has ingested a lot of chocolate. I will need to monitor her heart while I continue to remove the theobromine from her system."

"You can let go," I reposition my hands, one on her back over her heart, and the other over her stomach.

Megai grabs a towel and gently cleans the vomit from Railu's face. "What's theobromine?"

I find myself remembering what it is before Aime can tell me. "It's found in chocolate. In large enough quantities, it can make someone sick."

"Will the others get sick too?" she asks, concerned.

"I don't like chocolate," Arru answers as she walks in. "How's she doing?"

"She's stabilized, but Aime needs to keep removing the toxin and monitor her. I won't be going anywhere for a little while anyway." Seeing Tayla and Sada walk in, I quickly add, "Don't let the kids in yet. They don't need to see this."

Megai quickly gets up and retrieves a mop and bucket from the closet in the hall. I'm somewhat surprised when Larrah helps Megai clean up the mess. Megai then gently sprays something over the damp area and the leftover smell soon dissipates. Tayla and Sada then let the kids in.

As the other sit and watch, Railu starts to wake up, having blacked out during the seizures. "Ugh."

I lean over her, so she can see me easily. "Welcome back."

Megai kneels next to her and gently asks, "How much chocolate did you have?"

"I had a few bars at the fair," she weakly replies. "Why?"

"You also had all the chocolate syrup in the dessert pitcher," Arru adds.

"While the syrup was more concentrated, she would still need to eat another kilogram of the semisweet chocolate to account for the amount in her system."

"Railu, how big were the bars?" I ask.

She reaches into a pouch on her belt and pulls one out.

I take it from her, knowing Aime will scan it through the paper wrapping. "She had to have eaten at least six of these."

"How many did you buy?" I ask.

She looks at the bar and reaches to her pouch again and finds nothing. "I bought eight, one for each of us. Mine was so good that I had another as I watched some dancers. I must have kept eating them as I watched. I started feeling sick, so I came back here."

"You ate *seven* bars?" Megai asks skeptically.

"And a pitcher of syrup," I add. "No wonder you're so sick."

"I have removed most of the theobromine from her system. She will still have an upset stomach for a while, but she will be all right."

"Aime says you'll be okay, but you're going to have a stomach ache for a while," I gently inform her. "You should get cleaned up and get some rest."

"Get cleaned up, why?" she asks, puzzled.

"'Cause I had to make you throw up," I tell her as I help her sit up.

"That explains the taste in my mouth, but why does it feel like someone pulled my tongue?"

"Megai had to hold it to keep you from choking on it."

Railu gives me a startled look. "Why?"

"You were convulsing." I sit back and sigh. "Listen, chocolate contains something called theobromine. Like sugar, it's one of the things that make it so good, but it also can be bad for you. If you have a lot, it will make you sick to your stomach. Unlike sugar, if you have way too much, you'll have seizures and could even die."

I look at her and realize that everyone in the room is looking back at me, some startled, some scared. "Look, you can have it, just not a lot of it. A bar a day would be fine. Eat it slowly, enjoy the flavor, limit yourself. If you get an upset stomach, put the chocolate away until you feel better." I turn back to Railu. "Just don't have eight bars in an hour."

"Why does everything good have side effects?" Railu asks, holding her stomach.

I help her to her feet. "Don't let it bother you. Anything can be bad for you if you have too much."

"Not water," Kotu tries pointing out.

"Even water," Larrah corrects.

Kotu cowers as Railu starts for the shower. I take off my armor and sit down on a couch. Noticing the chocolate bar, I open it and break off a corner.

"What are you doing?" Tayla asks sternly.

Putting the chocolate chunk on my tongue, I realize she was talking to me. "Who, me?"

"You just watched her throw up all that and now you're eating some?" she chastises.

"It doesn't really seem to bother me, I guess." I put my head back and enjoy the flavor until the piece has dissolved.

Everyone else takes the opportunity to change back to their normal clothes as I sit and enjoy another piece of chocolate. Megai meekly sits next to me. "You are a warrior and a shaman?" she asks, sounding unusually small.

"Hmm?" I sit up, puzzled by both her question and her sudden meekness.

"A healer," she offers. "I heard Aime's instructions, and you did more than just follow directions."

I sit up for a moment, mentally reviewing what I did versus what Aime had told me to do. I realize that I did a lot more than she had instructed. "How did I know how to do that?"

"Maybe it was reflexive knowledge," Aime answers.

"What's 'reflexive knowledge,'" Megai asks, puzzled.

"Reflexive memory is basically things you can do without thinking about it. Things like eating, walking, talking, opening doors . . . stuff like that," I state.

She thinks for a moment. "So if that was reflexive knowledge, you've had some practice with seizures?"

I nod and add, "With how easily that came to me, I'd guess that I have more than practice."

"Is that good or bad?"

I think for a moment, trying to come up with a logical reason. "Considering it probably means I was around someone who had seizures, I don't know," I confess.

Seeing how uncomfortable I am, she changes the subject, "You told me Aime was your conscience, but she not, is she?"

I chuckle. "I'm not really sure how to describe Aime," I admit. "She lives inside me . . . keeps me healthy . . . teaches me a whole bunch of stuff. She also does what I tell her, or what my actions imply to her like when Railu was convulsing, she understood what I wanted her to do without me needing to say or think it."

Megai thinks for a moment. "She sounds like your helper spirit, and that would make you a shaman."

"I'm not a shaman," I insist, "and Aime is not a spirit."

She looks skeptically at me. "What makes you so sure?"

"Well, if Aime was my helper spirit, how many people would be able to hear her?"

She thinks for a moment. "Normally just shamans can hear the spirits."

I smile. "Okay, you've heard Aime."

Tayla comes out of her room as Megai argues, "But I have really good hearing."

"I've heard her too," Tayla offers, "and so has Larrah."

"Me too," calls Fey.

I shrug. "See, too many have heard Aime for her to be a spirit."

"Then what is she?" Megai asks, confused.

"I'm not sure how to describe her to you," I admit. "Aime?"

"In the simplest form, I am a tool. A very smart, complex tool."

Megai looks at me curiously. I just shrug. A knock at the door interrupts us and Megai opens it. Janik stands outside, says a few words to Megai, and then departs down the hall. Megai turns to us. "Please, excuse me," she says and, bowing, departs the room.

Tayla takes the opportunity to speak up. "See, we're not the only ones that thought you a shaman," she points out.

"I know," I counter, "if I didn't know better I'd think I'm a shaman too, but that's the problem. I *do* know better."

"Speaking of what people think you are," Arru interrupts as she exits her room, dressed in a more casual kimono-style gown, "when did the council start calling you master?"

I think for a moment. "This morning, when they called me over during breakfast."

She sits across from me. "Please tell me that they didn't ask you to be their leader," she says, shaking her head in dismay.

"Uhm, okay, what they really did was *tell* me I was in charge of the village." Her expression turns to one of surprise and her jaw drops open. Tayla half falls, half sits in the nearest chair, also surprised.

"What!" Larrah asks from the other side of the room, also looking at me in surprise.

"What?" I ask, confused.

Arru recovers slightly. "They put you in charge of the village. You're now the Sovereign of Arindell," she explains.

"Sovereign?" I stutter.

"That's why they've been calling you master."

I sit in shock, unsure of what to do or say. Tayla just stares at me, a mild look of shock on her face. Larrah sits with a puzzled look, her eyes darting between me and Arru.

"Aime, did Sage know about this?" I ask.

"He made no indication to me about the council's plans, though he did express his surprise at their actions."

"How could they have come to this decision without Sage knowing?" Tayla asks.

"Unsure. Sage had indicated to me that they had not left the chamber since their return yesterday."

I sigh heavily and then ask, "Could they have made this decision while they were at the Farm View?"

"If they did, they did it before we arrived."

"Great." I sigh, slouching on the couch. "Pendekar, Shaman, now Sovereign? What am I doing to myself?" I ask, looking up at the ceiling.

"It sounds like this was beyond your control," Arru consoles.

"Maybe, but I can't help but think I said something wrong."

"Did you?"

"No, he did not," Aime interjects. "If you like I can replay the entire conversation for you."

As if on queue, Sada walks out of our bedroom carrying a tablet and hands it to Arru. I pay little attention to the screen as Aime begins playing back this morning's meeting with the council, all from my point of view. Everyone else gathers around, watching the screen.

Almost immediately, Arru comments, "Oh dear."

"What?"

"They called you master right from the beginning."

"Yeah."

"That means that they had already conceded power to you. You did not have any say in the matter, or something got said earlier . . . Aime, I need to see the other visits to the council, from the beginning."

I lean back as the screen starts playing the first visit to the council, the day we arrived. I follow mentally as it plays. Suddenly Arru gasps, "Uh-oh," and pauses the playback. She puts the tablet down and takes a deep breath. "It's Sage's fault and I don't think he meant to do it," she explains. "He was just trying to explain his responding to you."

"Great, a slip of the tongue, and I'm in charge of a whole village. Aime, let's try to make sure that doesn't happen again."

"Agreed, adjusting the upload data accordingly."

"What? You're in charge of the village?" a drowsy Railu asks as she comes out of her room.

"Yeah, I am."

"Wow," she groggily exclaims, sitting in the nearest seat. "Now what? I thought we were leaving tomorrow."

"We are." I turn to Arru. "What can I say to the council to convince them to stay in charge?"

"You'll need to give them an assignment that will keep them occupied until you return."

"Until I return?"

"They will expect you to return, but if you don't, they should resume control."

"You did have them start clearing the debt, following Sage's instruction," Aime offers, speaking through the tablet for all to hear.

"That was what, a two-year plan?"

"Correct."

"You may want to remind them of that and let them know that you are leaving, to complete your own task," Arru suggests.

"When would you suggest I do that?"

"First thing in the morning, after breakfast," she states. "Then we leave. That way they can't argue with you about it."

A weak knock at the door interrupts us. "Come on in, Megai," I say.

She opens the door, bows, and steps in. "Supper will be in an hour." She starts solemnly passing out the menus. She saves me for last and sits down next to me as she hands me the menu.

I look at her curiously. "What's wrong."

She looks at me, then at the floor. "Pendekar, Shaman, and Sovereign? What am I supposed to call you? How am I supposed to act around you?"

I touch her cheek, gently turning her to me. "I'm no different than I was yesterday when you didn't know. Treat me no differently today."

She swallows, but nods, obviously still conflicted. "Megai, I don't claim to be anything. These are titles that others have given me. *I* didn't want them. I don't tell anyone about them because I want the people around me to be themselves." I gently put my forehead to hers. "I don't ask for any special treatment, especially from anyone in this room. That includes you."

"Okay," she manages to whisper. "I've never known someone so important before."

"You knew me before you knew that," I point out, hugging her. "So just keep being yourself."

She hugs me back. "I'll try."

"Thank you. I'm sorry to ask, but could you not tell anyone?"

She nods and then looks around at the others. "Welcome to the club," Railu says, smiling.

Megai looks up at her, confused. "Club?"

"It means, you know what they know." I tell her, "Seems to be more of a joke though."

She looks at me curiously. "Why?"

I smile. "How much do you know about me?"

She thinks for a moment, but Arru interrupts her, "That's the joke. None of us know more than the last three months of his life, except Sada."

"And her knowledge is from a very unique point of view," I add.

Megai looks at me curiously. "Why don't you remember?"

I open the menu and start browsing. "Amnesia. I slept too long."

She gets a confused look on her face. "How long is too long?"

Not looking up from the menu, I answer, "Thousand years."

"How?"

"Frozen," Larrah answers.

"And you're alive, how?"

"Aime," Tayla answers.

Megai sits for a moment and then asks, "Is there anything else?"

"Only that I'm going to a place known as the Dig." I point to the book of myths sitting on the table.

"That's a myth," she insists.

"I know many things in that book to be true," I confess. "I'm proof of at least two of them, and you know about Sage, also a myth and the beast that was outside the village was a karnesh."

"Really?" she gasps, genuinely surprised. "But how do you know the rest are real too?"

"Because they're all by the same storyteller," Tayla says, "my grand-mother."

Megai suddenly sits up. "Oh, I forgot, Tita's waiting for your supper orders."

Having been looking at the menu, I promptly give her my choice and how I'd like it cooked. The others take their turns, and Megai soon departs.

Sada sits next to me, giving me a curious look. 'Are you going to ask her?'

'I'm not sure. Would you have a problem with that?' I sign back.

'No. I was just curious. I could tell that you trust her.

'I can't help it, she's an honest person.'

"I hate it when you two don't include others in the conversation," Tayla chides.

"Sorry," I say as Sada goes over to her and hugs her.

I pick up the book of myths and start reading as Tayla asks, "So what were you talking about?"

"Choices," I answer, turning a page. "Choices that can change someone's life."

She sits down next to me. "Your choices, or someone else's choices?"

"Both," I confess, as I start to read about the Ghost of Garrent.

She gently leans on me, looking at the drawing on the page. "I wonder if it really looks that way."

Seeing the ameba-like shape of the ghost, I can't help but chuckle. "I would have never thought a ghost would look like that."

"What do you think it should look like?"

I look at her curiously. "More like it did before it died, but I don't believe in ghosts."

Tayla gives me a shocked look. "But you said that the myths were true!"

"I said the myth was based in truth, but even truth is subject to interpretation." I flip to the pages about the Great White Dragon. "Read the eye witness accounts and tell me what you think it is."

I hand her the book and grab the tablet off the table. While she reads the accounts I have Aime pull up an image of the rescue ship as it would have appeared on approach.

When Tayla puts the book down, I ask, "Well, what did you picture?"

She thinks for a moment. "Something like a der'ock, but more graceful."

"And flies during the day?" I ask.

She looks puzzled. "Yeah, that one I can't explain. Nothing flies that high during the day."

I hand her the tablet. "When I first read it, that's what I thought of," I say, pointing to the tablet.

She takes the tablet and looks carefully at the picture. She then looks back at the book, rereading some of the descriptions. Larrah, Arru, and Railu take interest in our conversation and circle around behind Tayla to get a look.

"What is that?" Railu asks.

"Remember I told you about where I woke up, the facility?"

"Yeah."

"This is a spaceship that came to try to save the people that worked there."

Tayla looks at me with a puzzled look on her face. She looks like she's about to ask a question when her face lights up. "So what do *you* think the ghost is?" she asks.

"Well, Garrent is an abandoned village. So if it was set up anything like the others, it's probably a very lonely, abandoned Sage. How long has it been abandoned anyway?"

"If the stories I've heard are true, about two hundred years," Arru states.

"I hate to think how he is holding up after all this time," Aime notes.

"Can it still fly?" Tayla's eyes fill with wonder.

"It needs some work, but it could," I confess.

"I've always wondered what it would feel like to fly."

"Keep to the ground. It's a lot safer," Larrah chides.

Tayla's face turns to a slight pout for a moment, but a knock at the door interrupts. "Enter," I call.

Megai enters with the supper cart, followed by Janik with a drink cart. We all set down our things and I set the book over the tablet to hide it from view. I find myself between Sada and Tayla again, noticing that this is getting to be a common seating arrangement. Supper goes well, Megai and Janik keeping things moving while the rest of us enjoy ourselves, knowing this is our last supper here.

After supper, Megai surprises us with a two-course dessert, coconut ice cream, and cake. She also doesn't bring any chocolate, something Railu is grateful for. This time, I indulge in a little mint syrup for my ice cream, finding it does a better job of covering the coconut flavor. The cake is cinnamon covered, much like the one I had at the Farm View. We all eat our fill of both.

Adjourning from the table, Railu grabs the book and sits down with it to read. Knowing Aime scanned the whole book when I flipped through it, I have her put up a copy on the tablet and continue reading. To my surprise, Tayla sits next to me and rests her head on my shoulder, purring. I find myself occasionally scrubbing her cheek to keep her purring, finding the sound as relaxing as Sada's, even if it is a bit different.

Sada stretches out on a couch opposite me and happily watches Tayla rest. Arru and Larrah both pick up a couple vouchers and head out, while Kotu and Fey quietly play a board game together.

The evening progresses rather quietly, with Railu and I both finishing the book. Arru and Larrah return just before twilight, both with a few new items. With the sun beginning to set, everyone gets ready for bed.

While I change for bed, Sada suddenly leaves the room, so I climb into bed and stretch out on my back. I'm about to drift off when I hear my door open. I open my eyes and see Sada crawl into bed, already wearing her pajamas. Then I notice a saddened Megai standing just inside the doorway, wearing a simple robe, apparently ready for bed.

"You're leaving tomorrow, aren't you?" she quietly asks, sitting down on the foot of the bed.

I sit up. "I have to."

She sighs. "Will you come back?"

Several answers come to mind, but I decide to go with the honest one. "I don't know," I confess. "I haven't really given much thought to what I'm going to do after."

She closes her eyes. I see a tear roll down her nose and realize that she's starting to cry. Sada also sees this and reaches out and wipes the tear away.

I take her hand. "Come with us."

She stays quiet for a moment, then answers, "I can't."

"Why?"

"What could I possibly offer to your group? I can't fight. I can't cook. I don't really know how to do anything but what I do here at the inn," she argues.

"I don't need you to do any of that," I comfort her. "I would like you to be with me."

She looks at me, then at Sada. "I would love to be with you. I feel at ease with you and your group, but I can't leave. My place is here." She fidgets with her gold bracelet and starts to get up, but I don't let her go.

"Then stay with me tonight."

She looks curiously at Sada and back at me. "With both of you?"

"To sleep."

A small look of relief crosses her face. "To sleep," she agrees and drops her robe to the floor, revealing a blue version of the bikini she wore yesterday.

I lie back, pulling the bunny girl with me to my right on the bed. Sada flips the blanket over us and curls up to my left side. Megai takes a little longer getting comfortable, settling on her left side with her hand on my chest. Sada nuzzles into my neck so I start rubbing their backs, making them both purr softly, and I drift asleep.

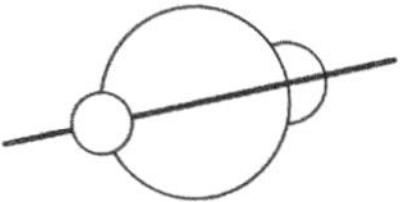

The sun starting to shine in a window wakes me up. With both Sada and Megai still asleep, I slip out from between them, grab some clothes, and walk out to the common room to dress. Finding the room empty, I quickly change into the light armor and pull a shirt and long shorts over top of it. I slip into my boots and walk over to the window. Parting the blinds slightly I stand and watch the sun slowly come up.

I keep looking out the window as I hear someone softly walk up behind me. "I'm gonna miss her," I find myself absently confessing. "I've known her for almost three days and I feel I can trust her with anything. I don't want to lose that." I pause for a moment, feeling tears roll down my face. "I asked her to come with us. I want her to come with us. She said her place is here. I won't force her. I have to respect her decision."

More tears roll down my face but I ignore them. "Three days, is it even possible to fall in love with someone in three days?"

I suddenly feel arms wrap around me from behind. "Yes, it is," Megai says, softly crying.

I turn around and wrap her in a hug, and we stand there holding each other, not saying a word. I feel my tears flow from my eyes, grieving the loss that is to come. As the sun gets brighter, we both realize that she has to leave. I put my forehead to hers. "I love you."

She presses her cheek to mine and whispers in my ear, "I love you too." Still crying, she quietly walks out the door.

Sada slowly comes up to me, and I see that she too has been crying. 'You hurt, I hurt,' she signs and gives me a hug that I gratefully return.

Arru is the first to come out of her room. Upon seeing me and Sada, still hugging, my face still tear-streaked, she walks over to me. "Tears of love and pain," she says, rubbing the streaks from my cheek. "Never easy to let go of someone you've come to care about so fast." She touches her nose gently to my cheek. "Come on, we still have work to do."

I reluctantly let Sada go as Arru hands me a wet washcloth. "Can't let the council see that you've been crying."

I wipe my face down with the cloth as I return to my room. Once there, I put on the rest of my armor. Sada comes in and helps me put on the cloak, positioning it so it looks like a cape. I pin it in place with my signet, the real one, not the copy. Sada hands me my weapons, and I position them in their usual places. She hands me the mask, but instead of putting it on, I put it over my left shoulder, so I can put it on after breakfast.

I have Aime use the converter to make some pictures. I put those in a pouch and then I quickly pack my things into my pack and carry it out to the common room. I set it next to a couch and grab the money box and dump it on the table.

I quickly separate the vouchers from the coins. Aime gives me a quick count of forty-five vouchers and thirteen thousand seven hundred forty-three in coin. I stop for a moment, wondering how the coin count went up, and then I realize that we've been dropping the change in the box, and only taking out vouchers.

I put the coin in a larger pocket on my armor. "Did anyone want to make any last purchases before we leave?" I ask, looking around. Getting only negative responses, I put the vouchers in the pouch with the pictures, and we head to breakfast.

The others get plates of food while I opt for pastries and juice. As I sit, I find myself both relieved and concerned that Megai is not in the room. Janik works the breakfast tables in her absence.

As I eat, I try to distract myself by mentally reviewing what I need to talk to the council about with Aime. After finishing my second pastry, I decide to go talk to the council. I finish my drink and put my mask on.

Walking into the council hut, I'm greeted once again by the lead mediator. She bows. "Welcome, Master Kyle. What can I do for you?"

I return the bow. "Is the council available? I would like to speak with them."

She looks at the door to the chamber, then back at me. "Let me check for you." She quietly opens the door and enters, then comes back out a moment later. "The council will be happy to receive you," she says, bowing again and holding the door open for me.

I enter, and she closes the door behind me. The council quiets quickly and all bow to me, so I in turn bow to them. "Council, I am leaving today, on business. I will be leaving you in charge until my return, so please continue in my stead. Remember if you need any assistance, guidance, or any help at all, please ask Sage. He will help you."

"How long do you expect to be?" the senior councilman asks.

"Unfortunately I do not know. It may be several months before I can return."

They look confused but seem to accept when they all bow. "We will respect your wishes, Master Kyle."

"Thank you." I return their bow and walk to the door. The mediator opens the door for me and follows me out.

"Best of luck to you, Master Kyle."

"Thank you, Mediator." I return to my room, feeling only partially relieved. Finding the others ready to leave, I grab my pack and head to the main counter.

Tita sees us approach and bows to me. "Master Kyle, what can I do for you?"

"Regrettably, we are checking out."

Her ears droop at my announcement. "Sorry to hear. We were really beginning to enjoy your company."

"And we were certainly enjoying your hospitality. Unfortunately, we have business to attend to and must move on. What is the bill?"

"Oh, there's no charge. The council's got it covered," she says, holding her hand up to stop me from paying.

I sigh. "Tita, you know that I'm Sovereign now, right?"

She nods.

"And I know about the lack of payment for your last ambassadors."

She sighs, but nods. Rummaging through a small stack of papers, she pulls out one labeled "bill to the council" and hands it to me.

I look at the total, two thousand five hundred. I reach in the pouch and pull out fifteen vouchers and hand them to Tita, along with the bill. "Thank you." I politely give her a small bow.

Looking shocked, she bows back and slowly counts them and puts them in a drawer with the bill.

I take a step to leave, but quickly stop and take off my mask. "Have you seen Megai?" I softly ask.

Seeing a tear roll down my cheek, she tilts her head slightly and nods. "Now I understand. She's in her room, crying." She points to a door to my left.

I walk over to it, but rather than knock, I softly talk to the door. "Megai, I know you can hear me. I have to leave now." I put my hand to the door. "I don't want to leave without telling you . . . I love you."

The door unlatches and slowly opens in. I watch as a very tear-soaked Megai appears, still in her robe. "You really mean that, don't you?" she weakly asks, looking heartbroken.

I take off a glove and run my hand through her matted cheek fur. "Yes, I do."

She straightens her legs, raising herself, and bumps my nose with hers. I take the opportunity to wrap my arms around her and kiss her, actually pressing my lips to hers. I see her eyes go wide in surprise and then she relaxes, closing her eyes, apparently enjoying the feeling of my lips on hers as she starts to gently purr. After a long moment, she slowly lets herself down, breaking the kiss.

"Are you sure you won't come with me?" I gently ask.

"I have to stay here," she weakly insists.

I kiss her on the head. "Then I want you to do something for me."

She looks at me curiously. "What?"

I hand her the pouch with the vouchers in it. "Take care of these for me."

Curious, she opens the pouch. Her eyes go wide in surprise. "I can't take these," she insists.

"Look, they're no good in any other village. Besides, if you won't come with me, and I can't stay here with you. Let this be my way of watching out for you. You can do whatever you want with them—spend them, save them, or even give them away if you want. I don't mind."

She nods and wraps me in another hug that I return. "I love you too," she confesses. "You should get going."

"I know," I admit, still hugging her. "I just really hate to say good-bye."

"Then think of it as 'until I see you again,'" she says, looking up at me.

"I'll try." I give her another short kiss on her lips.

Tita walks up beside her and puts her arm around Megai as I reluctantly back away.

Sada walks up to Megai and hugs her, nuzzling her nose into Megai's neck. She giggles in response and hugs her back. "Take good care of him, for both of us." Sada pulls back and nods, giving her a light bump with her nose.

Fey gives her a big hug, with a tear in her own eye. To my surprise, Tayla also hugs her while the others simply say their good-byes.

We depart for the gate to Dendros, and to our surprise, a familiar face stands guard. "Marl," Fey shrieks as we approach and runs to hug him.

"Fey! How you doin'?" he asks as he scoops her up in a hug.

"I got adop . . . adopit . . . I got a new family."

He chuckles. "I see that. I'm so happy for you." He sets her down as I approach. "Master Kyle, are you leaving us?"

I frown slightly, but let it go. "I have business to attend to."

He bows slightly. "I wish you a good journey then."

The group starts to move on, but I stop. "Marl, what happened to your accent?"

He chuckles lightly. "It's something I do for the children. My grandpa did it when I was little to cheer us up. I thought it would be good for the harvesters if I gave their kids something to laugh at. You know, cheer 'em up a little."

"I hope you don't stop just because the beast's dead."

"I wasn't planning on it." He smiles.

"Good." I extend my hand. "Take care, Marl."

He cautiously takes my hand and then smiles again. "You too, Master Kyle."

I catch up to the group quickly, and we walk on through the fields, watching the farmers work as we pass. Most of them wave to us, prompting us to wave back.

After a couple of hours, Tayla moves up beside me and asks, "What was in that pouch?"

"Seventy-five hundred in vouchers," I say, "and a couple dozen pictures of us."

She smiles and gives me a light bump with her nose as we walk. "That was very thoughtful of you."

CHAPTER 11

Having left the expansive farms behind more than a day ago, we set up camp close to a small stream, placing the tent off the main road near a cluster of trees.

After supper, we all sit around relaxing. Kotu carves small symbols in his new staff while Sada helps Fey practice some lessons on her tablet. Arru reads from one of her books, as Tayla and Railu both clean the arrows they used to fish. Larrah sits on a fallen tree, slowly rummaging through her pack with a sullen look on her face. I sit and watch everyone, slowly making notes on my own tablet as I review the map that Aime is making as we progress.

I find myself looking at an image of the council inn, in Arindell, wondering what Megai is doing. I can't help but miss her, wishing she had come along. I set the tablet aside as Larrah finds what she was looking for in her pack.

A flute.

Not a whistle type like Kotu makes, but a sectional, meditation flute. I find myself watching as she puts the sections together and adjusts them, aligning the fingering holes. After she's satisfied, she holds it crossways to her lips and practices a few notes.

This gets everyone's attention as the flute produces two notes at the same time.

Larrah closes her eyes and starts playing. The melody starts off calm and peaceful. I find myself trying to find out how she is able to actually control the airflow, not having the proper lip structure, like a human does.

She changes key, picking up some tempo, sounding a little more cheerful. I find closing my eyes allows me to pick up more of the subtleties of the song. I get the feeling that it's telling a story, and I'm along for the emotional ride.

Without warning, she plays a sour note, throwing discord into the song. Another sour note. Then another. The song takes on a dark and scary tone. I get a strange feeling of impending doom. She picks up the pace again, and I find my heart racing, as though I was running, trying to escape. With a sudden set of trills and an off-key note that she lets fade, I open my eyes to see everyone else watching with similar expressions of fear, everyone breathing hard like they too had similar reactions.

After a few heart-stopping moments, she starts again. This time the melody is slow and mournful. My eyes start to water as I look around. I see that almost everyone is softly crying even Larrah, but she plays on. The tempo and key both change again, sounding happier, upbeat until it finally comes to a hopeful end.

Still crying, Larrah sets down her flute and takes a deep breath. She then looks around. Realizing that she has a captive audience, she smiles, suddenly embarrassed. "Sorry, probably should have warned everyone first."

Wiping tears from my cheeks, I curiously ask, "What did you just play?"

She gets a sad look on her face. "It's called 'Garoshi's Ballad.' It tells the story of a warrior who found a life-mate. They conceived a child, lost the child when she got deathly ill. She slowly recovered and they eventually conceived another child." She sighs heavily. "My mate loved that song."

"Your mate?" I ask. "I thought you said you didn't have one?"

She sighs again, wiping a tear from her eye. "I used to. He was a kind, strong snow. Like Kotu, he was also an orphan, having lost his parents when he was young. He scored high in the Trials. You broke his records. He wanted a mate, chose me. I challenged him. He still won, so I accepted. I didn't expect to fall in love with him."

"What happened?" Tayla cautiously prods.

"We bonded." She smiles. "But after my third cycle, he was called to duty, went after some bandits." She starts to sniff and wipe a few tears from her eyes. "It was an ambush. No one in his squad survived." Tayla steps over to her and wraps her in a hug.

"I'm sorry, I didn't know." For the first time since I met her, she lets her emotions out, burying her muzzle in Tayla's neck and bursting into tears. Tayla holds her close for a moment, then something beside me catches her eye.

I turn to see what she is looking at. Railu sits between a distraught Fey and a solemn Arru, sobbing hard. Sada gently pushes me toward her, encouraging me to comfort her, but before I make it to her, she gets up and collapses into me, wrapping me in a hug, balling hard.

I wrap my arms around her and hold her to me. She cries so hard she shakes. Thankfully, someone puts a chair up to my legs, so I scoop her up and sit down. She reflexively curls up and I continue to hold her as she cries and slowly relaxes.

Larrah comes over and puts her head to Railu's. "I'm sorry. I play that when I miss my mate." She kneels and puts her hand to Railu's cheek. "I envy you. Your mate is still out there, still alive, and you are chasing after him."

She closes her eyes, swallowing back some of her own tears before continuing. "Something I never got the chance to do. I was supposed to bear him a child. I never took. I failed him." She pulls away to look her in the eye. "You will find your mate. You will make him proud of you."

Railu leans forward and wraps Larrah in a hug. "Thanks," she manages to whisper. After a moment, Railu leans back against me, slowly getting her emotions under control.

As I sit and hold her, I get a strange feeling of déjà vu. Trying to figure out what's familiar, a name comes to mind, and my eyes start to water. After a while, Railu sits up, notices where she is, and looks apologetically at me. "I'm sorry."

"Don't worry about it. I know that you miss him. If you need to cry on a shoulder, I'll be happy to soak up your tears."

She smiles and hugs me. "Thanks, I may need to." She slowly gets up and heads to the tent. Since it's starting to get dark, I pick up my chair and head in also.

Once in my room, Tayla comes in. "What was that about?"

I give her a puzzled look as I sit on my bed. "What was what about?"

"You cried."

"We all cried."

"Yes, we did, but you stopped, then you started again when you held Railu. What brought that on?"

I sigh, not realizing someone saw my own tears. "I remembered something while holding her."

"What did you remember?"

I frown, feeling odd confessing to her, but yet it seems right, so I take my boots off as I start talking. "I remembered holding my sister while she cried. I was small, she was smaller. I can't remember why she was crying though." I feel a tear run down my cheek and wipe it away.

She sits next to me and gives me an odd look. "Why does that make you cry?"

"I found myself missing her. I'll never be able to see her again."

She leans on me and puts her head on my shoulder while Sada sits up and wraps us both in a hug, purring. We sit like that for several minutes, until Sada sighs heavily.

"We need to get some sleep," I find myself saying."

"Mmmhmm," I hear Tayla mumble and realize that she too is purring and almost asleep on my shoulder.

Not wanting to disturb her, I gently pull her up on the bed. I then lay down between the girls and Sada rolls onto me, like she usually does, and we fall asleep.

Feeling Sada get up, I wake and quickly realize that at some point during the night, Tayla has rolled over and is now asleep on my right arm. Sada looks at me and, seeing Tayla still heavily asleep on my right arm, smiles, and walks out.

"Tayla," I gently say.

Getting no response I run my fingernails through her fur, following her spine. The sensation makes her stretch a little. "Tayla," I repeat.

She groans, apparently not wanting to wake up. "Tayla," I say a little more sternly.

"Hmmm," she groans, and then her eyes open wide. Sitting up suddenly and stammers. "Oh, I'm sorry, I didn't mean to—"

"Tayla, it's okay. You fell asleep and I didn't have the heart to wake you up. I'm sorry."

She gives me an apologetic look. "I didn't mean to fall asleep. You just seemed so sad."

"Well, thank you."

Suddenly puzzled, she asks, "Why?"

I give her an honest look. "For reminding me that I'm not alone and that there are people here that care about me like I care about them."

She leans over to me and licks my cheek. "You're welcome," she happily says, then gets up and walks from the room, her tail happily flowing behind her.

I sit there, for a few minutes, wondering what I said that made her happy enough to lick me.

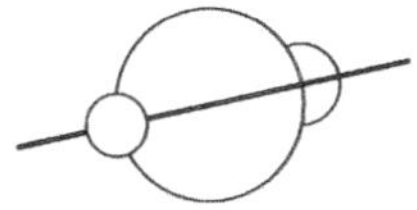

The night of First Moonstorm is here, and we are all staying up to watch it. Larrah had told me that this one starts the New Year, and is usually the best. Arru also stated that the event can sometimes change one's life if watched in the right company.

I have also learned that on these nights that the der'ocks do not fly until after it's over, as the storm provides too much light. Even though they are the only big creatures that hunt at night, we are all fairly quiet. Only the sounds of the numerous small creatures and bugs fill the air.

Standing in the small clearing, I find myself enjoying a cool night breeze when Fey pulls gently on my arm. I stoop down to her. "What's up?"

"I'm scared," she whispers into my ear. "Will you sit with me?"

Smiling, I answer, "Sure."

Taking my hand she leads me over to a chair between hers and Tayla's. She waits for me to sit and then pulls her chair as close to mine as she can before sitting in it. She stays there maybe a minute, before climbing up in my lap. She lies back on my left shoulder as she looks at the moons, still waiting for the storm to start.

After another minute, she's asleep, curled up in a ball, on my lap. Sada brings over some water, and seeing Fey, she retrieves a blanket from the tent and helps me wrap her in it. She then sits in Fey's chair and looks up at the sky.

I watch Fey's face for a little while. Seeing her eyes moving under her eyelids lets me know that she has indeed fallen asleep.

Turning my attention back to the moons, I realize that the smaller moon, Terr, has moved in front of larger Nai and is approaching alignment. I recline my chair back just a little and wait.

After a few more minutes, the show starts. I try to gently wake Fey, with no luck.

The flashes of light start subtly, but quickly intensify, in both brightness and number. Not being able to see the lightning directly, the larger moon reflects the light in localized areas, making it appear that the light is rippling across it like water. I soon realize that the lightning *is* in fact rippling across the surface of Nai. Aime had told me that if the storm was strong enough, it would start jumping around the heavy metal deposits on the surface, but I had not seen that happen yet.

This is a particularly strong storm, and it's still getting stronger. As Nai brightens, Terr seems to darken, being without any direct illumination. Around me, I hear several soft "oohs" and "ahs" whispered.

Kotu even manages an "oh, wow."

Suddenly, as the moons hit their closest, Nai brightens noticeably, and Terr seems to disappear into blackness. For almost a minute, they appeared to be one large rippling silver ring almost as bright as the sun.

Sadly, as the moons start to part, the storm quickly subsides, having used up much of its energy. There are still a few dim flashes, but as the moons spread farther apart, they don't last.

"Did I miss it?" a sleepy voice asks from my lap.

With my eyes still adjusting to the sudden return of darkness, I don't get to see her expression. "Yes, hun, you did. I had Aime record it for you. She sent it to your tablet so you can watch it when you're not so tired."

She brings her nose up under my chin, nuzzling me a little, a gesture that I promptly return. "Thank you," she says.

I help her climb down off my lap, and she takes Sada's hand as she looks at me.

I smile. "I'll be along soon." She nods and walks Fey to the tent. I look for Kotu and see him still watching the moons. I glance up at them, but the storm has passed completely. "Kotu."

"Huh?" He looks around, realizing where he is.

"Collect the remaining chairs and go to bed."

He sighs, but gets up and starts folding up the three remaining chairs. As he heads to the tent, I realize that I'm not alone. Tayla is still sitting beside me.

"Um, Kyle, can I . . . uhm, talk to you?" she nervously asks.

I turn to look at her. "Sure."

She tries to look at me but keeps looking back down at her hands, unable to hide her growing nervousness. "You remember that I didn't commit to being your guide, right?"

"Yes, I remember that you seemed . . . distracted."

Her ears slant back like they did that night. "I was."

"You want to talk about it?"

She thinks for a moment and then sighs heavily. "I know how my grandmother knew all those stories," she confesses, giving me an odd look. "She was an oracle. She didn't like the attention it brought so she really didn't tell anyone. My mother never got the gift she had, so it was assumed that I would not have it either. But I have . . . dreams. Dreams that come true."

"You mean premonitions?" I ask, allowing my interest to show.

"Yes." Her ears perk, and she sounds relieved that I know what she's talking about. "They only happen on the nights of Moonstorm."

Seeing her hesitation, I gently prod, "Why are you telling me this?"

Her ears sag again. "Because I'm embarrassed."

"Of what?" I gently ask.

She fidgets with her hands in her lap, then explains, "Three months ago, I had a premonition. In it, my village was visited by a stranger. He took with him two females, one as a colleague, and one . . . became his mate."

Not missing the similarities, I ask, "You think that I am that stranger?"

She looks softly at me. "I know that you are that stranger. I think part of me realized then that he was you when you took off the mask."

I sit up, realizing what she is inferring. "You want to be my mate?" I calmly ask.

"I have seen it. I accept it. That is the way of an oracle."

"What if you don't want it?"

"It doesn't matter. This is something I want. Don't you?"

I lean forward. "You're asking if I want you?" I smile. "I do. I'm not sure how long I've felt this way, but I do."

"What about Sada? Why isn't she your mate?" she asks, suddenly worried.

I sigh, realizing her dilemma. "That's not so much a choice than a barrier." I take my shirt off and point out the bite mark. "Sada has a defense mechanism that won't allow her to mate."

Tayla leans in close, touching the scars, as I continue, "We tried to, but she went feral and defended herself. I lost a lot of blood. We decided that we wouldn't try again." I hang my head for a moment, and then ask, "I thought you knew about Megai and me."

She sighs. "I didn't fully understand, but now that I do, our time in Arindell makes more sense."

"Now that you do, how does that change things?"

"Would Sada be okay with me being your mate?" she asks, worry returning to her eyes.

Glancing up at Sada, who now stands behind Tayla, smiling, I say, "She didn't have a problem with Megai. I'm pretty sure she wouldn't mind. In fact, I'm sure she'd be thrilled." Then to emphasize my comment, Sada bends down and gives Tayla a hug from behind, being sure to nuzzle her, cheek to cheek, purring.

Tayla's eyes widen in momentary surprise, and then, realizing what's happening, she returns the nuzzle. "How long have you been behind me?"

"Since the beginning," I offer. "You should have seen her face when you told me you wanted me as a mate." I chuckle.

Suddenly from above, we hear a loud cry, reminding us that it's past time to move indoors. Sada and Tayla quickly retreat into the tent, and I grab the chairs and follow.

'Bedtime,' Sada signs.

"Yes, I do believe it is," and I kiss her on her nose, then turning to Tayla, I ask, "So where does this leave us?"

She puts her hands to my face and pulls me to her. "Right about here," she whispers and puts her muzzle to my mouth, imitating the kiss I usually give Sada.

Taking the hint, I wrap my arms around her and return the kiss. To my surprise, she starts to purr softly and wraps her arms around me. We hold that for a moment and then she breaks the kiss to slide her cheek along mine.

"Marking me as yours?" I softly chuckle.

"Hmm, yeah," she purrs, putting her nose under my chin.

An unusually loud yawn from Fey interrupts us. "We should get some sleep," I whisper.

"Good night then," she whispers.

"Good night," I reply, giving her another kiss on the muzzle. I watch her give me a tentative look, then glancing at my room, frowns, and slinks softly over to her own bed and lies down.

Feeling a little confused, I follow Sada to my own bed and crawl in. Sada gets comfortable on my left arm, as usual, and starts to purr as I rub her back. I lay there for a while, quieting the thoughts racing through my mind, before finally closing my eyes.

Slowly I begin to realize that I'm being watched. Looking at the door, I see Tayla standing in the dark, watching me.

"Tayla?" I gently ask.

She slowly steps over and sits on the bed next to me. As I look at her face, I see confusion in her eyes. I reach up and touch her cheek, and she nuzzles my hand.

I gently pull her to me. Realizing my intent, she nervously asks, "What do I do?"

"Just get comfortable."

She rolls toward me, putting her head on my chest like she did the night she fell asleep in my arms. I feel her sigh heavily and tremble. "I'm scared," she whispers. "I've never felt so strongly about someone like I do about you."

"Why is that something to be afraid of?"

"I don't want to lose you like Larrah lost . . . hers."

I start scratching her back, starting at her shoulder blades. "There's no way I would let that happen, and Aime would make sure of it."

As I reach the base of her tail, her back arches slightly, and she starts to purr. "That feels good," she moans, and her body starts to relax. I start rubbing Sada's back the same way, getting a similar reaction. I lay there for a while, gently scratching both the girls' backs until the purring fades. Feeling more at ease than I have since I woke from cryo, I drift off to sleep.

I awake to the sensation of something moving across my chest. Looking down, I see that Tayla is lazily tracing along my ribs and muscles with a finger. Her head is still on my chest, just below my chin.

"I'm glad I'm not very ticklish," I whisper.

"Why don't you have fur?" she asks curiously.

"Because humans don't grow fur."

"What will you do when you find more humans?"

"I'll let them know what really happened at the facility, and Aime can relay the data she has."

"And after?"

"I don't know. Haven't given it much thought. Go back to Arindell maybe, see if Megai still wants me," I confess, wondering what she is leading up to. "Part of me would like to see Earth again, but I doubt it would look anything like I remember."

She stops tracing and lays her hand flat, feeling my heartbeat. "Tell me what you remember, of Earth."

Thinking for a moment, I say, "One moon, no rings. Most of the trees have green leaves. There are a lot more flowers, all sorts of colors and shapes. The creatures are a lot smaller. And there are a lot of birds. Most of them are colorful too."

"What's a bird?"

"Well, a bird is a small flying animal. Most are smaller than the dragons and could be held in one hand. Their bodies are covered with feathers, not fur or scales."

"Are they harmful?"

"No, most are actually pretty colorful. The whistling or chirping sounds they make can be relaxing."

"Can I go with you, if you go there?"

"I wouldn't go if you didn't come with me."

She cuddles in closer and we lie in silence for a while, listening to each other breath. She finally breaks the silence by asking, "Do you want to have children?"

So that's what she was building to. "Well, already having been a father, I can't help but say yes. I would like to have a little one . . . or two. As for how soon, I don't know, but I'd want to make sure we're ready first."

"We," she mumbles. "I'd like that."

I quickly realize that she has drifted back to sleep, apparently more than happy with my answer. I give her a kiss between her ears and let myself fall back to sleep.

As the sun starts to rise, I wake early. After slipping out from under Tayla and Sada, I get dressed for the day. After quietly setting up for breakfast, I sit back and relax while waiting for the others to wake up.

Railu is the first to awaken and gives me an odd look as she exits the tent. "You're not usually up this early," she states, then seeing everything set up for breakfast, asks, "What's going on?"

"You'll see, soon enough."

She gives me a skeptical look as she sits down in a chair and gets comfortable.

Arru and Larrah both come out at the same time, both looking freshly groomed and ready for the day. Larrah nods to me, smiling as if she knows something the others do not.

Sada comes out and, upon seeing us, asks, 'Do you want me to wake the others?'

'Send the children out.'

She gives me an odd look but nods and heads back into the tent. A few minutes later Fey comes out looking bright and chipper as she walks over and sits down next to me. When Kotu comes out, he looks like he just woke up. His fur plastered to one side of his face.

Sada pokes her head out of the tent. 'Now Tayla?' she asks.

'Yes, then you get out here before she does.' Sada smiles and disappears again, only to come out a few seconds later at a near run.

I stand up and position myself about ten steps from the tent's door.

Tayla opens the tent door but doesn't step out right away, looking around, suspecting something. Seeing the cautious look on her face, I call to her, "Pendekar Tayla of Pridewyn, I'm challenging your reserve."

She steps out of the tent, then realizing what was said, walks up to me and kneels on one knee, and bows her head.

I look down at her, realizing again how much I don't like this custom. "I stand above you as your superior. I'm looking for a mate. Do you accept this contract, or do you stand and challenge?"

She stays kneeling, ears drooped, thinking about her answer. "I challenge," she finally states, rising to her feet.

I nod to her. "What is your choice of combat."

She again thinks for a moment. "Unarmored, open hand."

I nod to her again. "I accept your challenge. Aime, armor off, no help, understood."

"Acknowledged, no armor, no augments." All my armor falls off of me as Aime releases it. I also remove my shirt, revealing my skin, to prove that I'm not wearing any armor.

We take a few steps away from the tent and chairs. Then Larrah steps up to us, assuming the role of ringmaster and bows. So we turn to her and bow, then turn to each other and bow.

We take our fighting stances and Larrah signals for us to begin. Tayla and I stand for a moment before she takes a few experimental swings at me. I easily block those, being careful to keep my hands open at all times.

As she steps back from her attack, I step forward and deliver a few attacks of my own, which she too, easily blocks.

After a moment we begin trading attacks and blocks. I find it somewhat refreshing that she's not holding back, so I return the favor of not holding back either, giving in to the fight and letting her have some of my better attacks. She blocks some and dodges others.

After a few feigns, she lets loose a rapid barrage that I find myself having to both dodge and block. We slowly return to the trading attacks and blocks. This time she tries to include occasional swats from her tail.

After a few minutes of this trade-off, I find myself wanting to bring the fight to an end. I feign a spin kick and use the momentum to get behind her as she blocks. I wrap my arms around her, holding my hands flat away from her, with her tail, and a leg trapped between my legs. She struggles for a moment, pushing her head against mine, and trying to twist and push out with her arms with no luck.

Larrah steps overlooking at the hold, making sure my hands are not closed.

Suddenly, Tayla stops struggling for a moment, catching her breath. "Do you yield?" I ask.

"No," she teases, starting to struggle again.

Feeling her hands closed around my wrist, I say, "You just did."

She stops struggling, realizing that she just forfeited the challenge. She relaxes in my arms, but instead of being disappointed, she starts purring and rubs her head against mine. "I am your mate."

I relax and wrap her in a hug. "And I am yours."

Having forgotten about our audience, I am surprised by their spontaneous applause. As I stand there holding Tayla, smiling, she turns around and wraps her arms around me, so I happily pick her up and spin around, planting a kiss firmly on her muzzle.

"Can we eat now?" a plaintive Kotu asks, interrupting our celebration.

"Party crasher," Tayla calls as I laugh.

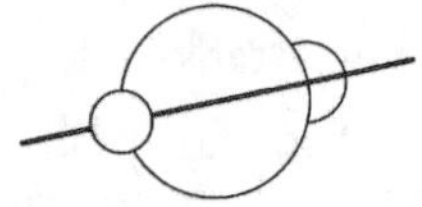

Walking into Dendros midday, I find this village very much like the others, except that the residents are primarily squirrels. With a quick look around, I see many varieties and colors, some I recognize and some I don't. We head straight to the inn as Railu heads off to find her new source of information. After shedding our packs in our rooms, I drop Railu's pack in her room and we set out for a café to get lunch. Railu shows as we eat.

"Where we going to next?" Tayla asks her between mouthfuls.

"Lorholt."

"Which way?" Larrah asks.

She sighs heavily. "Garrent."

"So we'll get to find out about that ghost after all," Tayla comments.

"How long do you think it'll take us to get there?"

She thinks for a moment. "Six or seven days."

"Then how long to Lorholt?" Tayla asks.

"Maybe eight or nine."

"How long would it be, if we went through Three Lands?" Larrah asks.

She sits back and takes a drink while thinking. "With the pass collapsed, maybe eighteen to twenty days, total."

"Well, unless something comes up, we should probably get moving in the morning," I offer.

"Agreed," Tayla admits. "We wouldn't want you picking up another title now, would we?"

Everybody chuckles, and I blush. "Yeah, can't have that now, can we?" I agree. "I'm going back to the inn. Anyone need any coin?" I ask looking around at the group.

Most shake their heads no, but Fey hops over and whispers something in my ear, so I give her a small handful of various coppers and a kiss. She then walks over to Sada, takes her hand, and they happily head off to the markets.

I flag down the waitress as everyone else leaves. When she comes over, I pay the bill and give her a generous tip, but before I can leave a soft, curious voice interrupts from behind me, "Are you starting a caravan to Lorholt?"

I turn and see a white mink, standing slightly taller than Fey, wearing a style of the green-and-silver robe that I've not seen before. "I wouldn't call it a caravan. It's just me and my group, but yes, we're going to Lorholt. Why?"

"My assistant and I missed the last caravan. I was wondering if we could accompany you."

I look at her curiously for a moment. "Will you be ready to travel by morning?"

"Of course."

I extend my hand. "Kyle."

She shakes my hand, bowing at the same time. "Niku."

"My group is staying at the South Gate Inn. Please meet us there an hour after sunrise."

"Thank you." She bows and departs, followed by a slightly shorter female gray squirrel, in a less decorative green-and-silver two-piece outfit.

I slowly wander back to the inn, wondering if I just set myself up for something else. Walking into the common room, I am pleased to find it unoccupied. I shed my armor and get comfortable in a chair. "Aime, how are you doing with your rescue program for Sage?"

"Thanks to my interactions with Sage Arindell, I have been able to loosely form some of the programs, but I will need to interact with Sage Garrent directly to see how bad he is before I can finalize anything."

"How long would that take?"

"Worst-case scenario, six hours to start him on a recovery."

"How long would recovery take?"

"Several days, minimum."

I rub my hands over my face. "Do I need to stay there for that time?"

"No, I can start the recovery and he can finish it."

"Ah, good. You had me worried that we'd have to stay there a few days."

"I would never interfere with your plans."

The door to the common room opens and Tayla steps in. She looks around. "Talking to yourself again?"

I give her a sour look. "You know I'm talking to Aime."

She smiles. "And you know I'm just teasing." She slides onto my lap, wrapping her arms around me, and leans into me. "It's nice to be alone."

I wrap my arm around her and start gently massaging her fur. She starts to purr in response and relaxes, curling her tail into her lap. I lean my head on hers and gently start playing with the tip of her tail.

"What are you doing?" she quietly asks, not moving.

"Does it bother you, me playing with your tail?"

"Feels weird. I normally don't let anyone touch my tail."

I let go of her tail. "I'll stop then."

She slowly slides her tail off her lap, but soon puts it back, landing it on my hand. "You can if you want," she purrs. "I've watched you with Sada. I trust you."

I kiss her on her head. "I love you." I gently resume playing with her tail.

After several quiet, long minutes, she quietly asks, "How long do you want to be with me?"

"What do you mean?"

She thinks for a moment. "As a mate, how long do you want me as a mate?"

I look curiously down at her, then remember what Arru had told me. "As long as possible."

She looks up at me, both hopeful and surprised. "Really?"

I kiss her. "My people usually choose to mate for life. I know that yours don't often do that, but I would like to try."

She smiles and leans back into me. "I'd like that too."

We sit in silence until the door opens and Railu walks in. Seeing us, she teases, "Aww, look at the cuddle bugs."

"If I didn't know you, I'd beat you," Tayla chides without moving.

Arru walks in. "Leave them be, Railu," she groans. "I'd forgotten how unusual squirrels are."

Tayla and I both look up at her, curious. I ask, "What do you mean?"

"They're so easily distracted," she grumbles. "Any little sound or motion and they turn away to see what it was and you almost have to start over with them."

Tayla chuckles as I bury my face in my hand. "Oh no."

Tayla sits up and curiously looks back at me. "What?"

"After lunch, a mink named Niku came up to me and asked if she and her assistant could accompany us to Lorholt."

"So what'd you say?" Railu asks, giving me a puzzled look.

"I said I didn't mind, and that we'd be leaving tomorrow."

"Well, what's the problem?" Tayla asks.

"Her assistant is a female gray squirrel."

"Oh," Arru says, a bit disappointed.

"Since she's an assistant, maybe she's more focused," Railu wonders aloud as Larrah enters, followed by Kotu.

"Assistant? Who's an assistant?" Larrah asks curiously.

"A squirrel," I answer.

"Whose assistant is she?"

"A mink named Niku."

"What's Niku do?" she asks, finding a seat.

"What *did* she say she was?" I ask myself, trying to remember.

"Herbal healer," Aime reminds me.

"Yeah, herbal healer, going to Three Lands to apprentice under a shaman."

Railu turns to me with an odd look on her face. "Herbal healer?"

"Yeah."

"Great," she sarcastically states, "just what we need is someone who believes that the plants and bugs can cure anything." She flops down on a chair, then realizes that everyone in the room is blankly staring at her. She shrugs. "What?"

Arru shakes her head. "Here you are, following your mate who is looking for a myth. You're getting help from a male who *is* myth *and* talks to someone no one can see, yet you have a problem with herbalism?"

Railu gets a rather odd look on her face. "Well, when you put it *that* way . . ."

Everyone chuckles at her words, even Railu. As the laughing fades, the door opens and Sada and Fey walk in. The first thing I notice is that Fey is carrying a box, big enough to require both of her hands to keep steady. She smiles as she walks over to Tayla and I. "We never really got to properly celebrate your union," she says, holding out the box.

Everyone watches as Tayla gently takes it from her. Opening the lid, we find a cake with white icing, hand-decorated with yellow and blue flowers, and other icing trimmings.

"Fey, this is gorgeous," Tayla gasps.

I take a closer look at the flowers. "These are *real* flowers, Fey . . . Thank you." Feeling a swell of emotions, I set the cake aside on a table and pull her to me, and Tayla and I both wrap her in a hug.

"You're welcome," she says, eyes watering. "I love you both."

"We love you too," Tayla confirms, giving Fey a gentle nuzzle.

As Fey pulls away, I notice Sada pulling something out of the converter. She walks over to us with a small stack of plates and a handful of utensils. Taking the hint, I grab the cake as Sada hands me the cake server and Tayla two plates.

I cut the cake and set the first two pieces on the plates that Tayla holds ready. Arru then walks up and takes the cake and server from me.

"Now, you get to feed each other," Larrah instructs, smiling.

"Oh, this is a custom I know."

Tayla hands me a plate and Sada hands me a knife. I cut a corner off and hand the knife to Tayla and she does the same. With her still on my lap, only having turned slightly to face me more, she gingerly picks up the piece on my plate. I nervously open my mouth, realizing that this is a test of trust between partners. She carefully places the piece in my mouth, getting only a little icing on my lips. I close my mouth on the cake, but before I can lick my lips, she leans in and licks them for me, an unexpected act that makes me giggle.

She gives me a lovingly nervous look as I pick up a piece from her plate. She opens her mouth as I hold it up to her muzzle. Deciding that she should trust me as I trusted her, I gently place the cake in her mouth, snagging a touch of icing on my fingertip as I do. As she closes her mouth on it, I touch her nose with the icing, drawing a small look of shock. I quickly lean in and lick it off her nose, in turn making her giggle.

"A mate can be won, but love and trust are earned," Larrah announces. "You two are off to a very beautiful beginning."

Everyone cheers and Arru picks up the cake and makes sure everyone gets a piece. Tayla and I continue feeding each other cake, giggling each time we accidentally get some icing or cake on the other but enjoying how we clean it off each other.

After we finish, Tayla leans back onto me, sighing. "We don't get enough alone time."

Sada walks over and sits next to me on the couch, giving her a pouting look.

Tayla gently scratches her behind an ear. "*You* are always welcome."

Sada smiles and purrs, so I wrap my other arm around her and pull her close. We sit for a while in a three-way cuddle, watching Fey and Kotu play their game. After a while, Sada gets restless and wanders over to the children to watch them play their game. She occasionally points to various pieces, apparently suggesting moves. I find myself marveling at how her personality can be so cat-like one minute and nearly human the next.

Feeling more mentally tired than anything, I spend the next few hours just watching the others. Tayla spends a good portion of the time on my lap, lounging against me, but when she's not there, Sada is. When suppertime nears, we all follow Railu to a café that she found earlier.

On our way, we are held up by a quartet of female squirrels having a very animated discussion. They are so focused on their conversation that they don't notice that they are partially blocking the road. Aside from a small line of carts, several people are trying to go around them, all at the same time.

As we funnel through the bottleneck, Fey decides to tap one of them on the shoulder and ends up getting all their attention. "Yes?" they all ask. Fey takes a step back, clearly not expecting all four to answer in unison.

"You're blocking the road," Fey stutters nervously, unsure of what they'll do.

Shocked, they suddenly look at each other, then at all the people trying to go around them. "Sorry, everybody!" they shout in unison and then quickly move out of the road.

Chuckling, I give Fey a gentle scrub. "Peculiar group, weren't they?"

After dinner, we turn in for the evening. I change for bed while Tayla and Sada brush out there fur for the night. I soon find myself helping Tayla brush out her fur, at Sada's insistence, so Tayla has Sada sit in front of her and she starts brushing out Sada's fur. As we do this, I find the quiet time we are sharing more rewarding than the time we spent snuggling earlier. Grooming is done, I lie down. Sada takes her time getting comfortable, but when she does, she quickly falls asleep.

Tayla, having watched Sada trying to get comfortable, softly asks, "Why does she act that way?"

Caught off guard, I ask, "Huh?"

"Sada. Why does she act so, I don't know, different?"

I think about what she said, then I realize what she means. "Remember the myth of your ancestors?"

"Yeah," she sighs, getting comfortable against me.

"She actually remembers what it was like to be that way."

"Oh," she whispers. I start rubbing her back, getting her to purr, and we drift to sleep.

CHAPTER 12

After an early breakfast, we all gather outside the inn.

"Kyle, there you are." Niku walks up with her assistant in tow. "This is Zoe, my assistant."

The squirrel waves. "Hi."

"Niku, Zoe, this is my mate, Tayla, my companion, Sada, my daughter, Fey, my charge, Kotu, and my colleagues and friends Larrah, Arru, Railu." Each nod or wave as I introduce them.

"Nice to meet all of you." She looks around at the group. "I'm sure he told you I'm an herbal healer."

"Yes, he did," Tayla confesses.

"Unlike some of the herbal healers out there, I am quite legit. I research all my methods thoroughly before I use them." She bows slightly with her conclusion.

"Well, I hope we won't need your services, but if we come into trouble, it will be nice to not have to rely solely on our own abilities." Tayla smiles at my subtle sarcasm but says nothing.

As a combined group, we make our way to the road to Garrent. Railu takes her usual spot in the lead, Tayla and Sada follow with Kotu and Fey close behind. Arru follows close behind, with Niku and Zoe. Larrah adopts a rearguard position.

I slowly start dropping back, letting the others pass, wanting to have a word with Larrah, but as Niku catches up to me, she asks, "Are we really going to Garrent?"

I pick up my pace to stay with her. "Yeah, not sure yet if we'll be going through or around it yet."

"Why not?"

"Well, we're following Railu's mate. He left Arroketh almost a year ago. She wants to find him. I need to go where he's going."

She smiles confidently. "If we end up going through Garrent, that's fine. I don't believe in ghosts."

Zoe hangs her head a little, then meekly states, "I do."

"You'll be fine," I assure her, and I start dropping back again.

As Larrah catches up, I cautiously ask, "Could you help me with something?"

She gives me a questioning look. "Like?"

"Could you tell me what 'bonding' is?"

She gives me an odd look. "What do you mean?"

"You mentioned last week, that you bonded with your mate."

Her ears droop for a moment, showing her sadness.

"I'm sorry, I didn't mean to pry."

"No." She looks back up at me. "You are curious. It shows you care." She nods slowly. "I will tell you."

"For us, cats, if both mates care enough about each other and want to become life-mates, we can choose to bond with one another. To do this, the female must be in unsuppressed heat. Both agree not to give in to their desires, but will instead sit with their mate for the duration of the first night." She gives me a curious look. "It may sound easy, but trust me it isn't.

"The process of bonding is often viewed as a single test. But it's really a test of many things: willpower, love, trust . . ." She takes a deep breath, seemingly fighting off the urge to cry. "There are dangers though. Mates can attack each other, or worse, one or both could have a heart attack from all the arousal." She looks at me again, smiling this time. "Those are rare."

Taking advantage of her momentary break, I curiously ask, "Unsuppressed heat?"

"Yes." She lightly chuckles. "We need to suppress our heat cycles to be able to function through them and to keep the males off. The Nao berries we eat suppress the cycle's effects, but don't keep us from being fertile." She gives me a tentative look and stops walking. She glances ahead to Tayla and then looks back at me. "Are you wanting to bond with Tayla?"

I first look at Tayla, then back to Larrah. "I'm thinking about it, for her, but with me not being a cat, would it even work?"

"I do not know," she confesses as we start walking again. "I know that for it to work, you would need to be affected by her scent, to feel the primal desire to mate with her." She thinks for a moment. "If you could do that, it may work."

We continue walking for a few minutes in silence, but my curiosity forces me to break it. "What was it like for you, if I may ask?"

She smiles. "I'll tell you what I remember." She looks around again. "I remember getting ready, both of us getting comfortable. As night fell, I started. I remember the intense urges, the nearly overwhelming desire to mate, how his musk was so thick in the air. Xander told me that he remembered me panting at one point. I don't remember though."

"Did he ever tell you what it was like for him?"

She thinks for a moment. "Not really, but I do remember him breathing hard, occasionally licking me, and I remember at one time he was trembling, or it might have been me, I'm not sure."

I frown a little, having his perspective would have been very helpful.

Apparently, noticing my frown, she says, "You *are* wanting to bond with her."

I smile. "Yeah, I believe I am."

"She would like that," she agrees, smiling. "What of Sada?" she asks. "Will she want to be a part of it?"

This time I'm the one who stops walking. "Is that possible?"

She turns to me. "I've heard stories of others who tried."

We resume walking and with a note of concern, I ask, "What happened?"

She scratches her head in thought. "In one, a female didn't like the other and they attacked each other. One of them died, I don't recall which. In the other, the male and both females came out with several scratches and claw marks, but it worked. They were closer than ever."

"It sounds like another type of test," I comment.

"This time for both the females involved," she adds. "Though, I think, if the trust and affection are there before, it helps considerably."

I look around, finding that I have a lot to think about. "Is there anything you would suggest to help get through it?"

She smiles. "If you are affected by her scent, you will lose most of your control. I would suggest trying to hold on to the fact you love her and to honor that love. Do not mate with her. It will be very difficult, but you must not mate during the bonding."

I look at her for a moment and then nod. "Thank you."

She nods back. "Good luck."

I pick up my pace, wanting to catch up to my mate, but Aime interrupts before I get close. "I may be able to approximate the proper reactions to her pheromones, but we'll need to have the DDS installed and some help from Kotu."

I slow down my pace to stay out of Tayla's range of hearing. *What kind of help?*

"I can reproduce Tayla's pheromones from her last heat and see how he reacts to them. I can then take that data and have your body react accordingly based on the strength of her pheromone."

I don't like using Kotu like that, but I'll ask him if he'll help.

"I have designed some sensors for him to wear to help me monitor his reactions. I will have the converter produce them when we are ready."

Okay, well, I suppose I should take the DDS now so you can start on it. I take off my pack and dig through it for the bottle. Finding it, I put the pack back on, and at Aime's direction, take each of the 2 DDS capsules.

Just before nightfall, I find Kotu idly whittling on his staff. I sit down next to him. "Kotu, would you be willing to help me with something?"

He stops whittling, giving me a curiously suspicious look. "Like what?"

I hesitate, trying to figure out how best to ask him. "Well, what I would like to do is have you smell various things so Aime can see how you react to them."

He gives me a slightly fearful look. "What kind of things?"

"Nothing bad, I promise," I confess, "but some may make you . . . feel different."

"Why?"

I sigh, not knowing any other way to describe my reason. "Do you know what it means to bond with a mate?"

He gets a slightly embarrassed look on his face. "Uhm . . . uh," he stammers.

"Yes or no?"

He slumps. "Yeah, a little."

"Okay, good." I sigh. "I want to do that with Tayla, but not being a cat, I won't react as you would, so Aime and I would like to see how you would react to certain smells, so she can have me react similarly. So both Tayla and I can do this for real."

"I'll be smelling *Tayla*?"

I chuckle. "Not like that, but in a generic way, yes. What will happen is, I will put these on you" —I hold up a few small sensor disks—"so Aime can monitor you, and you'll breathe through this, so you can smell what Aime wants you to. That's it."

He thinks about it for a moment and then nods to me. "What do I need to do?"

I place the sensors on his forehead, chest, and stomach, and my mask over his snout. "All you need to do is sit and relax, breathe normally through your nose. Now remember, you may not notice some of the smells, but your body will. Okay?"

He nods and gets comfortable. Aime signals ready. "Just relax and breathe." I watch Kotu and wait as she records his reactions. I don't notice any change in Kotu other than his eyes dilating a couple of times.

When Aime announces she has the information she needs, I pluck the sensors and mask off him. "I didn't really notice anything," he comments.

"Well, Aime was looking for how your body reacts, not how you as a person react."

He gets a puzzled look on his face, "Oh."

I give him a pat on the shoulder. "Thank you."

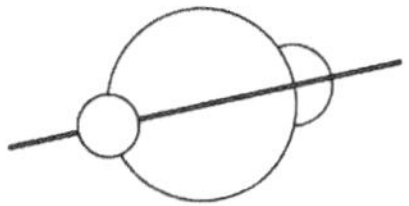

The next evening, we make camp. Seeing Tayla talking with Niku, I walk over and notice that Tayla has a worried look on her face. Concerned, I ask, "What's wrong?"

Tayla gives me a worried look, but Niku gives her an encouraging look, "He's your mate. He should know." She then steps away, giving us some privacy.

I give Niku a curious look as she leaves, then turn to Tayla. "I should know what?" Taking her hands in mine, I feel her tremble.

She squeezes my hands with a nervous tear in her eye. "I'm coming into heat." She looks down, ashamed. "And I'm out of Nao berries."

I gently lift her chin with my finger, bringing her gaze back up to mine. "Then maybe we should take advantage of this."

She gives me a tentative smile and an understanding look. "I'm not sure I want to have cubs yet."

"I was thinking more along the lines of us bonding."

She takes a small step back in surprise. "You aren't a cat. It won't work right."

I smile casually. "Aime's ready to take care of that. I'll react to you, just like a male cat."

She leans back into me. "Are you sure you want to do this?"

"I want you to know how much I love and trust you."

She quietly holds me for a moment. "Then I want Sada there too. She should be a part of this."

"I've already talked with her. She hoped you'd want her there."

She pulls herself away from me, eyes watering. "We should get ready then. I can feel it getting stronger."

I get Sada's attention. 'It's time.'

As she comes over, Larrah follows. "Is it time?"

Tayla nods. "Yeah."

Larrah takes her in a hug. "You have a mate to be proud of. He truly cares about you."

Tayla smiles. "I know."

Larrah noticeably sniffs the air. "Ooh, not much time. I will take care of things out here. Go, get ready." She ushers us into the tent.

Sada and I follow Tayla into our room. "Aime, can the bed be more like a shallow bowl?" she asks.

"Kyle?" Aime asks.

I name Tayla as my second executor. You should also begin with the alterations.

The bed suddenly takes on a nest-like shape, with softly stepped sides, big enough for the three of us. I notice that my sense of smell starts getting more acute, and I start hearing both girls breathe.

"Good," she says. She then looks at me as she strips out of her clothes. "To my mates, I offer myself. Let us bond and be one." She then steps into the nest.

I follow her lead, also removing all my clothes. "To my mates, I offer myself. Let us bond and be one." I then step into the nest and wrap my right arm around Tayla. Sada strips and steps into the nest. I wrap my free arm around her and we sit down. Sada takes Tayla's free hand and holds it in hers.

I can easily smell both of them, though Tayla's scent is quickly getting stronger, more enticing, getting me very aroused. Tayla starts to breathe hard, her scent now strong enough for me to taste. I close my eyes for a moment, enjoying her scent.

Suddenly I'm getting licked across my face, my mind unable to figure out who's doing it, so I lick back. It's Sada. Another tongue slides up my neck and I turn to lick that face: Tayla. I feel her trembling as I realize that Sada is also licking Tayla. I hear something else, something loud, both are purring.

I run my fingers up both their backs. I hear Tayla groan and feel Sada's claws sink into my back. Suddenly Tayla hisses and I reflexively grab their scruffs and press their noses firmly to mine. I let out a low growl and they relax. As their purring resumes, I let go and run my fingers down both their spines, to their tails. Tayla lets out a whimper and buries her nose under my chin, pushing up, while Sada arches her back and lets out a slow sigh.

Tayla leans forward and presses her body to mine. I manage to realize that she wants to mount me so I hold her tightly to me to prevent her from moving and she whimpers again. I bite her neck, not hard, but she screams with pleasure, and Sada rakes her teeth across my shoulder.

As I turn to lick her face, Tayla lightly bites me, right on the scar that Sada gave me. I run my hands up both girls' chests, right between their breasts. Sada grabs my hand and starts licking it while Tayla runs her hands over my chest.

We continue this behavior, licking, touching, feeling, and smelling each other, losing all sense of time. When one tries to mount another will gently stop them. Time having blurred, driven by instinct, we eventually start to fatigue.

After Sada falls asleep, Tayla takes the opportunity to explore my mouth with her tongue, lapping at me repeatedly. When she finally succumbs to fatigue, I pull both sleeping girls to me as Aime makes the bed flat again and force myself to sleep.

I wake up first and find myself quickly pleased that neither girl moved after I pulled them to me. Aime does a quick check and lets me know that Tayla's heat has greatly reduced in strength, her pheromone level having reduced to what it was when she's using the Nao berries.

Sada rolls over to face me. I quickly realize that she's awake, but just pretending to be asleep, so I gently run my fingers down her back, and she stretches out as best she can. She reaches out and gently strokes Tayla's cheek, straightening out the ruffled fur. Tayla returns the gesture, lightly giggling as she does.

"It worked," she happily, if sleepily, says. A tear rolls down the black stripe of her muzzle. Sada easily catches it and gives her a curious look.

"Tears of joy," she explains, giving Sada a rub. "I think I understand now how he feels about you." She looks up at me. "You're right. It's not easy to put into words." She kisses me, lightly licking my lips. "Thank you," she purrs.

"All your doubts gone?" I curiously ask.

She smiles. "Like they never were."

I kiss her. "Good."

"Hey, you're awake," Larrah calls through the closed door to our room. Sada quickly reaches for a blanket and covers us up as Larrah parts the door. "Oh, sorry, thought you were more awake than that."

"Don't worry about it. Come in," I call.

She turns back to us, looking a little embarrassed, but smiling. "All went well I hope?"

"Yes, it did," Tayla insists happily. Sada nods, enthusiastically agreeing with her.

"I seem to remember getting clawed," I comment, rubbing my back.

Tayla sits up a little, looking at Sada. "So do I."

Sada slinks down, apologetically. 'I don't remember doing it,' she signs defensively.

"But I have dried blood on my fur, here," Tayla says, pointing to her side.

I sit up to look but realize something else. "Wait a moment. You understood her?"

Tayla's face drops. "No, I didn't . . . I just . . . felt . . ."

Sada sits up, a puzzled look on her face, but doesn't sign anything.

"I don't know," Tayla says, then gasps, "Oh my."

I look between Tayla and Sada. "I thought you two acted alike before but reading each other's minds?"

"I don't think I'm reading her mind. It's more like, an emotion," Tayla cautiously states.

Without changing my expression, I curiously think, *What about me?*

She turns and looks at me curiously. "What?"

"I wanted to see if it worked with me too."

"I've never heard of this happening," Larrah interrupts.

I give Tayla a suspicious look and a thought of her grandmother.

She seems to understand that. "Maybe," she tentatively agrees.

"Maybe what?" Larrah asks, curiously looking back and forth between us.

Tayla looks at her, then back at me. I simply nod to her but give her an impression of trust, so she turns back to Larrah. "I will trust you with this, but don't tell anyone, okay?"

Larrah nods. "I will honor your privacy."

"My grandmother was an oracle. My mother never got the gift, so it was assumed that I didn't either, but I did. I'm not as good as she was. That book of myths was mostly her stories, the things she saw, far ahead or far back. I've only been able to see a few months ahead, mostly about myself."

"Why didn't you tell anyone?" Larrah asks curiously.

"I tried once," she sadly confesses, "but I had a vision that changed my mind."

I suddenly get a deep pang of fear and dread, so I wrap my arm around her and gently pull her to me. As Sada takes her hand to comfort her, I quickly realize that she must have felt what I did.

Tayla gently leans into me, taking a heavy breath before continuing, "Anyway, we think that this—understanding—we seem to be sharing may be linked to that."

Larrah sits in apparent shock for a moment and then her face seems to light up. "If I remember right, your mother didn't bond, did she?"

Tayla shakes her head. "No, my father didn't stay around."

"Did your grandmother bond with her mate? I know that they were still together when I started training you."

She thinks for a moment. "I'm not sure, but I'm beginning to think that she did. I seem to remember them having an understanding that no one else could figure out."

Larrah smiles, a tear coming to her eye. "This seems like a good move then, I'm so happy for you, all of you." Sada reaches out and wipes the tear from Larrah's eye and gives her a nuzzle, purring.

"Please don't take this the wrong way, but I've noticed a change in you. You're more relaxed," I cautiously compliment, getting a smile from her.

"Yes, you are, more confident, almost back to your old self," Tayla happily adds, reaching out to hug her former mentor.

She sighs, hugging Tayla. "I guess since you trusted me, it's only fair I trust you."

Tayla gives her a puzzled look. "Trust us with what?"

Larrah's eyes dart around like she's looking for an escape, but she sighs heavily, closes her eyes, and blurts. "I'm sterile, I can't have cubs." When she opens her eyes she looks heavily relieved.

"Why do you think that?" Tayla asks curiously.

"Because I did not conceive with Xander. We tried several times, but none took. Then he left . . . was ambushed . . . Now, I'll never be able to fulfill that contract." She sits on the edge of the bed, nearly crying.

Sada and Tayla gently pull her down onto our laps. "How do you know it wasn't him?" Tayla gently asks.

She sniffles. "He already had a cub."

Tayla gives me a stern look, and I get an impression to fix her. I gently put my hand on Larrah's belly. Aime immediately brings up a display for me to see. As Aime instructs, I slide my hand slowly down her belly, so it's over her womb.

"I am finding no problem with you," Aime reports. "You are very fertile; in fact, you will be starting your own heat in six days."

All three look at me puzzled. "Then why couldn't I conceive with him?" Larrah asks, confused.

"I would need to scan him to properly answer that, but as you are completely capable of carrying a cub, I would suspect that something happened, between the time of his last cub and you, that made him sterile."

Sada gently plays with her ears as she lies on our laps for a little while, thinking. "It's starting to get late. We need to get moving." She sighs. We help her sit up and she looks back at us. "Thank you."

I nod to her. "If you ever need to talk."

She nods again, this time with a slight smile. "I will." And she walks out the door, leaving us to get dressed.

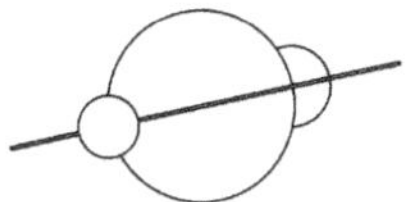

With the main path leading into the deserted village heavily overgrown, we find instead two paths diverting around the village, one path to the north, the other to the south.

"Which way should we go?" Arru asks.

Railu looks at me. "I'd bet that they went into the village. Amsel would not have passed this up."

"If that's the way they went, that's the way we go," I insist, drawing a complaint from Kotu.

I give him a look to quiet him. "Keep your senses alert."

Railu starts into the thicker brush, using her blade to clear a crude path. I follow, pulling my bow and readying an arrow, just in case. The rest follow in single file.

She leads slowly, pausing now and then to listen. Breaking through to the outskirts, we're pleased to discover that the roads are fairly devoid of plants. Looking ahead, we see the weathered gray huts standing barren. Their doors and windows open, appearing empty before us.

Fanning out, I notice that both Larrah and Tayla have readied their bows too. We proceed to walk slowly and quietly down the street to the council hut. The small dragons that have made this place home scurry away, but those don't concern us. It's the larger creatures that may be defending nests that are our concern. With our non-fighters in the middle, we hold our circular formation as we walk slowly, quietly toward the middle of the village.

Aime, are you ready?

A green thumbs-up appears in my vision.

Good.

With the council hut now in view, and having found no larger creatures, we relax a little and pick up our pace. Suddenly a loud wail pierces the silence. Everybody in the middle ducks and those of us with bows start searching for predators.

Another wail, this time I realize that it's not from an animal. It's from the council hut. Apparently I'm not the only one to figure that out, as Aime announces, "It is Sage."

Sighing, I say, "That was Sage everyone." I put my bow up and enter the hut. "Aime, talk to me."

Her voice comes from the hut, instead of from my ears. "He is in worse shape than I had anticipated. I have had to assert control of some of his systems temporarily. You may want to get comfortable. I need to upload and run the recovery program."

"Are we safe?" Tayla asks as she enters the hut.

"Yes, I do not detect any life signs larger than a ma'pai within the village. It would appear Sage's vocalizations kept predators away as well."

Tayla pokes her head out the door. "Come on in, we're clear."

Everyone files into the hut's foyer and sets down there bags. I drop my armor and get out my table and chair. Sitting down, I lean on the table. "I'm going to be stuck in here for a while. So if anyone wants to look around, make sure that you have someone with you. Aime says that there's nothing big in the village, but I still want you to be cautious."

Several nod. Railu, however, surprises me. "Anyone want to go for a walk?" Niku and Zoe both quickly grab an empty pouch and follow her out the door.

Fey pulls her chair up alongside me as Larrah steps up to the door. "Well, if no one else wants to go out, I'm going to look around."

"Go carefully," Tayla states. "I'm going to straighten up in here, make it suitable for sleeping."

"You could sleep at the inn across the street. I can create a pair of signal relays. While their range is limited, they should suffice for a night."

"Want to check it out?" I ask, looking at my girls.

As Tayla and Sada head across the street to check out the abandoned inn, I clear some debris from the window sill and watch for a moment as they walk down the open hall. When they enter the ambassadorial suite, I hear a door squeak behind me, I turn around to see Arru and Kotu come out of the central chamber.

"There's nothing in there," she states.

"What do you mean?"

"Nothing, no furniture. It's like they never used the place."

"They probably didn't. I had a chance to talk to an old Moku and he indicated that they abandoned their village after the humans disappeared."

"Why?"

Remembering my promise, I limit my answer. "They don't like staying put. They prefer to wander."

"The humans wanted them to be like the rest of us? Why?" she asks.

I think about that for a moment, I say, "I'm not sure." Then realizing that I've only seen one other Moku, I ask, "How many have you seen lately?"

She thinks for a moment. "Just one I'm afraid. They tend not to come to Arroketh anymore."

Realizing that we both probably saw the same one in Arindell, I say, "I wonder what their population is now."

"Last known population of the Moku was one hundred six," Aime offers.

"When was that?" I ask.

"Just before they abandoned the village."

"What and when was their highest population?"

"Initial population was two hundred forty-seven. Their number declined after that."

"They're dying?" Arru sadly states.

"That is the most likely conclusion."

I sit back down. "The researchers must have been trying to encourage them to reproduce, to save their species."

"Something that was obviously complicated by their wanderlust and a natural aversion to their own kind," Aime adds.

"Now I know why they don't like humans."

Tayla and Sada come back in, sparing me further grief. "The inn's empty."

"We know that," Arru states.

"No, it's completely empty, no beds, no furniture, nothing."

"Well, that matches what we found," Railu states as she walks in the door.

"Every hut we looked in was cleaned out," Niku adds.

"I couldn't even find a print, of any kind, anywhere," Railu adds.

"I found some coins," Zoe states, holding out a small array of coins.

"That's all that's left here, coins," Larrah states as she enters. "The Treasury has coins all over the place like they were just thrown in there by the handful." As if to reinforce her point, she drops a handful of gold and silver coins on the table.

I pick up a coin and wipe the dust off it. "Leave behind anything that reminds you of humans and trade-off the rest."

Arru sighs. "That's a sad way to live."

"They have a lot of animosity toward humans. Not much can be done about it."

'What are we going to sleep on?' Sada asks, changing the subject.

I sigh. "I'll set up the tent inside the main room." I grab the tent and head into the main council room.

"Let's make supper," I hear Tayla say as the door closes behind me.

I quickly set up the tent, centering it in the room. I expand it to fill the room, aligning the tent's door with the room's door. With the room being slightly smaller than the tent usually is, I adjust the rooms to compensate. Stepping back out into the foyer, I find supper waiting.

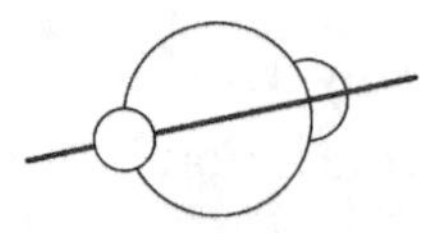

I wake up early and gently slip out from under Sada and Tayla. With a yawn, I make my way out to the foyer. With it still dark outside, I have a seat in my chair and grab my tablet. After pulling up the map, I select Garrent and start making some notations.

Suddenly, a pair of hands slide down my chest from behind me and I feel a muzzle slide along my cheek. It's Tayla. I recognize her smell. "What you doing?" she softly purrs.

I set the tablet down and gently hold her head against mine. "Still getting used to a little of you in my head."

She sighs. "Me too." She sits across my lap and leans into me. "Do you regret bonding with me?"

Feeling insulted, I say, "Of course not! I wouldn't trade what we have for anything." Then feeling an odd pang from her, I ask, "Do you regret it?"

She wraps her tail around her waist and tries to curl up in my lap. "There are times where it's great. I feel so happy, so loved." Her ears suddenly droop, and her voice changes reflecting her sadness. "But sometimes, like yesterday when we entered the village, it was hard to separate my feelings from yours and Sada's. It's a little scary."

"Give it some time. It's only been a few days."

She gives me a curious look, so I start to gently rub her back. "Well, you didn't learn to walk overnight, did you?"

"I don't see what walking has to do with this."

Thinking for a moment, I say, "Okay, think of it like this. I don't have a tail. You do. You've had it since birth so it's natural for you. For me, if I were to grow one, I'd have to learn how to control it, learn to keep it out of doors, away from wheels, things like that."

She gently shakes her head. "This isn't a tail we're talking about."

"No, not a tail, but it's still something new to learn how to control, something to get used to."

"I suppose, but sometimes, it's not easy."

I wrap my arms around her, letting my feelings for her flow freely through me. "Not easy." I kiss her muzzle and then rub my cheek against hers. "But worth it."

Her only response is a gentle sigh as she starts to purr, but the feeling of love I get from her tells me that she understands.

Light through the window wakes me and I find Tayla still on my lap, snuggling with me while asleep. I look out the window, watching the shadows slowly descend as the sun rises. As it gets brighter, Tayla starts to stir.

"Morning," I softly say, holding her to me.

"Hmmm, already?"

"Yeah." I kiss her. "Come on."

She slowly stands up and I gently let her tail slide through my hand. In response, she adds some wiggle to her tail as she happily walks into the tent to get dressed. I sit back and watch her go, smiling at how beautiful she is.

After the door closes, I sigh. "Aime, how's Sage this morning?"

"I am feeling much better this morning, thank you, Master Kyle," Sage answers.

"Good to hear. I apologize for fixing you up and then leaving you, but we must be moving on."

"Aime has already filled me in. I understand, and I hope you find them."

"Thank you."

Railu comes out of the tent and slowly walks toward me. "Mistress Railu, good morning."

Railu stops abruptly, eyes wide, obviously startled. "Who . . . ?"

"My apologies for startling you. I am Sage Garrent. I wanted to personally let you know that your mate was here, with the other three. While I was not able to communicate with them, I do remember their visit."

"How long ago were they here?" she asks, relaxing.

"Just over ten months ago."

She visibly shudders, suppressing emotions. "How were they?"

"The four of them were in excellent shape and very high spirits. Their three pack jata were also in very good shape."

"Three, they left with four," Railu states, showing her concern.

"They did mention something about losing one in a bridge col-lapse."

"That may explain the lack of a bridge crossing Pride River," I volunteer.

"I wonder what made them cross. They knew it wasn't safe for jata."

"Perhaps they were left no choice," Arru suggests, having come into the room unnoticed.

"That scares me."

"The important thing, if I may, is that when they were here, after the event, they were all healthy," Sage offers, trying to comfort her.

Arru sits next to her. "Take solace from what you know. Try not to fear what you do not."

As Tayla and Sada both come out, Sada comes over and pokes me. 'Get dressed.'

Puzzled, I look down at myself and realize that I'm still in my shorts. I put the tablet back in my pack and head off to get dressed.

CHAPTER 13

With Sage able to continue his own recovery, and Aime having given him enough raw data to keep him busy for over a year, we depart. Aside from the particularly rocky terrain, the trip is fairly uneventful. Kotu takes to collecting interesting rocks, and to my surprise, Sada and Zoe help him. By the time we reach Lorholt, they've collected enough that they have to trade off carrying the pack frequently.

Walking into the village late in the day, we agree to meet at a café for supper and split up. Railu heads off to find more information about where her mate and where he went, while the three "geologists" head off to try to trade off their bounty. Niku heads off to find the caravan. Larrah and Arru head off together, while Fey and Tayla accompany me to the inn.

After booking the rooms, we drop off some of our gear and set out to the markets. While Tayla and Fey browse the kiosks, I find myself spending more time marveling at the variety of patterns on the skunks, raccoons, and red pandas present. As one of the skunks passes by, I realize that he has a pattern I'm not familiar with.

Skunks can have spots?

"Of course, while the most common trait is black with white stripes, some are brown, gray, or even cream-colored. They could have one wide stripe, two thin stripes, or a series of white spots and broken stripes. Some also have stripes on their arms and legs."

I did not know that. Thank you. Feeling less curious, I turn my attention to the wares in the kiosks and follow Tayla and Fey as they browse.

After Fey finds a new outfit, we head to the café to meet up with the others.

Finding a large table, we have a seat. Larrah and Arru are the first to arrive, and as they sit, the three treasure hunters arrive.

"We managed to get thirty coins for the rocks," Kotu triumphs.

"How did you manage to pull that off?" Tayla wonders aloud.

Zoe smiles wide. "Jewelers love pretty rocks."

In response, we all chuckle, and Arru asks, "Did you share the profit with your partners?"

His jaw drops in both surprise and disappointment, but his honesty gets the better of him and he fishes out some coins. He hands some to Zoe, who promptly squeals happily and counts them, but when he tries to hand some to Sada, she closes his hand around them and gently gives him a nuzzle.

Arru smiles. "Profit is not profit at the cost of others."

He smiles and offers Zoe another coin. She squeals again, giving him a surprise hug. He manages to hug her back, despite being caught off guard.

As they find seats, I state, "Sometimes the reward you get is worth more than the coin."

Still embarrassed, he sits by Fey as Niku shows up. "The caravan leaves in the morning."

"So soon," Larrah asks.

"They've been here for a day already."

"So we leave for Three Lands in the morning," Railu states, finding a seat of her own.

"Tell us about the caravan," Larrah asks Niku.

"Well, there are a couple of families and traders being escorted by a pair of fighters."

"They need an escort?"

"Yeah, there've been some attacks lately along the road to Three Lands," Railu interjects. "I heard something about bandits, killings, and even some kidnappings."

"Traveling with the caravan seems like a really good idea," Arru offers.

The server brings drinks and menus. "Then we'll meet with them in the morning. I'm sure they wouldn't mind having the extra protection."

"I'm certain that they will allow us along," Niku states. "I was supposed to be with them. I'll vouch for you if it'll help."

Arru chuckles. "I'm certain that won't be necessary." Knowing what she is alluding to, the rest of us chuckle too.

Niku and Zoe look at us, confused, so I state, "You'll find out in the morning, but for now, let's eat."

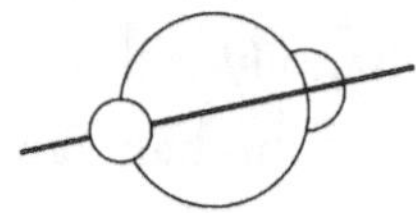

After breakfast, we find the caravan readying just outside the outfitters, near the middle of the village. Seeing us approach, a lioness in green lizard skin armor turns her attention to us.

"Larrah, Tayla, what brings you this far?"

"Mirra," Larrah coldly states.

"Contract," Tayla adds, equally cold.

She looks at the two and then at the signets on their armor. "Both for the same person. Who could have possibly beaten you in the Trials?"

I step forward, noticing that this lioness has light hints of spots on her arms and legs. "I hold their contracts."

She looks me over and grins. "How did you get into the Trials?"

"I entered him."

She looks at Kotu, then back at me. "Should I call you Pendekar?"

"My name is Kyle."

Her eyes widen. "Pendekar Kyle, Shaman of Pridewyn?"

"I am not a shaman."

"That's not what I heard." She chuckles, suddenly sounding friendly. "Well, is someone going to introduce the rest of your group?"

Tayla smiles and in a suddenly warm, friendly voice, says, "Mirra, this is Arru, Kotu, Sada, Fey, and Railu."

"I am Niku, and this is my assistant Zoe. We were supposed to catch you in Dendros."

Mirra nods and turns to her group. "Big guy there is Romo. Behind him are Hoke and Tret, traders. That's Nath over there with his friend Teza and her son. The rabbits over there are Tav, Insa, and their two daughters."

I look where she points as she introduces them. Romo's a big St. Bernard in near full plate armor and looks like he's carrying an axe. The traders are both ferrets, standing by their cart, arguing with each other. Nath is obviously a red panda, while his friend and her son are both raccoons. The rabbits also have a cart, which is good since their kits are very little.

Mirra looks around for a moment as if expecting somebody. "We did have another . . . Oh, there she is."

We turn to see a female skunk approach. She bears the look of someone with an education, holding herself properly, wearing a full-length red-and-black gown. She approaches me and extends a white hand to me. "Tria."

Responding in kind, I shake her hand. "Kyle."

"So do I pay before we leave or after we arrive?"

"You'll need to take that up with Mirra," I state, stepping aside.

"Half now, the rest when we arrive."

Tria bows and I instantly notice that she has three stripes on top of her head. As she hands Mirra a small handful of coins, I take a small step to the side and get to see that the three stripes continue down her visible back and tail.

Apparently noticing my look, she turns to me. "Yes, I have three stripes, first in generations."

To my surprise, I admit, "They're very fetching," drawing an annoyed look from both Sada and Tayla.

"So why do you travel to Three Lands?" Mirra asks.

"I heard that they were building a new school. I'm a teacher."

"Okay." She turns to me. "How about you and your group?"

"Three Lands is hopefully my last stop before continuing east."

She looks around at my group. "After the Dig, huh?"

I smile. "I am, yes, but she's after her mate."

Mirra turns to Railu. "A red fox who was also after the Dig?" Railu nods, turning her full attention to Mirra. "We met your mate and his party there. They headed out that way, oh, let's see . . . Romo?"

He tilts his head and then holds up three fingers.

"Yeah, almost three months ago."

"What took him so long to get from here to Three Lands?" Railu asks.

Mirra looks at her confused. "What'd you mean?"

"He was here almost ten months ago."

"Wouldn't know. We were in Lanketh then."

"Maybe we'll find out more once we reach Three Lands," I suggest.

Mirra turns to me. "So, anyway, are you wanting to be hired or what?"

"Not hired, just accompany."

"You bring three fighters with you. I can't overlook that."

"I also bring six to be escorted. *I* can't overlook that."

She sighs and bows. "I concede your point. Safety in numbers then."

With everyone ready, we set out from Lorholt. The weasels take turns pulling their cart while Nath and Tav each pull their own. Watching how Nath behaves with Teza and her son, I get the feeling that he wants to be more than her friend. He simply cares too much about her and it shows. Fey spends some time talking with Insa and ends up playing with her daughters. I find myself happy that she gets to be a little girl again, if only for a few days.

The first couple of days go smoothly, but we soon come across a broken cart that causes concern. Railu takes lead, watching for recent prints and traps. At night we take turns keeping guard, watching, and listening for signs of bandits.

After another two days, she finally finds fresh prints. Before continuing, we rearrange the caravan, making sure that the children are protected. Sada puts on her cloak, pulling the hood up and walks next to Fey, keeping her close. Those of us with bows make ready.

We proceed slowly and quietly; the only sound we make is that of the wheels as they roll. Everyone pays attention to what's around, not knowing where they may attack from. I keep my eyes wandering, trying to see everything I can.

Aime, let me know if you see anyone.

In response she quickly displays several crosshairs, indicating targets. Some are in the trees and some are on the ground. *Not good.* Feeling a sudden burst of fear from Tayla, I turn to look as Mirra shouts, "Get off the carts!"

I quickly unhook my cloak and throw it to Kotu. "Cover the kits!" I whirl and pull another arrow. Taking aim, I let loose the two arrows together at a pair of targets in a tree. As I watch them both fall, arrows shatter against my back.

I draw another arrow as I turn to see another arrow coming right at my face. Reacting without thinking, I raise my arm in defense. The arrow shatters harmlessly against my forearm.

I check my target to see that it's dropped from the tree, what I now see are two wolves charging at me. I let loose the arrow and drop the bow; the farther wolf drops to the ground.

I pull a sword and block the other wolf's first attack. I quickly follow with a cross-chest slash. His light armor and flesh split open and he collapses to the ground.

I swing at another attacker. My sword cuts through his armor, sending him to the ground. Suddenly I'm assaulted with a stabbing sensation in my left side and I hear a blood-curdling scream.

"Tayla!" I suppress the pain as I leap over the cart separating us, landing behind one of the hyenas surrounding her. As I stand up, I knock one of them aside with my elbow and then slash another with my sword.

As that one falls, Tayla again screams. In a blur, I see her pull the dagger out of her side and stab a hyena with it. That hyena collapses as Tayla drops to the ground. I throw a coyote aside as I rush to her.

I press my hands to her wound and feel her pain as she screams again. I know Aime is working hard to repair the damage. "I'm here love. I've got you."

I feel a tug at my quiver and then hear a yelp. I turn my head and see the coyote drop, an arrow lodged deep in his chest. Looking back, I see Kotu perched above me on the cart, Tayla's bow in hand. I look back down a Tayla and see her looking up at him. I see in her eyes the same mixed feelings that I have.

In that act, he's no longer a cub. He's an adult.

As Aime repairs the damage the dagger did to Tayla, I try to steel my mind. *My concern is Tayla. Kotu knows what he is doing.* As I feel another arrow being pulled from my quiver, my concern for him returns. *I hope.*

Sada suddenly appears holding her side. Noticing the confusion on her face as she checks herself, I conclude that she felt the pain too. Suddenly, Tayla tries to sit up. Reflexively, Sada and I stop her. "Easy, easy, not yet. Aime's not quite done."

Sada wraps her arms around Tayla and holds her, purring and rubbing on her at the same time. Noticing that Sada's not wearing her cloak, I conclude that most of the fighting's over.

"The jagged edge of the dagger did a lot of damage when you pulled it out," Aime states. "Just another moment, please. There, you will still feel some discomfort, but I have repaired most of the damage."

Sada and I help her to her feet and let her lean against a cart. As I remove my hand from her wound, I get to see that her blood trails all the way down her leg to the ground.

I look at Kotu, seeing him standing firm, bow drawn. I turn to where he's aiming and see the hyena that I elbowed, lying on the ground, holding his ribs. I glance back at Kotu and hold up my hand. He lowers the bow. "How many of you are there?" I demand.

The hyena looks at me, eyes quivering. "I...I don't know," he whimpers.

I pick him up by his tunic and hold him up to me. "How many?"

He tries to turn away. "I...don't count."

"You can't count?"

He shakes his head. "Never learned."

Sighing, I drop him. "Sit. Stay."

To reinforce my commands, Tayla lifts her blade and taps him under his chin. He immediately sits, still holding his side. I look around at the others. Larrah's tying two jackals together, and Railu is helping Mirra and Romo cover the bodies of the attackers that were killed.

"Aime, are we safe?" I ask and start taking a slow look around.

"I can detect no hidden threats. There appear to have been twenty attackers, most of which are now deceased."

From the center of the carts, a voice calls out, "Is it safe to come out?"

I step around the cart and lift one of the cloaks. "Everybody okay?"

Nath nods. "Scared, but okay."

Sighing, I say, "It's safe, but I wouldn't recommend coming out just yet, not unless you have a strong stomach. Let us get them covered so the kits don't see them."

Nath stands. "I will help you."

The females nod and Tria starts talking to the kits, keeping their attention on her with an entertaining story.

Arru stands. "I will let them know when it is safe for the children."

Niku also rises. "I will tend to the wounded." Zoe follows her as she starts to check the others for wounds.

We spend the next hour covering up the bodies, not for the sake of the dead, but so the children don't have to see them. With the bodies and the spilled blood covered by dirt or leaves, everyone starts checking their wares and belongings.

"Fey?" Kotu shouts. "Where's Fey?"

I see the others start looking around frantically, calling for her. "Fey!"

Looking at the closest captives, I ask, "Are there more of you out there?"

The jackals just look at me with contempt, so I turn to the hyena. With his ribs broken, we tied him up separately. "How about you, any more out there?"

He looks at me, then down to the ground. "The guards."

"Where are the guards?"

"Den."

"Where's the den?"

He looks around, then nods. "That way, I think."

"You think?"

"Not been out here before."

"What, is this your first time?"

"Yeah."

"What do you normally do?"

He hangs his head, apparently ashamed. "I, uhm . . . I, bring 'em food. I want to give 'em more, but I don't get enough to go around."

Realizing that there's more to what he's saying, I pry, "Give who more?"

He shakes his head, refusing to answer.

Rather than strong-arm him, I try an act of compassion to get him to talk. "Look, Fey's my daughter. Talk to me!" I put my hands on his ribs and his face relaxes as the pain subsides.

"The little ones," he confesses, crying. "Some of them like to keep the children."

"I found her trail!" Railu shouts.

"Where?"

Railu points to the softer ground at the edge of the road. "She went that way, and it wasn't by choice."

I turn and look at Larrah and Tayla. "Stay here, keep an eye on the kits."

Kotu approaches me. "I'm coming with you."

I put my hand on his shoulder and calmly state, "You should stay here."

"She's my family too."

Hoping I'm not making a mistake, I concede, "All right, but we do this quietly."

He nods, and I notice that he still has Tayla's bow. With a nod to Railu, we proceed into the forest. Walking single file, I follow Railu, walking in her foot-paw prints, in turn, Kotu walks in mine. I keep my bow ready as Railu skillfully follows Fey's trail. It seems, at first, Fey put a pretty good struggle, but the farther we go, we find fewer signs.

Abruptly stopping, Railu kneels to the ground. "Her prints are gone. She's being carried," she whispers, pointing to the ground. "See here. The other's prints are deeper, looks like a dingo."

"Is he alone?"

She looks at the ground for a moment. "Looks like it, but I can't be certain. His tracks have been difficult to follow until now."

Proceeding on, we get to a rocky hillside with a cave in it. We hide at the edge of the trees, checking for signs of guards.

Not seeing any, I say, "You two wait here, I'll check it out."

Both nod and I activate my armor's camo, once again making me invisible. I head down the cave, pistol ready. When it starts to get dark, Aime enhances my vision to compensate.

Entering a larger cavern, I see that there are few torches, providing a little light. There are also three anti-chambers and another tunnel that continues farther in.

In one chamber, I see a few carts, just small enough to make it through the entry cave. In another, I find a collection of bags, packs, and other gear, apparently loot from their other raids. In the third, a collection of weapons.

I continue down the cave, past a white wolf guard, and find a larger chamber with a stream running through it. There are several planks laid out across the stream, allowing easy passage over it. At the far wall, there's also an elevated pool, apparently used for fresh drinking water. At the opposite side of the room, there's a second pool below the floor level. From the look of it, I'd guess it was used as a bath. With two other guards in this room, I pick a stable board to cross and head deeper into the cave.

I quickly come across a makeshift door. Through the gaps in the boards, I see several children, all various ages, the oldest among them, Fey.

Aime, let Fey hear me. "Fey."

She rushes to the door, surprisingly calm. "Dad? Where are you?"

"Shh, not so loud," I whisper. "Are you ok?"

"Mostly, yeah. There's other children here, too."

I grit my teeth as anger makes me flush. "How many?"

She turns and counts, "Uhm, eleven." She then smiles. "I knew you'd find me."

"I'll be back for you in a few minutes. I need to make it safe."

"Please hurry. I'm scared, and they're hungry."

"I will, hun, I will."

I quickly return to Railu and Kotu. Deactivating the camo, I kneel next to them. "Three guards and almost a dozen children."

Railu's eyes go wide. "Children?"

"Yeah. Aime, can my pistol stun?"

"Not in the usual sense, but I can have it fire a dart that will keep someone stunned until removed."

"Do it." Then I look to the others. "Ready?"

Drawing my pistol, I lead them into the cave. In the first chamber, the wolf stands facing the entrance. From the shadows, I line up my first shot and fire. He quietly drops to the floor. Railu and Kotu quickly remove his weapons and tie his hands and legs. Leaving the dart in him, we move on to the other two.

How quickly can I fire two shots?

[1.5 seconds.]

Fast enough, I line up on the larger dingo and fire. He drops to the ground and the smaller dingo rushes to his side. As he looks up, I drop him too. We remove their weapons and tie them up. Railu goes to let the kids out. I follow close behind.

When she opens the door, most of the children run to the far end in fear, but once Fey happily hugs Railu, they start coming toward us. When Fey wraps me in a hug and calls me dad, most of the children swarm around us, realizing that they're safe.

We lead the children out to the other room and get them some fresh water. I pick up the larger dingo and remove the dart. He wakes up and starts growling and snarling, trying to bite me until I thump him on the nose. He instantly stops, realizing that he's tied and can't fight back.

"Why take the kids?"

"Alpha wouldn't let anyone pass through without paying in blood. None of us would kill the young."

I pull the dart off the other. As he wakes up he shakes his head several times. "What happened?" he asks groggily.

"What do you plan on doing with the children?"

Noticing that he's tied up, he thinks for a moment then answers, "I'm not sure." He then looks to the larger for help.

"Then why'd you take my daughter?" I ask, looking at the larger.

He looks at the ground. "I, uhm, I dunno."

Fey steps over and looks at the larger. "Then why'd you say I'd be a lot of fun?" She then turns and kicks him in the groin with her hoof.

I let him fall as he balls up, the smaller starts to scream at him, "WHAT? They're just children." He looks up at me, pleading. "I swear I didn't know."

I look over at him. "Who's in charge?"

"Khargh, he's a black wolf."

"He's dead," I state and then look at Railu. "Let 'em walk, but not run." As she reties their ankles, Kotu keeps ready, in case they try anything.

With those two and eleven children in tow, we head back out to the first chamber. Kotu sits the two dingoes next to the still unconscious wolf. Railu and Fey start helping the children through the collection of packs and bags, looking for more suitable clothing for them.

I pull the dart out of the wolf and as he wakes up, he growls and starts barking at me. "You're in no position to make threats," I chide him.

He starts to wiggle, struggling against the wire vine that binds him. As he continues to struggle, I notice that his wrists and ankles are starting to bleed.

"You're tied up with wire vine. You're not getting free. You're more likely to cut off a hand or foot."

"Maybe that's what I want," he grunts, struggling harder. Not wanting to put up with his struggling, I shoot him with a fresh dart.

With Railu and Fey having most of the children dressed in better clothes, I notice that none look older than seven. Aside from Fey being the only deer, there's also a rabbit, two raccoons, two ferrets, an otter, a red panda, and three squirrels.

"Most of these children are too little to walk far, and we don't have enough room on the carts," Railu points out, showing her concern for them.

I look around. "Well, we do have several carts over there." Getting a closer look, one is just like the long skinny flatbed that we used back at Arindell, but the other two are slung low with high walls.

I move one of the deeper carts over near the entrance, and despite their protests, Railu ties the two dingoes to the rings on its tongue. Fey then helps her line the wagon with blankets and some pillows from loot and start helping the children into it.

I grab the second cart and start loading the weapons and other gear into it. I drop the wolf on top and we set off to regroup with the rest of the caravan.

Once there we find that the dead are being cremated and that the others have found a suitable place to camp, nearly a kilometer away from where we were attacked. We tie the two jackals to the weapons cart and put the scavenged weapons in it. The hyena gets tied to the children's cart and we set off to meet with the families.

Finding camp, I see that we're set up near a stream. Seeing us return, Sada bounces happily over and wraps Fey in a hug. Tayla comes to me, pulls my mask off, and puts her nose to mine. "I knew you'd find her."

I put a hand on her wound so Aime can finish healing her, and I kiss her. "Vision?"

"No, I just knew." She then puts her hand over mine. "That feels weird, healing that fast."

"And I hope you never get used to it."

Catching my meaning, she agrees, "Me too."

Having managed to get free from Sada, Fey inserts herself into our hug and asks, "Did you get hurt?"

"Yeah, but I'm all better now. Are you okay?"

"He was mean so I kicked him."

Seeing me nod, Tayla says, "Good girl." She then gives her a gentle nuzzle, before letting her run off to play with the other children.

With almost as many children as adults, the camp becomes very busy. While Romo and I stand watch, all the children get baths. Fortunately Fey and Kotu help, making it a little easier for everyone.

With them now clean, we start to feed them. Aime makes sure to provide some extra vitamins and nutrients in their food, as they're showing signs of malnourishment.

I set up my second tent, making it quite large. I don't bother with any interior walls, preferring instead to let the children play inside the large room. This makes it much easier to keep track of them.

The prisoners we keep tied to the trees, under a lean-to. Not really my preferred treatment for them, but it's what most of the others agreed upon, without killing them.

After waking the wolf again and finding him more agreeable, I give them some food. Most of them, consigned to their fate, don't argue or fight, but the wolf still seems insistent on testing his bounds, though the way he's tied now, he can't fight his bindings so his struggling is useless.

Letting them eat, I have a moment to sit and relax. To my surprise, Fey brings the one girl rabbit that we rescued up to me.

"Dad, you need to see her," Fey states to me.

I look down at the little rabbit and I see a face that I haven't seen since Arindell. I try my best to keep my composure despite my feelings.

"Hi, what's your name?" I ask her.

"Amela." She then raises her arms to me and I reflexively pick her up and set her on my lap. She wraps her arms around me and relaxes. "Where's my mom?"

"What's your mom's name?"

She chews on her finger for a moment. "I dunno."

"Do you remember what she looks like?"

The little girl thinks for a moment and says, "She has dots, like me." She points to her nose and forehead. "And long ears."

"Fey, could you get one of the small converters, please." She nods and quickly returns with it. With a flash, a picture appears in the converter. As I pick it up and look at it, I sigh, realizing just how much I miss Megai. I turn the picture and show it to Amela.

"That's my mom." She takes the picture as I gently rub her back.

"How old are you?"

"Five."

"How long have you been away from your mom?"

She shrugs her shoulders. "Dunno, long time." She leans into me, still staring at the picture.

"How about your dad?"

"He tried to protect me, so they made him sleep." The way she says it, I know that she means that he was killed.

"I'm sorry," I whisper, giving her a gentle hug. *Aime, what do you think?*

"Surprisingly, Megai is a parental match, but my scan of Megai indicated that she never had a child."

Twin sister?

"Identical, maybe, matching markings are rare."

"Amela, do you know who Megai is?"

She keeps looking at the picture and finally shakes her head.

"That's okay." I give her another hug. "That's okay."

CHAPTER 14

After spending nearly a week traveling with a dozen small children, Three Lands is a most welcome sight. Finding some guards and a mediator, we explain everything that happened and hand over the six remaining bandits and the children.

I speak at length with the mediator about knowing where Amela's aunt is. The mediator assures me that if they cannot find any of her family locally, they would do what they could to contact her. After leaving the confiscated weapons and carts as a donation to help find the families, we part from the mediator.

Free and clear to pursue their own directions, the families quickly thank us and pay Mirra their remaining balances. Mirra then turns to us, offering us a portion of the pay. I politely refuse, again.

Saying our good-byes, we part our ways with the duo. Railu sets out to find information about her mate. Niku and Zoe set out to find the shaman while Tria heads off to find out about the school. The rest of us head off to browse the markets.

After a few hours, we all find our way to the café. I find myself beginning to like that all the villages have nearly identical layouts, even if the population here is primarily otters, weasels, minks, and the like. I realize that the location is perfect for the many water-loving people here, as it spans across the east and west branches of the Rock Falls River.

Waiting for our meal, we are approached by a mediator. "They council would like to extend their hospitality to you and your group, as thanks for taking care of the bandits."

I lay my head on the table, hoping I haven't just picked up another title. Tayla though, sensing my feelings, asks, "What does the council have in mind?"

"Nothing special, just a night's stay in the council inn for your party."

"No celebration in our honor, or anything like that?" Larrah asks.

Puzzled, the mediator states, "No, though Moonstorm is tonight and there will be a street fair after supper."

I sit up and ask, "Has this invitation been extended to Mirra and Romo?"

"Yes, another mediator is looking for them."

"Thank you, we'll accept," Arru states.

"I'll make the arrangements for you." She bows and leaves us to our dinner.

I sigh heavily and lean back in my chair. Tayla looks at me, curiously. "What's with the relief?"

"I didn't pick up a title this time." I chuckle.

Tayla purrs as she nuzzles me. "No, you didn't, but you still did a noble thing." Sada leans into me also purring, as everyone else chuckles.

Having just arrived, Railu takes a seat and asks, "What are you all laughing about?"

Larrah looks at her. "No new titles for Kyle today."

She smiles. "Good. I learned something interesting."

"What's that?" I ask.

"Roen came through here twice. The first time was about nine months ago. They went south then, to Burrowfield. The second time through they headed out east, having been through Lanketh and Pridewyn also." She takes a drink of water. "I wish I knew what they found out. We could cut several months off."

I suddenly realize that I may already have that bit of information for her. "The card!"

"The what?"

"The card that the councilor at Pridewyn gave me." I root through my pack for it. "I never even bothered to open it."

I hand it to Railu, who takes it and quickly opens it. After looking at it for a few moments, her jaw drops, "How . . . how did she know?"

"I have a guess," I glance suspiciously at Tayla. "She did that with most of us when we first left Pridewyn."

Seeing the cats nod, she smiles. "She's good."

"You better believe it. She sent us to find you," I state.

"And I'm glad you did," she states. "This allows us to bypass those villages, putting us about . . . two months behind." Her face lights up as she hears herself say that.

"Closer and closer," Larrah states.

I feel a sudden pang of regret, realizing that I'll need to be departing to the wilds sooner than I expected. Tayla gives me a sudden look of confusion as I suppress the feeling. I know she'll ask me about it later, or she may have already figured it out.

We enjoy our dinner, and I disperse some coin to those who need some as we set out to enjoy the festivities. With the future on my mind, I don't have a lot of fun, though I make a good show of it. After several game booths and a slow trip around the vendor kiosks, we watch the Moonstorm and then return to the inn.

I quietly change for bed and lay down, then Tayla comes in soon after and crawls up the bed to me. "What's wrong?"

Unable to stop myself, I say, "I have to say good-bye to some of you tomorrow."

"Only if you want to," she coos, "but I have a feeling that you may not have to."

"I know. I just don't want to put someone in danger if I don't have to."

She bumps my nose gently. "Isn't that our choice to make?"

Feeling a little relieved as she just provided me an idea, I rake my fingers through the soft fur of her cheeks, pulling her closer to me. "I love you." Hearing her start to purr, I gently kiss her muzzle.

"I love you too." She then gently bites my lower lip, letting her teeth slide along my skin as she pulls back.

"You're going to get me all wound up, you know."

"I know."

"And I know that you won't be in heat for almost a week yet."

"So?"

"So that means you want to torture me into something."

She gives my ear a light lick. "Maybe."

I release the straps on her armor and run my fingers down her back, all the way from her neck to her tail. Feeling her tail stand on end and her legs quiver, I know I found the right spot. "Two can play this game, love."

She collapses on top of me as I continue to gently scrub. When she moans gently and I feel her press herself into me, I stop. "That was cruel," she purrs.

Suddenly Sada comes in and crawls up next to us, purring hard and rubbing us both, extra friendly. "I think she felt your excitement."

Tayla gently scrubs Sada's head. "If that made you like this, how are you going to handle me being in heat?"

Sada's eyes go wide, as do mine. "Oh, that will be a whole new set of feelings for you to try to deal with."

She gives us a confused look, so Tayla explains. "I know that when we bonded, you started by imitating my behavior. Since you got wound up from what we just did, I worry that you'll feel everything, like you're in heat too." She gives Sada a nose-to-nose bump. "And I don't want to fight with you."

"And I don't want you two fighting either," I agree, "but this is something we'll have to figure out how to deal with."

"And soon," Tayla adds.

'Why?'

"She goes into heat in less than a week."

Sada's eyes go wide in surprise. 'Already?'

"Every month."

I find myself fighting a yawn, sleep wanting to claim me. "Is our conversation boring you?" Tayla asks.

"No, rather the opposite, but it is very late," I confess.

"We have some time yet. Let's get some sleep while we can." She then tosses her armor aside and they both climb under the light blanket with me. Once again, I fall asleep to the two-part harmony of their purring.

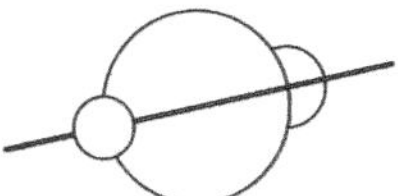

Standing at the eastern edge of the village, I look at my friends. "Larrah, your contract is up. You are free to choose your path from here. Arru, I know that you wanted to travel, but I don't expect you to continue beyond this point. The only one who needs to continue with me is Railu. I sincerely thank you all for coming this far with me, but out of my respect for you, I cannot ask you to come any farther."

Sada walks to me. 'I am always with you. I am your companion.'

"That word fails to mean what you are to me."

Tayla follows. "I am your mate. I am always with you."

I hug them both while trying not to cry. As they step behind me, I look at the others. Fey quickly wraps me in a hug. "I go with my family."

Kotu quickly follows. "Me too."

Arru casually steps to me. "I am with you, as your friend and advisor."

I give her a quick hug, as does Fey. I then look at Larrah. She stands in obvious conflict with herself, ears laid back, thinking hard.

I step up to her and softly state, "Your contract is up. I freely release you from any further obligation. What you do from here is completely up to you. Either way, no one would think less of you."

She slowly looks up to me. "I . . . I will come with you. You are the first to treat me equally, even when you had no reason to. That is an honor that I can never repay."

Seeing a tear flow from her eye, I extend my hand to her, "Friendship is an honor that is shared by both. There is never a need to repay." She nods in agreement as she takes my arm in hers.

After a moment, she lets me go. Seeing the smile on her face, I can't help but smile back. "Wow, I feel a lot better," she confesses, as she wipes a tear from her eye.

"Wonderful thing about confessions," Arru states, "they can make anyone feel better."

"Does your offer stand for us too?" I hear Niku ask.

We all turn to see Niku, Zoe, and Tria standing together, packs ready. "What happened to your prospective jobs?" Arru asks.

Niku speaks first, letting her frustration show. "That shaman was an idiot. She spent an hour talking with her 'spirit' only to tell her customer that he was fine. I had to lie and I gave him some berries that would help him."

"How about you?" Arru asks Tria.

"The school would have loved to have me, but they already have too many teachers."

"Zoe?"

"I go where she goes," she states, gesturing to Niku.

"You know we travel east beyond the wilds."

All three nod.

"Why do you want to go with us?" Railu asks.

Niku glances at Zoe, smiling. "I've always wanted to see what new plants, bugs, and other things are out there."

"And I see two children who could use some schooling," Tria adds.

"I cook," Zoe exclaims.

"It won't be all fun and exploration," I counter.

"We know," Niku and Tria state together.

I turn and look at the others. Receiving several nods and a shrug, I turn back to the three. "Very well, you may come along. Keep in mind that our first goal is to catch up to Roen and his group, hopefully before anything bad happens to them."

Seeing them nod, I continue. "We'll then proceed to the Dig, where we will, hopefully, find more of my kind." I smile at Tayla. "After that, we'll come back to the villages. I've no idea how long it will take, so is there anything you need to do before we depart?"

"We are ready," Niku states.

"As am I," Tria agrees.

"All right." I turn around. "Railu."

"As they left, they followed the tree line, staying in the open, so we'll do the same."

"Lead on."

She takes point and the rest of us follow her. I hang back a little and pull three tablets out of my pack.

"Now that you're going to be with us for quite a while, I'll give you each one of these. I know you've heard me talk to Aime, these will allow you to ask her questions too if I'm close enough. She can also learn from you, take notes for you, things like that."

I look at Niku. "She has a rather large encyclopedia of plants, bugs, and other creatures if you need to look something up. If you know something she doesn't, please feel free to add your own notes.

"For you," I look at Tria, "Aime has several tools to help you teach. Fey and Kotu both have one of these, so you can easily set up assignments for them. Aime will show you how.

"Zoe, you said you like to cook?" She nods enthusiastically. "Okay, you *love* to cook. There's a large library of recipes and dishes. Most are from my home, but I imagine that they can easily be altered. Feel free to add any recipes you know.

"I would like to caution you if there is something you don't want anyone else to know, please don't put it in these. While the rest of us won't look, Aime's not too familiar with the concept of privacy.

"When you're ready to start, just touch anywhere in this area," I state, gesturing to an area on the front of the tablet. "Have fun." I jog forward to resume my usual spot leading the main group while Railu scouts a fair distance ahead.

"You just made their world a lot bigger," Tayla states, taking hold of my hand.

"I know, but better they learn now, so they can get used to it like the rest of you already have. Besides, they're smart, shouldn't be much of a problem."

She sighs heavily and gently rubs her nose on my cheek so I return a kiss to the side of her muzzle.

Having set up camp for the evening, we sit down and start supper. While we eat, we notice voices from beyond the tall grasses. Our own conversations fall silent as we listen to the approaching sounds.

We start to make out two voices, one male and the other female, arguing over which way to go. The voices get closer, and we start to here footsteps. Suddenly someone trips through the tall grass into the open. He hits the ground face first causing the items from his pack to fall out, some bouncing off the back of his head. Not missing a beat with the argument he rubs the back of his head, saying, "See, I found the clearing."

As he puts things back in the pack, her response is somewhat satirical, if exhausted. "You couldn't find the clearing if you tripped and fell on it."

Hearing that, he rolls his eyes. Having repacked, he stands, puts on the pack, and turns to the grasses. "Over here."

As she approaches, she again chides him. "I know where you . . ."

He turns toward her voice, not sure why she stopped talking. "Ania? You okay?" He takes a couple of steps to his left and finds her, standing still at the edge of the tall grass, mouth hanging open. "Ania?"

He turns to look at what she is staring at and sees us, all curiously looking back at him. "W-what . . ." he stammers as he takes a step back, blocking our view of his companion. His sudden lack of motion allows us to get a look at him; he's a brown and tan otter. Aside from his pack, he is wearing a simple loincloth, a belt with several pouches hanging from it, and across his chest is the strap to a larger pouch hanging at his hip.

Fey suddenly calls out in an overly friendly voice, "Hello!" waving her hand enthusiastically.

He gives a small wave. "Uhm, hi?"

"Please join us," Tria calls out.

"Would you like something to eat?" Zoe adds.

He seems to want to come over, but a hand on his shoulder stops him.

"Well, if you prefer, the village is a day's walk that way," I offer, pointing the way we came from.

He turns and looks at his companion and then takes a step into the clearing. She then steps out of the grasses. Her markings are almost the same as his, but she has several thin stripes that travel up between her eyes, and we get to see that she is pregnant, very pregnant, so she is not wearing a pack, but instead a simple wrap dress and shawl.

"I'm Naro, and this is my mate, Ania," he nervously states as they slowly walk toward us. Kotu and Fey quickly set a pair of chairs up for them as they approach.

"Nice to meet you. Please sit and relax. I'm Kyle. This is Sada, Tayla, Larrah, Kotu, Arru, Railu, Fey, Tria, Niku, and Zoe."

They both sit. "We have food, thank you," he answers, starting into his pack.

Fey quickly sets up a table in front of them, as Niku chides, "Nonsense, we are offering. We have plenty. Here." She sets two plates of food, a mix of small berries with several strips of seasoned fish, on the table in front of them. Zoe brings a couple of drinking bowls with water.

Naro curiously eyes the table, seeming amazed at how it set up, but picks up the plates and hands one to Ania. She is less interested in the table and more relieved to be sitting, since she takes the plate, leans back, and breathes a heavy sigh.

"What brings you out here?" Niku asks, pulling up her chair to sit across from them, most of us follow suit, forming a loose circle around the table.

"We are going to see the shaman," he answers, nervous at all the sudden attention.

"I'm not sure what it is, but something is wrong. I don't feel right," she adds, rubbing her swollen belly.

"Do you still feel the pup kick?" Arru gently asks.

"Yes, but not like before. It's almost like they're weak, or I'm not as sensitive. I can't tell."

"They?"

"Oh, yes. I think there's two."

"When did you notice something wrong?" Niku asks as Zoe sets another bowl with more food on the table.

"A few days ago. I woke up and things felt different."

"Do you remember eating anything new the day before?"

"Not really, but we did have a family gathering a couple of days before, and there was a lot of food there," she admits. "I've had most of it before, but not while pregnant."

Niku thinks for a moment, then waves me over. "Kyle, come tell me what you see."

"Are you a shaman?" Naro asks.

"Not really," I admit, walking over to Ania.

"He's better," Tayla adds, making me smile.

"May I?" I ask Ania as I kneel to her left, holding my hands over her belly.

She nods. "What do you want me to do?"

"Just relax."

As I start to move my hands, she reaches her right hand out toward Naro, who turns his chair to face her and takes her hand.

To my surprise, Tayla comes up by Ania's head and reclines the chair slightly. "Better?"

"A little, thanks," Ania admits.

As I gently feel her swollen belly, I feel the gentle kicking of the pups. I find myself reliving a memory. In a moment I'm in bed, lying next to my pregnant wife. My hands are on her belly, getting kicked by my unborn son. Then just as suddenly, I'm back with my hands on Ania's belly, getting gentle kicks from her unborn. Feeling a tear run down my cheek, I look at Ania's face and she is leaned back, eyes closed. I look at Tayla and she is curiously looking back at me.

I focus my attention back to Ania. *Aime, let me see what you see.* My view of Ania's belly changes to that of the pups within. Looking at them, I find myself amazed at what I see. Aime starts showing me information about their weight, development, age, sex, and anything else she can learn.

Since Aime does not find anything wrong with them, I smile and look up to Ania's face, then at Naro's. "Congratulations, you are going to have three very healthy pups."

"Three?" they answer in unison, making both smile and happily look at each other. I notice that Tayla too, is smiling, but she is smiling at me.

Looking at the couple, I ask, "Would you like to know their genders?"

"You can tell?" Ania asks in disbelief.

"Yes, I can. Would you like to know?"

They hesitantly look at each other, then in unison answer, "No."

Behind me, I hear Fey chuckle, and Tria quietly shushes her.

I continue looking for a cause of Ania's discomfort. I move my hands around, helping Aime look for any problems. Naro keeps looking between me and his mate, a concerned look on his face. Since the pups are healthy, we turn our attention to Ania herself. Finding no problems down low, I move my hands higher and to her sides.

"I found a pinched nerve," Aime announces. "You'll need to put a hand directly to her upper back, on her spine."

"I'll need to put my hand under your back." I gently slide my hand between her back and the chair fabric. I feel her tense up, arching her back a little to give me room. Once I have my hand in position on her upper back, I say softly, "Okay, now just relax."

"She'll feel the difference immediately," Aime warns.

Continuing in the soft tone, I say, "I want you to take a deep breath. Now, slowly, let it out."

After a moment, Ania gives a small gasp, followed with "ooh, much better."

I pull my hand from between her and the chair. "There. Stay relaxed for a while and you'll soon have all your feelings back."

She looks at me, looking very relieved. "Thank you."

"You're welcome." I return to my chair, pick up my drink, and watch the girls gather around, taking turns talking to Ania and putting their hands on her belly to feel the babies kick. As I watch I notice that both

Railu and Tayla seem to be asking the most questions, and it seems that Ania is thoroughly enjoying the girl talk. Even Larrah seems interested despite herself.

I look around and notice that Kotu is practicing some fighting moves, obviously not wanting to participate in the gathering. While I watch him practice, I notice that Naro has moved his chair closer to mine, allowing the girls to encircle his mate. He turns to me and pulls a pouch off of his belt.

"We made these to offer to the shaman for her help." He holds it out to me. "Since you helped, they are for you."

"No, please, I'm not a shaman."

He puts the pouch in my hand. "Please you helped my mate. Maybe one of your mates would like them."

"Oh, they're not all my mates. Just Tayla." I find myself suddenly embarrassed.

"Why else would you travel with so many females?" he asks, puzzled.

"They chose to come with me," I admit, looking at the pouch.

He takes a good look at me as if noticing for the first time that I do not have fur or tail. A question crosses his expression but he says nothing as if he is not sure how to ask it.

"I'm human," I say, answering his unasked question.

His face reflects relief and that he doesn't know what a human is. Letting that go, he motions to the pouch. "Please open it."

I untie the strings and pour the contents into my hand. I'm astonished at what I see. In my hand is a matching set of ear wraps. They are large wire hooks that hang around the ear, from them are several thin strands of leather covered with patterns of light blue, white, and yellow beads, ending with a mix of detailed thin silver leaves, some with gold tips.

"You made these?"

"Yes. Ania helped with the design. I make the beads and leaves myself."

"These are nice."

"They're yours. Thank you for helping my mate and for dinner."

I look at the girls, still deep in conversation. "Your welcome, and thank you for the distraction"—I motion to the girls—"and for these," I say, looking again at the ear wraps.

"You're also welcome," he says with a nod.

"It's getting late," I note, looking up at the ringed sky. "We have room in this tent if you want to join us for the night. I also have a second tent if you prefer."

"Are there separate rooms inside?"

"There can be. Would you like one?"

"Please."

I look over to where Kotu was practicing. He's not there. I find that he's sat down behind me, carving more designs in his staff. "Kotu, could you please set up a room for these two, just off the door."

"Sure."

"Thank you."

We continue talking. He shows me some of the jewelry he has crafted. Some are simple, but some are elaborate with fine detail. I find myself impressed with his skill, and, to my surprise, Aime is also impressed. I make a few purchases and trades, supplying him with some wire vine and a few other items that he finds of value.

As the sun descends, we call it a day. We collect chairs and tables and put them just inside the door of the tent. I show Naro and Ania there room and wish them a good night. I then retire to my own bed.

Once I lay down, Tayla softly asks, "Can I ask you something?"

Figuring it must be important since she waited till night to talk, I say, "Always."

"When you started helping Ania, what happened?"

I sigh. "Putting my hands on her belly triggered a memory. I once had a human mate, and we had a son. I remembered her being pregnant, feeling my son kick my hands from within. I even remember him being born. I don't yet remember their names but I do know that I lost them both when he was very young."

Sada tears up and wraps her arms around me, putting her head to my cheek. I wrap my arm around her. "You know what happened, don't you?"

Sada wipes a tear from her eye as she sits up and nods. As she signs, I translate, "These memories are from before, when I was small."

"I remember the woman and small boy. They left and Kyle stayed. Later, Kyle was sad and had to leave. When he came back very late, he cried for a long time. I tried to comfort him, but he still cried. I never saw the woman and boy again." Sada puts her head back to my cheek and wraps an arm around me.

"Oh, I did not know you had a mate," Tayla says sadly, her ears drooping to match the feelings I sense from her.

Suddenly, I feel a rush of emotion as more memories come. As I start filling in Sada's story, tears fill my eyes. "Meagan was my wife . . . mate. Michael was my son. When he was a couple years old, he got sick. Meagan took him to the doctors, but there was an accident and they both died."

I feel tears roll down my face as I look at Tayla. She too is gently crying, holding her own tail in her hands like a tissue. "I'm so sorry," she manages to say and slides up to me and wraps her arm around me.

"That was over a thousand years ago," I mutter.

"But for you, it could have easily been just a few years," Tayla points out.

"Yeah . . . I suppose," I softly confess, putting my other arm around Tayla, as tears start to roll freely from my eyes. I feel the girls lay me down and curl up to me, Sada in her favored place on my left and Tayla on my right.

After breakfast, we pack up camp. Naro walks over to me and extends his arm. "Thank you, again, for everything," he says to me.

"My pleasure." I smile back, taking his arm in hand. Looking over at Ania, I admit, "She looks much better this morning, seems to glow."

He watches her for a moment and nods. "So where are you going?"

"East. Somewhere called the Dig. The same place Railu's mate was going."

"Oh, I hope you find what you're looking for."

"Thank you, good luck with your coming family."

As Ania walks over to me. I notice that she has a new basket full of various fruits, undoubtedly Niku's doing. She hands Naro the basket and hugs me. "I can easily feel them again. Thank you." She then reaches into a pouch on her own belt and pulls out an ear wrap, smaller than the ones that Naro gave me last night. Like the others, there are thin leather strips with several black beads accented with thinner red beads on them. The metal leaves on these are also black, accented with red tips.

"I made this just for you. Naro told me that he gave you the others, but I wanted you to have one too. I saw your armor last night and made this to match, my gift to you." She puts it on my right ear and makes subtle adjustments to make sure it fits. "It looks right on you," she concludes.

Looking around, I get several nods from my friends and Naro. "I . . . thank you. It will take a little getting used to, but I will wear it."

"Thank you again." She then turns to her mate. "Are we ready?"

"Yes." He smiles. "Let's get to the market."

With that, they walk off down the path to town, holding hands.

Tayla walks up to me, looks at the ear wrap. "It does look good on you. What are her pups anyway?"

I wait till they're out of earshot. "Three girls."

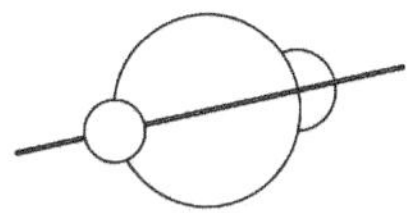

With the evening of Tayla's heat approaching, Sada starts feeling the effects. We quickly make camp and lie Sada down in bed as she starts trembling. I have Aime examine Sada to see if it's just mental or if it's also physical.

Tayla looks at me and says, "I'm used to the onset, so I can shrug it off for a while, but she seems to be going through her first heat. This won't be easy for her."

I hold a hand to Sada's cheek and one on her belly. "The emotional effects are strong enough to cause some physical ones too. It will be close to the real thing," Aime states.

Tayla kneels down next to Sada. "Sada, eat this, it should help." As Tayla tries to put the nao berry in Sada's mouth, she tries to bite Tayla's fingers. She hands me the berry. "You'll need to feed it to her. She's further in than I thought."

Sada curls on her side, holding her belly. I cautiously hold the berry in front of her nose. "Come on, open up," I gently coach.

Sada sniffs at it and then starts licking my hand. I try to get her to lick the berry but each time she does, she shakes her head. She then reaches out and pulls me to her and starts licking my lips.

Thinking quickly, I pop the berry in my mouth, crush it. I then let her lick the juice from my lips as she licks me. It works, and she soon begins to feel its effects.

'Sleep,' she weakly signs.

"She's scared," Tayla informs me as she lays her muzzle alongside Sada's. "You're okay, love. It's a normal feeling. It will get better." I hear Tayla start to purr, trying to comfort Sada.

'Make me sleep,' she signs as a tear roll down her fur.

"Aime, can her nanites help with the symptoms?" I ask, still holding my hand to Sada's cheek and belly.

"To a small degree, I can have them remove any surplus of hormones in her system, but since most of the symptoms are psychological, her suggestion of sleep may be the best solution."

Sighing, I sadly look into her blue eyes. "I did not want this."

'Not your fault.'

"I know." *Aime, do both, make her as comfortable as possible.* "Sleep well." I kiss her as she falls asleep purring. I check her vitals, making sure she is resting comfortably before I stand.

Sensing my guilt, Tayla wraps me in a hug. "You have no reason to feel guilty. None of us could have predicted this."

"I know, but—"

"She will get used to it, all females do. This is her first. The first is always the worst, even if it is false." She turns to Sada, giving her another nuzzle. "You will feel much better in the morning, I promise." She then leads me from the room. "We need to eat. It's going to be a long night."

After supper, we find that Aime has had the tent rearrange our room slightly. Sada now sleeps in a separate room, off our usual room, leaving the bedroom slightly smaller.

Feeling Tayla's nervous anticipation, I pull her to me and let my feelings for her fill me. She relaxes noticeably and starts to purr as she pulls me closer, gently licking my face. She stops for a moment. I feel her curiosity and fear mix. "I've never . . . will it hurt?"

I try to convey my love to reassure her. "Maybe, at first, we can go slowly." I start removing her armor, dropping it off to the side. She follows suit, removing mine, piece by piece.

I feel her nervousness fade and a mix of confidence and anticipation build inside her. I let her feelings fuel my own. She runs her hands over my chest, feeling me. I let my hands roam over her, ruffling her fur as I feel her body. She presses her muzzle to me, breathing hard.

I begin to realize that I can easily smell her, and feeling her urges, I start licking her, as she licks me, tasting her. In response, she presses herself to me. Feeling her closeness, I pick her up and she wraps her legs and tail around me.

As I sit down on the bed, her confidence builds. Instead of licking, she starts gently raking her teeth across my skin. I feel her hips get closer, then a sudden pang of fear and she backs away. I let my trust of her swell up, hoping she feels it.

She repositions her legs under her and she raises herself up. I feel her heat slowly envelope me as she lowers herself down. Her eyes go wide and I feel brief pain from her. I gently hold her, letting her know to take her time. She takes a deep breath as she rises up a little. She puts her hands on my shoulders and sinks down. This time there is no pain, only pleasure.

She lifts herself up again. I let her slide through my fingers as she sinks down all the way, coming to rest on my lap. Breathing hard, she leans into me. "Let's stay . . . like this . . . for a moment."

"When you're ready." I gently hold her to me, letting her decide when to start moving. Slowly, she starts rocking; the sudden stimulation brings my excitement rushing back. I feel her excitement build in turn and she changes to vertical movement.

Driven by passion, my hands caress her body. Finding her breasts, I massage them, stimulating her nipples. Hearing her moan, feeling another rise in her excitement, I curiously lick at one.

She gasps and I feel her body tighten and claws sink into my back. Catching herself, she withdraws her claws and pulls my head back to her breast. I take her breast into my mouth and let instinct and desire guide me.

Feeling Tayla resume her movement I start to lose the distinction between her pleasure and my own. Our pace quickens, feeling ourselves nearing. I rake my fingers down her back, once again finding the sensitive spot on her back.

The stimulation proves too much. I feel her body clamp down on me, hard. She screams out her orgasm as she arches her back, her claws sink into my back as she holds on to me, trying to force me deeper into her. My body returns her effort, trying to push deeper and I explode into her.

We slowly come down from the high. Her strength fades and she collapses into me, breathing hard. Feeling our mutual exhaustion, I lay back on the bed, carefully bringing her with me. I barely register the bed lengthening under my legs as I fall asleep.

The feeling of a tongue against my cheek wakes me. I open my eyes to see Tayla's face, eyes closed, lying on the bed next to me, still asleep. I turn my head and meet her lick with one of my own. The sudden sensation of my tongue on hers wakes her.

With her tongue still sticking out a little, she gives me a puzzled look so I lick her tongue again. She smiles, pulling it in, and snuggles up to me, purring. I wrap my arm around her and we happily drift back off to sleep.

Feeling the bed move, I open my eyes to see Tayla sitting up, absently pulling at the tip of her tail. I sit up behind her and gently wrap her in a hug. "What's wrong?"

She lets her tail drop to her lap. "I thought I'd feel different."

"How so?"

She sighs and leans back into me. "I thought I'd feel more mature now."

"Why's that?"

She takes my hands in hers. "Because I'm one step closer to completing the cycle. I've seen several others change after they mated."

Feeling her confusion, I say, "*You* are not like the others."

She turns her head to look at me. "What's that supposed to mean?"

"Well, for starters, how many of the others would choose a mate that's not a cat?"

She visibly thinks for a moment. "None."

"Okay, something else I learned while at Pridewyn, the males can be . . . persistent. I've noticed that both you and Larrah appreciate that I'm not like that."

She smiles. "Yes, we do."

"So you've not done anything you weren't ready for."

She leans back into me. "Are you trying to tell me that I don't feel more mature because I was already mature enough?"

I kiss her. "Mature, smart, beautiful, and most importantly, in love with the one who loves her."

She snuggles into my arms, purring. We sit silently for a while, simply enjoying each other's presence, and then I get an odd feeling from Tayla.

"Can we have cubs, together?"

I think for a moment. "Well, not that I'm aware of," I admit, suddenly feeling a little saddened by her question.

"There may be a way," Aime interjects. "I will have to perform some simulations, but I believe I can make it possible."

Tayla turns and looks at me again. "What do you mean?"

"Much like Kyle had me make some alterations so he would react appropriately to your estrus cycle, I should be able to recreate his DNA to permit conception."

She looks deeply into my eyes. "You can do that?"

"I will most certainly try."

"Thank you, Aime." She wraps her arms around me. "That would be so nice."

"To be a mother?" I ask curiously.

"To be the mother of *your* cubs."

I give her a long kiss on the muzzle. "You'll make a wonderful mother."

I see her smile as she puts her head under my chin. "You've already proved to be an excellent father."

Unexpectedly, Sada peeks through the door. "How are you this morning?" Tayla asks. Sada happily sits and wraps us in a hug.

"What's that for?" Tayla asks.

I translate as she signs, "For wanting a family."

"We are a family," Tayla states.

She waves her hands and signs again, changing the last word. "Ah, for wanting children."

"You were spying on us?" Tayla teases.

Sada starts purring again as she nuzzles Tayla under the chin.

Tayla lifts her head, trying to get away from Sada. "It's hard to stay mad when you do this."

"That's why she does it." I chuckle. I then scoop them both into a hug. "No arguing, my loves. It's too early. Let's get dressed and then eat."

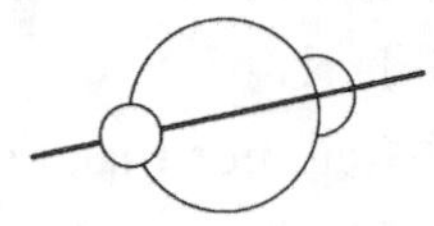

Railu hops up on a large embedded rock and holds her hand up, shielding her eyes from the sun. "We should be seeing one of them by now."

"What are you looking for?" Tayla asks.

"A marker. Usually, they're a tall stack of stones or one big one stood on end."

"Let me look." Railu hops down and Tayla takes her place. After a slow scan of the flat, eastern horizon, she says, "I see it. Still about four kilometers out."

"You can see that far?"

"Of course, I can see farther too," Tayla admits.

"It's a cheetah thing," Larrah states.

"What, we just have good eyesight."

"Lead on, sighted one," Railu jokes.

Tayla takes her by the arm. "Come on, you're with me."

The marker turns out to be a collection of flat stones stacked nearly two meters tall. Railu starts circling it, looking carefully at the rocks. "There's usually a box . . ." Suddenly she reaches out and moves a rock. "There it is."

She pulls out a small box, no bigger than one of the rocks. She clears an area on the ground and dumps out the contents. The others gather around and I sit down next to her on the ground as she starts looking through the small disks that came out of the box. I pick one up and examine it.

"They're signets."

Still looking, she explains, "The builders of these markers always put theirs in a box, either inside or under the marker. Explorers, scouts, hunters, everyone's taken to adding theirs, a way of claiming 'I was here' if you will." She drops a few in the box and picks up some more. "They should have come by this . . ." She abruptly stops, staring at the one in her hand.

"Whose?"

"Amsel's." She sets it aside and starts looking again. She sets another aside. "Sarn's." She holds another up, then squeezes it in her hand. "Roen's."

I see a tear roll down her face. "If his is here, that means he was here, right?"

"Yeah, it's an honor, of sorts, for a scout or an adventurer to put their signet in."

"Is Rami's there?"

She looks through the remaining signets, then dumps them all back out and looks again. "His isn't here. Why isn't his here?"

"Could he have forgotten to put it in?"

"Not a chance. He always carried extras." She sits back, a look of sadness overtaking her. "The only reason I know that would have prevented him is . . . is he didn't make it here."

"How well did you know him?" Tayla asks.

"He hired Roen a few times, for caravans. I never really got to know him more than Roen's talking about him."

Larrah kneels behind Railu. "We all feared this possibility, but your mate is not lost. Morn only the loss of his friend. Do not morn what you fear may happen."

Railu nods. "Won't be easy, but I . . . I will try."

"If ever you need to talk," Arru nods.

"I know," she concedes. "You're all like family."

"Remember that," Tayla states, smiling.

I gently take the three signets from Railu and put them back in the box. I then pull a copy of mine from my pocket and add it to the box. "I was here."

Railu takes one of hers from her pouch. "So was I."

I hold the box up as the others start dropping a copy of their personal signets in. Railu takes the box and puts it back in the marker. She turns east and stands, eyes closed in silence for a moment. "Welcome to the Wilds."

CHAPTER 15

After nearly a week's walk, a sudden loud, but a distant crack gets our attention.

"What was that?" Tayla asks Railu.

"I'm not sure," she confesses.

We hear another loud crack; this time followed with an unusual sounding yell.

"That sounds like a whip," I offer.

"Who would be way out here with a whip?" Larrah asks.

Two more cracks ring out, and another yell, this time sounding like they're in pain.

"Whoever it is, it sounds like there's someone on the receiving end. I'm going to go check it out." I set my pack down and make a quick check of the sun's position. "Might as well set up camp. Find a good place for the tent and get things set up."

"I'm going with you." Larrah sets her pack down and readies her staff.

Getting an invading sense of concern, I kiss Tayla to let her know that I understand her feelings. Sada slides up next to her, apparently sharing the concern, and I kiss her too.

Larrah and I head out through the trees, following the whipping sound. When we get close, we're able to make out two voices. Although we're unable to understand what is being said, we can tell they're arguing. We get in closer, trying to get a look at who they are.

We find two arguing figures standing over a third. They are all similar, being reptilian and standing on their hind legs. They have very long, thin tails that they are using like whips, trying to hit the other with them. The way the stand and move remind me of Earth's raptor dinosaurs, though without the massive claws, their arms are slightly larger and their eyes face more forward. They have no visible teeth and their scales are smooth, primarily green with brown stripes or spots.

Larrah looks at me, puzzled, and mouths, 'What are they?'

Aime? I mentally ask.

Unknown, she responds visually, prompting me to look back at Larrah and shrug my shoulders.

As we continue to watch, the larger one keeps bleating at the other, whipping its tail in the air, trying to get it to back up, which it reluctantly does, bleating back from a lower stance. Once the larger feels that the other is back far enough, it turns his attention to a third on the ground. This one has softer features, and several stripes running from its eyes to its tail, or rather its stump. The tail appears to have been bitten off.

As the larger leans over the softer one, it lets out a series of bleats and hoots, which the smooth one seems to understand as it lays flat on the ground, closing its eyes. The larger then starts swinging its tail and whips the smooth one across its neck, making it scream out in pain.

Aime starts to identify differences between the three, labeling the one on the ground as female and the other two as male. Getting Larrah's attention, I try to relay this to her. After a couple of attempts, I finally get her to understand and make a mental note that it may be a good idea to teach sign language to the others.

Looking back, we see that the smaller male has tried to intervene, as the larger male is again whipping and bleating at him. The smaller male tries to stand up for himself and whips and bleats back, trying to push the larger away from the cowering female. He doesn't succeed.

The larger charges and bites at the smaller, who manages to duck and hop back. The female picks up her head to watch the fight but the larger male turns and bites her on the neck, making her again call out in pain.

I hear Larrah reflexively growl and start a lunge, apparently wanting to aid the female, but she quickly stops herself. I turn back to see that both males are looking in our direction. They glance back at each other and then back in our direction. There's a brief exchange of sounds between them and they start to approach us.

I see Larrah bare her teeth, her hands tightly wrapping her staff, forcing her claws out. Hearing one of the approaching males make a gurgling sound, we both stand and assume our defensive stances. Both males lunge, the larger to Larrah, the smaller toward me. I see Larrah leap over the male attacking her as I turn to block an attack from the male attacking me.

Squaring off, his hunkered stance rivals my own height as he bleats in my face, so I do a spin kick that catches him alongside his face. He spins and uses the momentum to whip at me with his tail. It lands along my back, my armor absorbs most of the blow and I take a step to steady myself.

He starts slinging his tail furiously, repeatedly whipping me, trying to keep me off balance. I plant my feet, forcing the armor to adhere to the hard-packed ground. In between strikes, I manage to pull a sword. Timing his strikes, I start taking swings at his tail. Sparks fly as I make contact and pieces of his tail go flying

He quickly realizes that he's losing his tail and changes tactics. He extends his claws and bleats at me again, louder than he had before.

I take a step back into an attack stance and pull my other sword. He charges, claws out, mouth open. I feign an attack and fall back into a backflip kick, landing my boot squarely under its chin. He flies over me but manages to grab hold of my leg with his clawed hand. As I land flat on my back, he flips and slams to the ground, but quickly gets to his feet as I flip up and land on mine.

He charges again, this time holding himself lower to the ground. I jump up to flip over him but he lifts his head and bites my leg, stopping my momentum. As gravity takes over, I point my blades down, running both blades run through him as I fall on him.

I pick myself up and pry his mouth off my leg. Retrieving my swords, I scan for Larrah and find only her staff.

"Larrah!" I spin around, trying to see any sign of where she went.

Suddenly she comes out from between trees, running by me. "Look out!" She claws a tree, trying to change direction, but she loses grip and falls, sliding roughly on the ground.

Quickly realizing that I stand less of a chance against the larger male, I turn to face him as he comes out of the foliage. I plant my feet, the boots again locking to the ground. Balling up my fist, I pull back and drive my fist into the larger male's face, the combined force of my augmented punch, and his momentum crushes his skull and breaks my forearm. He collapses lifeless at my feet.

I grab my arm as I turn to Larrah, Aime tells me not to move the arm and hand, as I now have several broken and dislocated bones. I look at it, noting that from my forearm out, the armor doesn't fit right. Apparently my arm is shorter.

"You okay?" I ask Larrah as I help her up with my other hand.

She checks herself, making sure to give her tail a good look-over, "He got me a couple times with his tail, but he didn't get a bite of mine. How about you?"

I hold up my right hand, still balled in a fist. "Big one had a thick skull." As if to reinforce the point, my nanites pop a bone back into place, making me wince in pain. "He was trying to bite your tail?"

"Yeah," she confirms, shrugging her shoulders with her tail wrapped around her waist, protecting it. She walks over to the one that was chasing her, noting that his face is crushed in; she kneels to inspect the body. "I've never seen anything like this."

"Neither has Aime. It took her a while to figure out who was male and female. Still hasn't figured out the language." I wince again as other bones pop into place.

Suddenly something brushes against my left arm. I look down and see the female gently rubbing her head against me. Even though she is standing, she has assumed a very submissive stance, standing no taller than my shoulders but holding her head at my waist, under my hand. I find it odd that she can maintain her balance without her tail. To my surprise, she starts making a gentle cooing sound as she rubs on me.

"I think she likes you," Larrah comments. I note a touch of sarcasm in her voice.

I gently try to push her away, but she flinches when I put my good hand to her. Curious, I kneel and put my hand out to her, palm up.

She gives me a curious look, then puts her nose under my hand again. I slowly turn my hand over and gently rub her nose. She gently resumes her cooing.

"Well, at least *you* seem friendly."

She gives me another curious look, obviously not understanding what I said.

"You can use your hand again," Aime tells me.

The girl stops cooing and cautiously moves her head, attempting to look past me. She takes a step to the side as she looks. Apparently not finding anything, she again gives me a curious look.

"I think she may have heard you," I note aloud.

"I agree."

The creature takes a slow walk around me as she intently looks around, apparently searching for Aime.

I put my hands back out in front of me and she gently presses her nose into them, resuming her gentle cooing. As she stands there, I slowly move one of my hands to the side of her neck, to where the larger male had whipped her. "Aime, can you heal this?"

"I can try."

The girl seems to ignore Aime this time but does look back at my hand suspiciously. After a minute the wound starts to close. When I remove my hand, she cautiously feels the area with her own hand, searching for the cut that was there. When she finds nothing, she turns sideways to me and lies flat on her belly, cooing again.

"Looks like she wants you to finish," Larrah snickers.

"You think this is funny, don't you?" I chide.

"Of course, you seem to pick up another female each place you go. I think this one wants you to keep her."

I give her a curious look. "I think this one is used to being abused."

She slowly steps over. "What?"

I start pointing to various places along the creature's back. "Look at all these old scars. Here's some bite marks. It looks like her arm was even broken at one time and didn't heal well."

Starting her own exam, Larrah flinches noticeably and states, "It looks like her tail was bitten off, and there's even more scars over here." She sidesteps and keeps looking. "It looks like she may have a broken rib," she says point to a slight deformation along the creature's side.

I gently put my hands over the area and she noticeably flinches, her cooing changes to a whimper.

"It's a fresh break," Aime comments. "This will take a minute."

I nod to Larrah and she gently starts rubbing the girl's neck, hoping to keep her calm. When her cooing resumes, Aime sets the rib back in place. She yelps and jerks from the jolt of pain, but doesn't fight. Larrah resumes rubbing her neck prompting her to start cooing again.

"She seems to like that," I comment to Larrah.

"There's a lot of bite marks here. I figured it's a tender spot."

"Well, her ribs fixed. Should I check her tail?"

"I wouldn't worry. Vipers and dragons can regrow theirs. She probably can too. Besides we should get back to the others."

"What about her?"

"If we leave, she should go back to where she belongs."

"I hope so."

As we get up, the girl rises to her feet but does not stand completely up. I look at my arm and notice that the armor has finished repairing itself. I give the girl a gentle pat on the head, and we turn to head back to our group.

I start to look back but Larrah stops me. "Don't look back. It will only encourage her to follow."

Leaving the tree line, we easily spot the tent and I see Larrah's ear twitch. "She's following us, isn't she?" I ask.

"Yes."

Sighing, I turn and see her trying to hide behind some tall grass. I tilt my head and she tries to duck from view, so I walk back to where she's hiding. She realizes that she's been seen and walks over to me, holding herself low and cooing. I notice that she now has a small, hand-woven pack.

I give her head a rub. "I'm not going to get rid of you, am I?"

She rubs her head against me, still holding her body low, submissively.

Sighing, I submit, "Come on." Keeping my hand on her, I start walking again, and she gets the idea and follows.

Everyone stares as we approach. The girl tries to hide behind me, obviously afraid, and starts chattering, apparently trying to tell me something. I know Aime is trying to understand what she is saying so I let her talk. She apparently trusts me more than she fears the others as she sticks close to me.

Tayla cautiously walks up to me, giving me and the girl a curious look. "What happened?" she asks suspiciously.

"We found her and two males like her. Couldn't understand what they were saying, but they were apparently fighting over her."

Larrah picks up, confessing, "They didn't know we where there until I got mad, gave away our position."

"They stopped fighting over her and teamed up to attack us. Neither one of us was prepared for the way they used their tails like whips."

"One kept trying to bite my tail," she adds, wrapping her tail around her waist again.

"They could think tails are important," Aime offers.

"That's right," I add, "mine got real mad when I started cutting off pieces of his tail, and hers is nearly gone, bitten off."

Tayla looks down where the girl's tail should be. Seeing only a stump, she also wraps her tail around her waist. "Can you heal it for her?"

"I'm not sure. It took Aime a while to learn her biology. Aime?"

"We're starting to run low on power but I should be able to get the bleeding under control."

I turn back to the girl. "Let's see what we can do." I gently rub her neck, trying to let her know that I mean her no harm. Hearing her start to coo, I cautiously make my way to her tail. Apparently sensing what

I'm doing, she abruptly turns to face me, not allowing me near her tail. She ducks down submissively but gives me a soft throaty gurgle.

"Okay, I take it that the tail is off-limits." I hold my hands up and back away from her.

"Are you sure she's safe to be around?" Arru asks.

"That's the first time she showed any hostility. She's been submissive until just then," Larrah points out. "Wait, I was near her tail earlier." Larrah starts rubbing the girl's neck when the girl starts cooing again, she cautiously steps toward the girl's tail. She turns to look at Larrah but does nothing else.

As Larrah takes another step, the creature watches cautiously but does nothing. So she takes yet another cautious step. Now standing near her hip, Larrah gets a good look at the stump. She turns away, trying not to gag. "I can't...there's...something in the wound."

Niku gets up and cautiously walks over to Larrah and looks at the girl's stump. "Big warrior can't handle some bugs," she politely chides.

Larrah glares back. "Bugs on the dead I can handle, but that's worse than any infection. Seeing those on the living makes me sick."

Niku looks at the creature and cautiously reaches out to touch the stump. She watches Niku carefully but doesn't make a sound. Picking out one of the bugs, Niku takes a good look at it. "Some kind of larva."

Seeing the bug larva, the creature turns to get a closer look at it. This motion startles Niku, making her drop the bug while she backs up. The creature bends down and gets a close look at the bug. Seeming to know what it is, she gurgles, "Nush-ta kek," and crushes it with her fingers.

"Okay, she knows the bugs are bad," Niku comments. "Zoe, bring me my kit."

Zoe comes over with the kit, cautiously hands it over, and then nervously retreats. Returning to the creature's tail, Niku gets out a pair of tweezers and starts picking out the bugs, putting them in a bowl. The creature watches intently but lets Niku work undisturbed. Once Niku's satisfied she's removed them all, she pulls a couple of bottles and several leaves out of her kit.

She opens one of the bottles and sets one of the larvae on the ground. With a dropper, she takes some of the liquid and drips it on the things' body. Getting no reaction she squishes it and sets another larva out. She drips a few drops from the other bottle on it and it starts writhing and changing colors, from white, darkening to tan, eventually to brown as it stops moving. She adds a few more drops to the other larvae; they all react similarly.

Happy with her results, she gets out her mortar and pestle. She crushes some of the leaves into it, adds several drops of the liquid, and mashes them together until the mix is a paste. She occasionally adds another leaf or more drops and continues until it's a consistency she likes. "Comfort her," she says to Larrah. "This part may sting."

Larrah starts to gently rub the girl's neck but does not block her view of what Niku is doing. The girl watches curiously as Niku starts to gently apply the paste to the stump. She lurches slightly and then starts to make an odd trilling sound as Niku touches her stump.

Niku looks apologetically at her before applying some more. She flinches again, but not like before. Niku finishes, using all the paste she mixed and then disposes of the larvae in the fire. The creature twists around and looks at the paste on her stump, but doesn't touch it.

"Well, she seems to understand that it's good for her," Tayla states and then turns to me. "What are we going to do with her?" she asks me, genuinely concerned.

I have a seat in my chair, rubbing my head. "I really don't know."

"We tried to leave her behind but she followed."

Unexpectedly, the creature walks up beside me and sets down the pack. She then backs up a few steps, and says, "Tss ka-le. Ne'ta Oana sae ka-le." She then bobs her head a couple of times and gently nudges the pack with her nose.

As the creature lies down alongside my chair, Tayla asks, "What was that?"

"I believe that she just presented you with the pack and its contents," Aime suggests.

"Did you understand her?" I ask, hopeful.

"Sadly no, I have yet to learn the language, though it seems to be a rather delicate mix of both action and voice."

As I sit for a moment, looking at the girl, Tayla sits next to me. I reflexively put my arm around her, gently pulling her to me. I notice that the girl is carefully watching me do this and tilts her head slightly, as if curious.

Sada walks over to the girl and kneels next to her. They eye each other curiously for a few moments. Sada then holds out her hand. The girl curiously looks at it, then puts her nose against the palm of Sada's hand, sniffs it, and starts cooing. Sada gets an odd look on her face, which quickly changes to a smile as she puts her cheek to the girl's nose and starts to purr. In response, the girl closes her eyes and lays her head down, still cooing.

"Well, that was interesting," Tayla quietly comments.

I pick up the crudely made pack. Looking through it, I find several coils of wire vine, a few crudely made wooden bowls, several wrapped bundles of various leaves, and an odd-looking stone.

I pull out the stone and turn it over a few times, getting a good look at it. It's thick, flat, has a V-shaped notch on one side, and is very abrasive. "Aime?" I ask.

"It appears they use it to sharpen their claws. I'm finding large amounts of keratin on it."

"Keratin, huh, that's a little unexpected, especially, with all the metals around," I point out.

"Well, I have also learned that they are primarily herbivores, and apparently the closest thing to a native mammal this planet has, aside from the Moku. I have detected no genetic alterations. They apparently have evolved to this state naturally."

I think for a moment. "So the researchers were wrong. There is a sentient species on this planet."

"Obviously, though I do not understand how they could have missed it," Aime retorts.

I glance back at the creature, noting that Sada is now draped out across her back, apparently asleep, and the creature is still gently cooing.

I reach down to gently rub her head and she rises up a little to meet my hand.

A rumbling comes from her stomach, waking Sada. The creature turns and looks curiously at her stomach, then at me. I put the stone back in the pack and pull out one of the leaf bundles. She gives me a hungry look and holds her mouth open to me in anticipation.

I untie the bundle and pull out a handful of leaves and offer them to her. She eyes my hand curiously, then gives the leaves a few sniffs. She cautiously and delicately takes the leaves from my hand with her mouth. She stays next to me as she slowly eats, so I take one of the bowls and fill it with water from my canteen. When I set it down next to her she starts, pauses to sniff it, then looks up at me cooing. I put the rest of the bundle in another bowl and set that down next to the water.

We have our own supper, everyone getting used to the creature's presence. We all curiously watch her as much as she watches us. To my surprise, after supper, Fey sits down next to the girl and starts talking to her, apparently trying to get the girl to understand her name. After several attempts, the girl seems to get the idea and says, "Ay."

Fey giggles, very happy she got her to say something. She then says, "Ffffay."

She repeats this several times, and the girl makes a few sounds, apparently trying to find one like it. She finally comes out with, "Vey," making Fey very happy. The creature seems to understand this and she looks at me. I smile and she gets a similar look of happiness.

Fey settles down a little, then starts with Sada's name, prompting Sada to sit next to her. Sada watches Fey pronounces her name, she then watches as the girl tries to pronounce it. After a few tries, she does manage to pronounce it correctly, "Sada."

This achievement makes me smile more, and I also notice that the girl does not look at me this time before joining the girls with their little celebration. Kotu comes over and sits down, next to them. As the girl looks at him, she gets nervous and walks back over to me, cowering down at my feet.

Kotu looks a little confused by this. "What?"

I reach down and rub the girl's neck; she relaxes and starts to coo again. "I think you scared her."

"If what we saw before the fighting started is typical behavior, I believe she may see him as a rival male," Aime offers.

Thinking for a moment, then I get an idea. "Kotu, come here, stay where she can see you."

He tilts his head curiously but slowly walks over to me. I reach out and rub his head between the ears. "This is weird," he comments.

"Yeah, but I think she'll understand that you're no threat," I state, watching the girl watch me.

She slowly edges up to Kotu, "Put your hand out," I instruct him. He puts his hand out and she tentatively sniffs it and curiously looks up at me. I reach down and rub her head while I still rub his. She seems to understand and gently pushes her nose into his hand. He gently rubs her nose, smiling.

"Kotu," he says. She looks at him curiously, then back at me. I nod to her and she looks back at Kotu.

She makes a few clicking noises, then says, "Kotu."

He smiles, gently scrubbing her head. "Good girl."

"Kotu, she's not a pet," Tayla lightly scolds. "Treat her like a person."

I look at him, but seeing that he already was scolded, I instead say, "Fey, you think you could get her to tell us her name?"

She looks at me curiously, thinking for a moment. "Maybe."

Tria comes over. "Let me help you." They each take one of the girl's hands and lead her around the camp, slowly teaching her everyone's names. When they get back around to me, Sada has joined me and both she and Tayla have leaned on me. The girl looks curiously at me, then lays her head on my lap, cooing.

Fey chuckles, then points to me and says, "Kyle."

She looks at me curiously, then at Fey and Tria, "Vey, Tria, Oana sae ta-Kyle."

"I think she just said her name. Oana?"

She looks at me, cooing. "Oana sae ta-le," she states, this time pushing her nose into my hand.

I reflexively rub her nose but find myself disconcerted by what she said. Thinking for a moment, I give her a test to see what she may mean, "Oana sae ta-Oana."

She backs up, shocked, "Oana ea-ta sae Oana, Kyle sae ta-Kyle. Oana sae ta-Kyle."

Shocked, I sit back, and Tayla gives me an odd look. "What is it?"

Having forgotten for a moment that she can read me. "I don't like the way that sounded," I confess. "Aime, what do you think?"

"That was an interesting test. If I understand her context. The most likely interpretation is that she thinks she belongs to you."

"That's what I thought too," I unhappily confirm.

"She thinks you *own* her?" Tayla nearly shouts, sitting up suddenly, making Oana duck away, and lie flat on the ground, trilling.

Trying to calm her gently, I say, "Tayla, please. I don't want to *own* her, but she doesn't seem to understand that she can be free."

"Then we'll need to teach her. Nobody should be owned."

"We'll have to be gentle, though," I agree, then chuckle. "It'll be like raising a child."

"I don't mind," Tayla agrees. "I want a big family." She kisses me to reinforce the point.

Heading to bed, it becomes obvious that Fey set up the tent. The whole thing is a lot larger than usual, something I'm suddenly grateful for, with the added person.

"Where are we going to put you?" I wonder aloud as the others find their usual places and get ready for bed.

Seeing Tayla and Sada, Oana follows them into our room. I follow and find Oana curling up on the floor, at the foot of the bed. Both my girls watch her, slightly shocked. I find myself looking at her with sympathy, finding herself somewhere new, not knowing anyone, and unable to understand anyone.

Sighing, I bend down and rub the sensitive area of her neck, making her coo and relax. Once I'm sure she's well on her way to sleep, Aime has the tent raise the floor beneath her, giving her a bed to sleep on. I cover her with a blanket and then get ready for bed.

As I crawl into bed between my girls and get comfortable, I whisper, "Watch your step in the morning. She's right off the foot of the bed."

"Think she'll be all right there?"

"Yeah, she's got a bed and a blanket."

"You're a big softy, you know it?" she purrs.

"Yeah, I know."

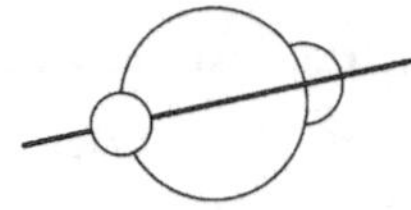

"Kyle!"

"Kyle, wake up!"

What?

"We have a situation."

Opening my eyes, I see by the little light that it's very early morning. *What's wrong?*

"I have engaged privacy on the whole tent. There seems to be a large creature right outside. From its size, I would speculate that it is a karnesh, but the tent lacks the sensor range and clarity for me to be more certain."

I gently pull myself out from between the girls and step over Oana on my way out to the common room. I look out the door window. "Oh great." It *is* a karnesh, standing just over twenty meters away. As I watch, it keeps licking the ground, right around the fire pit, where we all had gathered late last night.

"What do you think?" I quietly ask Aime.

"Well, I have adjusted the surface of the tent to reflect sound like a rock wall, but the tent itself offers little other protection."

As I continue to watch it lick the ground, it gets closer and closer to the fire pit, apparently following someone's footprints. As I wonder if there are any coals left, the thing suddenly sticks its tongue in the remains of the fire. I get my question answered as the beast suddenly howls loudly in pain, shaking its head violently.

Everyone suddenly piles into the common room, mumbling and holding their heads. To my relief, the tent windows fog over so no one can see out, but the light can still get in.

Desperate to get everyone calm, I tell them, "Shh, please, quiet. Listen, listen. Whatever you do, you must stay still and quiet. The tent is already working to keep us safe, but we have to do our parts too."

Railu hesitantly asks, "What was that?"

I sigh. "There is a karnesh by the fire pit." I hold my hands up again to get their attention again. "From its behavior, it seems to have been following our trail."

"How did it get so close?" Tria asks. "Aren't they bulky creatures?"

Tayla turns to her, "Don't confuse big with bulky. It may be a *big* creature, but it is in no way bulky. It can sneak up on someone quite easily."

I glance at Fey, noticing that Sada has wrapped her arms around her from behind, to comfort her.

"What are we going to do?" Larrah asks, bringing us back to what's important.

"How is it tracking us?" Railu asks, also voicing a point of concern.

I glance at Larrah, then look to Railu. "It seems to be tasting the ground," I confess, looking back out the now-cleared window. "As for what to do, I'm not entirely sure."

"Well, we can't stay here. If it's tracking us, it's only a matter of time before it finds the tent door," Railu states.

Sighing, "And if it does, I don't think Aime's rock wall effect will be any protection at that point." I turn to look around, "We could use the tent to shield our movement, keeping it between us and the beast until we're a safe distance away."

"We'd have to move quietly and cautiously," Larrah points out. "But it may work."

Sighing, I look back out the window, watching the thing lick at the ground some more, "Everyone, get dressed and packed," I state. "We're leaving this tent behind." I enter my room and get changed into the light armor and then start putting the sectional medium armor on over it.

"Preparing to fight that thing?" Tayla asks, suspiciously.

"Not if I don't have to," I assure her as I dress, "but I'd rather be over-prepared than not at all." I suddenly get a deep pang of fear and sadness; I quickly realize that this did not come from me, but from Tayla. I stop getting dressed and giver her a curious look, prompting her to turn away.

"I can't . . . ," she starts to say, but she begins to sob, so I wrap her in a hug.

"A vision?" I gently ask.

"Yes, one that I hate," she murmurs into my chest.

I kiss her on top of her head, "A bad one, huh?"

She nods.

I focus on how much I love her as I hold her, hoping she can feel it. Suddenly another set of arms wrap around us, I reflexively wrap an arm around her, knowing without looking, that it's Sada.

Reluctantly breaking the group hug, Tayla takes a deep breath, trying to get her emotions under control. She gives me a look, a very determined and meaningful look, "Aime, you keep him safe. Make sure we don't lose him."

"I will," she affirms. "My life depends on it."

Tayla nods and gives me a kiss, obviously worried; Sada gives me a rub with her cheek. A small part of me is curious as to what Tayla has seen in her vision, but we agreed, I would not ask, and she would not tell. Apparently, whatever is to come, she dreads more than anything.

I finish with my armor and pack since the beds were no longer needed; Aime has had the tent deflate them, rerouting the power to the walls and privacy field.

Hoisting my pack, I exit to the common room. Seeing everyone else already waiting, I take down the walls opposite the door and create a second door. "Everyone ready?" I tentatively ask. Getting several nods, I suddenly realize that someone's missing, "Where's Oana?" I ask puzzled.

"I believe that she is outside," Aime confesses. "With my attention on the karnesh and maintaining the tent's rouse, I did not notice her leaving the tent."

"It's not your fault," I say as I rush to the front and look out the window for her. "Aime, help me find her." Unexpectedly my vision changes, I'm suddenly seeing things in a red to blue color scale. I try to keep my calm, "Aime?"

"I have momentarily given you thermal vision," she advises me.

"Why?"

"You asked for help finding her, she is warm-blooded and it's still cool out."

"Oh, you could have just told me that when you did it," I comment, looking around, trying to figure out what is what. I quickly realize that the large green-yellow blob is the karnesh; most of the plants are showing in the blue to blue-green range. I note that the fire pit is still showing light pink.

"Oana should show yellow to red, based on her normal body temperature."

I suddenly catch a glimpse of a red object to my extreme left. "There she is," Aime confirms.

"Normal vision, but track her with a flag," I state.

"What's she doing?" I hear Larrah ask.

"I'm not sure, but she seems to be doing a good job of hiding as it's not noticed her yet." I continue to watch as her flag moves to the right, apparently circling around behind the beast. As she reaches the far side, it turns abruptly to face where her mark is.

"I think it knows," I tell the others and I hear someone gasp.

Keeping my attention on the beast and Oana, I try to figure out if the thing really knows or not. My question is soon answered when it turns around and starts licking the ground again. Oana starts moving again.

The karnesh roars, turns back to her, and charges. It was a bluff, it knew she was there.

Tayla panics, "Kyle!"

I rush out the door thinking. *What am I doing? I've only known her for three days?* I quickly brush that though aside, replacing it with, *She needs me.*

Bringing my thoughts back to the beast in front of me, I realize that I have the element of surprise, something it though it had. I run the short distance to it and leap, intending to land on its back.

Oana chooses that moment to leap out of its way. The beast turns to follow her, and I miss, landing on the ground right next to it. I pull a sword and jam it under a scale. It turns suddenly, knocking me down and I lose my grip on my sword. I hear it skitter across the ground away from me.

Realizing I'm down, the beast takes a sudden advantage. It raises a foot and tries to step on me, I roll quickly away, but I don't get too far before it swings its tail around. I feel the weight of its tail slam into me, sending me tumbling across the ground.

As I stop rolling, I suddenly hear an odd hooting sound. I turn my head to see what the sound is and I see Oana standing in the open, bobbing her head and hooting. The karnesh turns to her and lunges after her. I lie still as the creature passes by, hoping it doesn't notice me. I relax after I see its hind leg pass by, but then I see its tail come at me fast.

From somewhere I hear Tayla scream, "KYLE!"

CHAPTER 16

"Kyle!"

"What?"

"Kyle, I can't get up. My leg hurts."

I turn to see my sister on the ground in front of the swing, holding her left leg. I can see clearly that it's not straight. "Kayley, what happened?"

"I saw you jump out of the swing, so I tried too."

"You're only six. You're not big enough for that." I sit down next to her. "Looks like you broke your leg."

"It hurts. Help me."

"I'll need to go get help. Don't move."

"DON'T LEAVE ME!"

I cover my ears, shielding them from her scream. "Kayley, you're hurt, I have to. I'll be right back."

She starts to softly cry. "I'm scared. Don't leave me alone," she weakly pleads. "I need you to stay with me."

I kneel next to her. "But you need help. There's nobody here at the park and it's starting to get dark."

"Help me stand."

"But your leg is broke."

"Help me, Kyle. Help me."

"Kyle, help me. Hey, are you asleep." I feel something hit my head. "Wake up!"

"What?" I look up to Meagan on the ladder, reaching her hand down to me.

"Hand me a new roll of tape."

"All right, you didn't have to through the old one at me." I pick up the empty tape roll and toss it in a garbage can. I grab a new one from the table and hand it up to her.

"Well, if you didn't what to help decorate the gym for the dance, you shouldn't have volunteered."

Looking up at her, I say, "Meagan, I didn't volunteer. I was volunteered."

She laughs. "It was for your own good. Hand me more balloons."

I quickly inflate one, tie it, and hand it up to her. "What's this dance again?"

She tapes the balloon in place, as I inflate another. "Sadie Hawkins."

"Ah yes, the girls ask the guys. Here." I hand up another balloon. "So who you going to ask?"

She takes a balloon, and I inflate another. "You."

The balloon slips from my fingers as I try to tie it, flying off in a random direction, making her giggle. "It slipped."

"Yeah, right," she jokes.

Sighing, I inflate another balloon, tie it, and pass it up to her. "What should I wear?"

"I want you to wear a black-tailed tux."

"With red cummerbund and bow tie?"

"Yes."

"So I should get you a red corsage?"

"My gown will have red, black, and white." Meagan smiles as she puts her mouth to my ear and whispers, "I'll let you decide the flowers."

I smile and kiss her on the cheek. Having been dating her for five years, I've come to know her taste in flowers. She likes unusual ones, not roses or carnations, but things like lilies and orchids. "I'll be sure to surprise you."

"You always do. Remember, prom's in a month." She returns my kiss. "I'll see you later."

"Love you." I watch her leave, then I head to my mom's office. Pulling out her interior decorating catalogs, I sort through them. Finding the one on flowers and arrangements, I open it and start looking for something I know Meagan will love.

After looking through the catalog for over an hour, I close it and push it away. I rub my weary eyes, my tears have dried. "I'm sorry . . . I just can't do this right now."

The funeral director slides the catalog aside. "We still have time," he consoles. "Would your sister be able to help you?"

"Kayley's too distraught, losing Mom and Dad at the same time." I shake my head. "She's not doing well. Meagan's with her, but . . ."

"I'm sorry. Is there anyone else that may be able to help you, an aunt or an uncle?"

"Mom had a sister, but she passed years ago. Dad's an only child."

"Sorry to hear. Well, I'll be here all day, today, and tomorrow." He looks down at the papers in front of him. "Go on ahead and take some time with your sister and we can work out the arrangements when you're ready."

"Thanks." I leave the office and head to my car.

Sitting down in the passenger seat, I hand Kayley the keys. "There's only so much you can learn in the classroom."

"Sooner or later, you got to get behind the wheel. I know, I remember Dad teaching you how to drive."

"Good, you were paying attention." I swallow hard, suppressing my fear. I wonder to myself if this was how Dad felt when he taught me how to drive. "Start her up."

She puts the key in the ignition and turns. The engine starts easily and she tries moving the gear selector with no success. "Press the brake before you try to shift. Hold the brake until you're ready to move."

She nods and steps on the gas pedal. The engine revs hard in response, making her squeal again and pull her hands back.

"Kayley, calm down."

"Really, you're more excited than I am," Meagan agrees.

"But, Meagan, you two have been dating for, like, ever! I thought he'd never ask you!"

"Hey, it's only been ten years, and for most of those we were in school."

"And I wanted to make sure you were old enough."

Kayley looks at Meagan, suddenly confused. "Old enough?"

"To be my maid of honor."

"Eeeeeeeeeee!"

The ambulance siren wails as we hit a bump. I bounce in my seat while trying to get our patient set up with an IV.

"Sorry!" calls the driver. "Didn't see that one."

I again check the patient's eyes. One's dilated, one's constricted. Head trauma cases are unpredictable. My partner applies an oxygen tube as I check his pulse. His body stiffens suddenly.

"He's seizing!" I shout as I grab the anti-seizure medicine and prepare a shot.

My partner protects his head to prevent injury as I give the shot into the IV.

"We're at the hospital!" the driver calls out, "Get ready!"

The rear doors fly open and two of the hospital staff grab the stretcher by its foot. My partner grabs his side of the head, "Let's go, Kyle."

"Kyle!" The shriek comes from our bedroom.

I run onto the bedroom. "What is it? Is it time?"

She grabs my arm and holds tight to me, trying to stay standing. She nods frantically as she tries to control her breathing.

"How far apart are they?"

"Too close," she gasps.

Being a trained rescue paramedic, I keep my head and scoop her up. I carry her through the house to the garage. After setting her in the passenger seat, I run back and grab her bag. I toss it in the backseat and drive to the hospital.

Finding a parking space, I step out of the car. I follow a now-familiar path and take the elevator to maternity. I step out to find Meagan in a wheelchair, holding our son. "Michael, look," she softly coos to the newborn. "Daddy's here. Time to go home."

I smile, seeing her glow, and our son's smile as I pick up our things and follow, as the nurse pushes Meagan to the elevator. The nurse presses the button and we wait for the elevator to arrive.

The door opens and Meagan steps through. "Honey, I have someone you should meet."

I walk over to her, carrying Michael in my left arm, and kiss her. "Who's that?"

Meagan pulls a white ball of fur out of her coat pocket. "Meet Sada."

I take the kitten as Meagan takes Michael from me. Having been carrying Michael all day, the tiny kitten is practically weightless in my hands. "Hello there, Sada."

"I picked her up at work today." She then holds our son up next to the kitten, "Look, Michael, a friend for you to grow up with."

He squirms in her arms, trying to see the little white fluff ball with bright blue eyes. Sada purrs contently in my hands but watches his waving hands carefully.

"My, easy-going, aren't you?"

"I noticed that too. She hasn't mewed at all. Purred a lot, and hissed once, but not cried at all." A look of concern crosses her face. "I wonder if she can meow at all."

I hold the kitten up to my nose, imitating what I know to be a kitten's cry. All Sada does is purr and lick my nose. "Well, you are certainly comfortable with us, aren't you?"

"Her things are in the car. Could you get them please?"

"Her things?"

"You know, litter box, food, toys. Did you really think I would bring a kitten home and not prepare?"

"Well, fur ball, let's get you set up in your new home." I set Sada on my shoulder and step out the door.

I slowly walk across the grass and find my usual place on the marble bench. Looking down at the headstones, I feel all my pains and sorrows return. Fighting to control myself, I reluctantly begin, "Meagan, your mom saw me yesterday. She wants me to leave, to move on." I close my eyes, fighting back the tears. "I don't know if I can. It's been two years, and I still love you.

"I wake up each morning, expecting to find you by my side and Michael in his crib. I know she's right. I can't keep on like this. I also don't want to leave you behind either.

"I can't help but think that if I was on call that day . . . if it had been my crew that responded, you'd still be here." I swallow hard. "I know can't blame them. I know I shouldn't blame myself."

Taking a deep breath, I reach down into the bag I brought. "Today would have been our fourth anniversary, our fourteenth year together." I pull out a bouquet of red, orange, and yellow lilies and put them in the vase in the headstone. "Some of your favorites."

As I stand, I fold the bag. "Meagan, Michael, wherever you both are"—I swallow again—"I will be with you as you both are with me, no matter where I am."

I put the bag in the trash bin as I get in my car.

I sit in my recliner and Sada quickly hops up in my lap. Looking out the screened windows of my cabin's porch, I see a herd of deer grazing in the distance and sigh. I pull over my PC and check to see if I have any orders.

"Four longbows, two recurve. Due in a month." I look down at my lap and see Sada curled up like she's asleep. "Already? You just got there." Her response to me is a yawn and a stretch.

"All right, today can be a slow one. My jigs are all full. I've got plenty of supplies." I yawn. "And I'm tired like you are."

I lazily rub her head, watching the deer graze in the distance. Meagan would have hated it here. She was always a busy-body, had to be doing something. We never really needed to work but we did anyway, her as a marketing manager while I was a paramedic.

I chuckle gently at how I've managed to change my life. Now I live in the country, in a log cabin instead of the townhouse where I grew up. My sister lives there now with her growing family. Instead of being a paramedic, I'm now a bowyer, preferring to make everything by hand instead of buying pre-made parts. Life moves slowly out here, and to my surprise, I like it that way.

A loud buzzing nearby gets Sada's attention. She hops from my lap to the other end of the porch, to watch the hummingbirds around the feeder.

Smiling, I get up and head down the hall to my workshop.

Closing the door behind me, I shuffle to my chair. After I sit, Sada walks slowly from the table to my lap and lies down. I set my cane aside and start petting her. "We're both getting old, aren't we?" She purrs in response, something she has done a lot in her life. I've only once heard her make one other sound. When she once got her tail caught in the door, she hissed. She has never once meowed or made any other verbal sounds.

Looking out across the meadow, I again watch the deer graze while the hummingbirds flitter around the lilies and orchids just outside. I see a car approach, kicking up a cloud of dust behind it. I quickly realize that it's my home care nurse.

She comes in the door. "Morning, Kyle, I've got your prescriptions, and some other things for you."

She sets a small bag on the table next to me. "Thank you."

Sada picks up her head and looks at Alicia, purring. "Hi, sweetie." She gently rubs Sada's head. "I brought your meds too." She then takes a larger bag into the kitchen and I hear her put some things in the refrigerator.

When she comes back into the room, she takes my blood pressure, checks my pulse, respiration, and temperature. She then uses her stethoscope to listen to my lungs. After making her notes for me, she turns her attention to Sada and listens to her lungs and heart, checks her belly and paws, and then makes notes on Sada's chart.

She switches back to my chart. "How's the pain?"

"Bearable."

She checks my eyes. "How's your vision?"

"I can still see the deer grazing out there in the meadow."

She turns and looks, then chuckles a little. "All right. How's your strength? Is it still coming and going?"

I simply nod.

"How are your legs, still dragging them?" I nod again. "Is it getting worse?"

I sigh and nod, "Yeah, are they still thinking cancer?"

She sadly shakes her head. "They don't really know what to think anymore."

"Figures, well, there's really no need for you to stick around any longer today. I don't plan on doing anything."

"All right, is there anything you need?" She looks at me. "Any food, supplies, anything?"

"No, thank you, though."

"You know I worry about you two, way out here, all alone," she sadly admits, gently rubbing Sada's head.

I smile. "I know, I can see it in your eyes." I take her hand. "Thank you, for everything."

She gently squeezes my hand, trying to smile. "Well, if there's anything you need, if anything happens, please call me."

"I will," I nod.

She collects her things and gives me a concerned look. "I'll see you in a couple days?"

"I'll be here." As I watch her leave, Sada makes her way over to watch the hummingbirds. Suddenly feeling a familiar urge, I grab my cane and make my way to the bathroom.

Opening the door to my room, I find Sada lying on the bed. "Sada, come on, we've got to go." The cat-girl gets up and I take her hand. "It's time." I peek out the door, checking for the crew. "Let's go."

I lead her down the central hall, past the hanger to the cargo bay. "Uh, let's see, blue is for the hatch, green unlocks the safeties, red launches." I hit the blue button and we step through the door. I push Sada inside and hit the blue button again to close the hatch.

I try to quickly explain as I strap her into the seat, "Sorry, but Charles said they were about to pass through the shell. If we can get out in time, we should be safe."

She nods as I sit in the other seat and strap myself in. I press the yellow button and the light goes out, indicating that the safeties are disabled.

"Here we go." I lean back and press the red button. I hear an explosion as the escape pod launches. I look out the window and manage to see the ship's bulkhead disappear, only to be replaced with blackness.

Opening my eyes, I see a large moon and the ringed sky. From the angle of the shadows on the trees, the sun's low in the sky, though I can't tell if it's rising or setting. I try turning my head. Nothing happens. I don't even feel pain. "Hello?"

"*Kyle!*" Tayla suddenly appears in my vision. "Kyle, you're awake. Don't move. Aime said your back was broken." She gently starts rubbing my cheeks and I feel her tears land on my face as her nose rubs mine.

"Tayla, love, what happened?"

"You don't remember?"

"Right now, I remember too much. Help me sort it out a little."

"You were hit by the karnesh's tail. It sent you flying through a tree. I'd thought it killed you until Aime called to us."

"Aime. Aime?" Getting no response, I look at Tayla confused.

"She's recharging. She's been working hard to fix your body for the last two days. Niku's been helping her. Sada and I . . . we . . ."

As my senses start to clear, I feel her mix of emotions. "Get your nose down here." She put her nose to mine and I kiss her. A wave of relief hits me as she returns my kiss. "I love you."

More teardrops hit my face. "I love you too."

Suddenly another purring nose presses into my cheek. "And I love you too." Tayla backs off a little to let Sada in. "Hey there, furball." Sada suddenly tilts her head curiously and I smile. "I remember."

Sada's eyes go wide, her purring intensifies, and she licks my nose.

"Yep. I remember everything now. You, Meagan, Michael, Kayley, even the Obsession."

"The Obsession?" Tayla asks.

"How Sada got to be like she is now. When the time is right, I'll tell you all about it." Doing my best to look around, I ask, "Why am I still outside if it's been two days since I got hurt?"

"Aime said something about the solar power from the armor. Not sure what she was talking about, but she said that she needed it to help her fix you faster."

"How bad was I hurt?"

"Broken back, several broken ribs, and a cracked skull."

"That explains why I can't move. What's been fixed?"

"Aime had to fix your skull first, something about being compromised. Your back is only partially healed."

I frown. "Is it morning or night?"

"Morning, why?"

"When was the last time I had something to eat?"

"Of your own ability or what we've been trying to get you to swallow?"

I hesitate for a moment. "What have you been trying to get me to swallow?"

"Just a vitamin- and calorie-rich drink," Niku volunteers, appearing upside down above me. "Something Aime and I quickly came up with."

"What's it taste like?"

Tayla curls her lips. "Mud."

I smile and chuckle lightly. "I've had worse. Put a straw in it and I'll see how much I can stomach."

Tayla's face skews. "Straw? Why would you want nakku bedding in it?"

Realizing what I said, I tell her, "A drinking straw, think blowgun, but really small. Bring a converter, I'll show you." Hearing several shuffles, I realize that almost everyone is gathered around me, but being unable to move, I can't see many of them.

"What do I tell it?" Tayla asks, holding one of the smaller units.

"Bendable drinking straw."

She repeats it and takes out the straw. "What do I do with it?"

I see Sada reach across me and take the straw. She promptly bends it, and then puts the longer end in the bowl Niku is now holding.

"Now just hold the bowl low enough so the end of the straw can be in my mouth."

Feeling the end of the straw touch my lips, I grab it and tentatively suck on it. Tayla was right. It tastes like mud, but remembering some of the things I had to drink for medical tests, I slowly drink as much as I can.

After I let go of the straw, Tayla sets the bowl aside and lies on the ground next to me. "You had us worried."

"Sorry. Once I'm better, you can take it out on me."

She scowls at me. "You think this is funny?"

"Do you hear me laughing? I know now why I'm so protective of you." I try to look her in the eye, but all I can see are her ears. She raises her head a little and gives me a curious look.

"I had lost both my parents when I was your age and finished raising my younger sister. Then I lost Michael and Meagan." I sigh, wishing I could move. "I lost almost everyone that I loved in less than six years."

"So you're afraid of losing us too?" she states, leaning her chin on her hand. "I know you saved me when I was stabbed, but you're being unfair to us. We aren't your previous family."

"I know that, *now*, but I didn't have all my memories before. Now that I do . . ." I sigh. "I know I've put myself in harm's way to protect you, but that's who I am. I know I can take it, but I don't know if I could take losing any of you."

"Do you think that either Sada or I could take losing you? How about Fey? Kotu? Megai? Even Oana has gotten quite attached to you." She sighs, putting her nose against my cheek. "I'm not asking you to change. Just be more careful for the sake of the rest of your family."

I lay there for a moment, staring at the rings in the sky, watching the smaller moon beyond them. As I do, I realize that she has a point and that she just reminded me how large my family currently is. I sigh heavily. "Thank you."

She perks her ears toward me. "What for?"

"For reminding me of just how big my new family is."

She gently bumps my nose as she purrs. "I have a feeling that *our* family will be much larger before this is over."

"I'd like that," I admit, feeling relieved. "I'd like that a lot."

I spend the rest of the day lying in the sun, allowing Aime to charge using both the armor's power and the nutrient drink. My family takes turns sitting with me, holding the bowl so I can drink.

By supper, with my back repaired and my ribs mostly healed, Aime releases me from the induced paralysis. I eat heartily, not really caring what it is, but I still have some of the nutrient drink, making sure that Aime and her nanites can finish with me by morning.

Afterward, I head into the tent and drop my armor. I retrieve a fresh pair of shorts and a towel and enter the shower. As I wet myself down, I find that my ribs are tender to the touch and grunt at the pain.

"Are you all right?" Tayla asks, apparently just outside the shower room.

"Yeah, ribs are still a little tender."

"Careful."

"Yes, love." I slowly start to shampoo my hair, gently scrubbing my scalp, wary of finding more tender spots. Thankfully not finding any, I rinse off and proceed to washing the rest of me, being careful of my ribs this time. I rinse again and gently towel dry. After putting on my shorts, I pull my hair back into its usual ponytail.

Stepping out into the main room, I find Niku waiting for me. "Let me wrap your ribs. Get them stabilized before you go to sleep."

Sada comes in and takes the towel from me and steps into the shower. I raise my arms, giving Niku the room to wrap my ribs. As she starts, I look curiously at her. "Why did you want to train under a shaman?"

She glances up at me. "I wanted to learn from a shaman, to be a shaman. I want to be a healer."

I stand for a moment in slight disbelief. "You already are."

She carefully presses one of the wraps into place and gets out another. "I want people to recognize me as a healer."

"It's your knowledge and actions that define you, nothing else. Let the people learn from those. That's why I'm a Pendekar, a shaman, and a Sovereign, but I don't tell people because I don't think I deserve the titles. You have every right to call yourself a shaman. You know more than they do. You're better than they are."

"And you're better than me. I want to be as good as you are."

"You want to be as good as Aime is. She's the one that does all the work. You have the knowledge and ability on your own. I know that. Besides, where would I be right now if you hadn't come up with that drink?"

She slowly finishes with the second wrap, obviously thinking.

"I'd still be lying flat on my back, unconscious . . . or worse." I put my hands on her shoulders. "I can't begin to thank you enough for staying with us."

She starts to bow slightly, but I stop her. "You are a trusted friend and will always be welcome wherever I call home. You do not bow to me." I wrap her in a gentle hug.

She slowly returns the hug. "I don't understand."

Aime, make me a bunch of signets.

"There is a portable unit in the bedroom."

"Wait here." I retrieve the signets and return to Niku. "I Kyle, Sovereign of Arindell, Pendekar of Pridewyn, offer you, Niku, the position of my family shaman. Do you accept?"

She smiles as tears come to her eyes. "I humbly accept and thank you."

I take one of the new signets and pin it to the shoulder of her dress. "Your duties will include the health of my family and close friends. If you want to take on additional clients, I will leave that your discretion."

She reaches in her pouch and pulls out a necklace. I instantly recognize that it's a shaman's pendant. She holds it up to me.

"As shaman of Pridewyn, I recognize your abilities and knowledge. I present to you, your shaman's pendant," I place the pendant around her neck. "Shaman Niku."

She hesitates, but bows slightly. "Thank you."

I see tears in her eyes, so I bow back. "Least I could do for the one who helped save my life."

She wraps me in another gentle hug that I return. She leaves the tent and Tayla touches my back. "That was interesting."

"She wanted to be a shaman. She already knows more than they do, and she's earned it."

"Yes, she has."

I hold up the other signets. "She's not the only one."

She follows me into the bedroom. "What do you mean?"

I pull on a shirt, long pants, and step into my boots. "Come on."

We exit the tent and find Niku showing off her pendant and signet. "I can't believe he did this. I'm finally a shaman."

"Does he have the authority?" Zoe asks.

"Yes, he does," Arru states.

"How?" Tria asks.

"I'm Sovereign of Arindell, that's how."

"Sovereign?"

"Please, no bowing, calling me master or anything like that," I explain. "Now that I've regained my memories, I realize that I've been under-appreciating some of you."

"You've been out for two days. It's hard to appreciate someone like that," Arru states.

"True, but that's not what I mean," I correct, stepping up to her. "You've been with me since Arroketh. You've counseled me, not only as a professional but as a friend. I've confided in you and trusted your judgment. I know you did not want any compensation for that, but you have earned this." I hold up a signet to her. "I, Kyle, Sovereign of Arindell, offer you the position of my councilor. I ask only that you continue what you already do for me, for the rest of us as well."

"I would be honored," she states with a slight bow.

I pin the signet to her dress and return her bow. "We share this honor."

She nods, and I step back and turn to Larrah. "I know that you chose the contract to regain some honor. Neither of us expected more than that. Now though, things are different. I notice that you haven't worn the signet since Three Lands."

"The contract is complete. I have no further need of wearing it."

I nod. "Yes, true, so I'll offer you a new one. As Sovereign, my family and I will require a guard. I would be honored if that guard were you. I can think of no one with the ability, the honor, and most importantly, my trust, to protect my family and me."

She suddenly kneels, a look of disbelief and awe mixing on her face. "You would honor me that easily?"

"Your honor was never in doubt to yourself. You have proven that to me."

She bows. "I, Pendekar Larrah, freely and willingly accept your contract."

"No challenge?"

"None needed. Your word carries the honor for you." She stands and produces the signet from her pouch.

I take it and pin it to her armor. "Let your words carry the same honor." Seeing the tears roll down her face, I hug her.

She sniffs lightly. "Thank you."

As I pull back, Tayla wraps her in a hug, also sniffling. I turn to Tria. "Tria, you seek to teach no matter where it leads you."

She blushes and bows, embarrassed. "I am happy to pass on what I have learned."

"Indeed, that you would follow us into the Wilds to do so." I look carefully into her eyes. "You have more courage than a lot of warriors claim to have. I respect that, and I would like to offer you the position of teaching my children, present and future."

She blushes. "Well, the company is nice . . ."

"You're teasing," Tayla politely chides.

Tria smiles at her. "Yes, I would love to."

Smiling, I pin a signet to her dress. "Welcome to the family."

I turn to Railu. "Without you, where would we be?"

"Without you, where would I be?" she counters. "I owe you my sanity, my life. What more could you possibly think me worthy of?"

I extend my hand. "Friendship."

"A family," Tayla corrects.

I give Tayla a curious look, and she nods her head slightly. "What do you say? Want to be part of our family?"

"I already have a mate."

"Not in that way," Tayla states. "In the time we've known you, we've come to care about you. We want you to find your mate as much as you do."

Sada comes up behind her and gently puts her hands on Railu's shoulders. Railu looks down as her ears turn back. "I . . . I don't know."

"Then at least be our tracker, until you decide."

She looks up, her ears still crooked back. "I already am." She then perks up. "Why are you doing this now, when we're out here in the Wilds?"

I sigh, conceding the point of her question. "Now that I have my memories back, and with a little help"—I glance at Tayla and smile—"I've realized that this world is now my home, as much as it is all of yours." I look around slowly, making sure they understand before continuing, "I consider all of you my friends, my . . . family, and with my being Sovereign, I can give you all something you can't get from anyone else."

"Most of us can get jobs anywhere," Tria states.

"But from whom else could you get a position in a Sovereign's house?" I correct.

"But all you have is a couple tents," Zoe states, confused.

Tayla interjects, "Only because we have to travel right now. After this is over, we plan on settling down somewhere. We have money. You'd be surprised how much. We'll find a home large enough for Kyle, Sada, Megai, and me, plus our children. It'll be a large house, adding rooms for the rest of you would be a welcome expense. Railu, please, what do you say?"

Railu looks like she's about to cry. The words she speaks surprise us in many ways. "I cannot, not yet. I want to, but as much as you honor your mates, I feel I need to show mine the same."

I take her hand, putting two signets in it as I do. "I understand and respect that." She looks at the signets, then at me, puzzled, so I add, "Find your mate, talk with him. Bring them to me when you're ready."

She smiles, closing her hand on them and nods. "Thank you."

I turn to my charges. "Speaking of family, you both should be wearing one of these. Let these signify that you are both part of my family." I pin one on Fey's dress, prompting her to give me a nuzzle. As I pin one on Kotu's toga, I see a tear in his eye. I pull them both into a hug.

"Just like my mates, you both belong with me."

Sada and Tayla both wrap their arms around us. "You belong with *us*," Tayla corrects.

"What about me?"

Breaking the hug, I turn to Zoe. "I would not dare think to leave you out; however, you already having an employer does make what I would like to offer you a little complicated." I look at Niku, who looks back at me curiously as I think aloud. "What to do, what to do?"

"I have an idea," Niku suggests. She whispers into my ear and my face lights up.

"Really?" I ask and she nods. "I like it, and it'll work for both of us." I turn back to Zoe. "We have a mutual proposition for you to consider."

"I'll take it!" Her excitement barely contained.

"You haven't even heard it yet." I chuckle as she covers her mouth, embarrassed. "Your first responsibility will be to Niku. That won't change. I know, though, that you don't really have a lot to do for her, so I would like to put you in charge of meals. After those, your responsibilities are of your own choice."

To my surprise, she wraps me in a hug, with her arms around my waist instead of my ribs. "Thank you."

I return her hug. "You're welcome." As she steps back, I pin the last signet to her dress. She smiles happily and turns to Niku and wraps her in a hug too.

I suddenly feel a nose press into my hand. Without looking, I know it's Oana, and I gently rub her nose. "Feeling left out?"

She lifts her head but stops to sniff my ribs. "Ouch?"

My hand slides down her neck. "Yeah, ouch." She then starts cooing and puts her head gently against my upper chest. I start rubbing her neck, finding that spot that she likes. "I know you're sorry, but it's not your fault." I look down at her and smile. From the look on her face, I get the feeling that she seems to understand.

"Does she get one?" Kotu asks.

"Not yet, I want her to understand what it means first," I state, still rubbing her neck. "Besides, with her not wearing anything, I wouldn't know where to put it."

CHAPTER 17

Following Railu as she scouts, I watch as she switches from examining the ground to sniffing the air. Ever since finding Sarn's grave, she's been more intent on finding Roen, pushing us along faster and farther, making more progress than normal each day.

We continue to follow as she searches, seemingly not finding many clues until she abruptly stops, nose to the air. As she stands still, we manage to catch up to her. The first thing I notice is that she is standing with her eyes closed, taking long, slow breaths.

"What is it?" I gently ask.

"I smelled him, for just a moment. I *smelled* him."

Hearing her sincerity, I nod, *Aime, make my nose better.*

"Enhancing," she responds.

As my nose gets more sensitive, I'm flooded by smells, first of which is Railu, as she is standing right next to me, then I smell Sada and Tayla. I consciously start slowing down my breathing, resulting in more scents. I start mentally filtering through the variety of scents, searching for a match to the tufts of fur from Sarn's grave.

Finding it, "He was here," I whisper. Turning to Sada and Tayla, I ask, "Upwind?"

They both point to the right, so we all fan out and start walking, searching slowly in that direction, taking care to also search the large clusters of grasses that disrupt the otherwise rocky area. We spend almost an hour searching and find nothing.

Railu drops her pack and sits on it, burying her face in her hands to cry. I kneel next to her and put my hand on her back. "Hey, what's wrong?"

"I'm never going to find him, am I?"

"Yes, you will."

"But every time I find a trail I *lose* it."

"You found his scent. With a weak trail that's going to happen. You can't lose hope."

"But it's so hard to hope when I keep losing his trail."

Zoe walks up. "Maybe this will help. Come see what we found." She takes Railu's hand and leads her over to a rather large cluster of tall grass.

"Beds," Tayla states as she and Larrah pull the grass apart. Inside the cluster are two "nests" of grass, both with the surrounding grasses tied together over top, forming a crude shelter, each just large enough for a person to curl up in.

Railu sticks her nose into one of the beds, then the other. "He slept here," her voice a mix of relief and hope.

Kneeling beside her, I look at the other nest. "The dead grass isn't dried yet, and the rest hasn't started to stand back up." I look at Railu. "How long do you think? A week, maybe?"

She leans into Roen's bed and sniffs again, pokes around a little. "No more than eight days ago, no less than five."

Finding some tufts of fur around in the grass, I pick some from each of the beds for Aime to analyze. She quickly tells me that they both are slightly malnourished, but that's all she can tell from the fur.

I look at Railu again. I see that she is starting to cry again, this time happy tears. "He's healthy, doesn't appear to be hurt, and most importantly, we're catching up."

She weakly looks at me, tears rolling from her eyes. "Yes, we are."

"We'll camp here for the night," I state.

She crawls into the bed and curls up. Tears flow freely as she lays there. I can't help but feel for her. This is the closest she has been to her mate in a year.

We set up the tent right next to the beds. By the time that supper is ready, Railu has fallen asleep. By nightfall, she's still asleep, so Tayla covers her up with a blanket, and we wrap the tied grasses with a tarp in case it rains.

Before calling it a day, I check on her. Finding her still soundly asleep, I gently massage her cheek. "You will find him, have no doubt."

As I crawl into bed, Tayla asks, "Will she be okay?"

"Between the blanket and the makeshift tent, she should stay warm and dry."

"That's not what I mean."

I take a deep breath, knowing what she meant. "Finding where he slept should help her confidence a lot. I hope her emotions can hold out until we find him."

"What if we don't find him?" she asks as she snuggles in close against my neck.

"I don't see that being possible. She's too determined not to find him."

"What if he's not alive?"

I sigh, fearing that possibility. "Then she will need all our help to get through it." I pull her and Sada in closer to me for comfort, wondering if Railu would be strong enough to survive that possibility.

Awakened by Sada's absence, I slip out from under Tayla and nearly trip over Oana as I step out to the main room. She stands, looking out a window. Hearing me, she turns and signs, 'Raining.'

I walk to the door and peek out to check on Railu. Not seeing her in the bed, I look around and see that she is just standing out in the heavy rain, staring off into the darkness. Hearing her sobs, I dart out the door to her and walk her back inside. Sada throws a towel over me and uses another to start drying Railu's wet fur.

I quickly dry my hair and turn my attention back to the crying fox. "Railu, what happened? What's wrong?"

Still sobbing hard, she manages to say, "Rain . . . trail . . . gone."

I wrap her in my arms and hold her tight. "I know. We will find it again. We will find him."

Her sobs become uncontrollable, and she wraps her arms around me tightly, "I . . . miss . . . him."

"I know . . . I know." I rub her back trying to comfort her.

"I'm . . . alone," she manages to confess.

"You're not alone."

To my surprise, Tayla comes up behind me, puts her hand to Railu's cheek. "He's right. You are part of our family, this family. We are all with you."

"I . . . know," she manages to say, before passing out. Already having her in a hug, she doesn't fall, just goes limp in my arms. I scoop her up, planning on putting her in her bed but Sada stops me, pointing to our room.

Tayla nods. "She should not be alone. Bring her in here."

Sada lays down on her edge of the bed, prompting the bed to get a little wider. I eye her suspiciously, wondering what she has in mind. She pats the bed next to her, as Tayla tells me, "Put her down next to Sada."

Sensing my hesitation, Tayla sighs. "She can't be alone right now. She has been without her mate too long. She just spent several hours smelling his scent. She needs to feel him, but he is not here."

"So she's sleeping with us."

"She needs the company," she insists. "She sees you like a brother. I see her as a sister. Part of her is calling for a male to sleep next to, so she can remember her mate."

I sigh, feeling a little defeated, so stepping over Oana, I put Railu down next to Sada and watch as she snuggles up against her.

"Now you," she softly instructs. Sensing my hesitancy, she puts her nose to mine for a moment, softly saying, "I know you care for all of us. You can't help it. It's who you are. It's one of the many reasons I fell in love with you."

Relenting, I climb into bed. Tayla follows and curls up to me in her usual way. To my surprise, I feel Railu roll over onto me, as Sada normally would. She sighs heavily, tucks her nose under my chin, and relaxes.

"Thank you," Tayla whispers, lightly purring.

I squeeze her to me. "You're lucky I love you."

When I wake in the morning, I find myself alone. I dress and head out of the tent to find Railu looking out to the east.

I quietly step up alongside her. "How ya feeling?"

She turns to me and wraps me in a gentle hug. "Thank you."

I happily return her hug. "You're welcome."

"Why do you do so much for me?"

"Because you remind me so much of my little sister."

She sighs. "I've never had a brother."

"I'll be your big brother."

"You already are." She releases me from the hug and points to her shoulder. "Tayla put it on me this morning."

"I thought you were going to ask your mate first."

"He made a big choice without me. I can make this one without him. He can make his choice when we find him."

By evening, we find ourselves walking a pass a few kilometers wide, with a tall cliff to the north and a sheer drop to the south. Sensing Tayla's coming heat, we make camp early.

Sada comes up to me. 'Is it ready?'

Sighing, I turn to Niku. "Is it ready? It's time."

Niku looks at her tablet for a moment. "I believe it is. We started with the Nao berry and added a few things to help suppress the urges, but I'm not sure how well it'll work."

I look at Sada. "I still wish we didn't have to do this."

'It's not your fault.'

"I know, but you still have to go through it."

Niku hands her a drink. "This should help your urges. If not, I can get you something to help you sleep."

I watch as Sada drinks the juice, hoping that this works. I turn to Niku. "Keep a close eye on her for me."

Niku nods as Tayla wraps herself around me from behind, purring. "It's time."

"I know, I can feel it. Sada, how do you feel?"

'Okay, for now.'

"Let Niku know if you start to feel too much."

She nods and kisses me. 'Love you both.'

With her arms still wrapped around me, Tayla signs, 'We love you too.' She then pulls me back to the tent.

"Aime finished it, you know."

"She did?" Tayla asks, starting to nuzzle into my neck.

"Yes, she did."

She starts backing me through the tent. "Will it work?"

"Yes. Are you ready to be a mother?"

"Certainly ready to try," she purrs. "Aime, make us compatible."

I give the soft chirp-like bark that male cheetah's do to encourage their mates, something that Aime had to help my larynx produce.

"You don't need to do that bark with me, love, I'm already ready," Tayla chuckles as she backs me through the door to our room. Once inside, she lets her heat drive her. I feel her desire quickly build as we shed our armor. Her building desire mixes with my own, and for a moment, I wonder if doing this without the berries is a good idea. She pushes me back on the bed and crawls up the bed, looking very much the predator she is.

Even though I'm her prey, I feel no fear, only her need for me. She lets out a low growl as she lies down on me. Feeling her physically fuels my own desire, and I roll us onto her back as our rapidly growing passion takes over.

I wake up to find myself intertwined with Tayla. As I try to unwrap her from me, I find her claws stuck in my back.

Unable to reach her hands, I gently start to kiss her. "Wake up, love."

"Uhnn," she groans.

"Come on, love, wake up."

She puts her head to my chest. "My head hurts."

"And your claws are stuck in my back."

I feel her body twitch in surprise. "Oh." She then starts trying to remove her claws. One hand comes out easily, but her other seems to have a claw stuck.

"Just pull it out," I state, fighting the pain.

She stops for a moment, taking a controlled breath. "Sorry." She quickly jerks her hand away, pulling her claw free from my back.

Grimacing at the sudden jolt of pain, I roll off Tayla and sit up. The pain quickly diminishes as Aime accelerates my healing. I look back at the bed and realize that there is too much blood there to be just from her removing her claws.

Apparently Tayla sees that too as she asks first, "Aime, whose blood is this?"

"It is both of yours, and may I say, please do *not* do that again without berries. I nearly depleted my energy keeping both of you from bleeding out."

Tayla stands up and I quickly check her for any remaining wounds. As we take care of them, I confess, "I believe Aime may have a point, because I don't remember anything after I rolled us over."

With a puzzled look, she scratches her head and confesses, "I don't even remember that."

"Then we agree, berries from now on?"

She gives me a hug and nods. "Definitely."

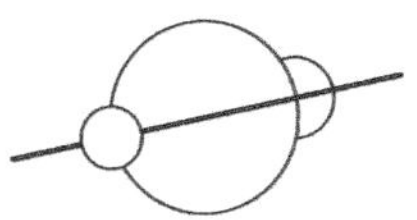

While walking through a lightly wooded area, our usual activities are interrupted by a series of loud crashing sounds. We abruptly fall silent, quickly determining that the sound is coming from ahead and not coming toward us. We proceed, quietly, listening to the sound travel off to our right.

We quickly come across a fresh path of knocked down and trampled trees. As the rest of us approach, Railu is already knelt down, checking for tracks and other signs as to what went through.

She looks up at me, then in the direction of the crashing sound. "Karnesh."

Suddenly the karnesh stops making noises, getting all of our attention. We all stand still and wait to hear what it does next.

The silence is broken by a male voice yelling, "Amsel! No!"

"Roen!" Railu gasps, taking off at a dead run.

I drop my pack and run after her. I manage to hear two more packs hit the ground before we are nearly stopped in our tracks by a deafening roar.

Recovering quickly, we resume running toward the karnesh. We come upon it rather quickly, as it approaches Amsel and Roen, who have their backs against a large rock.

Before we get a chance to do anything to help, Amsel darts to his right, and Roen to his left. Unfortunately for Amsel, he is slightly larger, drawing the karnesh's attention. He manages to get four steps before it lunges and grabs him in its jaws. Amsel lets out a blood-curdling yelp that's cut short, as it throws him in the air.

Roen turns to see his friend get thrown and screams, *"Amsel!!"* He stops running near the cliff's edge and starts waving and screaming frantically, trying to get the beast's attention.

It works, the beast forgets about Amsel and charges right at Roen. He freezes for a moment and then starts backing up until he right at the edge.

To my left, Railu screams, *"No!"*

Roen takes one last step off the edge and disappears.

"Roen!"

The karnesh, sensing the scream, tries to turn to us, but the speed of its charge takes it over the edge of the cliff, not far from where Roen stepped off. With another blood-curdling roar, it slips off the edge. We hear it crash through the trees and land heavily on the ground below.

We rush over to the cliff where Roen stepped off, and to our surprise, he is lying on a ledge about ten meters down.

"Roen!" she blurts and then starts climbing down the ragged cliff-side.

"Careful!" I call out. *Aime?*

"You're safe to jump," she states, anticipating my request.

I step from the edge and land within reach of Roen. Without touching him, I start at his head, checking to see how badly he's hurt.

Railu lands next to me. "Don't move him," I command. "Talk to him. Try to get him to wake up. He's got a concussion."

From above I hear Tayla yell, "Niku!"

Railu holds his head still as I continue to his chest. She starts gently licking his nose and softly calling, "Roen, love, come on, wake up." Tears fall from her muzzle and land on his face.

"Punctured lung, broken rib." I sneer. "Have to fix those now." I watch the visual overlay as Aime sets the rib and starts the healing process. "Not too much, just get him stable for now." Aime alters her target to the punctured lung, repairing the damage that the rib did. As she works, Niku appears, pulls out her medkits, and immediately starts dressing the numerous gashes and cuts to stop the bleeding before that becomes a problem. As she works, Roen finally starts to wake up.

"Roen, it's me, Railu. I've found you. Please, love, don't move. Let me know you're still with me."

"Railu?" he manages to say, as I move from the lung to check his left arm. "How?"

She pets his face, her voice reflecting her relief. "I'd thought I'd lost you."

"Compound break, upper left arm, Aime set it. Niku, need a splint right here." I watch as the bone realigns. Roen lets out a cry as it pops into place. Niku then changes sides with me and splints the arm. I check the right arm and then move to his lower body.

"We're starting to run low on energy," Aime warns.

"Keep at it," I insist, noticing another problem. "Ruptured spleen, repair it."

I see Oana appear nearby, wearing my pack. She looks at Roen curiously and then glances between Railu, Niku, and myself, but she stays back, careful not to get in the way.

With the spleen repaired, I move on. "His spine's intact."

"We're almost out of energy," Aime warns.

"Just a little more," I insist, moving down to his legs. I notice that Oana has settled on watching me as if trying to figure out what I'm doing. "His right ankle's shattered. Niku, splint it." I turn and call up to the others, "He can't walk. We'll need to lift him." As I turn my attention back to Roen, I see Oana turn and curiously look at her stump of a tail.

As I finish his right leg, the others lower a simple stretcher down to us, which Oana quickly collects. As Niku finishes wrapping his splinted ankle, I place the stretcher alongside Roen. It's simply made, consisting of a blanket and branches tied together. Not seeing any way to hold him on it, I turn. "Oana." She looks at me. I wave her over and get the portable converter out of my pack.

Looking at the stretcher for a moment, I tell it, "Five, wide, two-meter long cinch straps." After the flash, I pull out the five neatly rolled straps, each wider than my hand. I run them under the stretcher, at even intervals. Oana carefully puts the converter back in the pack while Railu, Niku, and I manage to slide Roen onto the stretcher. We pull the straps across him to hold him snugly in place.

I lean over him. "We're going to pick you up, try to stay still, keep your arms in, okay?"

He gives me a worried look but nods.

I look at Railu. "You better get up there. They'll need your help lifting."

"I'll see you at the top, love," Railu adds, giving him a gentle nuzzle.

She nods and starts climbing up the cliff, using the various roots and rocks as handholds. Oana, Niku, and I lift Roen into position, leaning him against the wall while we wait for the others to get ready to lift.

"Are you ready?" I ask him.

"No," he says with a frightened look on his face, "but I don't want to stay down here either."

"Okay." I chuckle a little. "Just try to relax."

"Ready?" Railu calls out from above.

"Ready," I reply and pick up one of the belay lines attached to the bottom end of the stretcher. Niku grabs the other.

As the others start pulling him up, Roen's face goes from merely scared to terrified, closing his eyes tightly and laying his ears back. They continue to pull him up the side, with Niku and me keeping him from swinging or spinning.

About halfway up the top, the stretcher snags on a clump of roots. They lower him down a little, trying to get him out from under the snag, but it doesn't work. Watching the difficulty, Oana suddenly darts up the cliffside, effortlessly climbing up to where Roen is snagged.

"Oana help," she proudly states, then starts using her claws to cut the roots. Once she is satisfied that the roots won't interfere, she waves her arm upward.

"Pull," I shout, and the others start pulling on the lines again. Oana makes sure that the stretcher does not snag on the roots and then climbs alongside it. Once it clears the top, they both disappear from view.

I help Niku pack up her stuff. "Up you go." As I watch her climb up, exhaustion hits me, and I lean against the cliff wall.

Taking a moment to catch my breath, I turn around and take in the view. To my right I see the massive furrow cut in the cliffside where the karnesh slid down, removing all the vegetation and protrusions as it went. I realize that if Railu had not screamed, the beast would have slid down right where I stand, killing Roen.

I look down below, trying to see where the karnesh landed. Seeing only a shadowed gap in the trees, I hope its armor's not strong enough to protect it from a fall from this height. Sighing, I turn back to the cliff and look for the best way up.

Finding a suitable starting point, I try to climb, but find myself too exhausted to get more than a start. Without Aime, the armor has no adhesive ability. I take a step back and look up.

"Oana help?"

Startled, I look down and find her standing right in front of me, slightly hunkered down so she is looking up at me. I notice she is not wearing my pack, apparently having left it above before climbing back down to me.

"Oana help how?" I ask, hoping she understands me.

She tilts her head, looking at me curiously for a moment, and then looks up the cliff. She turns to face the cliff and backs up against me. "Oana help."

Realizing her intent, I wrap my arms around her. She straightens up and lifts her stump of a tail between my legs, lifting me off the ground. I tighten my grip around her as she starts to climb up the cliff. In the short time it takes her to make the climb, I realize just how strong she is. Once at the top, she lowers herself back down, setting me on the ground.

"Thank you, Oana." I rub the side of her neck. She closes her eyes and turns her head, exposing the area to my touch. I let her indulge a little as she coos.

"What kept you?" Tayla asks, momentarily interrupting Oana's treat.

"The view," I say, hoping she doesn't ask.

"And?" she adds, not buying my first answer.

Giving up, I say, "And I'm worn out."

"How's Aime?"

"Recharging, she's out of energy too. Did anybody find Amsel?"

Larrah nods her head. "He is gone, most likely before he hit the ground." She indicates. "I have covered him."

I look at Roen, lying on the stretcher with Railu still showering him with her affections, and wonder how he will take it, being the only survivor. "Well, let's make camp and get Roen onto something more comfortable so he can rest." I make a quick check of the sun's position and add, "And maybe some lunch."

Finding a gap in the undamaged trees, Fey sets up the tent, making sure to add a room for Railu and Roen. After Railu and Tayla move Roen from the stretcher to a reclined chair, Niku checks his dressings, making sure that the bleeding is under control and the splints aren't too tight.

Tria and Zoe start fixing lunch while the kids start setting up the tables and chairs. Tayla and Sada corner me and put me in a chair next to Roen. I quickly realize that I'm too exhausted to argue with them. Instead, I sit and watch everyone else work. Fey passes out water, Kotu collects wood for the fire, Niku joins Tria and Zoe, working on lunch. Tayla and Larrah start searching for something among the fallen trees while Sada gets out plates and utensils.

Railu has calmed a lot, quietly resting her head on Roen's shoulder. I find myself smiling at the way he is returning the affection, his head on hers, eyes closed, and holding hands. A feeling of relief washes over me as I realize that she is whole again.

Sada gives me a curious look. 'Why are you so happy?'

I simply nod to Railu and Roen. She looks at them for a moment, smiles, and turns back to me and gives me a nuzzle, rubbing her forehead along my cheek. I smile and hold her to me for a moment. Pulling back, she signs. 'You did that.'

'No, she did that,' I sign back, correcting her. 'I just gave her the excuse to do it.'

'You saved his life, and hers.' She insists.

I think for a moment, but before I can respond, Arru and Oana approach, carrying the stretcher with Amsel's covered body on it. They place the stretcher across two logs that Tayla and Larrah placed at the edge of camp, keeping the body suspended above the ground.

Sada covers her mouth, in shock, her ears slanting back, and sits on my lap. Railu gasps at the sight, also shocked, getting everybody else's attention. We all fall silent for a moment, looking at Amsel's covered body.

"I'm . . . sorry," Railu quietly says looking at Roen.

Roen sighs, saddened by the sight of his friend. "I'm sorry too," he confesses. "I should have never left. I never believed the stories like he did."

"You believed in him, and that was enough for you. I cannot blame you for that, but I could blame you for leaving me behind. That was *your* choice."

"I know, and I regret it," he confesses sadly, "not to change the subject, but we need to get him buried soon, his beliefs and all."

"Manenic?" Arru asks.

"Yeah, I don't believe myself, but he was my friend. I'll respect his wishes."

"I am familiar with the burial needs," she states. "I will make the preparations."

"Thank you." He looks around, finally noticing everyone in the group. "Did you put all this together to come after me?" he asks Railu.

"Well, that was what I wanted to do, but he was already heading this way, so I tagged along with him."

He turns to me, seeing me clearly for the first time. His jaw drops open for a moment, eyes wide, and stutters, "Y-you . . . you're a—human?"

"Yeah."

"But legend says you're all gone."

"And yet here I sit," I politely tease, drawing a sudden scolding punch from Sada. "Oww!" I protest, rubbing my chest.

'Behave yourself,' she gestures, furiously.

Roen, suddenly confused, looks at me, then at Sada. "You certainly don't act like the humans I've read about."

Arru walks up, carrying a small bottle and a pouch. "That's because he is not one of *those* humans, even if he has some of their abilities."

"What do you mean?" he asks, looking at her, still confused.

"What she means is," I explain, "just like there's a difference between yours, Railu's, and Arru's personalities, there's a difference between each human's. We all think and act differently, and have our own personalities."

"But from the stories, they all seemed . . . emotionless."

"Well, from I learned, they were researchers. So I'd bet their indifference was really them trying to remain objective."

He thinks for a moment. "That does change a lot of things about them." He pauses for a moment and his face lights up. "Actually, it makes a lot of sense."

"I'm not a researcher. I'm more like a . . . searcher. I was looking for a place I felt I fit in. In our pursuit of you, I realized that I already found a group of people who I fit in with." In response to my confession, Sada nuzzles my neck, purring loudly, making me chuckle. Tayla also gives me a bump, and I return her kiss. "Some more than others."

Tria and Fey bring over several plates of food and pass them around. We continue talking while we eat, each taking turns introducing ourselves, telling a little part of our journey.

After lunch, Kotu surprises Roen with a crutch he made, which he gratefully accepts. We then see to Amsel's burial. Unable to dig through the rocky surface, we find a suitable place near the rock wall and cover him with stones. Arru performs the service, and then she, Railu, and Roen each collect a tuft of their own fur, dip an end in the bottle of sap, and stick it to the larger stone marker that Oana helped place. Roen then uses a black rock to write Amsel's name on it.

He stands silent for a moment, then says, "I'm sorry you never got to the Dig, but I thank you. You helped me find what's really important." He looks at Railu. "Family." She gently nuzzles him, with tears in her eyes.

Returning to camp in silence, most of us spend the rest of the day relaxing. Tria spends some time on lessons with Fey and Kotu. Arru sits with Oana, trying to teach her some more words. Sada curls up in a chair and takes a nap. Tayla sits on my lap, curling up with her head under my chin. I wrap my arm around her and hold her close, enjoying the moment.

"So . . . you have two mates?" Roen asks.

I think for a moment, looking at Sada curled up in the chair. "Well, yes and no. Tayla here is a mate to me like Railu is to you. With Sada, it's a little harder to explain. She's more than a friend, or companion, like a mate would be, but she's not a mate. She is happy to be with me, knowing that I care for her like she cares for me." I scowl, realizing that I still can't really define my relationship with Sada like I can with Tayla. "Does that make sense?"

"She's a soul mate," Tayla states.

"Yes, that would be a better way to describe it, thank you." I kiss her on her nose and she nuzzles my neck a little.

He gives us a skeptical look and then hesitantly asks, "Can you have cubs, together?"

"Roen!" Railu scolds.

"It's okay," I interrupt her. "Yes, we can."

"And we want to." Tayla purrs.

Railu look at him through narrowed her eyes and rubs her nose on his. "And now that we're together again, so can we," she coos.

He looks wearily at her. "Would that be a good idea, being out here in the Wilds?"

She gives him a patient look. "Aside from Kyle, you've had the worst injuries yet, and you're still here too. Together, there's nothing we can't handle."

"Very optimistic of you," he gently says to her, giving her a kiss and one-armed hug. He then turns to me. "How bad were you hurt?"

"Karnesh slapped me with its tail, threw me into a tree hard enough to knock the tree down, broke my back, three ribs, and cracked my skull, and I was wearing my armor at the time. It took Aime three days to fix me."

He looks around, suddenly confused. "Who's Aime?"

"She's . . ." I think for a moment, trying to figure out how to best describe her to him in a way he'll understand.

"If you think of him as a shaman, Aime is the spirit that helps him," Railu explains.

"I'm not a shaman."

"No, you're not," Tayla agrees. "You're better."

I sigh heavily and roll my eyes, not willing to enter that argument again.

He thinks for a moment. "How bad was I hurt?" he asks, afraid of the answer.

"You had a broken rib, punctured lung, and a ruptured spleen. You still have a broken arm, shattered ankle, and a concussion, and of course, the cuts and scrapes."

His eyes go wide, a mix of surprise and shock. "It sounds like I should feel more pain than I do."

"The first thing Aime did was to block most of the pain. She didn't block it all because you need to be aware of where you're hurt. It'll wear off in a day or two."

"Will I be healed by then?" Worried he looks at me and then Railu.

"When Aime has enough energy, we'll fix you up some more. I won't let you suffer."

Railu and I help Roen to bed for the night. Niku then starts changing his bandages and I address his concussion. "This is about all I can do tonight. Aime's still low on energy, but it's safe for you to sleep now."

"Thank you."

Understanding his meaning, I reply, "You're welcome, but you really should be thanking your mate. If it wasn't for her nose, we may not have found you in time."

He looks at her. "You finished your training?" he asks.

"No, I did not." Ashamed, she bows her head.

Noticing that she did not tell him why, I add, "It turns out that she's a natural at tracking."

"So you take after your mother after all," he comments, smiling at her.

"As much as I didn't want to, I'm glad of that now," she confesses.

Niku interrupts, "Okay, try not to roll over. It will disturb the medicine in your wounds. You need that to help you heal." She looks at Railu. "He needs his rest. Please make sure that he gets it."

Railu nods and Niku leaves the room. Railu then looks at him, smiling. I sigh realizing what she wants. "Go *easy* on him. He still needs to heal." He smiles at her, reaching up to her with his good arm to pull her close. I smile and close the curtain.

Stepping over a sleeping Oana, I crawl into bed between my girls. Sada immediately snuggles up to me and starts purring, while Tayla props herself up on her arm to face me. "Do you think she will be okay?"

"She will be fine," I admit, and hearing Railu start to giggle, I add, "I more worried about him right now."

She lies down and snuggles up to me. "He survived a karnesh. He'll survive her."

"I hope so."

"Let's give them some privacy," she whispers into my ear. I quickly realize that she was talking to Aime because the giggling suddenly disappears. "That's better." She then reaches across my chest and massages Sada's cheek, prompting her to purr louder. "Good night loves."

I give them both a gentle squeeze. "Yes, good night, my loves." I yawn, as Tayla also starts to purr.

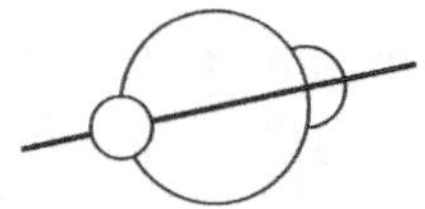

After seeing to Roen's remaining wounds, he stands and tentatively flexes his arm and leg. When he sees Railu step out of the tent, he stops and turns to me. "If that offer still stands for me, I'd like to take you up on it." He holds out the signet I gave Railu for him.

Taking the signet, I give him a curious look. "Tell me why you want this."

He sighs and looks down, ashamed. "I would like to say that it's just because I feel I owe you one, but that's not the only reason. Railu and I talked for a long time last night and she told me a lot of things, and I've come to realize that I owe her a lot, and in turn, I do owe you, but not for me, for her. So, I'm asking, to say thank you, for everything." He swallows hard. "And because she told me to."

"Starting to trust your mate?" Tayla asks.

"Learning that she's more mature than I thought she was."

"She has her moments," I chuckle, "but you're right. You do owe her much." I pin the signet on his bandolier, "Your trust should be the first thing you give her."

He nods. "I know." He bows and turns to Railu and rubs his muzzle along hers. "I regret leaving you behind, but I thank you for coming after me."

She wraps him in a hug. "Just don't leave me behind again."

He returns her hug, holding her close to him. "I won't."

CHAPTER 18

With time not pressing on us anymore, we make our progress at a more leisurely pace. Roen takes lead, with Railu close behind. With the passage we walk narrowing, the rock wall on one side and the cliff on the other, we really only have the one direction to go. I start sending up the drone again, only having it sweep the narrow passage before night.

Waking one morning, I find that Tayla has rolled to her side, and now has her back pressed against me. In the two months, we've slept together, she has not once turned away. I sit up and gently run my hand over her belly and head, allowing Aime to check her.

Feeling my hands, Tayla groans slightly as she wakes. "Why'd you roll me over?"

"I found you this way, love. Are you okay?"

"Yeah, why?"

I smile and gently rub her belly, marveling at the image that Aime's showing me. "Because you're pregnant."

Tayla sits up suddenly, as does Sada. "What?"

"It worked," Aime states. "I will need to monitor closely for a time, but right now you are the future parents of two, congratulations."

Her hands reflexively rub her belly. "I'm gonna be a mom?"

Sada sits up nodding happily, also putting her hand on Tayla's belly. "Isn't this what you wanted?"

She smiles. "Yeah, I was just surprised," she slowly states, rubbing her belly.

I bury my nose in her cheek fur and kiss her. "You'll be wonderful, don't worry."

"I'm not worried." Her face seems to drop as she adds, "Am I?"

"Yeah, a little," I admit as Sada nods her agreement.

'We should tell the others.'

"Oh, let them sleep in. I want to cuddle for a while." She curls up on my lap, purring. Equally happy, Sada curls alongside us.

I sit holding the mother-to-be, keeping my hand on Tayla's belly, marveling at the image of the developing cubs.

"What will they be?" she asks, catching me by surprise.

"The cubs?"

"Yeah, I mean, you and Aime set it up, right?"

"Well, to a degree," I admit, trying to figure out how to best describe the process. "There were some things we left alone, like the chance of boy or girl, but since some of my physical traits don't compare well to yours, we worked out a system to remove the ones that don't work and replace them with statistically similar traits that do work."

She gives me an odd look. "I've learned a lot with you but some of that was still beyond me."

"Sorry, we looked at how common certain traits are in cheetahs and compared them to how common my traits are in humans. We then traded the non-relevant human traits and replaced them with the ones that we still needed. I didn't even look at your traits until after Aime and I were finished."

"You're saying our cubs could be anything?"

"Boy, girl . . . yellow, white, king, whatever." I give her a kiss between her ears, "It just didn't seem right, picking anything specific for our child, well, children."

"So Aime doesn't even know?"

"Nope."

"That's the way it should be." She settles back into my arms. "Will you do the same for Megai?"

"If she wants kits."

She nuzzles me again. "I hope she does."

Her comment makes me smile and after a while, we dress for the day. Tayla decides against telling the others for now, not yet wanting to be treated differently until necessary.

Reaching the wider ground, our progress slows due to uncertainty of where to go. I continue launching the drone every evening, but with the sweep now being wider, Roen, Railu, and I spend much of the morning reviewing the scans for signs of life.

After nearly a week of this, I sit outside early one the morning reviewing the map. Having found something of interest in a southeastern direction, I have Aime start enhancing the detail in that area. As I wait, Railu comes up, grabs my hand, and holds it to her belly.

"Sorry, I've been feeling odd these last few mornings, today's worse."

As Aime begins to show me what she sees, I turn suddenly and drop my tablet, putting my other hand on her back. "You . . . you're . . . pregnant," I stammer

"I'm WHAT?" Her scream gets everyone's attention, and Roen runs over to us.

"You're pregnant," I repeat.

"I—I can't be. I wasn't in estrus."

"You certainly smelled like it," Roen states.

"I have to agree. I could smell you too," I admit.

"How? I'm not due for another week."

"Premature estrus," Aime offers. "Emotionally induced by reuniting with Roen."

I find myself agreeing. "Seems likely."

"What seems likely?" Railu asks.

"Railu, you were in an emotionally induced premature estrus."

She sits, clearly puzzled. "What's that mean?" Roen asks.

"It means, her body wasn't ready for this. I'm going to keep an eye on her and your kit, but . . . Niku, she'll need prenatal vitamins." I look at Railu. "We'll do all we can to help you through this."

"You might as well set me up with some too, Niku," Tayla states.

"You too?" Niku asks

"Yeah."

"I thought you didn't want anyone to know yet?"

"No need now, not since she is too." She hugs Railu. "We will go through this together."

"Together?"

"Yeah, I'm carrying twins."

"Congratulations."

"To you too."

"Well, I feel a small, sensible celebration is in order," Arru states. "To congratulate the parents-to-be."

"No," Roen and I say together, causing several of the others to laugh.

"You're outnumbered," Tayla states as she sits next to me.

"So I noticed," I moan.

"Never before have I been at the mercy of so many females," Roen states as he sits.

"Don't think you're going to get used to it either," Railu chides.

He gives her a loving look. "I doubt you'd let me."

Zoe proceeds to make a rather filling breakfast of breaded fish with fruit syrup, an interesting combination of the fish that Tayla loves with the sweet syrups that Railu enjoys. We all eat slowly and heartily, surrendering the morning to enjoying the meal.

After we eat, I resume looking at the map. I find that Aime has finished enhancing the area that I found interesting. As I zoom in on the area, I notice that I'm looking at looks more artificial than natural.

I look up and see that Railu and Roen are relaxed and talking calmly with each other. Picking up their tablets, I step over to them and casually place them in their laps. "I hope I'm not interrupting something important, but I need your opinion on what you see." With a flick of the screen, the image on my tablet replicates on theirs.

Roen picks up his and takes a look, prompting Railu to do the same. They both study the image for a while, moving the image around, making short comments to each other and pointing at each other's screen.

I suddenly feel a chair get shoved under me, forcing me to sit. "Fey!"

"Sorry, you looked like you needed your chair."

"Simply placing it behind me would have worked."

She giggles. "I know, but that's no fun."

"Sometimes 'fun' gets someone hurt," Tayla adds, coming up behind the girl. "Don't you have a lesson?"

Fey's face drops. "Yeah."

"Off you go then." Fey hops off to Tria, and Tayla leans over me. "What'd you find?"

"Paths. Human paths," Roen states.

"How do you know?"

"The ground is hard-packed, and there's a pattern to it, like patrols or hunters would use."

"Could it be Ootuku?" Tayla asks, looking over at Oana.

"Well, from what Aime's taught me, Oana's people all have claws, three forward and one back. If you look at her tracks, it's like she grabs the ground as she walks, digging all four claws in. These are all too smooth for that, not even hooves would leave the ground this smooth."

I sit back and pull Tayla to me for a kiss. "Looks like we finally have a solid destination. Plan a route for us and we'll head out in the morning."

When morning comes, Railu again complains of discomfort. After checking her, Aime and I realize that she's already showing early signs of a difficult pregnancy.

"Railu, I'm sorry, but you're staying back with me."

"Why? I want to help my mate."

"I know that, but for the safety of your child, I need to keep a close eye on you."

"It's okay," Roen consoles, then gives her a nuzzle and puts his hand on her belly. "It's for the kit's safety, and this time, I won't be far."

She hugs him. "For our kit."

After packing, Roen takes point, leading us in a southeast direction to the trails. Railu stays close to me but watches her mate closely as he leads. He consults his tablet a few times, but I get the feeling that he's really just taking it easy to make sure that Railu doesn't overexert herself.

We make slow progress over the next few days, stopping often to allow Railu to rest. I check her condition often, allowing Aime to fix what she's able, but with Railu developing multiple conditions, most of the treatments aren't much more than temporary fixes.

One morning, Aime wakes me up early. "Kyle, the drone found something you need to see."

Noting the faint light through the tent window, I ask, *Can it wait a while?*

"You also need to check on Railu, preferably before she gets up."

Sighing, I kiss Sada and slowly slide out from under her. As I climb over Tayla, whose sleeping on her side, her usual position now that she's pregnant. I kiss her too. After I dress, I look at my sleeping mates, despite how different this planet is from Earth, how different its people are, I'm home, and I'm happy to have them as my family.

I slowly open the door to check on Railu, and she quietly whispers, "I've been waiting for you."

Smiling at being heard, I step through the door and see she's lying on her side, her back to me, with her head on Roen's chest. He appears to still be asleep. "Well then, let's see how you and your kit are doing."

As I put my hands on her belly, she makes a sour face. "I'm sorry you have to do this."

I chuckle lightly. "Like you could have done this on purpose, stop feeling guilty."

She smiles, realizing I'm right. "I'll try."

After finishing with Railu, I grab a tablet, table, and a chair and have a seat outside. "All right Aime, what's so important."

The tablet comes on, showing me another pattern of paths around an odd-shaped structure. I sit up and zoom in on it. "Is that . . . ?"

"It is. I double-checked the tail numbers with the ones from the facility."

"We found them!"

"There are several small structures scattered around, all appear to be in use."

I zoom out and see some of the structures. "Those look prefab."

"They are indeed. I am surprised that they lasted this long. They are emergency shelters and short-term housing, really only supposed to last a year or two."

"Does the shuttle have a converter?"

"Several. They could be using it to make supplies."

"Would that mean that the shuttle is in working condition?"

"Possibly, there are no signs of vegetation growing on it, so they are likely maintaining it in some fashion."

"I suppose there's some sort of upgrade to pilot?"

"There is, however you can learn how without it, but it is more effective with the pilot package."

"I used to fly, you know, when I was a paramedic."

"A helicopter does not compare to an orbital shuttle."

Chuckling, I say, "No, I suppose not, but if standing on a book will help you reach the shelf, then stand on a book."

"I fail to see how standing on books will help you fly a shuttle."

"Aime, he means that he already has some background. Even I understood that."

I look up from the tablet to see Larrah set up her chair and sit across from me. I smile, "Morning, I thought that I'd be alone for another half hour yet."

"I heard you leave the tent." She takes a deep breath, enjoying the cooler morning air. "What's this about a shuttle?"

I hand her the tablet. "We've found them. They're using the shuttle along with several temporary houses, but there they are."

She looks at the image for a while. "So we're almost there. Then what?"

"Take care of them, then find a place of our own."

"I'd like that," Tayla purrs, wrapping her arms around me from behind.

"Morning."

"Why didn't you wake me?"

"You needed your sleep."

"No, I didn't."

"Okay. You looked so peaceful I didn't have the heart to disturb you."

She gives me a gentle bump with her nose. "That, I believe." She then notices the tablet in Larrah's hands. "Find something?"

"Shuttle," Larrah states, handing her the tablet.

As she examines the image, she sits on my lap. "Wow, we're almost there." She looks curiously at me. "And you aren't the least bit excited."

I set the tablet aside and put my hand on her belly, feeling the small swell of her baby bump. "I have all the excitement I need right here."

With Railu needing to rest a little more each day, our progress slows. Finally nearing the paths we spotted, we take a rest as I prepare them for their first encounter with humans. After tending to Railu, Roen takes point while the rest of us quietly follow a safe distance back.

After a few hours, Roen comes quietly back to me and nods. "I found their tents."

After, checking Railu's condition, I follow Roen down the path. When his ears perk, I realize he's hearing them.

"Bring the others here and wait for me to call out. He nods, and I casually walk out through a gap in the foliage toward the shuttle.

Entering the clearing, I'm greeted by several surprised human faces. I nod, trying to be genuinely friendly. I warmly greet them, "Hello."

An older man slowly walks up to me and looks carefully at my face. "Who are you?"

Holding out my hand, I reply, "My name is Kyle."

He hesitantly shakes my hand. "Marcus, where'd you come from?"

"I was sent to find you. I'm one of the last survivors from the facility."

His expression drops noticeably. "One of the last?"

"Yeah, we survived because we were in cryo."

"How many survived?"

"Three: myself, my companion, and Cayla Ryan." By now we're gathering a small crowd. Most of the people are in casual clothes, carrying various types of tools.

"Wait, Cayla was a caretaker. That would mean . . ."

"That makes me Alpha," I state tapping my signet.

His face lights up. "Your companion, where is she?"

I look around at the others who have gathered. "She's not like us, so please don't be afraid." I turn to the path I followed, "Sada."

Cautiously, she comes out and walks over to me. "Oh," Marcus gasps. Several others also gasp, and a few murmurs circulate.

Seeing their surprisingly calm reactions, I figure it's okay for the others to come out. "I have other friends too, all here to help me, and now, *we* can help you."

"Help us with what?"

I look to the crowd, to the one who spoke up. "Help you go home, or find a new, safer home."

"We can't go home," Marcus states. "There's a virus that will kill us."

"It's gone, burned itself out, long ago."

Several more murmurs circulate. "How can you be sure?"

"Because I was there. I saw what it did. My AI found no trace of it, and she's been checking the whole time."

"You . . . have an AI?" Marcus asks.

"Yes."

"Please, come with me." He leads me into the shuttle, where five very elderly people sit in reclined seats. "If you truly have an AI, they will know."

"Aime, if you please."

I look around curiously at the inside of the shuttle while I wait. This section looks more like an extra-wide bus or a passenger plane, with a door and a pair of large converters at each end of the cabin. There is also the larger door we entered through on the side. Through the forward door, I see the cockpit, the aft door is closed and the window dark.

"Upload completed," Aime states, interrupting my observations.

"Upload?"

"Apologies, these are the few remaining archaeologists."

"How? They'd be . . ."

"Two hundred seventy-three, for the youngest," Aime states. "I have learned much with the data exchange. For instance, we AIs drastically slow your aging process. That is how they are still alive, although they are nearing their end. They have also uploaded their combined medical knowledge and piloting skills. I don't need any additional hardware for piloting, but my healing ability will still be limited until I can upgrade my hardware."

"We welcome you," I hear one of them say, as they all open their eyes.

"Marcus, he is to be trusted. He is here to help us," another says.

"Trust his friends. They are dedicated to him."

"The dig site was natural, but it saved our lives."

"The facility is ruined."

"We thought we could not go back."

"Take us to Garrent. We will make it our home."

"You now have what you need to save Cayla."

"Aime has a data packet for the Sages. They will know what to do with it."

"You have done well, both for yourself and the people you have met."

"You would do well to accept their praise and guide them."

"That's not what I want," I protest.

"They need someone to guide them, to unite them."

"Some have already chosen you."

"Through a misunderstanding. I can't accept that," I counter.

"You will . . ."

"In time."

They all close their eyes, apparently signaling that the discussion is over.

Still trying to get a grip on everything I just heard, I follow Marcus out of the shuttle, back to where Sada waits. I call out to the others, and as they emerge from the foliage, I introduce them to Marcus. When Oana comes out several people back away, including Marcus.

"It's a . . . ," he stammers, obviously afraid.

"She's an Ootuku. She means you no harm. She's my friend."

"But they've been attacking us."

"Only the males are aggressive. She's harmless," I stress.

Oana hides behind me, cowering. "Ti-ku, Oana ti-ku."

"See, she's just as afraid of you as you are of her," Tayla states, as she gently takes Oana's hand and coaches her out from behind me.

"Oana scared."

I wrap my arm around her and rub her neck. "It's okay, they're friends."

"Friends?" she straightens up a little and starts cooing as I continue to rub her neck.

Hearing her coo and seeing her lean into me, Marcus cautiously approaches. "She speaks?"

"Yes, and she's surprisingly smart. She's learned just over a thousand words in less than three months."

"Really?" He reaches his hand out to her. She tilts her head curiously, then puts her nose to it, sniffing.

"Friend?"

Marcus smiles as Oana gently pushes her nose into his hand, trying to get him to rub her. He chuckles and rubs her nose. "You are friendly, aren't you?"

She starts cooing and bobs her head a little. "Oana like friends." She then takes a few steps forward, past Marcus, toward the others, still cooing. They all look at her curiously but a small girl reaches out to her. She bows down to the girl's hand and waits. The girl touches Oana's nose and giggles. Oana mimics the girl's giggle, making the little girl and many of the others around her laugh.

With the tension broke, Fey walks up to Oana and the little girl. "Hi, I'm Fey."

The girl looks at Fey curiously for a moment. "Sarah."

"Sarah, nice to meet you."

Oana tilts her head. "Sarah."

"What are you?" Sarah asks.

Fey giggles. "I'm a whitetail deer."

A few other girls join in, starting to ask Fey questions. I find myself relieved that I told my group to expect any kind of questions and to try not to be offended by them.

Everyone relaxes and my group slowly starts to mingle with the humans. Their mood changes from solemn to nearly joyous as they get to know each other.

After a while, everyone settles, and they start packing. Taking things out of a few of the nearer structures and putting them in the back of the shuttle. I tend to Railu, with the updates that Aime just received. She's able to do more for her, but we still agree on rest.

I then have a seat in the pilot's seat of the shuttle. Sada joins me in the copilot's seat and Tayla sits behind me. "What's our next step?"

"Well, I need to take a pilot's training course."

"You really think this will still fly?"

"Obviously, they all think it will." I look over the panels, realizing that they're not too different from the ones on the rescue ship. "Besides, if it does, you'll get your wish."

She smiles and nods. "What do you need us to do?"

I wiggle in the seat, trying to get more comfortable. Not succeeding, I look at her. "Make sure I don't fall out of the chair."

Tayla chuckles as Sada pats my leg. "All right."

I lean back and relax. "Aime, pilot training, please."

I close my eyes and drift off into the training program.

Waking up, I find myself still in the pilot's chair. Tayla now sits next to me instead of Sada. "Hey, you're back."

"Yeah." I turn around and look into the cabin. It's now half full of stuff, with nearly twenty of the forty seats packed with belongings. "Looks like they're almost ready."

"Just waiting on you."

"Okay, well." I turn back to the shuttle controls. "Aime, initiate main power cells, start preflight diagnostics."

"Unable to initiate main power cells, main power relay failure, insufficient power in capacitor."

"Can you divert power from elsewhere?"

"Available power insufficient. Proximity power is insufficient."

"Proximity power. The emergency cell?"

"Correct, direct connection is required."

"Where's my pack?" I ask as Sada comes in carrying the power cell.

Getting up from the chair, I take the cell and ask, "How do you do that?"

Receiving only a smile and a nose bump, I squeeze through the passenger compartment into the aft section. I'm pleased to find that this small room is not packed with belongings.

After attaching the cell to the engineering console, Aime speaks up, "Initiating main power, starting preflight diagnostics, five minutes to complete."

"That's better." I exit the shuttle and do a walk around and then climb up on it to check the wings, intakes, and exhausts. Finding all clear, I return to the cockpit to see the diagnostic panel showing all greens.

"That's a pleasant surprise."

"It appears they were diligent with their maintenance," Aime states.

"Good." I check several other displays, making sure that everything checks out and is ready. Finding everything set, I exit the shuttle again and find Marcus standing just outside waiting. "Everything checks out. It should fly."

"I know, I've been keeping her that way." He turns around and motions to a group of people standing near the shuttle. They board and sit in the remaining seats, surrounding the elders. "Your people ride command."

I look around and come up with the best first three. "Tayla will ride copilot. Sada, stay and watch the children. Arru and Larrah, you'll be coming with me."

"Why us?" Larrah asks, nervously eyeing the shuttle.

"Well, you and Tayla will be security while Arru helps them understand the layout of the village, just in case."

Arru nods. "Sound reasoning."

I follow them inside as Marcus calls out. "All clear!" I wait a minute for everyone to get clear before closing the door and starting up the engines.

The shuttle starts to rise slowly like a hot air balloon. I smile as Tayla's eyes go wide with wonder. I feel her flood of delight as she watches the ground fall away. I glance back at Arru and Larrah and they are holding tight to the arms of the chairs, eyes wide with more fear than wonder.

I chuckle softly to myself. "Aime, terrain mapping systems on, full scan."

Tayla looks at me, curiously. "Why do that?"

I give her a wink. "To see what we missed. Besides, the shuttle can do it so much quicker than Aime can."

"Course plotted to Garrent."

I turn the shuttle to the west and engage the engines. We accelerate quickly, but we don't feel much of it. We pass between Dendros and Three Lands, and reach Garrent, traveling the same distance it took us months to walk, in just a few minutes.

With the shuttle being slightly wider than the streets, finding a place to land isn't easy, though Aime manages to find the one intersection that has enough room to land, which happens to be right in front of the council hut. Setting down is surprisingly easy despite the limited space, though the street becomes largely impassable due to the bulk of the shuttle.

After powering down the engines, I exit the shuttle. Larrah and Tayla follow as Arru waits in the door. "Most of the dragons would have scattered from the shuttle, so set up a perimeter. Arru, try to keep them in the closer buildings for now. Let's unload."

The people start pulling out everything that was packed, and then they carefully carry out the elders. To increase the cargo room in the shuttle, we start removing some of the seats, starting from the back. They take five of them into the council hut with the elders. With the shuttle unloaded and half of the seats out, I shout an all-clear and board the shuttle.

After several trips and nearly a whole day, everything and everyone is in Garrent. Over the next couple days, most of us help clear the huts of any remaining critters as they get settled. Railu, however, spends a lot of her time resting in a chair or bed, obviously not wanting to be there.

By the end of a week, we have little to do and decide to head north to Arindell. Seeing us packing up, Marcus runs over to us. "Leaving us?"

"I have someone I need to see." Feeling a sudden pang of fear, I add, "If she'll have me." Tayla hugs my arm and leans into me, trying to comfort me.

He gives me a curious look, but nods his head. "I think I understand."

"If you need help, send someone north. Arindell's a week's walk on the north road. Have them tell the council that you need Sovereign Kyle's help. They'll know what to do from there."

"I understand, but we have communicators. We can call the shuttle." He reaches out to shake my hand. "The elders would like to offer it to you, as thanks for your help." He looks over at the shuttle and sighs. "Besides, you're the only one who can fly it, and it's blocking the road."

"Yes, that it is, but are you sure you can do without it? I know that you've been using the converters for food and stuff."

"We have a dozen portables we've been using for food and supplies. The ones in the shuttle, we've used for making the structures. We don't need those anymore."

I turn and look at my family and friends. They all stand in various states of surprise. "Thank you. I'll be sure to check in with you often, but I'll park it outside the village."

"Thank you . . . and good luck to you and yours."

"And to all of you."

With a bow, we board the shuttle and everyone drops their packs and scatters out, with only Railu and Roen sitting together. I'm joined in the cockpit by both Tayla and Sada, as I start the preflight check. Faintly I hear Marcus shout, "All clear!" Tayla then pressed the button to close the doors as I start up the shuttle.

We slowly lift off and turn north. "You're afraid she won't want you, aren't you?"

"I'm afraid she doesn't love me like she did, like I still love her." I feel Sada's hand gently grab my arm from behind.

"Give her a chance. She may surprise you."

"A vision?"

"Intuition."

Doing a scan for life signs as I approach the village, I set down at a still abandoned farm nearly an hour's walk from the village.

"Who's coming into Arindell with me?"

"With us," Tayla quickly corrects.

"How long will you be?" Railu asks, trying to adjust herself to be more comfortable.

"I'm not sure, really, an hour's walk in, minimum of a couple hours there. Half the day, maybe longer?"

"I'll go," Fey interjects, grabbing her pack. Tria and Zoe both join her.

"I'm going to stay," Railu states.

I kneel beside her, putting my hands on her belly. "You're having trouble again, aren't you?" She nods, grimacing at the discomfort.

As she starts to relax, finding relief in the treatment, Roen takes her hand. "I'll stay here with her."

"I'll leave the tents here, if it gets near supper and we're not all back, or you need to lie down, go on ahead and set one up." I look to the others. "Staying?" They nod and Oana trills as she lies on the floor next to Railu, something she's been doing more of lately. I give her neck a gentle rub, then put on my armor and pack.

Seeing the others ready, we set off for the village but don't get too far when we hear Arru shout, "Wait up, I coming too."

Epilogue

The guard gives us a bow as we enter the village, and we find our way toward the council inn. Feeling my nervousness, Tayla stops me. Sada takes some coin from the money pouch and hands it to Fey. Suddenly happy, Fey takes off, dragging Sada to the markets, following Arru and the others.

Now alone, Tayla looks me in the eye. "You amaze and confuse me. You join the Trials out of curiosity, kill a karnesh to protect a little girl, walk for months into the Wilds to find people you don't know, nearly get yourself killed, all without fear or worry. Here we stand mere meters from someone you love and you're terrified."

I swallow hard, my voice falters as I try to explain, "Tayla, rejection is something I don't handle well."

"Sometimes, the best way to handle what you fear is to face it."

As I turn back to the inn, I see Megai standing out front, looking at me, and I feel my heart skip. With a light shove from Tayla, I start walking toward her. I feel tears run down my face and I reflexively wipe them away. Megai suddenly sprints to me. As I catch her in my arms, I realize that she's crying just like I am and my fears evaporate.

"You're back."

"Told you I'd be. I missed you." I kiss her on her forehead and gently stroke her lop-ears while I hear Tayla sniff, apparently crying. "Megai, my feelings for you haven't changed. I still want you for my mate."

She pulls back slightly, wiping her own tears from her eyes. "I"—she takes a ragged breath —"I . . . can't." She turns and heads back to the inn.

Suddenly confused, I follow her. I find Tita standing, smiling at me. "Welcome back, Master Kyle, Tayla. It's a pleasure to see you." She steps out from around the counter, stopping me from following Megai to her room. "Are you here to take my Megai from me?" she jests.

"If she'll have me." I look to Megai's door curiously.

"She changed after you left, you know."

Tita now has my full attention. "How so?"

She gives me an odd look. "She stopped seeing males, and you should know about this." She hands me the paper and winks at me. "I think you'll know what to do with it."

I quickly read the paper and put it in my pocket as Megai's door opens. Seeing who walks through holding Megai's hand, I kneel, "Amela!"

The little girl runs to me and wraps me in a hug. "I never got to thank you for getting me to my aunt."

"Seeing you happy is thanks enough." I kiss her on her cheek and she giggles.

"How?" Megai stutters. "How do you know . . . ?"

"We saved her," I admit, setting Amela down. "I couldn't mistake her markings." I take Megai in my arms as Tayla picks up Amela and holds her. "At first, I thought she was yours, but Aime assured me that was not quite true. I didn't know you had a twin."

She looks down, saddened by my words. "I . . . *had* a twin sister, her mother. Her father was coming to see me when they disappeared. Wanted my help raising her." She slowly looks back up at me. "What happened?"

I sigh. "I'm sorry to say, they were jumped by bandits between Three Lands and Lorholt. He most likely died during the attack."

She sniffs, obviously shaken by the news. "How'd you find her?"

"They jumped us too. That time they lost, but one of them took Fey. We tracked them down and found a lot of children. She was one of them."

She sniffs again, her tears flow freely from her eyes. "I need to tell you something. Several years ago, after Amela was born, my sister got caught stealing. I got blamed for it, but I was here the whole time. No one believed that we had the same markings, so they punished me. My choice was slavery or exile."

"You were made a slave because of what your sister did?" Tayla gasps.

Megai nods. "Basically."

Tita adds, "Since she was already working for me, I bought her. I don't like her being a slave any more than she does."

"But you seemed free."

"Tita still treats me like an employee, but I can't own anything for myself." She leans back into me, and I wrap my arms around her.

"Wait, I gave you money. If you can't own anything, what happened to it?"

"You didn't give it to her. You *entrusted* it to her," Tita explains. "I witnessed it. You gave her permission to use your money. In turn, anything that she bought with it became your property. You found a way for her to get things."

"How does that work with Amela?" Tayla asks.

"The proof of love was complex. I explained that since I 'own' Megai, that in turn I would also 'own' her niece if no one else could claim her. After half a day, they accepted that and I wound up receiving a share of a reward."

I stand there for a moment, just enjoying the feeling of Megai against me, when Tayla asks, "If we know that she has a twin sister with the same markings, why is she still . . . a slave?"

Realizing that's why Tita gave me the paper, I turn to her. "Tita, may I borrow Megai for a few minutes?"

Tita looks at me with a smile and bows. "Certainly, Master Kyle, take as long as you like."

I grab both Megai and Tayla's hands and pull them across the street to the council hut. Stepping into the foyer, we're greeted by the lead mediator, who smiles. "Master Kyle, what can I do for you?"

I place the paper on the counter. "I need to annul this. The accusation was false."

She picks up the paper and reads it. "I'll need to show it to the council, a moment please." She bows and steps into the council chamber.

"Aime, have you shown our memories to Sage yet?"

"Yes, I have, I have also given him a copy of the data packet."

"Good. Thank you."

After a couple of minutes, the mediator comes back out, but holds the door open. "Please, they would like to see you." We follow her back in and walk to the middle of the room.

The head councilor bows to us. "Master Kyle, it is good to see you again."

"Thank you, Councilors. Have you come to a decision, or do you have questions for me?"

"Our apologies. We do have just a few questions. We wish to apologize to you and Megai. We were not made aware of the details regarding the little one's relation. I see now that she has the same markings that you have, a rare thing to have in common."

He looks from Megai to Amela. "How old is the little one?"

Tayla turns so Amela can face the council. "Amela, how old are you?"

She holds up her hand, showing all her fingers. "Five."

His eyes go wide for a moment. "Megai, how long have you worked at the inn?"

Megai thinks for a moment but Sage interjects, "If I may, Megai has worked at the inn for six years, seven months. In that time, I have no records of her being pregnant. Also, the data provided by Kyle confirms that Megai does indeed have a twin sister."

The council murmurs for a moment but quickly quiets. "Megai, it is my duty to declare your servitude annulled. Your rights are hereby returned to you." He takes the paper and writes across it in large letters. "Mediator, please remove her shackle."

The mediator steps up and unlocks a thick bracelet from her right wrist, something I had thought to be merely jewelry. Noticing that her fur's shorter where the shackle was, she rubs the area, trying to get it normal looking again. I gently take her arm and let Aime restore her fur, undoing the damage that the shackle has done.

Megai runs her hand over her wrist, feeling the restored fur. "Thank you."

The head councilor looks to his left. "And now for the child."

"Yes. Megai, I remember you wanted to claim her as your own. Do you still want this?"

"Yes, ma'am."

"For the record, please restate your proof of love."

"She is my twin sister's daughter." As if on cue, Amela turns slightly in Tayla's arms and reaches for Megai. Megai happily takes her, wrapping her in a small hug as Amela hugs her back, yawns, and snuggles into Megai's neck.

The female councilor watches this for a moment with a slight smile. "I accept your proof."

The head councilor, in a softer voice, adds, "Megai, she is now in your charge." He looks to the mediator. "Please let Tita know what we will refund her, and that the reward should be forwarded to Megai." The mediator nods her understanding so he turns back to us. "Unless you have anything further?"

All the councilors nod to us, and I nod back. "Thank you for clearing this up."

"Thank you for bringing it to our attention."

We find Tita behind her counter with a very large smile. "I knew you couldn't do anything like that. You're just not that kind of person." She places a pouch on the counter. "This is yours."

"What's this?"

"Your back pay and what you haven't spent of the reward."

"Tita, I can't . . ."

"I saved it for you. You earned it," Tita firmly states. "And you have her to care for now. You'll need it." She then leans forward, smiling like a child. "So are you going to take him or what?"

"I have a child to care for now." She turns to me. "You still have Kotu and Fey, right?"

I nod, as Tayla rubs her swelling belly. "And two on the way."

"Two?" both Megai and Tita gasp.

"Yep, and they're both his." To emphasize her point, she gently pokes me with her nose.

"What do you say, Megai? Want to be my mate too?"

She looks at me, then nervously at Tayla. "You're . . . uh, okay, with . . ."

"I fell in love with him after he fell in love with you. I accepted that, I still do. I can feel his love for you. It is real and it is strong, like it is for me, and for Sada." She reaches out and gently rubs Megai's cheek. "He's following his heart."

"You've gotten to know him quite well, haven't you?"

"More than you know," she admits, "but don't let that bother you."

I kiss her on her nose. "I carried you with me in my heart. I couldn't stand the thought of losing you again."

She looks at Tayla and then to me as Tita states, "He's taken away your excuses. You're free. You've been thinking about him every day since he left, and you haven't even given another male a second look." Tita reaches out and touches Megai's shoulder. "What's stopping you?"

Seeing her eyes water, I gently take her free hand. "Do you still love me?"

She nods. "Yes."

"Will you be my mate, alongside Tayla?"

She nods, her tears start to flow freely. "But I don't want to have kits yet."

"You don't have to have kits for me if you don't want to."

Tayla gently takes a sleepy Amela from her as she nods again. "Yes." She falls into my arms, crying happily.

I hold her to me, kissing her. "And I am your mate too." After a few moments, I pull a signet out of my pocket and pin it to her wrap.

She pulls back a little, looking at it. "Your symbol. You claim me as part of your family?"

Tayla gently hugs her. "His family, my family, and now, your family."

She gently rubs the emblem as Tita asks, "So where are you gonna live?"

Tayla and Megai both look at me. "I was thinking nearby, but I haven't had a chance to look yet."

Tita chuckles. "Go see the officer of deeds. They'll help you find something."

Megai takes our hands, leading us. "We should find something close. I don't want to leave Tita without training a replacement."

"You could keep working for her if you want to," I suggest. "You don't need to change for me."

She smiles happily. "I'll think about it."

I kiss her and pull her and Tayla close as we walk. I find myself enjoying the moment when Fey comes running up. "Dad! Dad! Look what I got!"

"Shh, not so loud, Fey." I point to Amela, nestled in Tayla's arms.

"Oh! Amela? Megai!" Fey quickly wraps her in a hug. "Did he ask?"

Megai points to the signet. "I said yes."

"I've got another mom!"

Megai chuckles. "You don't need to call me that."

"I call Tayla mom. Besides, I want to."

"Do you call Sada mom too?"

"She's not a mom. She's a friend. Dad has to correct her sometimes like he does me and Kotu."

Megai gives me an odd look. "Sada may be my companion, but she has a very unique outlook on how to behave. Sometimes she acts mature, other times . . ."

"She can be more childish than the children," Tayla finishes for me. Sada gives both of us a dirty look, obviously disagreeing. "Well, you do."

"But she sleeps with you."

I can't help but smile. "Most of the time. Sometimes she'll curl up with Fey or Oana."

"Who's Oana?"

"A slave girl he rescued."

"Who still doesn't understand the concept of freedom, but she's learning."

"Oh yeah, I wanted to show you what I got." Fey pulls out four rolled cloths and unrolls them, showing us carvings resembling Tria, Niku, Zoe, and one of a green viper lizard. As I pick the last one up to look closely, she sighs. "It's the closest they had to Oana. I had him repaint it."

I chuckle a little. "Maybe we'll bring her by some time, so he can make a real one of her."

"I'd like that."

Arru arrives, followed closely by Zoe and Tria. After introductions, they proceed on to the shuttle leaving us to talk to the officer of deeds.

With me now carrying Amela, who's still asleep, we enter the deeds office. The buck behind the counter smiles as he sees the sleeping girl and softly greets us. "Master Kyle, how nice to finally meet you. How may I help you?"

"We want to know if there are any available homes."

"How many rooms will you need?"

I do a mental headcount. "At least fifteen."

His eyes go wide for a moment. "Fifteen?"

"Rooms for my family and my staff."

"Ah, of course." He pulls out a small stack of papers and starts looking through them, abruptly stopping at a page. "Will you want to farm the land?"

I look to Megai and Tayla, who both shrug, so I state, "Not likely."

"All right." He passes that one by, flipping a few more pages before stopping and pulling out a page. Placing it on the table before us, he says, "This one has fifteen bedrooms, two kitchens, and a main room."

We look at the rough floor plan. The layout is nearly a long hall with the rooms off of it. "That looks like an inn," Megai states."

"It was, before the beast showed up."

"We want something more family-friendly," Tayla adds.

"Ah, of course." He puts that page back and keeps looking. Finding another, he pulls the paper out and stops. Before he lays it down, he says, "This is an older one, outside the village. It was meant to be a farm estate, but the land around it is not very good for growing."

He lays the page down. "It has twenty bedrooms, a master suite, a large kitchen, and a dining hall. It also has several other rooms that could be used for offices and such."

As we look at the layout, we see that it's a large central hall with smaller rooms added on to the sides, shrinking in size as they get farther from the center. They're arranged in wings, giving a definite front and back to the home.

He points to the area in the front. "This area had a good foundation of pealli moss, making it perfect for children to play. This area out here is almost a solid slab of stone. There are stables and a garage along this side, facing the slab. There is also a pond off this direction." He points to an area off the page. "And a spring in the middle of the main hall."

The girls all look at me, smiling, so I say, "Sounds perfect. How long has it been empty?"

He turns the paper and looks at it for a moment. "Nearly fifteen years."

Megai looks up at him. "Why so long?"

"All the people who want to live outside the village want to farm. This sits right in the middle of rock and moss. It's almost an hour walk in any direction to fertile ground. No one really gives it a second look."

"Where's it at?"

"Along the south road, just over an hour's walk. Look for a large gate on the east side with this symbol on it." He points to a symbol on the corner of the page. "Then follow that into the front door."

"I wonder what kind of shape it's in," Megai asks.

"You can go look if you want to. If you want it, let me know and I'll put your name on it."

"What's it cost?"

"Since it's outside the village, and the previous owner just abandoned it, there is no cost, just a few formalities."

"Thank you. We'll go look and let you know."

Returning to the shuttle, we find everyone relaxing around a small fire. As we approach, I call out, "Who wants to go look at an estate?"

Everyone turns to look at me while Zoe exclaims, "ME! ME! ME!"

"Megai!" Railu exclaims, resisting the urge to jump up. They hug, greeting each other warmly.

Arru comes over to me. "Estate?"

I set Amela down, letting her go play with Fey, and shrug, "Gotta live somewhere. Besides, it's big enough for all of us and then some."

"Have you bought it yet?"

"No, and it's been vacant for nearly fifteen years. I want to see it first anyway."

"Long time."

"It's floor plan looks great though. I hope it's in good shape."

"Yeah, me too." She pats me on the back as she turns to look at Megai. We stand there for a moment, watching everybody greet her warmly, each telling her a little story about our travels. As a pang of sadness hits me, I know what story just got told. I walk over to Megai and give her and Tayla a hug. Tayla quickly hugs me back, reassuring herself that I am all right. Megai is a little too into the story to do more than lean up against me.

After an early supper and several more stories, we fly the short distance to the estate. After parking the shuttle in the front "lawn," I look at the outside of the building. Seeing all the different levels of roofs, I get the feeling that I've seen something like this before.

"Looks like a ziggurat," Aime comments.

Smiling, I say, "Yeah, it does." I look at Tayla and Megai. "The layout on that page did not do this place justice."

"No, it didn't," Tayla agrees."

With it getting late in the day, we grab our packs and head inside. The first thing I notice as we step inside is that the drawing of the layout was not to scale. The great hall is literally huge, almost large enough to park the shuttle in, wings and all.

I pull out my flashlight, as do many others, and start looking around. We spend over an hour exploring, before settling around a stone table in the great room.

"I know what I think, but I want to hear what you think." I look around at the others, honestly hoping they all liked it as much as I did.

"Would this be our first 'official' house meeting?" Arru asks.

I smile and nearly laugh, realizing that I'm the only one standing and everyone is sitting around the table, looking at me. "Sure, why not. It'd be appropriate, I guess, to have our first house meeting about the house itself." I look at Arru. "What do you think?"

Arru shifts position slightly. "It's in surprisingly good shape, stone walls and floors. There are plenty of shelves upstairs for a library, and a few of the rooms off this one are perfect for offices. I really like it."

I look to Roen, who happens to be sitting next to her. "I agree. The bedrooms are fairly large. I would consider setting up one or two as nurseries. I like the layout, hard to get lost."

Railu speaks up, being next to Roen. "I really like this room. With a little more light and the right décor, it could make anyone feel welcome."

Niku speaks next, following around the table. "There's a large room, next to the kitchen. I think it might have been for grain storage or something, but I could set it up for my office. It'd give me easy access to the kitchen's cold storage and pantry for when I need to make medicines."

"The kitchen's big, with cold storage, pantry, drying room, three ovens, two places for pit fires and cauldrons. It's like a dream." Zoe states while hugging herself. "There's a pair of doors leading to the dining hall, easy to move the food in and out. The dining hall has a large table too, seats thirty I think."

"There's plenty of room upstairs for me to teach. It'd give me and the children easy access to the library, if that's what you do with the shelves. There are also a few small rooms up there. I could use one for setting up classes, research, or whatever."

"The garage is large enough for eight wagons. We could use some of that for a training area. If you want more security, I could also set up a room or area in here as an office."

"I like how large it is, plenty of room," Tayla adds. "Our room is large enough for all four of us, and there are rooms close by for our children. We could add a door from ours to one for the nursery. There's also a rather large grooming room attached to ours."

We both look at Megai, who's blushing. "I noticed," she states. "There are four more down here and a small one upstairs." She looks up at me. "With the number of utility closets, I think the house should have a regular staff, at least one to help with the cooking and maybe two others for serving and general cleaning. After the children are born, a nanny would be a good idea."

"Good points, all of you." I look around the table. "Did anyone see anything bad, signs of leaks, vermin, anything?"

Several shake their head no, but Roen speaks up, "Nothing eats the pealli moss, so there's no reason for bugs or critters to get close. The only signs of water I've seen are over by the spring."

"Well then," I softly clap my hands together and smile. "Seems we're all in agreement. Welcome to the Sovereign's Estate. Welcome *home* everyone."